# The Hypnotist

# The Hypnotist

## David S. Jones

AuthorHouse™
1663 Liberty Drive
Bloomington, IN 47403
www.authorhouse.com
Phone: 1-800-839-8640

First published by AuthorHouse    08/24/2011

ISBN: 978-1-4567-9047-9 (sc)
ISBN: 978-1-4567-9048-6 (ebk)

# ABSOLUTE COPYRIGHT

# THE HYPNOTIST

## DAVID S. JONES.

*The Mirage*
*Sitio Da Ramalhete lote 1*
*Praia-da-Luz*
*8600-163 Lagos,*
*Algarve,*
*Portugal.*

*Tel 00351282788237.*
*Mobile 00351912674565.*
*e-mail davidjones@sapo.pt*

# 1

# SANDHURST

His name was Nick, Nick Trevelyan but this was about to change when
he became Officer Cadet Trevelyan and, if all continued to go well,
would move on to be Lieutenant Trevelyan. It had been his dream to
become an officer in the British Army for as long as he could remember.
Looking back and recalling how green he was at that time still made him
wince. The only thing that he could remember wanting to do ever since he
was a small boy, was to be a soldier. Now he had reached the point where
that dream was finally to be realised. He had worked hard at school, and
gained a military grant which had seen him through University. Now,
with a degree in Modern History under his belt he was about to set out on
his chosen path. His background was modest; his father had been a long
service soldier whose career sadly never amounted to much. Home was a
series of army accommodation ranging from Hong Kong to Germany. His
father was often away either on exercise or overseas duty. What time he
did spend at home was divided between family and the mess. Thankfully
his mother made up for the absence of Dad, and his sister and he were
spared the discomfiture of a father who, as the years passed, sank deeper
and deeper into a culture of alcohol.

Now he stood at the threshold of a new adventure, all of his dreams
fulfilled. Finally the day had arrived when he would enter Sandhurst,
the world's most renowned military academy, as an officer cadet. He was
confident that he could handle the tough regime that this establishment

would throw at him but he never in a million years expected to encounter the pitfalls that were to have such a devastating effect upon his life.

# First meeting with TR-B

Why did he have to be the one who caught the delayed train from Waterloo His first day in the army and he was already late. Somehow, he didn't think *"leaves on the line"* would go down too well. He stared nervously out of the train window as it slowly dragged itself into Camberley Station, several minutes behind schedule. He couldn't help but notice the tall, upright, military figure standing on the platform, head and shoulders above the rest of the commuters. *'My escort, no doubt,'* How best to make a good first impression? *'Well, here goes. If I can't exert my charm to effect on this sergeant, then I really am in trouble,'* he thought.

Pulling himself up to his full height of 6'2", and putting on his most winning smile, he bounced off the train directly in front of the imposing figure of the attending Sergeant, hand outstretched.

'Ah, good morning, Sergeant, I'm Nicholas Trevelyan. So sorry . . . .' he started, only to be interrupted by a tremendous roar that caused him to take a hasty step backwards.

'Colour Sergeant! That's what I am—Colour Sergeant McGarrigal and don't you forget it! But you can call me *'Colour'* because that's how we do things in this man's army. Now then Mr. Trevelyan, shut up! You're late! I have no intention of listening to your excuses—join the other recruits who are waiting for you in the car park by the minibus, before I decide to send you back to Waterloo on the next train.'

The broad Glaswegian accent was like a blistering wave of heat that washed over Nick. Even at three feet distance he could feel the Colour Sergeant's breath buffeting him in the face. He froze with disbelief at this unexpected assault. The Sergeant's eyes were barely visible, shielded by the severely slashed peak of his forage cap. His clipped moustache bristled and the square jaw jutted forward in a passable imitation of Desperate Dan.

'Now make a note of this, Trevelyan: fortunately for you, I don't happen to be your particular troop Colour Sergeant, but should I ever have the misfortune of bumping into you again, you will address me as *'Staff'* and nothing else. If you annoy me in any way, shape or form between now and the time that I deposit you at your Company Offices, I will have you parading in front of the Adjutant before you've even been shown where you are going to lay those lovely curly locks tonight. Understood?'

The Colour Sergeant's voice rose or decreased in volume, according to the severity of his message; his accent grew harsher or softer, sinking to an acceptable Sean Connery burr when, on the odd occasion, he wasn't using his vocal cords at their usual screaming pitch. Nick made a mental note to check out whether regionality had any significance on the way the directing staff taught the Cadets, and if this did have some bearing on the matter, silently prayed that he would be spared too much contact with any northern cousins.

'Uh, yes, Sir—I mean Colour.' He gathered his belongings and beat a hasty retreat to the nearby station car park where a regulation Sandhurst minibus stood waiting, surrounded by seven other, apprehensive-looking potential officer cadets. He climbed aboard looking as nonchalant as he could; hoping no-one had heard the frantic exchange that had taken place only minutes before on the station platform. Although, with the Colour Sergeant's penetrating roar still ringing in his ears, there was little doubt that most of Camberley had been privy to the tongue lashing that he had just endured.

## Tristram Wrath-Bingham

'What's the matter—didn't your mother wake you up on time? Your tardiness has caused us to wait here in the cold.' The other cadets fidgeted nervously. Nick cast a quick glance at the rear view mirror where he spotted his smirking protagonist at the back of the coach. His elegant attire and handsome, but rather weak-looking face immediately gave away his upbringing as one of the privileged aristocracy. Nick wanted to tell them all that he was sorry for keeping them waiting and that British Rail was the real culprit but the other mans superior attitude annoyed him so much that he decided to keep quiet.

The irritating nasal laugh reached his ears again as the minibus pulled out of the car park and headed for its destination, The Royal Military Academy, Sandhurst. Within minutes they had arrived at journey's end. The Colour Sergeant nosed the vehicle up to the main gate entrance barrier, carefully placed his treasured forage cap back on his head, meticulously adjusted it and got out of the vehicle. He walked over to the entry security control cabin, chatting to one of the soldiers on duty. He waited until a bomb search of the vehicle had been completed. Then, positioning himself seventy feet in front of the bus, he bellowed:

'Everybody out!'

The eight would-be officer cadets scrambled out of the bus, tripping over one another in their eagerness not to be last. They formed some semblance of a straight line in front of their tormentor, who waited patiently for them to settle before he spoke again.

'Now, gentlemen,' growled the Colour Sergeant. 'This side of that barrier you belong to your mothers. But once you cross the line, you will belong to Her Majesty's Forces, and that means that myself and the other instructors at this Academy will be your new mothers! It may have crossed your minds as to why such a pleasant chap as myself has been given the privilege of baby-sitting you little orphans this morning. Well, it's because I'm considered to be a pussycat and I won't upset you little darlings too much before you meet the other nasty old instructors that work here. I therefore suggest that if any of you thinks that perhaps you have made a mistake and want to go home to your mummies, now is the time to do so! Because once you cross that line, I promise you all that your feet will not touch the ground for the next forty-four weeks.'

The Colour Sergeant clasped his hands behind his back and rocked from the heel to the toe of his immaculately polished boots, staring above our heads. None of us said a word, afraid to speak; our apprehension obvious. No one moved.

'I deduce from your silence, Gentlemen, that you have all decided to trade in your mothers so that I and my nasty colleagues can nurse you all for the rest of time that you are going to spend here with us at this academy.' Nobody took up the offer.

'In that case, there is nothing more to do here. I therefore require you all to form up in a straight line on the other side of that barrier.' The last words were said in an almost fatherly tone; and then the air exploded as his subsequent command ripped through the sound barrier.

'NOW MOVE!'

They flapped about like a flock of startled ducklings, which had been injected with the fowl equivalent of Mad Cow Disease. The Colour Sergeant looked pleased with himself, contemplating the terror that he had inflicted upon his unfortunate charges with such ease. Nick was mesmerized by this man who had the ability to transform, within the blink of an eye, from a benevolent father figure into a deranged monster. The Colour Sergeant strolled over.

'Right, Gentlemen. My name is Colour Sergeant McGarrigal. My Regiment is the Scots Guards. And I promise you now, that if any of you put so much as one "little pinkie" out of line, I will be down on you like a ton of bricks. Gentlemen, I shall be your worst nightmare. Stand at ease if you can manage that, and wait there.'

Colour Sergeant McGarrigal strode back to the minibus, carefully took off his forage cap and got in. He lovingly placed the prized cap on the engine cover and started the engine. He drove the bus past the now open barrier, pulling up alongside the bewildered recruits. Thinking that it was expected, they all broke formation and moved forward as one to climb back into the bus. The sound barrier ripped open again.

'WHERE THE HELL DO YOU THINK YOU'RE GOING? GET OUT!'

This time the shout resembled a scream and Nick winced at the noise the man made which was a sound more terrifying than any other he had heard in all of his twenty-one years. It felt as if they had personally insulted the Sergeant.

'You don't actually think that you are going to ride in here with me, do you, Gentlemen?'

The cadets turned from one to another, hoping that someone would say something that would appease this madman, but none dared to speak.

'Fall in behind the bus. Now! And God help anyone whom I spot in the mirror dropping behind!'

There was light drizzle in the air when they, like eight ducklings, set off behind mother duck. The distance from the barrier to the main induction block was all of a mile, and by the time they arrived, they were looking less than pristine. Everyone was soaked through, partly from the rain and partly from the sweat that was pouring from even the fittest as they were all wearing coats and ties. The more unfortunate had alighted from the bus carrying hand luggage, which severely slowed them down.

Nick was lucky. He was fairly fit thanks to all the rugby he had played both at school and university. His greatest discomfort was self-inflicted, because, as they set off after the bus, a sense of rivalry immediately developed between himself and the aristocratic recruit who had complained at the station. Each determined to beat the other. In the short time that they had been in each other's company it was obvious to Nick that this man had decided that he disliked him intensely and he wasn't too keen on him either. They ran their own private race and pushed themselves much harder than they probably needed to, had they just kept pace with the rest of the group. Both began to tire towards the end and fell back from leading the other men to finish neck and neck in the middle of the pack. They exchanged meaningful glances that signalled the start of what was to become a very long and troubled relationship. It was a pretty sorry group that gathered around the bus, when, thankfully, it came to a standstill. Colour Sergeant McGarrigal put on his forage cap with all the pomp of the Holy Father donning his papal mitre. He walked up to the steaming, coughing, bedraggled recruits as two stragglers staggered the final few yards.

'Dear, dear, dear, dear! This won't do now, will it?'smirked the Colour Sergeant.

The last recruit to arrive was a tall, stocky, fair skinned guy whose eyes were bulging from his head at the sudden, unexpected exertion. His bright red face was a distinct improvement on the several shades of purple he had turned throughout the run. The unfortunate recruit attempted to loosen his tie but McGarrigal had been ready for this.

'You're not thinking of taking off your tie are you, lad?'

'No, Colour' spluttered the young man as he continued his chameleon-like pursuits.

'Now all of you line up! Stop wheezing like a bunch of geriatrics. When I give you the order, disappear smartly to your destinations before I decide to run you all back again, NOW MOVE!'

McGarrigal's final command proved remarkably effective in making everyone disappear with commendable speed, their ears still reverberating, as each mega green novice scurried off in search of any safe haven that would surely prove to be more welcoming than the horrible experience they all felt that they had just been through.

After a cursory introduction to his Platoon Colour Sergeant, another Scotsman called McGregor; Nick devoted himself to hurrying from one appointed destination to the next as swiftly, and with as little fuss, as possible. He received his army number and plastic name tag, then hurried to his designated classroom where he made sure that he blended into the background while his new Platoon Commander made clear to everyone exactly what was expected of them.

They then returned to their barrack rooms to contemplate the impending reality of the harsh regime that they had volunteered for and were about to embark on, all wondering if they had made the right decision. Also to make the most of the only decent night's sleep they would get for the best part of the next five weeks. A grey drizzle greeted them the next morning. Initially everyone lined up with trepidation outside the Academy hairdresser's. A bewildered looking line of scalped recruits filed back past the waiting cadets at a precisely regular interval of one every forty-five seconds. After taking their turn in the barbers chair, they ruefully rubbed their newly acquired haircuts. It was obvious that the barber not only believed that, "speed is of the essence" but also in economy of style which consisted of extremely short with no variation whatsoever. Through persistent rain they hurried to the Academy Quartermaster's Stores where they gathered mountains of kit and clothing that was to see them through their period of training.

Nick noted that the dispensing of military clothing definitely lacked the personal touch and came to the conclusion that the Lance Corporal in charge of fitting should never contemplate leaving his present position with a view to taking up a career in Savile Row.

He hurried along the half mile journey back to his quarters to drop off his kit, anxious to be in time for the introductory talk due to start shortly. His muscles ached as he held the huge pile of uniforms in his outstretched arms. Swiftly, he caught up with a small group of cadets ahead of him and was about to overtake them when his boot sank into a rut in the path, which had become disguised by the downpour.

The pile of equipment flew from his arms as he tripped and the heavy steel-heeled drill boots, resting on top of the kit slowly spun through the air as if in a slow motion film sequence. In front, in response to the scuffling behind and his muffled yell, a fellow recruit slowly turned his head. The heel of the boot caught the other man squarely on the cheekbone, before it somersaulted onto the muddy grass beside the path. Nick raised himself up from the ground where he had landed on his hands and knees. Surveying his scattered kit, he despondently started picking up the crumpled, muddy effects. As he reached out, an arm grabbed his shoulder and a voice snarled.

'If you've left a mark on me, I'll make you pay. I've had enough of your amateur fumbling from the moment that you arrived. You're not going to last five minutes on this course if you go on like this, and if you do, by some miracle get any further, I'll see to it that life is as uncomfortable as possible for you!' he shouted over his shoulder as he puffed off, adding.

'Your bloody sort are always trouble.'

Nick's feet were planted on the hallowed ground that was Sandhurst; his ambitions were about to be fulfilled. It had been an up-hill struggle to get to this point and now he was jeopardizing it all by his own clumsiness and the terribly bad luck of encountering the most arrogant upper class idiot imaginable. Of all the recruits he could have bumped into, it was just his luck to hit the one who had already made his dislike for him obvious at the station yesterday.

He strode away angrily, blood seeping through the fingers that he held over the wound on his cheek. Nick stared after him despairingly. Another recruit started picking up the kit of the injured man after placing his own in a neat pile on the path.

'You certainly know how to go out of your way to make friends, don't you?' smirked the man whom he had noticed was usually in the company of his new tormentor.

'You've just booked yourself a rough ride.'

'Thanks for that—and you are?' Nick asked the unwelcome commentator.

'I'm Timothy Harcourt, a good friend of Tristram's,' he replied, 'Because I certainly wouldn't like to make an enemy of him.'

'Tristram?'

'Yes Tristram Wrath-Bingham. I'd check him out if I were you.'

'Thanks for the advice,' Nick called after Harcourt, as he walked away, laughing but staggering under the burden of the two piles of kit.

'*I'm sure you have my best interests at heart,*' he thought to himself as he leant over to pick up some more of his equipment.

## Steve Craig

'Want some help, my friend?' asked a cheery voice from behind.' You look like you've come a bit of a cropper!' Nick turned and smiled, putting out his hand.

'You can say that again. Nick Trevelyan, Pleased to meet you.'

The fellow recruit standing before him was about the same age and height. He had short cropped fair hair which was not of the Academy barber's styling, and a slightly more rugged appearance compared to the other cadets.

'Hi, I'm Steve. Bit of friendly advice, Mate: you'd better shift this stuff double quick and make tracks for Colour Sergeant Macgregor's tea party before your "friend" gets in first and starts telling tales. You're in deep shit already, but if you get your side of the story in first, you might end up cleaning the toilets with a scrubbing brush instead of a toothbrush', the friendly face warned.

'I've come up through the ranks so I pretty much know the score already. You shouldn't ruffle too many feathers in your first week, although it looks like you've given it a fair bashing already.'

'Thanks for the advice,' Nick replied. 'You're right. I'd better go and do some serious grovelling. See you later—if I don't end up in solitary confinement. Although at least I'll have the comforting picture of Wrath-Bingham's now less than perfect features to keep me amused.'

'Shame it didn't crack him on the nose; it might have improved his looks.'

Nick trudged back to his quarters with the sodden equipment before making his way to Colour Sergeant Macgregor's office. He knocked on the door and entered at the bellowed command. As he stood to attention, he was suddenly painfully aware of the muddied picture he presented, and by the look on the Colour Sergeant's face he could tell that Tristram Wrath-Bingham had already been in to see him.

'You are a sorry excuse for a cadet, Mr. Trevelyan. We've hardly got you in a uniform and you're being accused of assaulting a fellow recruit! What do you have to say?' roared the unimpressed Colour Sergeant as he rounded the desk, and thrust his face closer to Nick.

'It was a complete accident, Colour. I tripped and fell. Mr Wrath-Bingham's face happened to be in the way.' Nick shouted in response.

'Yes, Mr. Trevelyan! We know it was an accident but you are still a blundering idiot! Next time you decide to rearrange a fellow cadet's features, try and make sure it's not someone as pretty as Mr. Wrath-Bingham. He'll need a fair number of stitches in that wound and we don't think he's very happy about his first battle scar! Get out of here and make sure that kit is clean and ready for inspection first thing tomorrow morning. Now get to your lecture and report to the duty NCO after supper for Restriction of Privileges. Meanwhile, try to keep out of trouble, Mr. Trevelyan.'

'Yes, Colour!' he shouted and left the office, feeling humiliated. Nick hurried to change, and only just made it into the lecture on time. He could hardly fail to notice the Platoon Commander's withering look.

It's going to be a long day. he thought, his only comfort being the sight of Bingham, as he entered the lecture room shortly afterwards, sporting a one and a half inch raised wound on his cheek, with half a dozen stiff stitches bristling along its length. Wrath-Bingham shot him a venomous look. Nick thought that an apology was in order but he could tell from the scowl on Wrath/Bingham's face that it would have been pointless.

# 2

The Royal Military Academy Sandhurst; world renowned training grounds for potential officers who would eventually lead by excellence in a variety of Armies spanning the globe. The institute stood in seven hundred acres of magnificent countryside, boasting playing fields, woods and lakes which formed a backdrop to the rigorous program of training that had only just begun for the latest intake at the Academy. The Old College building stood as a monument to the illustrious military history of the nation. The main accommodation buildings—New College and Victory College—were less impressive externally but Nick found them quite comfortable. He had been expecting fairly Spartan accommodation so there was no shock factor.

It was the former College building that was to become home for him and the other graduate recruits throughout the intensive training period, designed to transform each one into an officer and (potentially) a gentleman. In spite of the unfortunate early confrontations, he immersed himself in the daily life of Sandhurst. The pace of the activities ensured that there was little time for anything apart from training. He soon learnt that the first five weeks of instruction was a period of intensive acclimatization, with the finale being the Cadet's Passing off the square Parade. The five weeks were equivalent to the twenty-one weeks that a private soldier takes to reach a similar standard of drill. These weeks passed with a relentless concoction of physical training, lectures, weapon training and drill.

Life was one big rush from one session to another, changing into a different type of uniform for almost every lesson. The cadets hotfooted from one discipline to the next at a continual trot. The time was utilised in such a way that it necessarily coerced the platoon into a unit that was more cohesive and mutually supportive than the original band of strangers would have thought possible.

The platoon consisted of twenty two men and two women. They all knew from the beginning that some of their number wouldn't make it to the end; some would fall by the wayside for various reasons. Within the platoon, individual friendships were formed, Steve and Nick became firm buddies. They had quickly discovered that they had much in common and shared similar aspirations. Nick was particularly grateful for the advice Steve had to offer based on his previous experiences in the ranks. As they were the two who came from more ordinary backgrounds, this created a bond between them. Tristram Wrath-Bingham and Timothy Harcourt also appeared to have paired up although the relationship was slightly unusual. Steve thought that the weasel ways of Timothy, coupled with Tristram's strutting air of supremacy, gave them a "Tom Brown's Schooldays" theme. But then decided that his opinion of them was that Timothy played Robin to Tristram's Batman.

The endless cleaning of kit was a ritual played out every evening. Steve and Nick got into the habit of doing this together so that they could use the time to chat about the day's events.

'Steve, do you remember the first day when I cracked Tristram's face with his boot?'

'Bloody right, I do! It made my day, no, actually my week!' He laughed.

'So I did what Timothy suggested and looked up the Wrath-Bingham family tree.'

'Don't tell me they are six generations of fish merchants from Billingsgate.' he quipped.

'No you daft prat. They are practically blue blooded'.

'Well you would know all about that given that you spilled some of it for him!'

'Their family tree goes back centuries, always military, very impressive. There appears to have been a Wrath-Bingham commanding British troops since the time of Charles ll. So where does that put you, Nicky-boy?' said Steve, a little more seriously.

'I would say in deep shit as Tristram's father is a serving General.'

'He might be a General but he can't actually do you any harm . . . I don't think.' he added a little unconvincingly.

'I don't know why, Nick, but you certainly do seem to ruffle Tristram's feathers without even trying.' He laughed. 'A day doesn't pass without him finding something to dig at you for and that toad, Timothy, is right behind him with his nose up his arse.' Steve was making an attempt to take the sting out of his discovery.

'Yep, I can't think why he has taken it upon himself to have this vendetta against me. It's almost an obsession with him.' Nick replied.

They carried on with their kit cleaning both wondering what might happen next.

The training was tough but exhilarating, and after their platoon passed off the Drill Square, they were given a long weekend leave. Everyone headed for London and hopefully some fun as they had been deprived of any form of off-camp distraction during this initial period.

The occasional skirmish with Wrath-Bingham had kept things interesting, but generally Nick did his best to keep out of Tristram's way. Despite Wrath-Bingham's initial blustering, he had family traditions to maintain and with a little help from his Colour Sergeant, certainly showed that he had ability in his quest for the elusive officer's pips.

Time in the class rooms and lecture hall was a welcome break from the hours spent on the parade ground, assault courses and on road runs. There were many academic as well as physical lessons and the academic side of the course was generally undertaken by civilian tutors. Everyone was required to give several lectures when the rest of the platoon would be the audience. Finally, when the debate was thrown open for discussion, an opportunity to criticize was entered into with enthusiasm. It was Tristram's turn to give his lecture which he did with all his usual bluster. After all, talking to the troops was something that was in his genes. His talk on the spread of the British Empire was actually very well done. As the lecture drew to a close, knowing that it had gone well, he was unable to resist the opportunity to slip in a snipe at Nick.

'And so from this great legacy, institutions such as the one we are attending at this moment were born. Here an attempt is made to make an officer and a gentleman from even the lowest material.' said he, smugly. A discernable groan went around the room and Steve and Nick looked at each other and smiled, knowing that the pointed remark was obviously aimed at them. Who would answer? Nick decided that it had to be him.

'Gold braid and fine uniforms don't necessarily make a good officer', he said. Tristram's face was turning decidedly red as Nick stole his thunder. It had tripped off the tongue quite nicely Nick decided. He could see that Tristram was taken aback so he added another analogy that seemed to fit the occasion quite nicely.

'If a dog sleeps in a stable it doesn't make it a horse!' There was a cheer from the other cadets none of whom, apart from Timothy, thought too highly of Tristram who by this time was fuming. Nick expected a barrage from the speaker but another voice intervened and he was grateful to be spared the conflict.

'Your remarks are nothing but sexist,' shouted Louisa Aldridge who was one of the females in the platoon and renowned for her feminist viewpoint.

'*An Officer and a Gentleman indeed!* How chauvinistic can you get? Have the two women in your platoon suddenly become invisible? You will need to choose your words more carefully when you speak to your soldiers when you get to your regiment or suffer the consequences of a tribunal,' Sally fumed.

Nick was grateful for her intervention which took Tristram's attention away from him as he squirmed to get out of a self-made tight spot. He was not a happy man and although it was Louisa who had really put the boot in, there was no denying that Nick was the real focal point of his anger.

Nick became intensely focused on the daily demands of the course, and the overall objectives of his training. If he could strip away the unhappy events caused by TW-B, then his time at Sandhurst could have been close to idealistic. His knowledge of Military History was something which stood him in good stead. His love of rugby was also very useful; soon he became an important presence on the rugby field and ended up captaining the Academy team. Elsewhere he proved himself during the demanding outdoor activities. Steve matched him stride for stride, and the hard edge of competition between the two spurred them on to an impressive catalogue of performances in the field as the cadets were pushed from one punishing exercise to the next.

It was at about this period of the training, when they were beginning to show signs of specialist interests that various army units started courting cadets whom they thought might serve them most usefully. Those showing a particular flair for engineering, having got an appropriate degree already as a prerequisite, were, for example, hunted down by the recruitment officers from units like REME, The Royal Engineers, and The Royal Signals.

It became apparent that, equipped with his degree in Modern History, Nick was showing promise for modern tactical warfare in the infantry. The Argyle and Sutherland Highlanders noticed him and started to take an interest. All other contenders for his talents fell by the wayside, as he was more than delighted to make his career in this famous regiment. Wrath-Bingham's constant hounding had become an obsession with him and was a constant nagging thorn in his side which meant that any time spent away from his tormentor was indeed quality.

Steve and Nick also demonstrated a healthy competitive spirit in the pursuit of girls and parties and the weekend saw them vying for their attention. The selection of female company was often planned with similar military precision to the exercises carried out at the Academy. Winning girlfriends was an important sport; it provided yet another way to prove themselves.

The social backgrounds of the cadets were diverse, to say the least. Every new intake boasted a few titles, and, amongst the overseas contingent, a couple of foreign Princes or members of leading families from far-flung places. Then there would be the usual selection of offspring from well-connected and wealthy origins as well as those few of slightly more humble backgrounds. Steve and Nick were in no doubt of their standing on the social scale but sometimes they found this to be advantageous The women that they tended to attract ranged from Norland Nannies to 'Sloane Rangers'. Most were remarkable for either their looks or their social connections with little attention being paid to any intellectual requirements by either side. On the whole, many liaisons were based on tacit agreements that both parties were 'in it' for fun only, and so it was with such mutual understanding, partners often changed at a fast and furious pace. Steve and Nick pretty much fell into this pattern of socializing, but as time progressed, Nick started feeling the need for steady female company that was a little more stimulating, less shallow, and longer lasting. He voiced this opinion as they set off together in Steve's car for a weekend-long jaunt to an estate in Suffolk. They had been invited as guests of the Stanford family, whose son, Jonathan belonged to the same intake and with whom they both got on well as he was as keen on rugby as were they.

'So, are you expecting to see any familiar faces this weekend, Nick, or are you ready for the hunt again?' Steve inquired genially, as they sped through the Suffolk countryside.

'Last weekend, I finished with that little nurse from Slough that I'd been seeing for a few weeks; well, actually, she dumped me for a doctor, so I'm a free agent again. I'm beginning to think it might be nice to see someone for more than a couple of evenings. I fancy getting myself a woman who's going to phone me every night, who I can go away for weekends with, instead of having to look at your ugly mug, a girl who might remember my name when I come back from an exercise,' Nick mused.

'My God! You're going soft in your old age! What makes you think anyone with half a brain is going to want to hang out with you for longer than a couple of beers? You've got no money, no car and you're not even good looking. In fact you are something of a freak.'

'A freak, what do you mean by that?'

'Well look at you—even your eyes don't match; you have one blue and one brown. You are, in fact, asymmetrical.'

'That's hurtful, but hey it didn't do David Bowie any harm and some girls find it charming. Didn't you ever read the story about the princess and the pea? The gods added my mixed eye colour to mar what would have otherwise been a perfect creation.'

'Fortunately for you some unfortunate woman would need to be standing close to you to notice your abnormality and I can't see that happening any time soon. Finding a colour blind woman could be the solution to your dilemma. Unless you can find someone who can name all the members of the England rugby team over the past five seasons, or recite the military history of our glorious nation over the last six centuries, you're going to strike out. Let's face it; I'm the one all the girls fancy and you just pick up the crumbs. I'll see if I can point someone passable in your direction this weekend. How about that Sloaney type, Sophie, who I saw a few times? She's going to be there this weekend. She's always good fun.'

'Thanks, friend,' Nick interrupted. 'You're a tonic for my confidence. Might I remind you that you're the one with so many "Dear John" letters that you could paper your ceiling with them? I'm quite content with the progress of my love life, thank you; at least I have some morals—I phone them when I dump them; you just turn up at the pub or a party with another woman.'

'I just like to pass on my experiences of life to as many poor unfortunate souls as possible; it's my duty to do so.' Steve explained.

'Oh, shut up!' laughed Nick. 'You're far more of a soft touch than I'll ever be where women are concerned; you just can't bear to get too involved in case someone turns round and wounds your delicate male ego.

I, on the other hand, am willing to take risks in the search for ultimate fulfilment.' Nick finished, smugly.

## Stanford Manor

At eight o'clock, when the sun was not far from setting over the lush Sussex countryside, Steve turned the car through the pillared entrance to the Stanford's estate. This heralded the start of a drive winding through green fields and paddocks for half a mile before entering an enclosed residence which was then reached by sweeping round a curve of gravel that ended in front of a manor house. The house was surrounded by immaculately kept gardens. There were half a dozen expensive cars parked in front of the house as they drew up.

Steve parked his ancient Ford Fiesta behind the adjacent stable block and they walked towards the house. As they approached, Jonathan Stanford bounded down the elaborate steps of his family home and warmly greeted them.

'I thought you'd got lost! You were meant to be only five minutes behind me and I got here an hour ago! Anyway grab your bags and come in and join the party.' Jonathan hurried them through the entrance hall and showed them to their rooms, so that they could quickly freshen up and join the rest of the guests for pre-dinner drinks.

They had both previously stayed at the house but could not fail to be impressed by the good taste that surrounded them. This was a large old manor but it had a relaxed feel about it. It felt like a home and not a stuffy museum which from the exterior it could easily have been. Each of the dozen guestrooms had an en-suite bathroom and every other possible comfort, including elegant furnishings that made you immediately feel comfortable. All a far cry from the circumstances of their present home at Sandhurst and Nick's parents' terraced house in Windsor.

He showered, shaved and changed his clothes. Steve and he met on the landing and joined the party. It felt good to be in different surroundings where they could relax away from the ever present regimented regime of the academy staff. Dinner was excellent and slowly Nick began to feel himself relaxing.

The next day, the Stanford's had arranged for their guests to have the choice of either riding on the extensive estate, helping Bernard Stanford give his stunning collection of vintage cars a run out or else entertain themselves as they pleased

'I'm off to do a bit of riding; what are you up to?' said Steve.

'I'm going to hang around here and check out the cars with Bernard; he's got some really amazing machines,' Nick answered. They went off to dress appropriately.

## Enter Marina

Later in the morning, Bernard, another of the guests and Nick were tinkering with a vintage Morgan at the front of the house when a Bentley Convertible drew up. Bernard hurried to greet the occupants: a tall, extremely attractive, leggy blond and a powerfully built, slightly balding older man. The man shepherded the girl in a protective fashion and Nick guessed that they were father and daughter. He wandered over to the group and was introduced by Bernard to Warren and Marina Fisher. Warren shook his hand powerfully and greeted him with a penetrating stare. Nick made a mental note that this was a man with whom you did not mess; he had an immediately formidable presence radiating total confidence. Marina, on the contrary, gave Nick the warmest of smiles and he allowed himself a glimpse of hope that this weekend might turn out to be more interesting than he had anticipated.

The Fishers disappeared to their rooms and Nick didn't see anything more of them until the early evening when everyone gathered for pre-dinner drinks. It was Gillian Stanford's birthday, and a few more people had joined the party for the evening, After dinner Nick managed to corner Marina for coffee in the lounge, having only managing to speak to her briefly earlier in the evening. Despite the lack of contact throughout the party, the two had managed to make eye contact as the evening progressed. When they finally sat down together on one of the sumptuous Chesterfields in the drawing room, he could feel an overwhelming attraction between them. This would have been obvious to anyone, had they been observing body language. In the company of the other guests they weren't able to have a particularly fulfilling conversation. Marina seemed to have no great qualms about hiding her attraction for Nick. Then, when she had finished her second brandy, she casually leant over to say goodnight.

'See you in an hour!' before swiftly turning away to say goodnight to the hosts and leave for her room. Nick stared after her with a mixture of surprise and unexpected anticipation. This really was turning out to be an interesting weekend. He spent another fifteen minutes talking to the Stanford and then left, buzzing with excitement at the implications behind Marina's whispered promise. He hurried to his room, threw off his jacket, tie and shoes, brushed his teeth nervously in the bathroom and sat in the comfortable chair in the corner of his room to wait. He woke with a start and felt cold. Nick glanced at his watch; it was four-thirty in the morning. His confused mind slowly woke up and he remembered why he was still sitting in the chair and not lying in bed.

'*Oh, great,*' he muttered to himself as he slowly undressed and crawled into bed. '*Trust me to pick the tease. I guess I've learnt my lesson here.*' He fell asleep dreaming of what might have been, to be awoken by the alarm in what seemed to be far too short a time.

He saw Marina at breakfast but didn't get a chance to talk to her. Nick cast a few discreet, but puzzled glances in her direction and although he caught her eye a couple of times, she didn't respond in any way, other than to give him a brief smile before continuing her conversation. After an extremely lavish, but frustrating, Sunday lunch, Nick still hadn't manage to corner Marina and he had almost given up hope of talking to her. However, after lunch, everyone gathered in the front hall to go for a walk and Nick disappeared to borrow one of Jonathan's Barbour jackets. Suddenly, he found himself alone in the cloakroom with Marina, who had sneaked up behind him and slipped her arm around his waist.

'I'm sorry about last night, Nicholas, but Daddy insisted in stopping in my room for a nightcap and fell asleep in the chair. He's incredibly possessive so I let him doze and by the time he woke, I thought it was probably too late. I can't really talk any more now but if I don't get a chance to speak to you again, here's the address of my shop in London; give me a call next week.' She had gone before Nick had a chance to respond, and he stared after her in amazement. As he drove back to Sandhurst with Steve that evening, Nick told him about his encounters with the mysterious Marina.

'Well, all I can say is, go for it, you lucky sod. She looks like a really hot proposition and I think you might well have some fun there. Just one word of warning. I spoke to her old man for quite a while. He made a lot of none too discrete inquiries about you and he seems quite unnaturally obsessed by her. I think there's some kind of story behind that. In the meantime though, I think Mr. Fisher is a bit of a tough cookie. If you're going to play around with his daughter, make sure you find out what his ground rules are as quickly as possible, or you might get yourself into trouble.'

'One day, you're going to make someone a wonderful wife, Steve.' laughed Nick. 'Don't worry; the situation is under control.'

When Nick got back to Sandhurst, he decided to give it a couple of days before phoning Marina. So it was much to his surprise that the night after his return, he received a phone call from none other than her father.

## Warren Fisher

'Nicholas, good to talk to you again! Our meeting at Monkton Hall was all too brief,' boomed Warren Fisher. 'I hope you had a good trip home on Sunday?'

'Fine, thank you, Sir,' Nick replied guardedly, wondering what on earth Marina's father could be calling him for; after all, nothing had happened with Marina. He could hardly be playing the outraged father role. Warren Fisher continued in his usual self assured manner.

'I enjoyed meeting you over the weekend, Nicholas, and I'd like you to join me for dinner on Wednesday night.' The invitation was issued far more like a command that he did not expect to be disobeyed. Nevertheless, Nick was relieved that evening was free as he would not have liked to have been obliged to say no.

'That's most kind of you, Sir. I'd be delighted to accept. Will we be having the pleasure of Marina's company?' Nick enquired, cautiously.

'Naturally,' replied Warren. 'She hasn't stopped talking about you for the last twenty-four hours. I wouldn't be able to keep her away. But beforehand, there's some business that I shall wish to discuss with you,' he finished abruptly. Nick's allotted time with the enigmatic man seemed to be over so they swiftly made the arrangements and said goodbye. He repeated the fascinating conversation to Steve later that evening in the cadets Mess and Steve agreed that it promised to be a most intriguing encounter.

Wednesday night came and Nick arrived at the rather exclusive destination immaculately turned out in his smartest navy blue blazer and cavalry twill trousers. He was slightly early and went into the hotel lobby, he was shown to the nearby bar where he ordered a vodka and tonic. Very shortly afterwards, the powerful figure of Warren Fisher strode in, precisely on time. He greeted Nick in a businesslike fashion and led him to a table in a quiet corner, a suave looking hotel manager appeared at Warren Fisher's shoulder.

'Mr. Fisher, a pleasure to see you here. We've missed your company these last few months.' the man was extremely smooth, with classic dark, French good looks, but unable to entirely hide the nervous edge in his voice as he spoke to the daunting figure before him. Nick took note of this as the manager continued:

'Please accept a bottle of Champagne with my compliments and I trust you will be joining us in the restaurant later? Pierre will be delighted to prepare your favourite dish for you.' The Manager paused nervously then added. 'And will your daughter be joining you?'

'You're very kind, Andre. Yes. Please have a table prepared for three at 9pm. This is a business associate of mine, Nicholas Trevelyan. He will be joining my daughter and me for dinner.' Warren concluded, charmingly.

Nick exchanged pleasantries with Andre, who then bid them an enjoyable evening and left, shortly to be replaced by the head wine waiter who, with a flourish, produced a bottle of Bollinger vintage champagne and then retired, finally leaving them alone. By this stage Nick's curiosity about this unfathomable man had been well and truly aroused. Cautiously, he tried to start a little polite small talk but Warren Fisher immediately interrupted as he prepared to launch into the 'business' for the evening, without any unnecessary preamble.

## The Offer

'Nicholas, I don't believe in wasting time; mine is very valuable so I won't beat about the bush with you. My daughter appears to like you. I have made a few inquiries about you with contacts at Sandhurst and it appears that you are a man whom others respect and feel that you have demonstrated much promise. You obviously move with ease in circles that you perhaps would not have been privy to, had you not decided to go into the army. I admire this adaptability and the natural facility you have for getting on with people and extracting the best from them. I believe you would be a most acceptable escort for my daughter. It would please me greatly if you decided to continue seeing her. I'm sure she would find your way of life most stimulating and rewarding. I would ensure that you were not wanting for anything that might prove an embarrassment to you. All I ask is this: my daughter is the most important person in my life and I am quite determined that she will only experience the best in every possible way. She may not be able to provide you with a great deal of intellectual stimulation but should anything happen that shows me you are not capable of meeting this simple brief, I should warn you that I am not a man that is easily crossed. However, less of that. Please let me know what you think about the possibility of this arrangement, Nicholas?' Warren concluded.

Holly shit! Warning bells rang in Nick's head rang as he wondered how on earth he had stumbled into this situation and how he could possibly get out of it again. As he had previously deduced, the man sitting in front of him was not someone you could easily say no to, and Nick's mind raced as he tried to think of some plausible way to escape. He realised that it would be unwise to make an enemy of Fisher but, at the same time, he had no intention of becoming part of some bizarre "deal" designed to turn him into an approved gigolo, signed sealed and delivered, with Marina as his taskmistress.

This man was blatantly trying to buy Nick for his daughter and threatening him in the process. Nick began to wish he had never set eyes on the stunning Marina and desperately tried to think of a way to gain some extra time to figure out how to deal with the situation. It was obvious that Warren was starting to become impatient for a response. He drummed his fingers on the table. Nick guessed that he had expected an instant reply and wasn't accustomed to being kept waiting. Before Nick could mumble some inadequate excuse, the very lady herself swept into the bar, distracting them both, along with every other male present. The figure-hugging designer dress that she wore showed off her fabulously proportioned body to the best possible advantage. Nick was temporarily left speechless as he recalled the potency of the immediate physical attraction that they had both experienced the weekend before. Marina reached the table, leant forward and planted a kiss on Warren Fisher's forehead, before sitting down and breathlessly announcing:

'Sorry I'm late, Darlings, but the damn taxi man got caught in a snarl up around Hyde Park corner. He wouldn't go and sort things out so we just had to sit there, would you believe! Anyway, I'm here now. Nicholas, I'm so glad you came. Daddy's been dying to talk to you and I've been longing to see you again.' Marina had a habit of over emphasizing a large number of syllables in her speech; this had a curiously mesmerising affect on him. Nick had to swiftly pull himself together to make the appropriate response as they moved off to go into the dining room. Realising that the shock and resistance which he had felt in an automatic response to Warren Fisher's bazaar offer were slowly fading away to be replaced by a yearning that he knew he was not going to be able to ignore or control. The closeness of the gorgeous Marina, the fragrance of her perfume stirred primeval feelings within his loins which had been the downfall of many men before him. His brains and common sense were rapidly disappearing to a new location below his belt and between his legs. He was totally aware of this and, worryingly, did not care.

Warren had shrewdly noticed the play of emotions across Nick's face from the moment Marina had arrived, and Nick felt he was currently reading his expression with ease for it was a look he'd seen on many men's faces before. Silently in his head Nick knew that Warren was thinking it was a "done deal" and, although he tried very hard, he could not stop looking at Marina.

The meal was lavish and exquisitely prepared. Traditional French cuisine at its best, a seafood platter which looked as if every fish and invertebrate in the Mediterranean was represented. The setting was discrete, the décor tasteful. But he might as well have been sitting in a bus shelter eating fish and chips! However, he managed to conduct myself with sufficient composure but his mind was on one thing and one thing only. Testosterone was in command. His brain was in overdrive, trying to think of a way to either get rid of Warren Fisher, or get away somehow to be alone with Marina.

Suddenly, Warren signalled to the Maitre D' who had hovered subserviently around the table all evening.

'Pierre, please continue to serve my guests with whatever they require for as long as they desire to stay. I shall be going now. Thank you for another most pleasant evening.' announced Warren Fisher. He made a deliberately slow and theatrical job of crumpling his napkin before standing up and holding out his hand. Nick swiftly drew back his chair, and stood up, thanking him for a lovely evening, hardly believing his luck. Warren kissed Marina briefly, fondly stroking her hair in a manner that was more proprietary than paternal, and then hurriedly left the restaurant.

## Marina makes the running

'Oh, thank God,' declared Marina, taking hold of Nick's hand. 'I do love Daddy, but he doesn't always catch on too swiftly when he's not wanted. Okay. Grab your brandy; let's go upstairs.'

'I'm sorry! What do you mean?' Nick stammered. He was still trying to get to grips with the game that seemed to be being played out around him at a hell of a pace.

'Shouldn't we pay first?' he added lamely.

'Don't be silly Darling.' she laughed. 'Daddy is a senior partner in this place. Now, come on! Let's go. I have booked a lovely room for us upstairs and I don't want to waste another moment.'

Nick was temporarily stunned at this blatant admission of premeditation, and for a brief moment a wave of panic washed over him as he realised he was being drawn into a situation over which apparently he had no control. But then a much more dominant, primeval emotion took over and he eagerly followed Marina across the lobby to the lifts and up to the fourth floor, where a sumptuous suite with bathroom, lounge and bar awaited. Nick sat down on the softly inviting bed while Marina disappeared into the bathroom saying.

'Make yourself comfortable Darling.'

Darling! A little premature Nick thought realising that he had had quite a bit to drink; they had tried many different fine wines throughout the meal in addition to the Champagne and he was feeling a little heady.

He kicked off his shoes. *"Right, he thought. They've been playing all the cards so far; time for me to take control".*

Nick was no stranger to women and sex. At an early age he had savoured the delights and revelled in the pleasures that are to be derived from a romantic or simply lustful relationship with, at first, girls, and then later graduating to women. He considered himself a lucky man. He was tall, fit, and young. He had realised the natural attraction that he seemed to have for women and had been swift to capitalise on this and taken full advantage of it. But no amount of preparation could have qualified him for what he was about to experience.

Marina walked out of the bathroom and strode across the sumptuous hotel suite, her bare feet sinking into the thick pile of the white carpet, her hips swaying in a deliberately exaggerated manner. She stopped four feet in front of him, legs slightly apart. Her hands were held as fists that were defiantly placed on her hips. She wore a gossamer silk full-length negligee that was completely transparent.

'Well Nicholas, do you like what you see?' she asked in a low husky and deliberately sexy voice. As the question ended she tossed her head with an almost Flamenco air, causing the golden hair that was cascading over the exquisite features of her face to fall back over her elegant shoulders. The effect of this sudden movement caused her breasts to quiver and the robe to fall open revealing her pert nipples.

Nick sat in stunned silence. The woman who stood in front of him was perfection. Everything was in proportion, her breasts, her thighs, her calves, her perfectly flat stomach, everything. Marina's long naturally blonde hair cascaded over her shoulder and completed the vision of beauty. But there was something else, something that only very few women possess. Marina was voluptuous, sumptuous, luxurious, and sensual. A woman, through and through. She positively radiated sex.

The heady combination of drinks that had been consumed during the evening was having its inevitable effect upon his brain. Just a few days earlier Marina's father had guarded her like an over zealous eunuch. Now he was handing her over on a golden platter. This sort of thing just doesn't happen, he told himself. Not to me. Every single nerve in his body was tingling; he fought hard to retain a resemblance of control. He dreaded to hear the sound of his voice as he answered her redundant question, expecting that only a burbling gaggle of non-coherent babble would emerge from his dry anaesthetised mouth. Did he like what he saw? How dumb can you get? Yeah dammed right, he liked what he saw, every delicious inch of it.

'Marina, you are a truly beautiful woman.'

He heard the words and for a split second thought that another man had entered the room, so calmly was the sentence spoken that he doubted that it could have been him who had uttered it.

'I'm so happy that you like me, Nick,' purred Marina. 'I know that I can make you so happy.'

Every ounce of Nick's common sense told him to run, that something was seriously wrong. This was all too good to be true. But what the hell. There could be no man alive on the planet who could resist what was on offer. Marina slowly slid her hands from her hips and took hold of the negligee by her finger tips easing it back over her shoulders, letting it drop silently to the floor. She moved forward opening her long, tanned legs straddling his legs and pushed her soft stomach towards his face. He gently kissed the perfectly formed navel.

Lowering herself onto his lap their faces were level. Their eyes were locked.

Marina brought her right hand up across his arm over his shoulder and caressed his neck. Slowly she drove her long sensuous fingers into the hair on the back of his head; then suddenly and without warning, she grabbed a handful of hair, violently jerking his head backwards. Nick was caught off guard and his mouth opened as if to let out an agonised scream but before he had drawn breath, Marina's mouth had covered his and was pressing lip to lip with a powerful force. Her wild tongue sought every hidden corner of his mouth. As the passion rose within her she twisted and jerked in ecstasy never letting the pressure between their lips relax. The violence of the jerking caused her teeth to cut into his lips and he could taste the salty blood. Initially the shock had hit him like a baseball bat between the shoulder blades. Marina had taken the initiative entirely up to that point. But now he was aroused and fighting back with equal passion. Slowly he brought his right hand up across her arm over her shoulder and caressed her neck. Then he drove his fingers into the hair on the back of her head, then suddenly and without warning, He grabbed a handful of hair, violently jerking Marina's head backwards. Now he really had the bit between his teeth and gave as good as he had received plus a little extra. They held onto each other's hair as they writhed and kissed in a crazed embrace. Nick allowed himself to be pushed back onto the bed. At the same time he slowly turned and levered himself so that he was now on top. He raised myself up onto his knees and with a violent tug wrenched their mouths apart. He retained his hold on Marina's hair; her grip was lost in the sudden violence of his movement. He pulled Marina's head backward with his eyes fixed on hers. There were smears of blood on her cheeks and at the corner of her mouth. Her expression was of feigned pain although Nick knew that he must have been hurting her. He released his grip and stood up. He was still fully dressed. He took off his clothes whilst Marina squirmed on the bed with delight, occasionally whimpering with anticipation.

When his feet left the deep pile white carpet to climb into the bed, it was more than four hours before they touched the carpet again. This was the opening to a night of sex that he would never forget. It was also the prelude to a erotic and tempestuous relationship. Within three days, a gleaming black Porsche 911 was delivered. courtesy of Mr Warren Fisher. Nick was now the proud owner of an icon vehicle which was generally accepted as the signature car for all well heeled British army officers. Things were certainly looking up.

## The Cane of Honour

They fell into a full time relationship and Nick continued to be mesmerized by the stunning Marina as the course at Sandhurst progressed, but by this stage there were other matters on his mind besides partying. The rivalry between Steve and Nick brought out the best in each of them. As the final weeks of the course approached, a shortlist of cadets who were the most likely candidates in the running for the prestigious prizes that were to be handed out at the Sovereign's Parade. Steve and Nick appeared to be in friendly contention for the coveted title of Cane of Honour, while Nick had also been earmarked for the Modern History prize.

Tristram Wrath-Bingham had shown he had a keen political brain and was likely to walk away with the award for Politics and Economics. With the exercises finally behind them, they apprehensively looked forward to the programme of rehearsals for the all-important Sovereign's Parade and the prize that they had all been striving for: their commission and officer's pips.

## Tristram's Verbal attack

Tristram chose the location for his final move against Nick with supreme cunning, added to which his timing was immaculate. Catching Nick alone in a corridor he stopped to talk. Initially he appeared quite friendly but as he progressed with the one sided conversation he changed to his more typical obnoxious mode. His criticisms were insulting to begin with, moving on to downright offensive. He was winding himself up with a rant of abuse which initially shocked Nick coming as it did out of nowhere. He made a move to walk past but Tristram had angled himself to block the corridor. Was he taking the opportunity to finally make his feelings felt before they went their separate ways? This was a man who had done his homework in detail.

'You'll be following in the footsteps of your illustrious father, Trevelyan. It shouldn't take too much effort from what I have heard. His army career amounted to a waste of taxpayer's money; the only people to benefit have been the pubs and breweries.'

Nick stood thunderstruck at the unprovoked verbal attack, his emotions were boiling. This pompous idiot was obviously enjoying every offensive word, but why, why did he harbour such hatred? His finger prodding and abuse were proving to be too much but amazingly Nick kept his cool, until Tristram delivered his final coup-de-grace which pushed Nick over the edge.

'And, Trevelyan, as if your father wasn't bad enough, your mother . . . .' but he never finished the sentence. He had exceeded his limits of reserve. Finally enough was enough and Nick snapped. Lunging forward he grabbed his verbal attacker by the throat and took it to physical level. Slamming Tristram against a wall, Nick pinned him with his left arm and drew back his right fist, ready to land the blow which he had anticipated would inevitably happen from the moment he had met this obnoxious man. All common sense had left him and reasoning was abandoned. Nick knew that he had descended to the law of the jungle but it felt good.

'What the hell are you doing, Trevelyan?' the familiar voice of Colour Sergeant McGarrigal came through the mist of anger. Nick released his grip on the dishevelled Tristram who slid down the wall.

'I want this incident reported to the Adjutant immediately' demanded Tristram, sounding like a spoilt schoolboy.

'This is something that you two should resolve privately' advised the Colour Sergeant.

'Colour Sergeant, I said that I want this incident reported to the Adjutant now!'

'Very well Mr Wrath-Bingham you leave me no alternative. Mr Trevelyan, I'm afraid I will have to report what has happened here.'

'Do your job, Colour. It's not your fault.' Nick had recovered his calm and was watching Tristram who was looking supremely pleased with himself. He had achieved exactly what he had set out to do and Nick had been an unsuspecting idiot who had jumped into his trap with both feet.

# 3

# INSTRUCTORS AT SANDHURST

The instructors at Sandhurst Military Academy are by any standards a remarkable group of men. Sandhurst is unarguably the best officer training academy in the world. Any instructor has to be top quality, and is drawn from Officers and non commissioned officers from every conceivable unit in the British Army and brought to Sandhurst for their expertise in their own particular subject, whether this is drill, small arms, self defence, physical training or whatever. Much emphasis is paid to drill in the formative weeks, teaching recruits to move and react as a single body, and forging the adjustment necessary to becoming part of a team. Drill instructors are usually drawn from the Brigade of Guards as these regiments are highly regarded for their rigid discipline and immaculate drill.

The lowest non-commissioned instructor rank at the Academy is a Sergeant whilst the highest NCO rank is The Academy Sergeant Major, holder of the Queen's Warrant Officer First Class. All units of the army have Sergeant Majors whose titles vary slightly, depending on their regiment or corps but there are two uniquely, prestigious and unusual appointments which a Guards WO1 can hold: The first is Garrison Sergeant Major, London District, and the second is Academy Sergeant Major, Sandhurst. It is traditional for these two appointments to be filled by a WO1 from the Brigade of Guards. The posts are highly respected within the army; therefore, whoever fills the post must be a formidable character.

# Dusty Miller

This was very much the case while Nick was at Sandhurst. Discipline was metered out by the iron fist of Academy Sergeant Major Miller, B.E.M. Grenadier Guards. "Dusty" was a formidable chap. He stood six feet four inches tall and weighed eighteen stone, all of which was hard muscle. His close cropped, greying hair topped a face which was more squared than rounded. His small broken nose was hardly noticeable above the wide black moustache and the piercing blue eyes were barely visible below the Guards style slashed peak of his forage cap. One of the many noticeable features of this massive man was that he appeared to have no neck. It was as if his head had grown straight out of his shoulders, All of WO1 Miller's spare time was dedicated to his awesome body. He worked out, pumped iron, and threw his tremendous frame over the various assault courses that were scattered around the academy's extensive grounds, whenever time permitted. Nick found it hard to decide just which of WO1 Miller's many outrageous attributes he considered to be the most striking. Eventually he settled the matter in a discussion with Steve when they agreed that it had to be the voice. "Dusty" as he was affectionately known by the recruits, was doubtless the possessor of the loudest voice in the world. Even his speaking voice was a dozen or so decibels above the norm, although there were few enough occasions when he actually just talked. But his Drill Square voice was something to behold. Everyone, bar none, stood in terror when the huge lungs expelled the air that carried forth the word. His eagle eyes were capable of detecting the most minute flaw in a recruit's turnout. But it was not only the cadets who needed to be faultless in their appearance: anyone who put a foot onto "his" Square was subjected to meticulous scrutiny, and should anyone be found to be less than one hundred percent perfect, he took it as a personal affront. The tongue-lashing that Nick could expect to receive from the Adjutant would be severe but in order to get to the Adjutant, he would have to pass through the office of the A.S.M. and that was a fate that every recruit dreaded. When he got the summons to appear before the Adjutant, his heart sank. A junior cadet had been sent to take him to the office of the Adjutant. Upon arrival, the company clerk told him to wait in the lobby for the ASM and it was here that he now found himself, sitting on a wooden bench, feeling like a schoolboy waiting for the headmaster from hell. His heart was in his mouth. He told himself to get a grip. After all, this was only a man; he would not be able to inflict any physical punishment Nick reassured himself. It's only words. Suddenly, the door was flung open and ASM Miller walked in. Nick sprang to his feet, determined not to allow his terror get the better of him. Miller strode across the room and stood toe to toe with him, their faces only inches apart. Being a tall man himself, Nick had never suffered from any feeling of inadequate height. But now, with the ASM seemingly towering above him, he felt positively dwarf-like. His immediate reaction was to take a step backwards, but this would have been a negative move and he denied himself the luxury, fixing his gaze on the ASM's knotted tie. He was surprised. He had expected that the effect of such close proximity to another human being would inevitably mean that his breath would be overpowering, but was amazed to observe that the gorilla in whose shadow he was standing actually had sweet smelling breath.

'Mr. Trevelyan,' began ASM Miller conversationally—which threw Nick a little as he had been prepared for an ear shattering shout.

'It may come as a surprise to you, but I have been taking a particular interest in your progress through this Academy, and after a shaky start you have settled down and shaped up very well. Your instructors speak highly of you and you have acquitted yourself well on the sports field. In fact, Mr. Trevelyan, you are as near as can be considered to being a model cadet. I have also checked into your background and I have observed that you do not have the same advantages as the majority of your peers regarding family ancestry and finances, as I'm sure hasn't escaped your notice. Now, Mr Trevelyan, here is something that I do not do very often. I am going to offer you some advice: be very careful. The old money, which you will see so well represented here, will always look after its own. You cannot infiltrate their ranks; they make bad adversaries and will have no compunction in trampling you into the ground. He stepped backward one pace.

'Mark my words well, Nicholas; it could spare you unhappiness in the future. Now, Cadet Trevelyan, I am going to march you into the Adjutant's Office and you had better move yourself. Orders, orders, 'shun! By the front, double quick march! Left, right, left right, left right, left! Right turn! Mark time! Halt. Salute. Cadet Trevelyan, Sir.' with this resounding demonstration of his usual character, ASM Miller left the Adjutant's office.

# The Adjutant

'Officer Cadet Trevelyan reporting, Sir!' Shouted Nick, standing rigidly to attention. The Adjutant was sitting at his desk. He looked directly into Nick's eyes from the moment he marched in, scrutinizing him as if he was an alien who had been brought in by Luke Skywalker from another planet. Nick stared intently at a spot on the wall about six inches above his head and braced himself for the impending ordeal, fully aware that his indiscretion was about to invoke a fearful response. The Adjutant stood up and walked around his desk, slowly he approached Nick. So far he had not uttered a word and the muscles in Nick's neck were aching with tension as he steeled himself for the roar of verbal abuse that was sure to burst at any second. The Adjutant seemed determined to enjoy his discomfort for as long as possible, but as he relaxed his muscles the merest fraction, the Adjutant suddenly screamed into his left ear.

'MR. TREVELYAN! I do not want to hear your excuses; I do not want to hear you so much as breathe. You will listen to what I have to say, and then you will give me your best reason as to why you think you deserve to make an appearance at the Sovereign's Parade in three days time, and not be dismissed from this academy or at the very least back squadded. I have had cause to see you before me many times in the last twelve months, Mr. Trevelyan, the cadets of your platoon have collectively tried my patience to its limits with your inadequate attempts to reflect the standards of behaviour which are demanded of you as Officer Cadets at this Academy'.

All of this was actually a gross exaggeration of the truth but there was nothing Nick could say in his own defence. He was expected to accept without argument this verbal punishment. He continued his exploration of the spot on the wall. Twenty percent of his brain was listening to the tirade of words whilst the other eighty percent was contemplating the real reason why he was here. Could it be that Tristram was right? Had he shown that perhaps Nick was little more than a mongrel who had revealed his lack of breeding and reverted to violence when a well-bred man would have solved the dilemma in an altogether more civilized way? The aristocrat had discovered Nick's Achilles heel and had exploited it to his advantage. The part of his brain that had been keeping watch warned the rest of his mind that the tongue lashing was drawing to an end; he prepared myself mentally for the climax.

'Finally, however, finally, the expert attentions of Colour Sergeant Macgregor seem to be having an effect, and I have come to expect that the members of your platoon will actually pass out as meritorious representatives of this establishment.'

'Sir, I . . .' Nick interjected when the bellowing Adjutant finally stopped, briefly, for breath.

'SHUT UP!' He roared in anger, 'I have not finished with you yet, Mr. Trevelyan. One more word from you and I'll have you shovelling manure in the stables for the next forty-eight hours. Mr. Trevelyan, you will shortly be graduating from this Academy. However, you can be sure that, apart from your usual drill rehearsals, your feet will not touch the ground from now until the Sovereign's Parade. Additionally, be assured that your copy book has been well and truly marked which will be evident to anybody in the future who, for whatever insane reason, decides to take any interest in your career. Don't say a word, Mr. Trevelyan! I don't want to hear any of your miserable whining. Get out of my sight. I will see you first thing in the morning and make sure your appearance is quite resplendent. Because Mr. Trevelyan, if I see as much as a crease or speck of dust I'll . . . . just get out of my sight until I have the misfortune to have to lay eyes on you again.' Nick trudged back to his quarters in a daze, feeling utterly shattered.

## The Sovereign's Parade

Finally the morning of the Sovereign's Parade arrived. They all prepared for the occasion feeling excited to have reached the end of the course. First stop was the Academy Chapel where parents were briefly met and a stirring service started the day's proceedings. Nick greeted his mother and father who were accompanied by Marina, looking great as always. Nick had been worried that she would wear something outrageous or too revealing but was delighted to see that she was dressed with stylish good taste. The designer suit was the height of sophistication but nevertheless the slit at the back of the superbly tailored skirt was cut high giving tantalizing glimpses of Marina's gorgeous legs. The snug fitting jacket had a low cut neck-line allowing a view of her voluptuous cleavage. When Nick had first introduced Marina to his parents he worried that her obviously sensuous appearance might be a problem but his mother took an immediate liking to her and as for his father, well the biggest problem for him was not to be seen leering, given that Marina was capable of raising the blood pressure of any man, irrespective of age. After attending to their guests the cadets hurried to pick up their rifles and belts. Then the platoon formed up for the last time in front of the Adjutant on New College Square.

Nick's apprehension was heightened by anticipation of the Award Ceremony at the end of the Parade. He knew that he had long been earmarked as a strong contender for the Cane of Honour but after the events of the last few days he had become increasingly anxious that he might have screwed his chances. It was with a certain amount of relief that he anticipated his commissioning and the disbandment of the 'newly fledged' officers to their various regiments and units. Nick had made many friends at the Academy, but there were certain influences that he would not miss. Certainly, he hoped it would be a long time before he was to have the misfortune of bumping into the poisonous duo of Bingham and Harcourt again,

He returned his thoughts to the day's parade, which is a very special event and something that will stay in the memory of anyone who has been fortunate enough to take part. Pageantry is something that they are exceedingly good at in Britain. The military bands and precision marching stir the soul of those who hear them.

## Prize Giving

As the parade reached its conclusion, everyone lined up in front of the royal visitor in anticipation of the award ceremony. Nick stood rigidly to attention. As the winner's name for the Cane of Honour was announced, he didn't flinch when the award went to Steve. He was genuinely pleased that, if it wasn't going to him, then Steve was equally deserving of the prize. He was more worried about his parents' reaction; having mistakenly talked to them about the possibility of his receiving the award, he knew he could rely on his mother; but his father was likely to make his disappointment known in no uncertain terms. As further prizes were announced, his disappointment was alleviated by his being announced as recipient of the Military History prize. Some recognition at least for his hard work.

With all the relevant ceremonial duties performed, the climax to the parade approached. The ranks of cadets who had passed out marched up the steps of the Old College in slow time to the accompaniment of Auld Lang Sine, to be followed by the traditional mounting of the steps by the Adjutant on horseback. Once beyond the entrance, the elated cadets handed over their rifles and belts, and then hurried to meet their guests and dignitaries for the Sovereign Parade's Luncheon.

Nick approached the gathering and spotted his parents to one side of the throng. He smiled for what felt like the first time that that day. His mother turned and caught his eye. She wordlessly conveyed to him across the room her feelings of pride in his achievements, giving his severely bruised confidence a well-deserved boost. The look on his father's face was an altogether different picture. Thomas Trevelyan's face was marred by a grimace that seemed to ward off the possibility of social advances from any of the other circulating guests. Nick walked up to them and greeted his mother and Marina with a hug, then stood stiffly and held out my hand to his father.

'Hope you enjoyed the Parade, father,' He said politely.

'Splendid affair, but tell me Nicholas; what happened with the award ceremonies? I thought you'd been boasting about the fact that you were going to win the Cane of Honour. How did you manage to screw that up?'

Nick smiled nervously, aware of the proximity of the other guests and of the fact that his father had obviously already indulged in a couple of large whiskies.

'If you don't mind, I'd rather talk about that later, father, this is meant to be a celebration lunch,' he muttered, tersely. 'I've got to take you and introduce to some of my friends. Do you think you can manage that without embarrassing me?'

'Huh! You seem to manage to embarrass yourself quite well enough. What am I meant to tell our friends when we get home? retorted his father, bluffly

'We'll tell them that our son has passed out from Sandhurst Academy as an Officer and a Gentleman. We'll tell them that we are very proud of him and look forward to hearing of his successes in his new regiment. Now, please can you two stop for just one day so that we can enjoy ourselves as a family, for once,' his mother interrupted quietly, but firmly. Both men looked shamefaced, reprimanded by the composure and dignity of the woman beside them whose serenity and understanding was a constant source of amazement to Nick. He discreetly smiled his appreciation of her intervention. His father coughed nervously.

'Certainly, my dear. Just as you wish. I think I'll just pop and get another drink while we're waiting.'

'No dear. No more drink until lunchtime. We've a busy day ahead of us and we're going to meet lots of different people. You'll never remember their names if you drink too much, and you know how much that irritates you.' interjected his mother again, resolutely.

'Quite right, dear . . . . very well. Come along then, Nicholas. Lead the way. The sooner we can sit down to lunch the better, as far as I'm concerned.' Nick allowed himself a silent sigh of relief. Once more, thanks to his mother, this might not turn out to be as much of an ordeal as anticipated. After lunch, his parents, Marina, and all the other guests, went home or to hotels to change for the dinner that evening.

## His Father

Nick's father was one of the last of the "old school" soldiers; he had spent twenty-two years in the army during which time he had only managed four promotions. His contemporaries had risen steadily upwards through the ranks, but his father had hardly moved up the promotional ladder at all. This was largely due to the bitter memories he retained of his own father's catastrophic demise and the effect this had had on his attitude to life. A huge chip which he carried that was sadly less positive than was expected of a potential army officer. His grandfather came from a rather well heeled family and inherited a reasonable fortune. Slowly, with the help of alcohol, he squandered it all away and died from sclerosis of the liver in his late forties, leaving his wife and son to fend for themselves during the austerity years after the war. His father felt cheated of the lifestyle that he thought he had been born to. He was too introspective to be a team player and too negative to be an inspirational leader. He stuck with the army life because it was an institutionalised existence which, if it was the path you chose, required little thought. He made the best of a bad job and ended up spending as much time in the regimental mess and various local watering holes, as possible. His greatest regret was that he had never received a commission and so it was left to Nick, his only son, to fulfil his father's dreams and join the army as an officer cadet. Nick however, had his own agenda, and was not joining the army just to please his father whose alcoholic antics left him cold. He made a pledge to himself that he would never allow himself to stay in the army if he were not an efficient soldier. It appeared at this point in his life that the world was his own particular, khaki oyster.

## The Sandhurst Ball

That evening, at the Ball, Steve and Nick were standing together opposite the doorway of the Academy gymnasium. It was a long standing tradition at Sandhurst that the insignia of the cadets chosen regiment or corp was covered and not revealed until midnight. Nick and Steve were dressed in their individual Regimental Mess Dress, worn for the first time that night, proudly sporting one pip on each shoulder. The evening boasted an array of entertainments that exceeded even the army's renowned organisational ability. A string of linked marquees housed all kinds of attractions, whilst the main buildings resounded with loud music from a variety of discos and bars.

Marina was in her element, attracting glances from so many good looking young men and she revelled in it. Nick was happy to have such a stunning woman on his arm and was also enjoying the fact that he was the envy of just about every male present. She flitted about between him and his parents, who seemed to be the people that she felt most comfortable with. This was a one-off occasion and she wanted to make the most of it.

Nick had long since left his mother to capably deal with his father's excesses of behaviour. They were sure to leave shortly as it was well past midnight; the remaining revellers would stay on long into the night. In the meantime he took the opportunity to have a quiet chat with Steve before they went their separate ways. Nick had been accepted as a second lieutenant with the Argyle and Sutherland Highlanders whilst Steve had the company of the men of the Parachute Regiment to look forward to.

'I really can't quite get used to you in that skirt.' said Steve, amused to see his good friend in a kilt for the first time. 'There's obviously not a drop of Gaelic blood stirring in my veins, as I'm afraid I feel most unmoved by your tartan togs. However, I would like to say that I think you have a lovely pair of legs and any man would be proud to have you standing by his side.'

'Thanks for the compliment. I do my best to keep in shape. Might as well show them off. I think you're just jealous of my rather splendid apparel because you're not having much luck with the girls. Whereas I can have my pick because of the extra added novelty value of dancing with a man in a kilt and the anticipation of whether or not he's going to reveal the secrets of the sporran.' Nick retorted, smugly. Steve laughed and fell silent as he contemplated broaching the subject that Nick suspected had been bothering him all day.

'Nick, about this Cane of Honour,' he started.

'Please, Steve,' It's no big deal. I'm just glad it went to you. I just messed up with one of the big guys and there were bound to be repercussions. I can't honestly say it wasn't unexpected. It's water under the bridge. I achieved what I wanted from the course and I'm proud of that. Now it's up to us to make the most of our careers. I'm looking forward to moving on; particularly to moving away from that specimen, Wrath-Bingham and his toady henchman, Harcourt. They'd better not cross my path for a while or I won't be answerable. In the meantime, let's not let that little maggot spoil our fun. Come on. I'm going to find my parents and put them in a taxi. Then we can really get stuck in. I've also left Marina alone for too long and there are plenty of admirers who will have noticed my absence and might be contemplating moving in. Let's say I meet you at the Champagne Bar in thirty minutes.'

Nick found his parents at their table in the Cocktail Bar. They looked tired but contented as they engaged in an animated conversation with another couple at the table. Steve had introduced his parents to Nick's and the four appeared to have hit it off rather well. Marina was looking a little bored with the older company and was happy to see Nick return. She gave him a smile and he knew exactly what she was thinking as something along the same lines was going through his head. It would be great to make love to her in his Sandhurst bed. Tonight would be the only opportunity. He noted that his father had certainly had enough to drink. He had seen the signs plenty of times before, but he was far from behaving in his usual belligerent fashion and must have mellowed in the engaging company. Nick reflected that it was a shame his father didn't have more friends like the Craig's. He was sure that the army friends whom he still met up with and his local drinking cronies back in Windsor did little more than aggravate his drink problem. If his father spent less time mulling over his regrets about his army career, he would be able to enjoy his life far more. Nick firmly believed that his mother and father would lead a much more contented existence. As it was, instead of moving forward and accepting new challenges, his father was trapped in the past and drinking had become his only real means of communication. His mother's steadfast support over the many years they had been together was his only real lifeline to reality, connecting him to everyday life. Without her, he would be lost.

'How's everybody doing? Enjoying yourselves, I hope?' Nick asked cheerily as he sat down.

'Couldn't be better! We could stay all night,' replied William Craig, a tall, imposing, heavy-set figure with a friendly face.

'But I don't think we shall.' interrupted his wife, Anne, smiling as she leant across the table and rested her hand on his forearm, a comfortable gesture that intimated the many years of easy companionship the couple had enjoyed.

'Yes, Darling,' laughed his mother. 'We've had a marvellous time certainly, but your father and I would like to go back to our hotel now; could you order us a taxi, please?'

'Of course! Mr. and Mrs. Craig, can I do the same for you?' I asked.

'No thanks, Nick,' replied William Craig. 'We'll say our good-byes to your parents now, but we'll wait a little longer in the hope that our errant son might turn up to say goodbye!'

Nick laughed and walked across the Cocktail Bar towards the door, idly noting that the Entertainments Committee had done a good job in transforming the normally plain lecture room into a colourful and atmospheric bar. As he reached the exit, a group of three people stepped round the corner, blocking his way. With a sinking heart he recognized the upright figure in the Regimental Mess Dress of the Life Guards.

'Trevelyan!' exclaimed Tristram Wrath-Bingham with mock delight. 'How marvellous to see you, and there was I thinking that you were going to leave without saying goodbye. Do come and meet my parents: General, Sir Michael Wrath-Bingham and Lady Wrath-Bingham, Nicholas Trevelyan.' Seeing no way out Nick reluctantly followed Tristram who made the polite introduction to his parents Nick gave a courteous reply extending his hand to both in turn, hoping that he was managing to inject enough warmth into the accompanying smile. He couldn't believe his bad luck; out of the hundreds of people milling around the Academy and its grounds, these were probably the last three people he wanted to bump into.

'Trevelyan!' barked the intimidating figure of Sir Michael Wrath-Bingham. Nick was well aware that Bingham's fearsome father had a reputation which preceded him and that he had been known throughout the British army as someone whose bite was definitely as bad as his bark. Confrontation with the fiery old war dog was to be avoided at all costs.

'My son has told me everything about you. I understand you are destined for great things. I believe the regiment you are headed for is the Argyle and Sutherland Highlanders; fine body of men; fine history. I know their Commanding Officer very well. He's a marvellous chap. I shall have to give him a call and let him know you're on your way so that he can keep a special eye on you!' announced the General.

*'Yeah, I could imagine the venomous remarks that he would convey to his new boss.'*

'Thank you so much, General, but please don't go to any trouble on my behalf. It has been a great pleasure to meet you both. I'm so sorry to rush off but I'm on an errand; I have to get a taxi for my parents and I don't want to keep them waiting,' Nick replied, sighing inwardly. *'What the hell had that little rat said to his father about me? Can't imagine that it could have been complimentary.'* Nick shook hands all round, finishing with Wrath-Bingham Junior.

'I wish you every success in the Cavalry and hope that you have the good fortune to be posted to many far-flung, exotic locations, where you will be able to prove yourself to be the stalwart leader that we all know is well within your capabilities. And who knows? Maybe one day, our paths will cross again, and we'll be able to chat about old times and all the fun we had together.' He delivered the short speech while unflinchingly meeting Bingham's penetrating gaze.

'I'm sure we shall,' replied Bingham, smoothly.

The message had clearly passed between the two of them and as they went their separate ways, there was a mutual, unspoken understanding that any future confrontations might not turn out to be so cordial. Wrath-Bingham had yet again managed to spoil the moment and Nick was angry. Yet there was something that he could do to alleviate the annoyance. After arranging his parent's taxi and saying goodbye. Nick took Marina by the hand and immediately she knew what he was thinking. Like two naughty school children they sneaked away to his bunk. All of his belongings had been packed up ready to leave but the bed was still made and it was all that they needed. As they arrived at his bunk and before he had finished carefully locking the door, Marina had practically torn her clothes off,

'Hurry up Nick; I want you so much.' she urged, then eagerly assisted him to undress and they fell onto the bed locked into a steamy session of unrestrained lust. The regulation army pattern bed was never designed for the gymnastics that were taking place on it at that moment and as they had been used to the luxury of Marina's king size bed at her flat, they came close to falling out of it several times. Another problem was that Marina was very vocal during sex. She always entered into the affair with her heart and soul, completely without inhibitions. Nick realised that this could be a problem and it was necessary to hold his hand over her mouth in an attempt to control the noise. This only had the effect of making her squirm and giggle even louder. Having sex in a location that is out of bounds adds to the excitement and this made it all the sweeter.

## Military Life

Nick joined his regiment in Northern Ireland as a rookie First Lieutenant. He learned quickly. When the tour ended his report said that he had served with distinction. Upon the return of the regiment to the mainland Regimental HQ they quickly found themselves dispatched to the Arabian Gulf, one of the few infantry units to be involved in the war known as *Desert Storm*. A happy reunion took place in the Gulf when he met up with Steve. Having spent a couple of years with 1 Para he had applied to join the Special Air Service and after the usual tough initiation course, had became a member of that elite regiment. He was sent to the Gulf as part of a unit assigned to free a couple of military hostages, taken prisoner by the Iraqis. Steve and Nick managed to spend a few evenings together, renewing their acquaintance with the ease of old friends who had been through much together. They vowed to keep in more regular contact when they returned to England. Neither could have imagined that such an opportunity would arise eighteen months later under circumstances that neither could have ever dreamt of.

The deployment of the regiment to Iraqi was sudden and the time spent there caused all of them to grow from what was, in Nick's case, a boy, to a man. It was hot, dirty and dangerous and they were all grateful that the hours, days and weeks of training stood them in good stead for the tasks that they were to encounter. Surprisingly the war didn't last as long as everyone had predicted and after a few short months they found themselves packing up in preparation for their return to the UK.

When he returned from the Gulf he was a Captain and it was generally acknowledged amongst his fellow officers that Nick was destined for a fine career in the army. His ability to command men in a modern manner, by leading from the front and by example, coupled with his aptitude as a military historian and tactician were qualities much sought after in the modern British Army. He loved every minute of every day that he spent in the army.

His relationship with Marina continued. When Nick was away on active duty or unable to get back to London, Marina seemed to be quite content to spend the time alone or with her father, running her boutique and shopping. The time that they spent apart only served to enhance the intensity of the reunions which can only be described as the clash of the sexual Titans.

Within a year after returning from the Gulf, Nick was guaranteed his promotion to Major, and from there, with his knowledge of modern conventional warfare, there was a strong possibility that, in time, he would be offered a position at The Staff College and the rapid rise in rank that went with the post. After leaving Sandhurst, he had had little contact with the other cadets from his intake, as they had all moved on to different sections of the army. Steve was the only one whom he corresponded with regularly. He crossed paths with Tristram Wrath-Bingham at a couple of weekend balls when he was stationed in England, but the encounters were brief and inconsequential. Nick would never forget what had happened between them, though with time he thought that it had faded into insignificance. Currently, he was far too intent on pursuing his career to let personal vendettas cloud his vision. However, that original encounter with Wrath-Bingham at Camberley station when he first heard his affected drawl was a pivotal point in his life, although Nick could never have guessed it at the time.

## Edinburgh Tattoo

While in the UK his regiment, in common with most of the British Forces, was occasionally called upon to undertake certain ceremonial duties. They were required to furnish a drill display team that would accompany the regimental band of the pipes and drums at the Edinburgh Tattoo.

Nick was called into the Colonel's office. The Colonel had decided that Nick looked good in uniform. He added that because of Nick's appearance, bearing and proven communication skills, he had chosen him to lead the Argyle detachment which was to attend the annual military display in Scotland. Wonderful thought Nick, so if I had been a scruffy git I would have been spared the privilege! The Tattoo stretched over a period of four consecutive days. The Argyles were required to mount a display of marching and rifle drill accompanied by their band; once in the afternoon and once in the evening. Nick arrived with his detachment and they were all taken to their various places of accommodation. It wasn't long before he realised that he was going to have his hands full keeping an eye on his men.

There were the inevitable occurrences of soldiers getting drunk which usually resulted in his being called to the local police station to recover one or more of his men. But this was only to be expected as the Jocks rarely had the opportunity to operate on their home territory. As a large percentage of the Edinburgh police were either ex-servicemen or sons and daughters of ex-service men, there was never too much hassle in retrieving his wayward soldiers.

He had developed a relationship with his men which was based on mutual respect. The men of the Argyles were hard and uncompromising but, if accepted, you were rewarded with their loyalty, and you knew that their allegiance would be unquestioning, no matter what the circumstance. If you did not earn this respect, your position as a leader would be a wearing, uphill struggle. Nick had spent long, arduous hours with his men in the turbulent and close-knit conditions that prevailed not only in Northern Ireland, but also during the Gulf campaign where he appeared to have won their respect and had secured a rock solid devotion from a group of tough and tenacious soldiers.

The whole Tattoo event took place in the imposing setting of Edinburgh Castle. It looked even more magnificent at night when it was floodlit. Inside the castle, there were the inevitable Messes, the most elaborate being for the officers. There was also a Senior NCO's Mess, which although well decorated could not compare with the lavishness of the Officers' Quarters. The two other Messes were temporary affairs, set up in tents, only for the duration of the Tattoo; these catered for the Junior NCOs and other ranks.

Traditionally, the Edinburgh Tattoo brought together a variety of armed units from all over the Commonwealth and this year was no exception, with contingents from the Ghurkhas, New Zealand and Canada. There were also British units from the RAF, Royal Marines and Royal Navy, with a musical ride performed by The Household Cavalry. All this made for very mixed and interesting bouts of serious drinking in all of the Messes. Nick had not long arrived at his quarters in Edinburgh when he received a message to be in the bar of the George Hotel at 8pm. Intrigued by this little mystery, he washed and changed and arrived at the appointed destination shortly before 8.00pm. He sat down at the bar to await his mystery "date" and it wasn't long before in through the door walked the welcome figure of Steve, grinning hugely as always.

'I don't believe it,' Nick shouted delightedly. 'What the hell are you doing round these parts? I haven't heard from you for a couple of months so I thought you were off on some top secret mission somewhere,' he joked.

'Maybe I am.' replied Steve, tapping the side of his nose. Nick knew better that to ask any more of his SAS buddy and guessed that he was probably there on close protection duty. He grabbed his hand and pumped it ruthlessly, so happy was he to see his old friend. They settled down for a welcome evening's entertainment catching up, with Nick filling Steve in first.

'Things have been somewhat boring since I returned from the Gulf. You have so much to sort out in your mind when you come back from something like that and it takes an awful lot to keep you occupied enough not to find yourself thinking about it all the time. I guess I'm still a bit hyped up. But generally, I've been reasonably busy and feel I must be getting closer to Staff College so I'm looking forward to that. I'm still seeing Marina although she couldn't come to the Tattoo; two weeks skiing in Val D"Isere but, after coming back from the Gulf, it's becoming more apparent quite how vacant she is. It really is all tin soldiers to her and I know I can't realistically expect any kind of sensible support from her. She's a sweet girl and I've enjoyed being with her and her old man is a hell of a meal ticket. I've still got that Porsche he gave me the summer that I graduated from Sandhurst; I reckon he might even update it soon! I suppose I could do considerably worse, I guess I'm just feeling a bit jaded! Take no notice of me. So how about you? A girl in every port I suppose?'

'Well, funny you should say that, but after having joined the Regiment there really hasn't been much time for gadding about so I was most definitely without for a while. Then I went for a two week series of lectures all about something very top secret. The lecturer was this fantastic woman. She's forty and amazingly intelligent, and the rest. Made me feel like a schoolboy in one minute. I couldn't keep my eyes off her! The more she brushed me off, the more I went after her. I chased her for two weeks and she finally let me take her out. I've seen her a few times since, but the most incredible thing has happened. I've stopped looking at other women! Can you believe it?'

'I guess even a leopard can change his spots eventually.' Nick laughed, 'I wish you health, wealth and happiness; keep me posted.' He added, giving Steve a friendly pat on the back.

'I certainly will, but there's one other bit of news that I don't know whether you're aware of yet; guess who else is in town? I bumped into him not half an hour ago and exchanged a few unpleasantries.' Steve said.

'I give up,' Nick replied. 'Surprise me.'

'I've got a feeling it won't be a very pleasant surprise, Mate: it's His Honourable Righteousness, Captain Tristram Wrath-Bingham no less.' said Steve, raising his eyebrows.

'Of course!' Nick exclaimed. 'He'll be in charge of the mounted detachment. I should have guessed. That's just the kind of cushy number he'd go for, with plenty of opportunity to show off.'

'Oh well, I guess you've got to just hope he's grown up and become a human being, but don't hold your breath, there's bound to be trouble if you two meet—so steer clear.' replied Steve.

The next evening, after dinner Nick was to find that steering clear of Wrath-Bingham was going to be a nigh impossible task. He was clearly enjoying the occasion immensely and immediately he showed up in the Mess, made straight for Nick as soon as he realised he was there.

'Trevelyan! How marvellous to see you!' he drawled. Nick felt an immediate flash of déjà-vu as he stretched out his hand to renew his acquaintance with his old adversary.

'Pleasure's all mine,' Nick replied, smiling warmly, allowing his eyes to linger on the thin scar on Tristram's cheekbone which became a livid red as he saw the direction of Nick's eyes.

'Are you well?' The smile that Wrath-Bingham returned was as false as that of a Cheshire cat, decidedly lacking in warmth, and as their eyes locked, Nick couldn't help but sigh inwardly. '*So much for steering clear of trouble.*'

'I am in excellent shape, Trevelyan. I look forward to seeing you on the parade ground.' He abruptly turned away to return to his entourage and spent the rest of the evening ignoring Nick completely, to his relief although he wasn't naive enough to believe this would be the last of their confrontations over the course of the tattoo.

Initially the assembled units spent time rehearsing the drills for the Tattoo. Finally, the full dress rehearsal reached the point of the finale and all of the participating service personnel were ranked up in the close confines of the castle parade ground. Nick's detachment was standing alongside two mounted troops from the Household Cavalry fronted by the upright figure of Captain Tristram Wrath-Bingham. There had been a Wrath-Bingham in The Household Cavalry since before the time of Wellington. Tristram's father, General Sir Michael Wrath-Bingham had only recently retired after a distinguished career in the army.

As Nick watched him, he epitomized all that was the very worst of British aristocracy and whilst he appeared popular within his own group, there were many officers who made a point of keeping out of the way of the swaggering, loudmouth buffoon.

Nick was aware that most of his men were distinctly unhappy about having to stand so close to the huge cavalry horses, which was not surprising given that most of them came from the tenements and council estates of Glasgow or Edinburgh and had never been closer to a horse than watching the racing on TV. The Jocks had no alternative but to remain rigidly to attention while the black mounts of the troopers were only three feet distant. For the most part, the horses were well-trained and stood obediently still while the ceremony continued, but one or two of the horses became fidgety and threatened to trample on the feet of the motionless Argyles. Nick could feel the anger rising within his men, but the rehearsal passed without incident, much to his relief.

He knew that the pranks played out in everyday army life could sometimes border on the excessive, but he didn't seriously believe that even Wrath-Bingham would jeopardize the continuity of such an important ceremonial occasion. He had a few encouraging words with his men at the end of the rehearsal and thought nothing more of the moments of friction that had marred the rehearsal for them.

At dinners and other Mess functions he had miraculously managed to pretend to consume the required quantities of whisky and had escaped being labelled a wimp by a hair's breadth. At times it appeared that one of the hardest tasks he had been asked to perform since joining the army was not to lose face as a non-whisky drinking Argyle. Although he was not a hard-drinking man himself, he loved the atmosphere within the Mess, with officers from all of the participating sections resplendent in their individual Mess dress. It was expected that an officer in a regiment such as the Argyles, or indeed any Scottish regiment, should participate in taking the national drink. Nick knew better than most the power that the amber fluid could have over men who drank it. He had witnessed too many times his father's arrival home, creating hell in what was otherwise a happy home.

The first day that the Tattoo was open to the public was Monday and within reason, all went well. Nick made two more visits to the local police station to retrieve another four of his flock who had gone astray and Tuesday passed without incident, although the close proximity of the Jocks and their equine neighbours was a potentially volatile situation that he kept a close eye on.

Wrath-Bingham continued to be an irksome presence. Nick tried to keep his distance from this old foe to ensure that there was as little opportunity as possible to renew previous conflicts.

Tuesday evening in the Mess was as enjoyable an evening as the others had been, but spoiled by the stupidity of Wrath-Bingham and his entourage, who had taken up residence in the most prominent position in the room; in front of the massive fireplace. This position gave him the vantage point that he clearly enjoyed as from there he was well placed to "take the piss" out of whoever was unfortunate enough to cross his line of sight. Nick watched with suppressed annoyance as he witnessed Tristram pick on some of the overseas officers who were not quite up to the banter that was aimed at them. He had been a pompous idiot when Nick first met him but he had now taken it to a much higher level. Inevitably, Tristram's eyes settled on Nick.

'Hey there, you in the plaid skirt! It appears as if your fellows are about to piss themselves with fright when my horses are around. I do hope that the rumour about you types not wearing anything under those skirts is only a myth or there is bound to be a lot of splashing going on tomorrow.' This outburst was directed at Nick but meant for all in the Mess to hear.

Nick smiled politely and nodded. Inwardly, he was seething and wished that he had used the opportunity to let Bingham know exactly what he thought of him, but tradition and etiquette prevented this, along with the indoctrinated service ethics that he was proud to uphold. Nick watched Tristram gather his crowd of cronies and leave. The incident was over in seconds but he felt disgust, not only for the posturing Wrath-Bingham, but also for himself for not returning his fire and giving as good as he got.

The Wednesday afternoon display proved to be a trial for Nick. It was obvious to all of the Jocks that the cavalry had been primed to push their horses even closer to the Argyles in order to give them a hard time. It was very easy for a trooper to irritate his mount with one of the huge swan neck spurs, which was out of sight on the inside flank of the horse. Nick knew that Wrath-Bingham was behind this prank and he also knew that, having made it so simple for Tristram to verbally bully him with no response, he had made himself an easy target.

A deputation led by Lance Corporal McTaggart asked to see Captain Trevelyan.

'We're not gonna take it, Sur!' argued McTaggart. 'Those bastards Donkey Wollopers on their fucking black horse's cannee treat us like this. We're gunna gie over te their barracks's and gie em a kicking, Sur.'

Nick sympathized with his men but it would have been unthinkable for him to allow such a thing to happen, although inwardly he wished that he could let the Jocks deal with this affair in their own inimitable, age-old way. Instead, he had to lay down the law and threaten to place under arrest any Argyle who was seen within one hundred yards of the Cavalry Barracks.

That evening in the Mess, Bingham was occupied with other matters and only occasionally did Nick catch a glimpse of him looking in his direction with a smug grin on his face. Thursday afternoon brought the longest two hours of his life. The Cavalry were having a great time making their horses do a veritable tap dance right up to the highly polished toecaps of the Argyles' boots. Nick expected that at any minute, one of his Jocks would leap up and drag a gleaming Cavalryman down onto the cobbles, and if it did happen, how would he deal with the incident? God only knew. Miraculously, the afternoon passed without any major disaster. Nick knew that by the time the evening display took place, the Jocks would have had a few drams and that would be the dangerous time. He took the unusual decision to go to the mess bar after lunch, and there he made the even more unusual decision of having a couple of scotches to help him through the afternoon. By the time that the evening display had arrived the tension in the air was electric. Nick had tried to reduce his own personal pressure by having a couple more swift drams before marching out to lead his men. They had now performed the sequences a dozen times and could carry out the required drill with their eyes closed. They had become used to the crowds of spectators and even the TV cameras held little interest for them. All went well to begin with.

Any man or woman who has ever marched to the sound of the pipes and drums will tell you that there is something magical that stirs latent feelings of pride from deep within. The Argyles were certainly big on pride and for good reason: their forbears had bequeathed them a magnificent legacy that every member of the regiment held in great respect. Eventually, the massed troops were again ranked up for the finale. Wrath-Bingham walked his charger into position at the head of the two troops of Cavalry. There was no denying he looked good astride his magnificent horse. He wore the officers' ceremonial scarlet State Uniform and exuded total confidence in a way which only those who are borne to the aristocracy, know how.

At first, Bingham cantered himself upon the leading section of cavalry, but upon giving a sideways glance and recognising Nick standing rigidly at his side, he edged his mount over until he was directly alongside.

## TR-B's Revenge

'Chilly evening, Trevelyan. Cold enough to freeze the balls off a brass monkey, or the bollocks off a Jock' Nick made no effort to reply. He continued to stare forward, quelling his feelings of anger. The policy of not being drawn into dialogue with Wrath-Bingham paid off as he soon became bored and returned his gaze to the crowd. He obviously considered all had paid their entrance fee in order to catch a glimpse of him, resplendent in his magnificent uniform astride his splendid steed. The mounts of The Household Cavalry are big horses. They undergo long and extensive training before they are considered fit enough to take part in ceremonial occasions. Captain Wrath-Bingham's charger was aptly named Hercules. He stood eighteen hands high and had a neck like a carved chess piece. Hercules was a massive horse and he possessed an equally enormous bladder. Although the training of a military horse is extensive, there are some things which cannot be controlled. The two actions that every horse will perform, no matter what the circumstances or the company is to urinate and to defecate. The Cavalry have a procedure when a horse decides to pee. The rider leans forward in the saddle in order to relieve the pressure on the animal's kidneys. But as it is not always evident to the rider that his mount has decided to take a leak, the rider directly behind will pass on the order, "Lean forward". And so it was on that eventful evening that at that time, in that place, Hercules decided to pee. The trooper directly behind Captain Wrath-Bingham shouted:

'Lean forward, Sir.'

Tristram's immediate reaction was one of annoyance at being given an order of any description by a Trooper even though this was a standard procedure. However, as the possibilities of the situation dawned upon him, Tristram was delighted to ease himself forward in the saddle and await the outcome. When it came, it was better than anything that he could have hoped to contrive. Hercules dropped his penis in the prescribed manner, arched his back and let go the plug. The distance from the end of Hercules' penis and the ground was in excess of two and a half feet. This had the effect of causing the six pints of warm yellow liquid to splash everywhere. Nick could do nothing to avoid the tidal wave; his legs deflected most of the deluge. His feet, boots and socks were soaked almost up to the knee, and there was absolutely nothing that he could do other than continue to stand rigidly facing forward. The steam rose upwards into his nose, carrying the pungent smell which burned the membrane of his nostrils. The warm liquid ran down his legs and as an added bonus to the insult, Hercules deposited a large pile of steaming dung neatly in front of him, with all the agility of Father Christmas delivering a Christmas parcel. Tristram Wrath-Bingham leaned back in his saddle and gave a barely audible snigger of pleasure. He then slowly turned his head and looked down at the unfortunate infantryman at his side.

'Warmer now?' he inquired.

There was no need to add anything more. The actions had spoken far louder than any words could. The ultimate humiliation was complete. When the Tattoo was over Nick marched his men back to their start point and dismissed them. He was struggling to face them and shouted out the words of command staring above their heads where before he had always made a point of looking directly at them. He gave the command to dismiss without feeling, wishing them to disappear as soon as possible. In the privacy of his bunk he tore off his soiled uniform and threw it into a corner. He sat on his bed and took a long swig from a bottle of J&B fifteen year old whisky, a present from his father from his time of graduation from Sandhurst that he kept in the top drawer of his dressing table. For some unknown reason as a last minute thought he had thrown the bottle into his holdall before leaving for Scotland. He probably sat for an hour, gazing at the wall, and wondering how such a thing could happen without there being any possibility for recourse on his part. Once more Bingham seemed to have the upper hand. The old resentment and memories welled up as he remembered their earlier encounters. It appeared that little had changed since the time of Wellington. Wealth and parentage obviously still ruled.

The advice that Nick had received from ASM Miller rang through his mind. He eventually snapped back into some semblance of reality and took a hot shower. He had arranged to meet Steve for a final quick drink, although he did not particularly feel like facing the throng in the Mess which was bound to be in a loud party mode after the stressful few days of ceremonial duties.

He slowly dressed in his mess uniform. At ten o'clock, he walked into the officers' mess, feeling as if all eyes had turned towards him; that all were aware of the humiliation he had suffered on the parade ground that evening. He walked up to the bar and ordered a double whisky. He caught sight of Steve chatting to a group of people. Steve was probably busy so rather than try to attract his attention, Nick sat down in a corner by himself to nurse his whisky and wait for Steve to finish his conversation and come over. At 10.15, there was a general increase in noise volume, and as if preceded by his very own state trumpeters, in strode Tristram Wrath-Bingham. At first he took up his usual position at the fireplace, but upon sighting Nick, he walked out into the centre of the room and pointed straight at him.

'You Argyle chappie!' It was remarkable how Wrath-Bingham appeared to have completely eradicated the events that had taken place not two hours previously.

'Hey, you Argyle chappie!' he repeated. 'We have locked up two of your roughneck privates. They were at our stable trying to cause trouble not half an hour ago. Be a good chap and take them away, would you? They're making the place look terribly untidy.'

Nick looked up, slowly focusing on the posturing figure. He was alert enough to realise that he was dangerously close to snapping as far as the goading Bingham was concerned. He tried desperately to quell the waves of anger that were starting to cloud his vision and reasoning. He felt that he had just about got himself under control when with one last prod, Wrath Bingham pushed the balance to tipping point.

'Maybe if you didn't wear a skirt, your men would have more respect for you. They probably fancy you and are at this moment planning manoeuvres on how to take you unawares from behind!' Wrath Bingham slowly turned back to his group of attendants, laughing in his unique lazily nasal way. Nick rose to his feet as if in slow motion.

## The Fatal Punch

Out of the corner of his eye Nick saw Steve turn and shout something that he couldn't hear. It felt as if it took a lot of time to cover the ground between himself and Wrath-Bingham, but in reality, the look of amazement on Bingham's face betrayed how swiftly he had actually moved. Nick grabbed Tristram by the shoulder and turned him to face him.

The punch when it connected was directly to the point of his aristocratic chin and the sound of his jaw breaking was heard by all present. The punch lifted him off his feet about four inches, and sent him back across the room to fall in a heap at the feet of his startled fellow officers. There then followed total silence. Nick stared in disbelief at the crumpled mass that seconds before had been an elegant Cavalry Officer. Silence, W-B was out cold

A Major from The Medical Corps moved across the room to render First Aid to the broken bundle on the floor, which eventually broke the silence. A Grenadier Guards Colonel glanced around the room, and realising that he was the senior officer present, walked over to Nick and said,

'Go back to your quarters, Captain, and remain there, please.'

The rest was a blur. There was not even time to have a quick exchange with the startled looking Steve. Nick went back to his room and lay on the bed. At midnight, an orderly knocked on the door and told him to return immediately to his unit in Canterbury Kent, and to be there for Colonel's orders at ten o'clock the next morning. He drove south throughout the night, expecting that at any moment, he would waken up from the nightmare that had unfolded in such a short time. There was a dull ache in his right hand which was quite swollen, and he suspected that he had broken one of the bones. There was also a pounding headache right behind his eyes. Slowly, it was dawning that he was suffering from a hangover. The realisation that he had consumed a lot of whisky during the day was slowly making him aware that his actions of the previous night might have been those of a man whose judgment was clouded by alcohol.

## Resignation from the Argyles

Colonel Angus Dumfries was a father-like figure; his red hair and enormous eyebrows gave him a faintly eccentric appearance, but he had proved himself time and time again to be a fine leader. At the same time, he was known to be a harsh judge if crossed. His punishments could be excessive, but the worst punishment was the tongue lashing that he could unleash on the unfortunate soldiers whose bad luck caused them to be brought before him. As he waited outside the Colonel's office, he contemplated what his chastisement might be. Transfer to a loathsome desk job somewhere in the middle of nowhere? A one month punishment of being confined to barracks as permanent orderly officer? A harsh fine to accompany the punishment and, of course, a good bawling out by the Colonel whose voice was often to be heard all over the barracks as he castigated some poor unfortunate sole.

'Captain Trevelyan, you stand before me on a grave charge. You have brought the name of the Argyles into disrepute by striking a fellow officer and you have behaved in a manner unbecoming an officer holding a Royal Commission.'

Colonel Dumfries had not lifted his eyes from the charge sheet when Nick entered the room, nor had he lifted his eyes as he read the charge. But now, when he looked up his eyes were sympathetic and this made Nick feel suddenly uneasy. The Colonel continued.

'And worst of all, you fool, you hit the son of a very powerful man. Nick, in all my time as an officer, I have rarely seen a man with such capabilities as you, but now you have thrown everything away in a minute's indiscretion. Captain Trevelyan, I must ask that you formally resign your Commission forthwith.'

The words hit Nick like a ton of bricks and he feared that his knees would start to shake as he struggled to take in the words he had just heard.

The prefix, "Ex" is probably one of the most widely used and well known in the English language. He was already on the "Ex" files as, for example an "Ex" Windsor Boys School pupil and also as an "Ex" student of Surrey University. The first "Ex's" were rather like punctuation marks in his early career, marking the advances he had made through the educational system. But the term "Ex-serviceman", was something he had not contemplated would happen for at least another twenty years, and it was a title he detested.

It was now almost two weeks since the fateful night that he had broken the jaw of Tristram Wrath-Bingham at Edinburgh Castle and the aftermath had been harsh and swift. Within four days of the incident, he found myself driving through the barrack gate of his "Ex" regiment as an "Ex soldier". He had considered appealing. The whole affair appeared to be totally unjust, but the Colonel advised him to face up to his lot and move on, as there would never be a future for him in Her Majesty's Forces. And so it was, Nick turned his car away from Dover towards the M25 to return to Windsor.

## Return to Windsor

At this point there was no alternative but to go back to his parent's home and lick his wounds while he considered what to do next. His parents had always kept his room ready so that whenever he decided to come home on leave it was there waiting for him. Their pride in their son "The Officer" had been total and he knew they would be devastated by the events that had taken place. As he parked his car outside the terraced house on the Windsor council estate where he had grown up, his mother came immediately to the door to meet him. She greeted him in such a comforting way that he experienced an instant calmness that he had not felt for the past two weeks. She quietly fussed over him and told him not to worry, that everything would be sure to turn out for the best.

His father was a very different matter. He pottered around in the garden grunting and talking to himself quietly under his breath hardly acknowledging Nick's presence in the house. The inevitable whisky bottle was never too far away and Nick knew that as the days drew on, he could be relied upon to cause a scene. He only hoped that the unpleasantness could be kept to the minimum for the sake of his mother. He had been at his parent's home for a few days when Steve rang to bring him up to speed with events. Although he had left the Tattoo shortly after Nick, he had been in touch with members of the Argyles with whom he'd become friendly to see if he could get the full picture of what happened after Nick had been dismissed. He said that Wrath-Bingham had been whisked away in a private ambulance, back to London where he was admitted to a highly reputed private clinic. He had lorded it over everybody, sending messages of progress on his injury back to his squadron leader indicating his need for a lengthy convalescence and threatening all kinds of grievous action against "that Grammar School thug, Trevelyan."

It took little longer than a week before his CO called him stating that if he wasn't back at his billet within the week he would be around to fetch him himself. Wrath Bingham duly turned up for desk duties within forty-eight hours, sporting an attractively wired jaw, grumbling incoherently, about injustice, revenge and other such matters that few of his colleagues were interested in. Nick mentioned to Steve that he had tried to get through to Marina a few times but had met with a wall of silence. Steve informed him none too delicately that ever since he had been given the boot and Wrath-Bingham had returned to London, she had been sniffing around The Right Honourable injured Tristram in the most solicitous manner. These were attentions that Wrath-Bingham was only too pleased too encourage as the pettiest of revenges against Nick, but as time passed, it became apparent that it was also a liaison, of which Mr. Fisher himself once again approved and encouraged considering it a superior deal to the earlier one that he had brokered on his daughter's behalf. Time would tell whether it would be Bingham or Marina who would first have cause to regret the pairing. But on the other hand they might be a well matched couple. Nick allowed himself the briefest of regrets for he had to admit that he had begun to tire of Marina's self-indulgent ways, but he had also to admit, she had been a most satisfying and decorative arm-piece in many ways, eye candy that no man could ignore, and the financial assistance from "Big Daddy Fisher" had been useful in the extreme. Fingers crossed; there had been no men in black suits turning up to collect the car. The papers were after all in Nick's name and above board, so he allowed himself a little hope in that direction as the Porsche was certainly a useful asset. Warren Fisher would have written the car off to expenses long ago.

Given all of the circumstances, he considered himself lucky to escape from the relationship unscathed. Finally, Steve reassured him that the men of the Argyles under his command were universally of the opinion that Wrath-Bingham, "Hadn't got haff as gud a kicking as he deserved."

They all thought that Captain Nick had suffered a grave injustice and were devastated that they would no longer be serving with him. He was much encouraged and touched by this show of support and on this positive note said good-bye to Steve, promising to keep him in touch with his plans for the future. Shortly after this call, Nick received a small package through the post. On opening it he found it to be a chunky, silver plated cigarette lighter embossed with the Argyle and Sutherland's coat of arms and engraved with the words.

"Set the world alight." It was from his men in the regiment. He was deeply moved by this token of regard from the bunch of Highlanders that he had served with. He was also much amused by the incongruity of the gift as he didn't smoke. This would always serve as a reminder of their sense of humour and staunch loyalty. He again felt a sting of regret at what could never again be.

Nick certainly had plenty of thinking to do, to try to redirect his life after the bitter disappointments of recent events. During the day his parents were at work and this gave him the space he needed. He was able to consolidate his thoughts and get on with planning his future, although he felt that he had made little or no progress.

He summarised his position to himself. He was twenty-eight years of age; he had an honours' degree in Modern History from Surrey University. Additionally, as it was he who had resigned from the army, in consequence, his military record still looked OK. In more practical terms, he was fit, intelligent and had a bank account in which he had managed to save several thousand pounds. Plus of course, the car. These attributes, he felt, could be his saving grace. But what to do next? He still felt that he was a soldier and a good one at that, but where could he make use of his skills?

He made inquiries about becoming a mercenary but there wasn't much going on that looked interesting enough to be worth the risks. The days passed and the feeling of no longer belonging in the family home washed over him once again as it always did after the first week of leave. He continued to miss the regiment and, in particular, the men of his platoon. "Crazy Jocks" they may have been, but he had learned to understand them and respect their way of looking at the world. He missed the Mess and his fellow officers, the horseplay and the camaraderie. The full impact of what had happened was only now beginning to take effect.

## Steve Beckett

His father was a man who had made many acquaintances during his time in the army as is only to be expected after twenty two years service. Luckily for Nick there was always someone calling in to take his father down to the pub for a pint and a jaw about old times. While staying at his parent's home, it was one such friend of his father's, Chris Beckett, who arrived at the house one evening. Nick had always liked Chris, who would turn up once or twice a year when he was back in the UK. He now lived on the Algarve where Nick remembered hearing his parents saying he was involved in the tourist industry. He was not as loud nor pretentious as the majority of his father's friends, and there was something relaxed and reassuring about him.

'Your father tells me that you have had some trouble, young Nick. Don't judge him too harshly; I'm sure you probably think he's giving you a hard time considering what you've been through. It will take him a while but he'll come round in the end. He's had many disappointments in his life and so desperately wanted you to succeed where he failed. He thinks the world of you; you know that, don't you? That's why he puts on the pressure,' Chris explained. Nick was a little shocked to think of his father in such a way. He would certainly bear in mind what Chris had said. He continued, 'I joined the army at the same time as your father but after three years walked away from the life that I loved and it's something that you may understand. I had quite a few run-ins, near-misses with officers. I was young and could never quite come to grips with the inequality that existed between the enlisted men and the commissioned officers. The divide in all of the Guards' regiments is enormous as you have experienced yourself, first hand and there is a lot of unfair privilege that I just could not agree with. So I decided that it would be better for all concerned if I left the army. After all, who was I to think that I could change something that had existed for centuries? I have to say that although I agree with you I do feel that it's all changing now and much of the class consciousness is diminishing. Having said that, there are some places where the aristocracy still holds the reigns.' he commented.

His father's phone call had ended and he walked into the room, ending Nick's conversation with Chris. 'Are you ready, Tom?' Chris asked.

'We'll be at the pub, Nick, in case you fancy a pint later on. Come and join us.' Chris offered.

The two older men left and Nick turned on the TV. He looked at the screen but his mind was miles away. Towards 10 o'clock he pulled on a sweater and headed off to the pub to join his father and Chris.

Nick knew that his father would not cause a scene while his old friend was around. The pub was full. His father and Chris were part of a large group. They were being entertained by a local wag who was in great form, keeping his audience in hysterics with his jokes. Nick joined the edge of the group and managed to attract Chris's attention and draw him away so that they could continue their earlier conversation.

'If you ever want to get away for a while, come down to the Algarve and pay me a visit. You'll be very welcome, and it's a great place to relax and decide what your next step will be.'

'I might well take you up on that.' Nick replied.

He had returned to his parent's home, the place where he had grown up but it was obvious that it would be wrong to stay on there. By leaving home and joining the army he had flown the nest. But now by returning he had made a negative move which was acting upon his sub conscious. He slept badly and dreamed a lot. His personal daemons were haunting him. Two more days passed. He had looked up some old friends from school and pre-army times. They arranged to meet up and have a drink. Although it was nice to see them again, they now shared nothing in common the topic of conversation lingering around children and mortgages. Early the next morning, Nick was busy making phone calls. He called the local travel agency in Windsor and inquired about car ferries to Portugal. There were several options including crossing the channel by the shortest route and driving through France, Spain and then into Portugal itself. The option which required the least driving was to board a ferry in Plymouth sail up the Channel around the Brest Peninsular, and from there across the Bay of Biscay. Thirty-six hours later the ferry would disembark its passengers and vehicles at the port of Santander in Northern Spain. Nick decided that the second option sounded the more interesting. He phoned his insurance company and arranged cover for the journey.

Eventually, when he felt happy that everything was in place, he made a long distance call down to the Algarve to Chris Beckett. He was delighted to hear from Nick and yes, of course, his offer still stood. Shortly afterwards, Nick set off from England to sample the delights of Southern Portugal.

# | 4 |

# THE ALGARVE

**N**ick took every opportunity to read up on his new objective which wasn't difficult as it was a popular tourist destination at there was plenty of literature available. He read:

The Algarve is a strip of land at the southern end of Portugal, approximately one hundred miles long by about twenty miles wide. At the Eastern end is the border with Spain. The frontier being the Guardiana River which divides the two countries at this point.

At the Western extreme lies the windswept Cape St Vincent, the most south westerly point in Europe. To the North, the Monchique Mountains divide the province from the rest of the country and to the South; the Atlantic Ocean washes the entire coastline. The old capital of the Algarve was Lagos, which is a walled city whose history is long and varied, dating back to before its occupation by the Romans.

Chris Beckett lived in the village of Praia-da-Luz, which was located three miles west of Lagos. Luz was a pretty, old fishing village, with a large sandy beach protected at one end by a magnificent rugged cliff and at the other end by a picturesque church and a handsome fort. There are hundreds of attractive beaches on the Algarve but by far the most appealing feature for this region of the Iberian Peninsular is the fabulous weather which gives virtually wall to wall sunshine for most of the year. The fantastic growth rate in the region earned it the title of The California of Europe. Portugal has also benefited greatly as a whole from its membership of the

European Common Market. As one of the poorer and smaller members there was nothing for it to lose by becoming a member, and everything to gain.

The Algarve has known and survived many invasions. The Phoenicians, Romans and Moors are some of the better known ancient civilizations that have conquered and occupied the region. But perhaps the greatest and most widespread invasion ever to take place is the twentieth century invasion of tourism. The invading army is multi national with the largest contingent by far being British. This intrusion has certainly not had an adverse effect on the province; in fact, quite the opposite. There has been huge investment which has brought with it prosperity and employment into an area which was otherwise pitifully poor. Of course, as in any newly developed society, there have been problems, but generally speaking, the Algarve has advanced while retaining much of its old personality and charm. The invaders who have conquered the Algarve in the past have left behind them many monuments to their periods of occupation which are to be found in the language, culture, architecture, food and indeed the character not only of the land but its inhabitants too.

The twentieth century invasion has also brought with it reforms which are to be found everywhere, creating its own transformation of not only the land but also the people. There are inevitably some that mourn the way things were in the past.

The Algarve, because of its remote location was virtually cut off from the rest of Europe until the late fifties, giving the region the feel of the land that was left behind. Indeed, the Moorish title "Algaharb." means "The Land Beyond." But now the region is being dragged into the twentieth century, not kicking and screaming as is the popular terminology, but rather shrugging and yawning, reflecting the attitude and character of the Algarvians themselves. The region stayed in the medieval period until the twentieth century.

## The Mirage Bar

Nick pulled up in front of the Mirage restaurant at 7.30 on a Monday evening. He had driven the best part of ten hours since leaving Salamanca in central Spain that morning. The drive had been pleasant and the Porsche made it all the more enjoyable, this was what it had been built to do. He had coasted along at a comfortable speed, enjoying the scenery. Having crossed the Spanish/Portuguese border at Badajoz, he noticed immediately there was a marked difference both in the quality of the roads, which were not as good on the Portuguese side of the border, but more dramatically, in the standard of driving. It had been reasonably good in Spain. Now that Nick had entered Portugal, it appeared that every driver was filled with an uncontrollable death wish. The desire to overtake seemed overwhelming no matter what the prevailing situation. Quite often he would find himself being overtaken on a narrow road where the overtaking driver had absolutely no view of the oncoming traffic. By the time he arrived at the Mirage in Praia da Luz, he was stressed out and tired. The place was far bigger than Nick had imagined from Chris's description. He knew that Chris had built the property some years before and ran it himself.

Nick walked into the bar and ordered a beer which, when it arrived, was thankfully chilled. The first beer went down quickly and felt wonderful. His thirst was enormous so he called the barman over and ordered a second beer, preparing himself to attempt to communicate with the man using the smattering of Portuguese words learnt from a phrase book that he had purchased on the ferry. The barman smiled at his pitiful attempt to speak his language

'I believe what you are asking me, Sir. Is for me to call Mr. Beckett?' inquired the barman in English.

'Er, yes.' Nick replied, feeling more than a little inadequate. The barman turned around and picked up the telephone. He spoke a few words in Portuguese, and then turned again to face Nick.

'Mr. Beckett sends his apologies, and will be here in twenty minutes. My name is Tony he has also told me that you are to be given whatever you need.'

The bar was beginning to fill up with holiday makers, all looking extremely healthy, sporting their newly acquired sun tans. Nick felt decidedly washed out and drab in comparison, but the beer gave him a pleasant glow within and he began to relax. Chris Beckett arrived as promised twenty minutes later. Nick had started to calm down from his tiring ten-hour drive.

'Hey, Nick great to see you. Welcome to the Algarve.' Chris strode across the bar and pumped his hand warmly.

'I hope Tony has been looking after you?' The barman smiled genially. Nick nodded his appreciation for the most welcome glasses of cold beer and genial conversation that he had been supplied with while waiting for Chris.

'You must be starving; have you eaten?' Chris enquired.

'No, I haven't. I must say I'm a bit on the hungry side.' Nick confessed.

With a meal and couple of glasses of wine inside, he was definitely feeling very relaxed. He was shown to his accommodation which was a studio apartment that was fully equipped and furnished. Nick threw down his suitcases and took a shower, unpacked a few clean clothes, dressed and wandered back into the Mirage bar. It was crowded with a mixture of Portuguese locals and holidaymakers. The atmosphere was terrific. The doors to a tropical garden were open and many of the customers were sitting outside, enjoying their drinks in the warm evening air. Chris buzzed backwards and forwards dealing with the inevitable problems that constantly arise in a catering business. Nick found a comfortable stool at the end of the bar and ordered another drink. In between organising the staff, Chris still managed to find time to sit with him.

'Everything OK in the studio?' he asked.

'Couldn't be better Chris, I'm very much obliged to you,' Nick replied. Chris dismissed the thanks.

'Please don't mention it. Tomorrow, when I start introducing you to some of the residents who live around here then you'll know you've really arrived. But I warn you, be prepared for a culture shock, There are a lot of unconventional characters about.' Nick settled back on his bar stool. So far, everything that he had seen, he liked, and there appeared the promise of plenty more to come. What more could he ask for? His decision to come to the Algarve seemed to have been a good one.

As the weeks passed, Nick became more and more relaxed, which caused him to wonder whether he had ever known how to unwind in his previous lifestyle. His hair grew longer than it had ever been in his entire life and he obtained a deep healthy tan. Some days, he didn't bother to shave, missing the daily ritual that he had carried out religiously, every morning of his life, since he was fifteen.

Of the two suitcases full of clothes that he had brought with him from England, all but a tiny percentage were folded or hung neatly in his studio wardrobe, having never been worn. His everyday attire was a pair of shorts, occasionally a T-shirt and flip-flops. Only at night did he "dress up" but this only required a pair of casual slacks and shirt. Each day was completely different from the last. Nothing was structured as it had always been in his life, particularly in the army. Nick spent his days swimming, playing tennis and golf or riding, followed in the evenings by the slightly less healthy pursuits that were offered by the nightlife of the Algarve.

The numerous bars and restaurants situated on every corner of every street were waiting to lure the ever willing band of tourists and locals alike. Also as promised, Chris introduced him to a very mixed bunch of residents. He was frequently invited to drinks parties and dinners. For the most part, the company was fine, but as in any society there were the inevitable bores and idiots. Chris steered him through the minefield of personalities with the expertise of a U-boat captain.

One of the holidaymakers whom he spent some time with, was a man called Tom Holland. He came regularly into the Mirage bar and they struck up a good relationship. Tom and his wife were on a two week holiday but by the evening his wife was tired and went early to bed leaving Tom to pop out for a couple of beers before turning in himself. He and Nick had plenty in common. Tom explained that he had been in the army for twenty-two years and had achieved the rank of warrant officer. He left the army aged forty-two which gave him plenty of time to have another career and a second pension. His new job was in security. He was now the manager in charge of vaults which were located in Chancery Lane, London. Tom was proud of his position and chatted regularly about the unusual circumstances of his employment. During the two weeks he was in Portugal they spent several enjoyable hours chewing the cud.

## Quinta Da Felicidade

'I have to go over to a place called Cama Da Vaca, which translates to "Bed of the Cow." It's just along the coast about three miles west of here. A friend of mine has a home there,' explained Chris one morning a few weeks after Nick had arrived.

'If you fancy a drive out, you will find it interesting I promise.' He smiled. Later that morning Chris picked Nick up and they drove the three miles west towards the village of Burgau. It was a typically hot Algarve day, and it felt good to be driving through the countryside with all the windows of Chris's jeep open, allowing a welcoming breeze to blow through the vehicle. The air was scented with various wonderful aromas from the exotic plants, shrubs and Atlantic herbs that grew in abundance along the roadside.

'We're going to visit a friend of mine. His name is Felix Bartholomew. He's an ex actor who owns and runs a boarding house and restaurant in a wonderful old manor house called Quinta Da Felicidade. You may find him a little eccentric but I'm sure you'll cope.' explained Chris. 'I'll fill you in on a few details which may be of use to you,' Chris continued. 'The Quinta Da Felicidade is rather like a Portuguese version of Fawlty Towers, with no fewer oddballs than its TV counterpart. As a generalisation, it could be said that people who have stayed there would themselves have to be either adventurous or slightly eccentric. It is one of those places that you either love or hate. Many of the guests have been coming back year after year because they enjoy the atmosphere so much.' Chris slowed the jeep as they approached a large colonial estate house.

'The main house boasts six suites that Felix rents out. In order to avoid confusion the rooms are colour-coded. There is a yellow suite, a blue suite, a mauve suite and so on. At the back of the main house is a cottage. This was a barn, which had been converted into a renting unit. Through necessity, everything has been done with minimum expenditure. Felix has struggled to pay the bills for most of the thirty plus years he has lived in the Algarve. All of this has made him an expert in the field of endurance. He could teach the SAS a thing or two about survival. I have never met anybody who has perfected the art of robbing Peter to pay Paul more effectively than Felix. Behind the house there is a large plot of land, which on occasions will support the odd caravan that has drifted in, plus a donkey or two. As Felix has a substantial amount of accommodation, has been around for some time and is well known, it quite often happens that people will turn up and ask for a cheap room, because they can't afford to stay anywhere else. Very seldom does he turn people away but quite often, he ends up losing out and not receiving the rent when his guests do a moonlight flit. There are people staying at the Quinta Da Felicidade who can't find the rent and come to an agreement with Felix to work their ticket. These are people from all backgrounds. Some will wait at table in the Quinta Da Felicidade bodega style restaurant, a treat you really must experience; while others do a little gardening or maintenance in return for free board and lodging. Felix calls the people who fall into this category, "His slaves". They seldom last for more than a month and almost never honour the agreement that they have made with him.' Chris summed up. 'The only thing about the Quinta Da Felicidade that can be relied on is that there is always something new and outrageous occurring on a day to day basis'. Ah—there is one other thing that I think I should mention, which is that Felix is a homosexual. He is very effeminate but quite harmless. No need to worry!' Chris added the final caveat with a wry smile. The though passed through Nicks mind, *experience had taught him that when someone says "Don't worry" that's exactly the time to start to worry.*

'When he meets you he will expect you to kiss him.'

'What! You have got to be joking.' Nick was doing a quick calculation of the distance they had come and how long it would take him to walk back.

'No . . . no, don't worry! Think of it like a Russian thing. We're not talking lips here.' Chris was laughing out loud, unable to suppress his reaction to Nick's sudden panic.

'Are you sure?' Nick asked gingerly.

'Trust me.'

As they drove into the car park, on the right hand side of the road, set back fifty meters stood a beautiful old period building. There had been a devastating earthquake that had flattened most of the old buildings in southern Portugal two hundred years before. And therefore it was unusual to come across anything so exotic in a rural setting such as this.

Pulling into the car park, it became evident that the Quinta Da Felicidade was in a sorry state of repair. Paint was flaking off of the walls that were themselves missing rendering in many places. The wooden window frames were dry, split and completely bereft of paint. The garden, which had at some time in the past been formally laid out, was overgrown and unkempt except for a few patches where lawn must have at some time existed and had recently been cleared to allow some broken items of tatty garden furniture furniture to stand. Growing up the front of the house were several brightly-coloured Bougainvilleas which extended to the eaves and over the roof. They looked as if they had not been pruned for years and had virtually taken over the front of house. Weeds grew through the cobbled pathway and there were pieces of furniture, broken toys and other discarded items lying around.

Quinta Da Felicidade must have once been an, elegant building but was now sadly much neglected. It was crying out for help; but, even through all the apparent neglect, the old house retained a certain degree of elegance. Perhaps there was still time for it to be restored to its former glory.

Chris and Nick got out of the car and together walked over to the main entrance. Two overweight scruffy dogs stirred themselves as the strangers approached. They made a lazy attempt to bark, thought better of it and decided to continue dozing in the shade of a magnificent dragon tree that dominated the driveway.

Once inside, the house was remarkably cool. The walls had been decorated with a marbling effect which must have, in its prime, looked spectacular, particularly around the central wrought iron staircase that was illuminated from above by a pyramid shaped glass apex.

## Felix Bartholomew

'Felix, are you at home?' called Chris.

'In the dining room, Darling.' came the reply and they walked towards the source of the voice.

Felix Bartholomew was sitting at a dining table that was strewn with plates, cups and the remains of breakfast. He was a large man in his early fifties; his grey hair was cut very short and his face, still handsome, spoke of earlier years when he must have been a very good looking man. He wore a large Fedora hat which accentuated his theatrical appearance. Nick couldn't be quite sure, but would have hazarded a guess that Felix was wearing some kind of eye liner. But by far the most striking feature about him was his voice. Nick placed the accent as being somewhere between mid-Atlantic and well educated English, to which was added a wonderful gravely quality.

'Hello, Christopher.' greeted Felix warmly as they entered the room.

'Good morning, Felix,' replied Chris, walking towards him.

'Kiss, please.' demanded Felix and Chris dutifully bent over and kissed him on both cheeks.

'And who is this handsome young man whom you have brought with you?'

'Felix, I would like you to meet Nicholas Trevelyan.' replied Chris.

'He may kiss me too.' Felix made his second demand in as many minutes. Nick walked over and kissed Felix on the cheek, eyes squeezed closed trying to dredge up images in his mind of Russian leaders congratulating meritorious soldiers.

'Both sides!'

Wow, three demands in as many minutes, Nick smiled and bent again to kiss the other cheek.

'And now, Nicholas, what brings you to the Quinta Da Felicidade? Do you want to use my beautiful house to make a film or as a location for a fashion shoot? Or are you an emissary from a horrible bank who wants me to pay them some money?' he enquired demandingly.

'None of these things, Felix, this is purely a social visit.' Nick replied politely. 'Well, if you're not here to make me some money, that is bad; but on the other hand, if you are also not here to take my money, well then that is good. So, Mr. Nicholas Trevelyan, you are welcome at the Quinta Da Felicidade.'

Nick felt an immediate liking for the eccentric owner of the remarkable property. He could not help but warm to his larger than life personality. They spent another half-hour talking to, or perhaps, being talked to, by Felix before leaving to return to the Mirage.

As they drove out through the gates of Quinta Da Felicidade, Chris turned to Nick with a huge grin on his face and enquired,

'Well, Nick, what did you think of our little visit?'

'I feel as if I have been well and truly entertained for the past thirty minutes. It was most enjoyable—that man can certainly tell a tale.' Nick replied, laughing.

Slowly and lazily the days rolled into weeks and the weeks into months. Nick found that as he awoke each morning, it became increasingly difficult to remember which day of the week it was—so indistinguishable was one sunny morning from the next. He also noted that while he had once been only too happy, willing and able to jump out of bed reasonably early in the morning, breakfast on the terrace, often with Chris, and then disappear eagerly to pursue some energetic activity, he was now starting to spend more time in bed in the morning, often lying in until midday. He wasn't unduly worried by this development as he knew that he was fit and he felt that it was perfectly reasonable to be making the most of the local entertainment as he was after all, meant to be relaxing. Such was the lack of structure in his new lifestyle that he was beginning to lose track of the days, mostly because it didn't really matter too much, given the laid back life style of the Algarve.

He did however notice with a little concern that his bank balance was starting to look less healthy. He realised that this down-swing seemed to correlate quite distinctly with the increase in the amount of time he was spending in the local hostelries. In reality, he was living very cheaply as his needs were few and his living costs minimal. Chris charged a very reasonable rent for his studio apartment and the rest of the money that Nick spent amounted to hardly anything. He duly dismissed this slight slide in his fortunes as an inconsequential blip; after all, soon he would have figured out what to do with his life, and money wouldn't be a problem. Meanwhile, he was there to take advantage of the opportunity to relax and enjoy himself.

## The downward spiral begins

As the warning bell rang unheeded in the distance, Nick continued his pursuit of the Algarve pleasures. His recent problems were all but forgotten, and Chris found moments between running the Mirage to pass some time with Nick. They spent many hours sitting in the gardens, discussing life and people-watching. Chris had lived in Portugal for fifteen years during which time he had had plenty of opportunity to observe the odd assortment of folk that had passed that way. Some stayed and set up home there; others were only passing through, like ships in the night. There were some who would have loved to have been able to stay but were not made of the right stuff and lost everything they had. A smattering found it necessary to get out quick usually leaving a trail of unpaid bills in their wake.

It was late in the afternoon, the sun was scorching and the sky, as it had been on just about every day since Nick arrived, was cloudless. Its colour was an almost unreal, incandescent blue.

'It all looks idyllic but don't be taken in by the obvious charm. This place takes no prisoners, I can promise you that. There have been many times that I thought that I would be the one making the one way journey to Faro airport myself.'

Nick reflected that Chris certainly had many regrets about his life so far in the Algarve which to most people would have looked idyllic. He had started to feel a little uneasy about the way Chris seemed regularly to be emphasising the pitfalls of the place, rather than the more obvious attributes. Was he trying to warn Nick? Had he noticed the signs of his downward spiral? No. Nick was just imagining things. After all, he was still riding on the crest of an Algarvian wave. Whilst naturally concerned about his future, he wasn't yet ready to come down from his perch to confront the reality of his existence as well as that of those around him. He found it particularly easy to make friends with the lively and fun loving groups of holidaymakers who passed though the resort. They were there to have a good time, as was Nick, and Nick slightly resented the more cynical outlook of the local ex-pats who appeared to increasingly be trying to spoil his fun with their tales of woe. It was with some reluctance that he patiently prepared to listen to Chris as he came to the end of his sermon for the day.

'We all tend to live our lives these days thinking that TV, films and the books we read are a true reflection of real life. No matter how much life piles on the problems, in the movies there always seems to be a wise person who takes the time to explain where the unfortunate victim has been going wrong and from there on the victim becomes the hero and life becomes worth living. In real life there are no wise men.'

Chris emphasised the last sentence, making it a statement. Nick nodded sympathetically and made his excuses, leaving Chris to his thoughts, relieved to return to the apartment. There Nick showered, changed then headed for the bar and some welcome early evening refreshment.

After three months in the Algarve, his lifestyle had slipped into a quite recognizable pattern, one that the region had witnessed many times before. As most did, he found it difficult to get to grips with the language that was universally proclaimed by all foreigners to present a considerable challenge to any newcomer. He therefore tended to hang out with English speaking people whether they were holidaymakers, ex pats or locals, many of whom spoke English very well. While he made no particularly lasting friendships, he did have enough acquaintances to be assured that he could walk into almost any bar in Luz and be assured of an entertaining evening's worth of conversation. Then there was always the Mirage bar to finish up at, where a welcome "one for the road" and Tony's ears to bend were always awaiting him.

## Another casual affair

A couple of days after Chris's rather depressing lecture on what he called 'Algarve Fever' in the Mirage gardens, Nick found himself woken in the usual fashion in his studio. The bright midday sun had crept round and up into the sky, high enough to find the familiar crack in the curtain through which a penetrating ray of glaring sunshine pierced his state of semi consciousness. As he struggled to raise himself slightly to turn and escape the painful wakeup call, his head seemed irredeemably glued to the pillow. He gave up trying and became aware of distant scuffling and rustlings in the far corners of the apartment. Painfully, he attempted to open his eyes to try and detect the source of the puzzling and unwelcome noises, but continued to be thwarted by the ever-present blast of white-hot light from through the curtains. As he finally managed to prize them open a fraction, he witnessed an alluring flash of tanned back as someone pulled on a T-shirt over a pair of cut off denims. As he heard the patio door open, a whispered voice called

'Thanks Nicky, See you next year.' and then she was gone.

With some difficulty, Nick managed to pull himself up onto his elbows. He furrowed his brow painfully, mumbling incoherently to no one in particular,

'Who?'The events of the night before, as was often the case, still remained a fuzzy blur. He was damn sure he had had a good time, but where and with whom, of this he couldn't be sure. It would undoubtedly come to him later. In the meantime, maybe a little nap might help him remember. It was mid afternoon before he managed to find his way to the shower and it was not until a comforting snake of soapy water was cascading down his back that he blurted.

'Sherry, Sharon no, Shelley from Walthamstow no, Wanstead Hah! Never forget a name, or was it . . . . ?' as he dried his hair, he felt the familiar stab of remorse at the undoubtedly cavalier fashion in which he would have treated the girl in his undoubtedly drunken state the night before. He managed to comfort himself with the knowledge that probably, she had simply been another of the many holidaymakers who passed through, looking for nothing more than a fleeting contact, a holiday romance or memory to be able to boast about when returning home. The encounter had been a fair deal for both of the parties' involved.

## Officer Braga

It was very obvious that Nick's car was something of a rarity in these parts. Chris had warned him to be careful as the local police would have certainly taken a keen interest in it. He was soon to realise exactly what Chris meant. The car was fast, expensive and had British number plates.

Driving in the countryside with the hood down was a delight and a pleasure that Nick treated himself to when boredom surfaced. It was just one of these excursions that he was enjoying when he approached the traffic lights at the junction of the Lagos-Luz road. The lights were about to change as he got to within fifty metres. It was one of those split second decisions and as he had a fast car, he floored the accelerator and roared over. Immediately there was the unmistakable sound of a police siren. Nick pulled over, stopped the car and rolled down his window. A smartly attired GNR (Guarda National Republicana) officer arrogantly strolled towards him, smoothing the creases in his immaculate uniform as he approached. He leant down to speak through the open window, touching the peak of his cap, and enunciated in almost perfect English.

'My name is Officer Braga. Can I see your driving licence, please Sir.'

Nick smiled outwardly and groaned inwardly. This wasn't going to be as easy as he had thought.

'Certainly, Officer.' He fumbled in the glove compartment and produced the necessary documentation.

'That's very good English that you speak, Officer Braga. Where did you learn it?' Nick's query was completely ignored and the stern mouth, framed by a well trimmed but luxuriant black moustache stayed firmly closed. The officer turned back to his jeep and had a seemingly casual ten minute conversation with his colleague, punctuated by laughs of amusement and much gesticulating finally lighting a cigarette. Officer Braga returned, leant down to the window again and asked politely.

'Please could you step out of the car, Mr. Trevelyan?'

Nick sighed deeply and did what was asked. The officer took a final nonchalant drag from his cigarette and threw the butt onto the floor. Slowly he continued the travesty that he quite obviously appeared to be enjoying immensely. He stood with his hands clasped behind his back, a politely inquiring yet disquietingly smug expression on his face. Nick felt a horribly familiar feeling of déjà vu as he was vividly transported back to the drill square of Sandhurst and some particularly unwelcome encounter with Colour Sergeant Macgregor that he knew was going to lead an unpleasant form of disciplinary action. He snapped himself back to reality and smiled nervously at Braga, shrugging his shoulders. He raised his palms in a show of bewilderment. Braga was obviously unimpressed by Nick's display and removed a notebook from his breast pocket. After having written slowly and deliberately in it for several minutes he turned to Nick and announced.

'Mr. Trevelyan, you must appear at the Lagos GNR post indicated on this paper within the next twenty-four hours with full documentation and suitable reasons for having taken up valuable police time. There is also a fine of two hundred Euros for having crossed a set of red lights, payable as indicated.'

He tore off the sheet he had been writing on and handed it to Nick, then turned to go.

'But you can't do that.' Nick stammered lamely.

'Yes I can,' replied Officer Braga smugly but firmly, with a look of satisfaction on his face.

'And unless you would like to come down to the police station with me now, I suggest you leave right away."

Nick turned quickly, got into his car and drove away slowly, to return to the Mirage.

## The Mad Hatter's Tea Party

When he arrived at the Mirage car park Chris cornered him, he didn't feel like chatting at that moment but was obliged to feign interest.

'Another bit of good news I forgot to tell you about when I saw you earlier. We've had an invitation this morning from Felix, asking us to join him for dinner tomorrow night at his place. I won't be able to make it but I strongly suggest that you go along as it's bound to be good fun if nothing else; it will fill another page or two in your memoirs.'

With some semblance of an enthusiastic smile on his face, Nick agreed that it was an opportunity not to be missed. After a light supper in the restaurant and a few more drinks with Chris, he returned to the apartment, weary to the bone. He had been to a couple of Felix's soirees and if you were in the right mood, they would offer an interesting feast of eccentricity. If you weren't in the right mood, it was like being caught up in a bad dream, such was the disarray that could be caused by the eccentric bunches of people who often gather together at Felix's home. This time, there was no escape. Chris had said yes to the request and he would have told Felix that Nick had accepted his invitation. Nick hoped that he would be in a good mood tomorrow and fell into a troubled sleep.

He awoke the next day at about two o'clock. What a difference from early morning reveille in the army. He felt rested but in low spirits so he busied himself with minor domestic duties such as shopping and a little mild tidying up to distract himself. As the evening approached he found that he was feeling a certain curious anticipation of the impending events and hoped this meant that he was in the right mood for the party. He went along to the local adega and bought a bottle of acceptable Dao red and another reasonable Casal Garcia, a popular Portuguese green wine. Then he returned to the studio and showered. He dressed, spending some time in deciding what to wear. The clothes he was most comfortable in were dirty or inappropriate for dinner at the "Manor House". With reluctance, he opened the wardrobe door to reveal a selection of clothing he had barely set eyes on since he had arrived in Portugal. Nick had quickly discovered that, by and large, the casual look was the only look out there. He contemplated a jacket and regimental tie, thought better of it and plumped for a pair of dark trousers and a white collarless shirt. The final touch was a pair of socks under the smart black brogues that he hadn't worn once since his arrival. This felt decidedly odd, it had been months since he had worn socks but he was happy about the end result. As he slicked the last stray wisps of hair down in the mirror, he thought to himself *'not bad—not bad at all.' He* walked to his car feeling happier than he had for many weeks and found to his relief that he was actually starting to look forward to the evening ahead. His biggest problem of late, which was the motoring fine, had been paid and although it hurt to part with the money, he was able to consign the incident to history and hopefully erase the sting of it from his memory.

At eight on the dot, he drove through the gates of the Quinta Da Felicidade. There were several other cars in the car park. As he walked towards the house, the usual two dogs waddled over to greet him. They were obviously feeling quite sprightly in the cool of the evening as each managed to bark twice before returning to their bed at the base of the dragon tree. The front door to the house was open as it always was. Nick recalled that Felix had mentioned that the key had been lost some years before. He walked into the entrance hall, waited a few minutes then called Felix's name. There was no reply so he continued on through the downstairs hallway towards the dining room, where he could hear laughter and voices. He knocked on the door, pushing it open at the same time.

'Nicholas, darling, I'm delighted that you have been able to make it.' boomed Felix who was wearing another huge fedora hat even more extravagant than the others that Nick had seen. Felix was famous for his collection.

'Do come in and meet my friends, but first you must kiss me.' he demanded.

Nick dutifully kissed the host on both cheeks and allowed himself to be dragged around the room as he introduced him one by one to the assembled guests, with all of the panache of a best of breed owner at Crufts.

The dining room, whilst not overly large, was of adequate size. The walls were half panelled and the high ceiling was decorated with a very elaborate moulding effect which on closer inspection turned out to be plaster, cleverly made to imitate wood. There were two French windows that looked out onto a raised patio, commanding a view over the land to the rear of the house. The patio had been originally designed by the architect to take advantage of the view from the back of the house. But now, alas, the patio was home to a collection of dead refrigerators and rusting washing machines.

The furniture that adorned the room was probably best described as "elegantly aged", having been elaborate in its time, but now well used. The flooring was made of bare boards worn fashionably smooth with age. The assembled guests numbered about fifteen. Of the more noticeable was a fun couple who Felix introduced as "my very rich friends." They were from Surrey but now lived in America; he was "in computers" and she, interior design. They were both in their early thirties with an eighteen-month-old baby boy who was accompanied by a very young English nanny.

Another interesting duo was two young women from Los Angeles. Felix explained that they were in the film business and extremely important. They were obviously very much in love with each other and made no effort to hide the fact. *'Perhaps they are on honeymoon.' Nick thought.* He was beginning to reach a conclusion that there were no descriptive words in Felix's vocabulary which were less than *brilliant* or *wonderful*. Nobody was allowed to be ordinary or average. Mediocrity had no place in Felix Bartholomew's life. Felix referred to those who were working for their keep as his servants.

The incumbent "servant "appeared to be a man named Paul. Nick was somewhat begrudgingly introduced to him, which caused him to deduce that Paul was perhaps coming to the end of his stay at the Quinta Da Felicidade. Felix explained that Paul had been a producer at the BBC, but a messy divorce had caused him to lose his job and by Nick's estimation, the best part of his dignity. Paul moped about, serving drinks and offering around the hors d 'oeuvres. In addition, there was a German couple who were on a walking holiday and had wandered, by chance, into the Quinta Da Felicidade; they had not yet decided whether their stumbling across the place was a stroke of good fortune or very bad luck. So they stood in the corner, resplendent in their leather shorts, braces and crag-hopping boots looking very bemused. A fair-haired Norwegian with a goatee beard introduced himself as Carl. He explained to Nick that he ran an alternative health clinic in the hills and should Nick ever require his services, he had only to give him a call.

The last people to be introduced were a couple from Wales. Geraldine was a flamboyant lady of about forty-five; everything about her was outrageous from the top of her blonde hair to the tip of her six inch stiletto heeled shoes. Her dress, a little designer rubber number, fitted like a second skin and she was adorned like an Indian bride with the most extravagant jewellery. But by far her most conspicuous features were her ample bosoms, which strained within the confines of her dress, threatening at any moment to burst from this unwelcome restriction, as she wobbled from one place to another. Her husband, by contrast, wore a very sober tie and jacket and appeared the sort of man that might be an accountant or bank clerk.

To all other men present, he simply appeared to be a very lucky man. Nick noticed his shoes were built up to give him extra height. A late arrival appeared at the doorway causing a flurry of attention from Felix, who dutifully made a block introduction to all those assembled, of Charlene who was a forty-year old psychiatrist from California. Charlene sported bright red hair and wore a most revealing dress. After very little time in her company, Nick concluded that she was completely mad.

'Sit down everyone! We are going to eat now.' Felix ushered his guests to the table like something from a sheep dog trial.

'Nick, you will sit at my right hand and help Paul to serve the wine.'

Perhaps Felix had missed his vocation in life, Nick thought, for he would have made an excellent Sergeant Major in the Argyles, keeping the Jocks in line. No one would have argued with him. The long table had not enjoyed the luxury of polish for many years and the chairs were of varying pedigree, very few pieces of crockery matched, but the food was delicious, all served by Felix from the head of the table and passed along from guest to guest.

Felix stood, an imposing figure, dishing out food whilst engaging all of his guests in conversation. He was a remarkable host, of that there was no doubt. He was also extremely clumsy. He constantly knocked things over in his exuberance to feed everyone and food was splattered about all over the place, but Felix appeared not to notice. As is normal at such dinner parties, the conversation to begin with was pleasantly polite, punctuated on occasions by the Germans in the leather hose who, every now and again interjected in very broken English, adding something totally irrelevant.

But as time passed, and the wine took effect, the barriers began to fall and Felix's dinner guests relaxed. During a quieter moment, while Felix was engaged in the kitchen resolving some inexplicable crisis, Nick took the time to sit back and collect his thoughts; something had been in the back of his mind since he had sat down to dine. What was it that this party reminded him of?

In a flash it came to him, "The Mad Hatter's Tea Party" of course!

On cue, the Mad Hatter returned with a selection of sweets, leaving a trail of juice in his wake. Early on in the proceedings, the young nanny, who up to that point had not uttered a single word, proceeded to knock back a couple of glasses of wine and then suddenly, to the amazement of all, let rip with a torrent of conversation about her parents, severely boring all within earshot. Then as equally suddenly as she had started, she stopped, sat still for five minutes and then proceeded to burst into tears. Her employer made the necessary excuses and packed her off to bed, explaining that this was the first time that she had been away from home and she was a little homesick.

The evening continued at a pace with much of the conversation revolving around spiritualism, astrology and faith healing. Nick recalled that Chris had told him about the local popularity of these subjects. In his current, troubled frame of mind, he wasn't really in the mood to be discussing the nature of the universe and the whys and wherefores of existence, but gamely humoured his fellow guests and participated in the proceedings as enthusiastically as he could. Felix produced a collection of children's colouring crayons and some paper and then proceeded to scribble like a demented chimpanzee on the paper, selecting different crayons at will.

'This is your wonderful colour chart, Nicholas,' announced Felix proudly, and proceeded to read Nick's fortune with the help of the colourful mess that lay before him. Nick found the experience more than a little incomprehensible as the chart had become adorned with unexpected supplements, to help or hinder the reading—such as gravy, sauce, cream and a healthy dollop of caramel pudding.

At the far end of the table, Charlene was whipping up a storm with her Tarot cards, predicting Geraldine's future. Nick was also able to predict the future for Geraldine. Given the intake of wine and the excitement of having her fortune predicted by the mad woman with the bright red hair, in the very near future her barely contained bosom was going to take a giant step forward for mankind and burst onto the dining room table, possibly injuring someone in the process. Geraldine jumped with delight as Charlene related yet another revelation in her future.

'V*underbar*!' shouted the German crag hopper and was smartly kicked in the shins by his partner's size nine crag-hopping boots. Carl in the meantime watched the proceedings with distaste, leaving the party tricks to the amateurs; after all he was a professional. The Californian lesbian lovers gazed into each other's eyes, blissfully unaware of the chimp's tea party that was now well underway. The time had arrived for coffee. Felix was organising this event, standing in his usual position at the end of the table, dishing out cups, saucers and orders. The seating arrangement had altered slightly, guests had moved around as conversations were struck up with other diners. Nick noted how most of the men had managed to position themselves at an advantageous point from which they could better observe Geraldine's sumptuous heaving cleavage. None wished to miss the magical moment of release that could surely now not be too far away.

Suddenly, from upstairs, there came an ear-splitting scream, shocking the group into silence. Nobody moved except Felix who continued to serve coffee, completely unfazed.

'Perhaps you would like a little more milk Nicholas?' he asked politely. Such was the shrillness of the scream that the chest-watching fraternity momentarily lost their concentration, but they quickly regained their composure and settled back down to observe the matter at hand. After a time, the interior-decorating mother left the room to investigate. She came back five minutes later, sat down and informed the assembled guests that the ornate plaster ceiling in the green room had collapsed onto the bed where the nanny was sleeping. Nanny was not injured and was now asleep in the blue room. There was then a wonderful exhibition of telepathy as Felix, without a word fixated his slave, Paul, with a steely stare for ten seconds. After which Paul threw down his serviette and sloped off to clear up the debris After a period of fifteen minutes he reappeared dragging several black bin liners full of plaster through the dining room and deposited them in the refrigerator graveyard out on the patio looking most disgruntled about the whole episode. Felix, in the meantime continued as if the event had never happened. The port was passed around and gradually the guests made their excuses and left.

Geraldine's fan club were bitterly disappointed that they were not to be treated to a grand exposure and left; and the German hiker went off to the yellow room to bathe his badly bruised shins and suffer the wrath of his heavily built Fraulein. Geraldine's husband left with a wry smile on his face, knowing that he alone would savour the delights that the other men could only dream of.

'Well Felix, I have to go, too'. Nick said. 'I must thank you for a most enjoyable evening,' he added, and it was true. He had enjoyed himself. As he walked towards the front door, he contemplated the past three hours and the eccentric charm of Felix's home. Anyone seeking a bland, homogenized experience really doesn't deserve to dine or stay at Quinta Da Felicidade. The evening had certainly been entertaining, but the diners' rather desperate antics had stretched his powers of endurance to the limits. He was looking forward to getting back to the Mirage bar where he could have a quiet drink with Tony and calm his nerves. Everybody was running round in circles looking for the answer to life; well, Nick had enough of his own hang-ups without having to suffer those of everyone else.

'Thank you for coming. We enjoyed your company, Nicholas.' Felix replied as alone they walked towards the open front door, then as they reached the reception area, Felix stopped and put his hands on Nick's shoulders and looked into his eyes.

'Oh-shit.' Nick thought, what the hell is this?

'Nicholas I knew that I was right; you do have different coloured eyes.' Felix was holding Nick's shoulders and peering straight into his eyes, looking very excited.

'Err . . . . yes, it's something that most people don't notice. You're very observant Felix.' Nick replied, wondering where this would go next.

'Nicholas, that's so wonderful, I'm sure that this must mean that you have mystic powers'. Felix and his group of whacky friends were looking for the occult and esoteric in whatever they could. Nick needed to make good his escape quickly before Felix decided that he was a Druid chieftain.

## The Book

In the reception area of the entrance stood a tall bookcase full of old dog-eared paperbacks. Nick saw his chance and swerved the conversation onto another tack.

'Would you mind if I borrowed a book Felix, I haven't stopped to read for months; it would make a nice change.' Nick enquired, ducking from under his arms and walking towards the bookcase.

'Yes, of course. Please help yourself. I have some wonderful books.' Felix offered enthusiastically. As soon as Nick began to read the titles, he realised that this move had been a mistake. Kind of out of the frying pan and into the fire. For all the books were on the subjects of spiritualism, astronomy and other allied supernatural matters.

'I'll take this one.' Nick decided, grabbing any book so as to be able to make good his escape.

'Oh! That's a fantastic book; you will absolutely adore it.' Felix encouraged. Nick took a look at the title for the first time.

"TEACH YOURSELF HYPNOTISM".

'Wonderful I'm sure that I'll enjoy this one', he lied. He kissed Felix on the cheeks in the prescribed manner, thanked him again for a marvellous dinner and headed off to the car park. As he passed the two sleeping dogs under the dragon tree, he called to them.

'Teach yourself bloody hypnotism!' and laughed wryly. The two dogs made no attempt to move.

## The First Hypnotic Experience.

How fickle and unpredictable life can be. In his wildest dreams, Nick could never have imagined that the book which he took from the Quinta da Felicidade could possibly have such a profound and instantaneous effect on the rest of his life. He had thrown the book into the back of his car on the night that he drove home from Felix's dinner party and there it had stayed for over a week. Then one day he picked it up and took it into his studio where it remained untouched for a further ten days. Then suddenly, and for no apparent reason other than boredom and a lack of reading material, he picked it up and casually browsed through the pages.

Nick had dismissed the book out of hand as not being worth the paper that it had been written on. It was a forgone conclusion in his mind that this must be something of a literary joke. "Mumbo Jumbo." aimed at those who sought the answers to life in the exotic and absurd. Inside the fly-leaf was a smudged, cheap rubber stamp that proclaimed that the book belonged to the Algarvian Book Club. It had probably been donated to the club along with a pile of others by somebody who had cleaned out their garage, and from there it made its way to the Quinta Da Felicidade. The print date was 1932 and the pages were yellowing. Nick settled back on his bed, ready for a doze, but instead picked up the book again and started nonchalantly flicking through it.

To begin with he browsed through the pages more from boredom than anything else. He was amused as he read with unexpected interest how to hypnotize whoever he wished and he laughed at his own stupidity for continuing to read such rubbish. The book was about as credible as a "do it-yourself" manual on brain surgery. Eventually, he slammed the book closed and was surprised to note that he had spent over four hours with his nose in the nonsense that lay on the table before him. He made a mental note to supply himself with some more worthy reading material as it was apparent that he needed to occupy his mind with something other than sun, sand and sea. This kind of crap was only going to addle his mind even more than it already was, although there were some sections that he found interesting and thought provoking. The reading had delivered him to a far too thoughtful frame of mind, so he decided to return to the bar for a nightcap. He realised with a sense of hopelessness that he was starting to find it difficult to get to asleep unless anesthetized with alcohol, but despite this sobering acceptance of reality, he left his room in search of a large tumbler of whisky. It would have been simple to have sunk into a depression had not a group of holiday makers whom he had befriended dropped in and swept him up into a bar crawling evening which ended with a party on the beach.

The next morning he found himself sitting in the Mirage garden. He was feeling decidedly fragile and was starting his second coffee by the time that Chris arrived to sit with him.

'Well you certainly look as if you've had a good night,' smiled Chris as he sat down to join Nick for coffee and read his mail. This was something that had become a ritual over the preceding weeks.

'I guess it was all worth it.' Nick replied, somewhat dreamily.

Chris carried on working his way through the pile of letters. He occasionally grunted and tutted. Then with a huge grin on his face he looked up and exclaimed,

'How about this! It's from my accountant in England; the Inland Revenue has given me a rebate of six thousand Pounds. Bloody hell! I can't believe it.' He was thrilled and promised to take Nick out for a meal to celebrate. Nick was delighted that Chris had received some good news at last but his thoughts were miles away.

'Chris,' he said in a low voice.

'Um.' Chris's mind was still with the Inland Revenue.

'Chris, look at me.' Nick repeated again in the same low voice.

'What's the problem, Nick?' enquired Chris, still having trouble dragging himself away from the good news that he held in his hand as if it might suddenly dissapear.

'Look into my eyes.' this was said half as an order and half as a request.

'Do what?' asked Chris, a little confused but complying with the request before he had time to think of what he was doing.

'Look deep into my eyes Chris, very deeply into my eyes.' Nick was quite enjoying playing the hypnotist; he had been a little bored and felt quite at home taking on the role.

'Bloody hell, Nick! I never noticed that before—you have different colour eyes.'

'Your eyes are beginning to become tired, you are sinking deeper into my eyes, deeper, deeper your eyes are becoming more and more tired.' Chris blinked lazily; he was going along with the charade.

'Your eyelids are becoming so heavy that you can't keep them open.' Nick directed. Immediately Chris's eyed banged shut like the doors of a double garage.

'You are now totally at my command.' Nick announced triumphantly.

'Yes, came the reply. 'I am at your command.'

Nick leaned back lazily in his chair stretching his legs out in front of him. He stared at an aircraft that was cutting a silver swathe across the pale blue morning sky. It was probably taking sun tanned tourists back to the greener shores of England, clutching their bottles of Port and green wine. Chris sat motionless, eyes still closed, breathing deeply. Nick sat opposite, waiting for Chris to become bored with the game and break the silence. Then he decided to carry on with the charade.

'Chris, you are now at my command and whatever I ask you to do, you will obey because you know that no harm will come to you. Do you understand?' Nick asked.

'Yes, I understand,' replied Chris obediently.

'Chris, open your eyes, walk out into the car park, turn around three times and then come back here and sit down.' Nick further instructed. Chris's eyes sprang open, he was sitting directly opposite Nick no more than a meter away across a garden table but his eyes looked straight through him. He stood up and walked out through the garden gate and into the car park. There he slowly turned around three times then walked back over to where he had previously been sitting and sat down. And there he sat, his gaze fixed rigidly forward with an expressionless look on his face. By this time, Nick was becoming more than a little apprehensive. Chris was making a great job of going along with the joke. Or could it be possible? Could he have actually hypnotized his friend?

'Touch your nose Chris.' Nick said in a calm voice, although he was now starting to become a little unnerved by what was happening. Chris obeyed and touched his nose as ordered. Nick studied the man sitting in front of him. His eyes gazed forward and he really looked quite normal apart from his general overall quietness, noticeably reduced movement and the slightly glazed look in his eyes.

'Surely not.' Nick murmured. Chris's eyelids fluttered almost undetectably, instantly giving Nick cause to think that he was going to jump up, claiming a victory at playing Nick along at his own game. But still there was nothing. He continued to stare ahead.

'Oh shit.' Nick's mind was moving towards panic. Chris remained virtually statuesque. In Nick's estimation, ten minutes must have passed since the incident had started. Surely it would be impossible for anyone to keep up the pretence this long. Chris must be hypnotized. The thought at first made him want to laugh. After all, it was so ludicrous. He continued his observation of the man sitting across the table, who, Nick was now convinced must surely be in some sort of a trance that he had induced. Now he began to worry about his friend. Could there be any lasting effects?

Could there be a possibility of some deeper psychological damage? Would this incident have any long term effect on Chris? He looked around the garden, slightly in desperation and partly in search of some inspiration. The curtain in his nearby apartment fluttered momentarily in the breeze.

'That bloody book!' He whispered angrily to himself. He slowly got up from the table, not knowing what effect this might have upon his subject. He half expected Chris to get up and follow him but Chris continued to stare into space. Once Nick had walked slowly out through the garden gate, occasionally looking over his shoulder to reassure himself that Chris hadn't moved, he sprinted the twenty metres around the building to the studio door. Fumbling with the keys in his haste to get the book, he burst into the room like a deranged maniac. He grabbed the book and started to scan the pages for the section that he remembered seeing about bringing the subject out of a trance. It was then that he heard the voice, just outside the window.

'Senhor Chris?' enquired a female Portuguese voice.

'Oh, Senhor Chris?' the voice again enquired.

'*Shit, shit, shit.*' Nick could barely contain himself. He ducked down and moved over to the window carefully so as not to be seen, pulling back the bottom corner of the curtain. He peered out into the garden. A middle-aged Portuguese cleaning lady with a dustpan and brush in her hand was addressing Chris. Presumably inquiring of her boss his opinion on yet another of the continuous stream of minor problems that arose. Chris stared forward, totally oblivious of the woman who was becoming increasingly impatient.

'Oh Senhor Chris!' There was obvious impatience in the cleaning lady's voice. She inquired for the third time. Nick was tempted to show himself and attempt to make some sort of lame excuse for *Senhor Chris*'s lack of attention, but he knew little or no Portuguese and was equally convinced that the cleaning lady knew no English. There was nothing that he could think of doing that would help the situation so he had to be content to observe the bizarre scene that was being enacted in the tranquillity of the garden and hope for the best. His prayers were answered. After two more attempts to attract the attention of her "patron," the cleaning lady stormed off in a huff to resolve the problem herself. Nick tore around the building like a demented greyhound and reached the garden gate. He stopped before entering the garden in an attempt to get his breath back. Now that he was armed with the book it should be a relatively easy matter to restore Chris to normality before anyone else came into the garden and found him on cloud nine.

'I'm going to count backwards from ten to one.' Nick explained. 'By the time I have reached 'one' you will be wide awake and feeling great. You will remember nothing of what has happened to you, just a good feeling all over. A feeling of well being.' If this didn't work what the hell would he do?

'Ten-nine-eight, feeling happy and slowly waking up. Seven-six-five, more awake. Four-three, even more awake and feeling good. Two-one, wide awake and feeling great.'

Chris sat in his chair with a puzzled look and a faint smile on his face. He was still holding the letter from his accountant in his hand. He looked down at the letter and then across at Nick.

'What was I saying Nick?' He asked.

'You were telling me about your tax rebate.' Nick reminded him.

'Err-yes. Great news . . . err, come at a good time too.' Chris's composure was returning rapidly. 'That's the best bit of news that I've had for ages.' he enthused.

'Know what? That's made me feel bloody marvellous.' By this time Chris was beaming all over his face, while Nick looked on bewildered. He was the complete opposite, covered in perspiration, his T-shirt was soaking from the exertion and worry and his hair was stuck to his forehead and neck. His heart was still pumping wildly. The panic was over and he slumped down into the chair. Chris looked across at him and remarked in a fatherly fashion.

'Nick, you look bloody awful! I don't think that these late nights are doing you much good.'

'I think you could be right.' Nick admitted.

'How about a drink to celebrate your good luck? I'm gasping.' Nick said, sorely in need of some refreshment.

'It's only ten a.m!' Chris replied, surprised. 'Go to the bar and help yourself,' he offered. 'I have to go to and sort out some problems with the cleaners.' and with that he bounced off across the patio obviously a happy man in a very good mood. Nick staggered to the bar and poured himself a large beer, hardly able to believe what had taken place in little more than twenty minutes.

# Second Encounter with Braga

The mood of despondency that he had now felt for some considerable time clung to Nick like a dark cloud. He found it very difficult to find anything to do or anyone to talk to that either interested him or managed to lift his mood. He was even starting to find Chris's company trying, as he felt unable to communicate his dejection, which left him feeling even more inadequate and isolated. He took to spending much of his afternoon walking on the beach or wandering across the rocks, sitting for long periods, pondering his situation in an aimless and futile fashion. He could find no answers to his current predicaments and didn't know where else to look. The only method of escape were his evenings in the bar. He had even stopped going to other places and making friends with the passing players. He just wanted to sit alone and drink until he could no longer remember. This was a trick he had now most successfully mastered. The Mirage also extended him a line of credit that was most welcome as his funds continued to dwindle seemingly in proportion to his inability to deal with his situation.

The next day was Sunday. Once more he got up and squinted out through the curtains at the burning mid afternoon sun. The warmth of the sunshine and the brilliance of the blue sky no longer gave him any pleasure; it might as well be a grey, grim drizzly February weekend in Windsor.

Nick dressed and quietly walked round to the car park, not wishing to meet anyone, for he was not in the mood for conversation. He climbed into his car and slowly pulled out of Praia-da-Luz. He passed through Lagos, casting a disdainful glance at the determinedly cheery holiday makers as they swarmed around the walled resort town like scavenger ants, desperately seeking a good time.

Thankfully he headed away from the scene and put is foot down as he moved out onto the Route National 125. He had not been on the road for more than five minutes when, looking in the rear view mirror, he caught sight of a GNR police jeep three or four cars behind. Nick smiled smugly, glancing at the speedometer, knowing that he had been keeping well within the speed limit and they had no reason to approach him.

*'Not me today, Mate! You can pick on some other poor bastard,'* he thought with satisfaction. There was no denying that the Porsche did stand out rather blatantly, even though it was now less than spanking new.

The previous brush with the police had, in some measure, emphasize the fact that a police officer's wage could never finance such a vehicle, which was a rare sight on these roads. The police jeep hung back in the traffic for some minutes. Then, when the flow allowed, it gradually caught up with him. Slowly pulling out beside Nick's car, the driver motioned for him to pull over. He couldn't believe it.

'What the hell is it now?' he said to himself, angrily, as he coasted to a halt on the hard shoulder. This really was all he needed. He sat for a minute, rigidly holding the steering wheel, staring ahead trying to compose himself. Then he turned and rolled down the window as the approaching officer took off his cap and lowered his face to the window. Nick could not help but close his eyes in dismay. Unfortunately, the bristling moustache and dark piercing eyes of officer Manuel Braga were firmly imprinted on the inside of his eyelids.

'Any problems, Officer?' Nick asked calmly, refraining from using Braga's name as this might indicate a familiarity he was not desperate to remind him of. He noticed with regret that, by the glint in the officer's eye, he was fully aware of who Nick was. *'Maybe it's time to try a different tack,'* he thought.

'Nice to see you again, Officer Braga. I trust you're well? If there's anything I can do to help?' Nick left the question hanging, remembering too late that from previous experience, his antagonist didn't respond too encouragingly to the niceties of such occasions,

'Papers, please, Mr. Trevelyan and step out of the car if you will.' said the unsmiling Officer. Nick decided to adopt the line of least resistance and say nothing more unless requested. He complied with Braga's wishes and waited silently to find out which particular game they were playing today.

'How long have you been in Portugal, Mr. Trevelyan?' Officer Braga inquired, looking down at the registration documents that Nick had given him.

'Five or six months.' Nick replied, helpfully.

'Perhaps you could be more precise, Mr. Trevelyan?' Braga intoned, coldly. Nick silently cursed his stupidity in allowing the man this obvious opening. He didn't like the way this conversation was going at all.

'Sorry, officer I came in the third week of April and it's now the end of September that would make it either five months and one week or,' he paused to calculate, 'twenty two weeks.' He finished, trying to sound confident, although without the help of a calendar, it was difficult to be so spontaneously correct. Officer Braga smiled, seemingly satisfied with the response.

'I see that you have a British MOT certificate that is dated 15th October 2003, and is scheduled to cover a twelve month period from that date.'

'Yeess,' Nick replied, cautiously, as is mind started working furiously, and a cold feeling of anticipation started prickling his stomach

'Which means, please correct me if I'm wrong, Mr. Trevelyan, that this certificate became invalid precisely eight days ago.' Braga could now barely suppress the smile of satisfaction that twitched at the corners of his moustache curtained mouth. To assert his authority even more he stopped the proceedings to light a cigarette.

'Well, yes, Nick replied curtly, I suppose you are correct.' He could think of no other way to respond. His mind had been so preoccupied recently (with precisely nothing) that he could barely remember what month it was, let alone what date. Now he had committed the ultimate stupidity of letting something as simple as getting a new MOT pass him by. And here, there was no tolerant British bobby to tell him off for his misdemeanour and send him packing to get the discrepancy rectified as soon as possible at the local garage. No, there was only this mini Hitler, who probably slept in his highly polished black boots and chewed nails for breakfast. Nick felt numb with resignation and succumbed to the remainder of his ordeal with a weary lack of resistance. Braga lectured him on the severity of the oversight, cited the laws that he had broken and invited Nick down to the station to further discuss this serious offence. He duly stepped into the police car with the smirking Manuel Braga, as the other officer had already radioed for a tow truck to come and fetch the Porsche, and he braced himself for the impending ordeal.

Two hours later, Nick returned to the studio by taxi. It was late afternoon and thankfully no one seemed to be around to witness his humiliation. He sat on the bed staring blankly, registering nothing. He felt totally desensitized, bereft of any emotion. As he reached out to smooth down some imaginary creases in the covers on the bed, in a gesture that was meaningless, he noticed absently that his hand was trembling. Braga had strutted and preened before Nick, gloating at his little victory. He must have felt most annoyed by Nick's total lack of acknowledgement of his position. Apart from the perfunctory answers to any questions required to fill in paperwork, he sat staring unmovingly ahead. This was scant compensation for the anger and frustration that he felt.

The officer, however, was determined to have his day, and took great pleasure in reading him the riot act. He impounded his car until further notice, and imposed a fine on me that he wasn't going to be able to pay in three months of Sundays, let alone within the fourteen days that Braga gave him by law. Apparently the alternative was a possible custodial sentence as the cars insurance was now also invalid. Nick was not contesting the charge, there was no point. Impounding his this beloved car seemed to be the irrevocable outcome.

## The Rock

Later that evening, sitting alone on a huge rectangular rock at the base of the towering black volcanic cliffs, the brilliant low rays of the early evening sun caused him to squint and create a shade for his eyes with his hand. He looked out towards the horizon. He saw the tiny fleet of wooden fishing boats moving westwards from their cosy berths in Lagos harbour across the calm surface of the Atlantic winter sea to the fishing grounds of Cape St. Vincent thirty kilometre's distant. The boats slid across the smooth surface of the water like a collection of snails across a pane of hammered glass. As his eyes became accustomed to the powerful light, he slowly realised that there were several flocks of seagulls lazily soaring on the invisible thermals, way, way out to sea, spiralling upwards as if they were on some unseen moving staircase. Nick often came to this rock and looked out to sea, vaguely hoping that, somehow, the mighty ocean might in some way provide him with an answer to his problems. In recent weeks, he had become an all too frequent visitor to the rock. He left the rock and wandered along the beach, allowing the soft Atlantic waves to wash over his feet. Looking up at the huge dramatic wedge of volcanic rock, he made an estimate of its height as being two hundred and fifty, three hundred feet perhaps. He picked up a small black pebble. Thousands of years ago it would have fallen from the black rocks that dominate the eastern end of the beach and for centuries it had rolled and tumbled in the surf. A reminder of how insignificant our time here on this planet really is. He wondered if other folk had such a place where they could go and contemplate their deepest, innermost feelings. He decided that most people seemed immune to depression or in some cases oblivious to any feelings at all.

Nick had tried hard to lose himself and search for oblivion in the bottom of a bottle, as so many visitors to the Algarve had done before him. But drinking had not been the answer. "Algarve Fever", Chris had called it. No matter how much alcohol Nick consumed, he always retained a certain sense of awareness. He could never get so smashed that he lost touch with the reality of the world around him. He almost envied those hardened drunks who were at least able to push their minds beyond sensibility and sink into another world where personal pride had no meaning. There appeared to be no way forward, no reason to continue. How could an end be brought to the mess that his existence had become? If only he could close this chapter of his life, wake up and start again with a clean sheet. When would the nightmare end? How do you give up? He churned the question over in his confused mind. To whom do you shout?

'Ok I give up! Stop the fight.' Who is the referee in this unfair contest of life? Supposedly you could lie on the floor and admit defeat, but to who? Sooner or later the floor would become cold, hard and uncomfortable and you would be forced to get up. What nonsense. What crap. His logical mind moved on. OK So what's the point of prolonging the agony, why drag out the misery. Who the hell is going to miss a loser like me? he asked himself.

This was a question to which he did not know the answer. Yes, of course his mother would be devastated; his father, too, but time heals and they would get over it. With a jolt, Nick suddenly realised what he was contemplating. Ending it all; hara-kiri; topping himself. He managed a cynical smile. How strange that something so serious could have so many flippant titles. But yes, it appeared to him at that time to be the only way out.

## Nick attempts to end his life

Right, the problem had been set. Now, how best to undertake this challenge? The whole thing felt like one of the officer cadet initiative tests that he had so often encountered at Sandhurst. His thoughts returned to the Gulf and Northern Ireland. He had witnessed death many times, savage death. But worse, far worse are the poor bastards who don't get killed outright and hang on with horrific wounds. It's something that never ceases to amaze all who are involved in warfare and witness at first hand the carnage that it brings. Just what it takes to stop a human being from being alive. They can be torn apart or burned beyond recognition, but still they hang on to life. Nick was young and even after all of the abuse that his body had endured in recent months from the submersion in alcohol that it had undergone, he was remarkably, still quite fit. His body would be one that would take some stopping and the job would have to be done properly.

The logic of his analytical mind went into action for the first time in months. The most obvious answer, given the location and terrain, was to take himself to the top of the black rock cliffs and launch himself off. This would probably do the trick, but there was an element of doubt. The drop was not sheer, therefore his body would be bound to hit one of the many rock outcrops on the way down, which would break the fall, probably culminating in a broken mess on the beach but without the guarantee of certain death. The leap into oblivion was therefore a non-starter.

Another cynical smile crossed his troubled face as the thought process continued. How strange, the trivial things that we retain within the hidden corners of our minds. As a kid, Nick had been a Boy Scout. He had derived great enjoyment from the meetings of the 3rd Windsor Troop, and was eventually elevated to the heady rank of patrol leader, Swift Patrol. In its infinite wisdom, the scout movement pays great attention to the correct tying of knots. And so it was at one of the weekly meetings of the troop that Mr. Jackson was invited to come along and give a demonstration of knots and lines to the lads. Mr. Jackson had been a sailor, and by his own admission, (several times during the evening), "What he didn't know about knots and lines wasn't worth knowing." Apart from the occasional "lamp swinging" memoirs, Mr. Jackson proved to be, as he had himself admitted, "an excellent teacher", whom the Scouts had been lucky to get. He certainly knew his way around a rope and impressed all present. To finish up, he demonstrated some fun knots, the last of which was the official hangman's noose. The scouts were all duly inspired and from then on, Mr. Jackson became a regular visitor to the scout hut. The hangman's noose was a particular favourite of Nick's and he taught himself to tie it. Now, after all those years, this trivial accomplishment might be of some practical use. The best way to complete the deed would be to drive his car to the cliff top, tie one end of a rope to a secure part of the vehicle and, wearing the neatly tied noose around his neck, jump over the edge.

The first hundred feet was clear of outcrops and a thirty feet fall would be sufficient to break his neck. And then it hit him, what car? His was in the compound in Portimáo along with dozens of others that had suffered a similar fate.

Mentally, Nick placed a tick by the word '*Hanging*' on the macabre list he held in his mind. It would be interesting to watch the Lagos fire brigade trying to recover the body as it hung by its rope from the black rocks, looking out to sea with bulging eyes, sporting the telltale wet patch at the front of the trousers, he mused. The wet patch was bound to have dried up hours before the body was pulled to the cliff top, but he would not be too worried by that time.

Another possibility was to join the Lagos pistol-shooting club. He had paid the club a visit just after arriving on the Algarve, but the place was so badly run that he had decided to give it a wide berth. Now, that inefficiency could well be used to his advantage. All that he had to do was go along, rent out a heavy enough calibre pistol to complete the job; wander off into a quiet corner and do the deed. The Portuguese were so laid back that it would probably take a week or so for them to notice anything unusual. This method was certainly one worth considering. In the end the technique that he decided upon was carbon monoxide poisoning, using the exhaust fumes from a car. He had read that the fumes act as a sedative and the whole experience might even prove to be pleasant. He had also read that this was one of the most popular forms of suicide, which meant that plenty of people had done their homework. He walked back along the deserted beach having made his first positive decision in months. Now that the conclusion had been reached, the matter at hand took priority in his empty life.

He regretted that his over sensitive mind dwelt on the less savoury aspects and end results of his objective but he found it difficult to prevent these thoughts from entering his mind. He had observed death on many occasions and in most cases the loss of control over the body's muscles allowed the bladder to empty its contents. Suffering the indignity of being found dead, with a huge wet patch at the front of his trousers was a concern that frequently haunted him. Another thought that passed through his head was the gold capping that he had on two teeth. He had heard of mortuary attendants knocking out the gold from their charges' teeth with a hammer and chisel. Apparently, it was considered to be a perk of the job. He did not want to end his days being disfigured by some unconcerned apprentice mortician eager for a fast buck. But it seemed that he would be unable to pursue these concerns to their logical conclusion; when he was dead it was hardly going to be of any consequence to him what his appearance was.

Nick went to bed, for the first time in ages, without paying a visit to the bar. Having not taken the customary night cap or two to help him sleep, the long, lonely night stretched before him intolerably. What little sleep he did manage to get was plagued by ludicrous dreams filled with endless rows of bodies laid out on mortuary slabs, all wearing nappies, heads tilted backwards, and their gaping mouths wide open and toothless. Dwarf like men in white coats busied themselves hacking lumps of flesh from the blue corpses.

The next morning, he got up early but hollow eyed through lack of sleep. He took a shower, shaved and paid particular attention to his appearance, not wishing to attract any undue attention. His first stop was the local rent-a-car shop. As he had lost the Porsche, he needed transport. In the past, when he had needed to have the car serviced, he had negotiated very reasonable terms with the local dealer who spoke excellent English. Luckily he had a car available for three days hire, so Nick paid the deposit and cheerily waved him goodbye. '*Poor bastard*,' Nick thought grimly as he drove off. The dealer might not get the rest of his money, but at least no harm would come to his car which could at worst be cleaned.

By ten o'clock, he was on the road to Lagos. His next stop was a large builder's merchant in town called Raminhos & Raminhos. He had been there several times in the past with Chris, buying odds and ends that were needed for maintenance jobs. He purchased five meters of plastic hose, a jubilee clip to fit the same, a screwdriver and a sheet of medium fine emery cloth. Next he drove on to a *papelaria* or stationers', where he bought a roll of extra wide masking tape. Then he I went on to the garage where he filled up the car's tank with petrol. From Lagos, he took the main 125 Route National towards Villa da Bispo. After ten minutes, he turned off to the right and headed along a bumpy, pot holed, minor country road to Barao San Joao. Cutting up through the sleepy little village, he entered the Parque Nacional an area of natural beauty that had been set aside for conservation. There was a particularly secluded spot, nestling in a scrawny forest, that he rather liked. He parked the car, got out and mooched around.

'As nice a place as any to end one's days,' *he* commented to himself 'wonderfully picturesque and very lonely.' The reconnaissance of his suicide site was now completed. He drove slowly back to Praia da Luz, parked the car opposite the beach, took off his shoes and walked to his private block of sandstone. He sat looking out to sea for the best part of three hours, thinking the whole thing over and over in his troubled mind. It really did appear to be the most logical solution; the location was ideal, it was remote and no one else would be involved. He wondered how long it would take before his body was found.

'Who cares, I'll be out of it anyway.' All of the time that he sat on the rock there was always the possibility that perhaps, just perhaps, someone would come along, strike up a conversation and unwittingly give him a reason to go on. A reason to not do what he was contemplating. No other human being on the planet knew what he was planning, so the chance of someone coming along and begging him to "think again" was nil. No siren arose from the deep Atlantic waters to offer him solace and so he gave up and wandered back to the car. He sat in the brilliant winter sunlight and gazed through the windscreen at nothing. Eventually, he started the engine and drove off.

He considered stopping off at the studio and writing a farewell letter, but he couldn't think of anything worth committing to paper. His worldly goods would more than likely be rejected by Oxfam. Anything of value appeared to be in the hands of the local police, guarded by the ever-efficient Officer Braga. So there wasn't much point in listing the beneficiaries. It was Monday afternoon, '*what better or worse time to end one's life,*' *he* thought, with weary resignation. The car moved inland as if driven by some other person. He felt like a passenger, almost an onlooker, witnessing a play being acted out by someone else other than himself. He passed through the little village of Espiche and out into the vine covered countryside. He could see the Parque Nacional in the distance. Suddenly, he was overcome by an awful sadness such as he had never experienced before. Up until this point, Nick had felt very depressed, but this was something else. A feeling deep inside that made the very foundations of his soul ache. Then he started to cry, tears flooding down his face until it became hard for him to see the road ahead. The countryside slid past the windows but his concentration was consumed with trying to negotiate the bumpy road through the floods of tears and violent sobbing that he was unable to control.

The village of Barao San Joao passed by the window and the car pushed on into the park. Miraculously the vehicle halted at the chosen destination. He sat for a while, making a concerted effort to compose himself. Eventually he got out of the car and walked round to the boot; his hands were trembling as he fumbled with the key before managing to open the boot lid. He picked up the emery cloth and tore it into two. Then with one piece of the cloth, he cleaned the end of the exhaust tail pipe so that the plastic hose would grip firmly. Next, he secured the hose to the pipe with the jubilee clip using the new screwdriver, making sure that he had created a gas-tight connection. He fed the free end of the hose in through the rear window of the car, laying the end carefully onto the rear seat. The window was wound up so that it held the hose firmly against the top of the window frame. This created a slot at the top of the window that he neatly covered with the masking tape.

The whole operation took about seven minutes to complete and the activity had returned Nick to a reasonably calm state. He walked off ten paces from the car and took a leak, thereby reducing the "wet patch" worries to a minimum. Resignedly, he walked back to his prepared coffin and slid in behind the wheel. He had no conception of time and was totally preoccupied by his own morbid thoughts that were now enclosed within the limited metal sphere of the car. It was perhaps another fifteen minutes before he leant forward, turned the key in the ignition and started the engine.

## The boy and his goat

A young boy strolled along the familiar path through the eucalyptus wood. His skinny, brown legs and shoeless feet poked out of rolled up, faded canvas trousers that were several sizes too large for him and the picture on the dirty torn T-shirt that he was wearing had once advertised Pepsi but now was faded almost beyond recognition. In his right hand he held a thin length of whippy bamboo with which he occasionally poked and swiped at the gently meandering, aged Billy-goat before him. Behind him followed a scampering pup of no obvious origins that ran around his ankles and snapped at the goat's underbelly from time to time. The boy was in no hurry, the goat had strayed too far from his compound, an unenclosed field of dusty ground with scant grazing possibilities on his grandfather's farm, half a mile away. It was his responsibility to look after the scrawny animal. He had been ordered to go and find it and it hadn't taken long. Senhor Caracol, for this was the goat's name (Mr. Snail) with which the boy referred to his charge, was a creature of habit, and not known for his racy lifestyle. He had a couple of favourite spots within a mile radius where the vegetation was a little more luxuriant. If he couldn't be bothered to wait for the boy to take him on his daily stroll to feed him, he would take off on his own at a sedate amble that took him circuitously to one of these favourite feeding places. The boy, who couldn't have been more than six years old, took his responsibilities seriously, but today, he was taking advantage of the little excursion to wander through some of his favourite haunts.

He was also not keen to return too soon, as he did not enjoy his next allotted task for the day that was to feed the pig. He hated having to step into the ancient, oversized, foul smelling rubber boots and sludge his way through the inevitable pig muck, which led to the decrepit wooden trough where he had to empty his pail of potato peelings and scraps of cabbage and other decaying vegetables that stunk to high heaven. No. That was a chore that could quite happily wait until a little later in the day. Now, he approached the small open space in the middle of the forest, which was at the end of an unused, rutted old track that once extended further through the trees. It was a familiar resting-place of his, where he could lie back on the grass, stare at the sky and dream. And if he was in the company of Senhor Caracol, tether him lightly to a tree on a long rope and allow him to graze for a while on the green vegetation beneath the trees as a treat. The boy threaded his way along through the last of the trees, and stepped into the clearing. He stopped with dismay, his plans for the day rudely shattered. It seemed that an intruder had invaded what he considered his personal territory and had spoiled the tranquil aspect of his hideaway.

A metallic green Fiat Punto was parked at the end of the track and sat incongruously and motionless in the middle of the glade. It certainly didn't look neglected and had obviously not been there very long. From where he was standing, it was difficult to tell whether someone was sitting in the driver's seat. The boy stared at it, unmoving, for a while, and then his curiosity got the better of him, and he gingerly approached the vehicle.

As he moved around the back of the car he became certain that there was a dark shadow sitting behind the wheel and he trembled with trepidation. It was an unusual sight at such close proximity. He was more used to the primitive contraptions used on his grandfather's farm. The boy had seldom travelled too far from the farm and, whilst he had often seen such cars at a distance, seeing one so close up was a treat, and a story he would retell again and again to his friends and family. He crept towards the driver's side, immediately noticing with interest, but no comprehension, that it was adorned with a long black plastic pipe which seemed to have been placed into a pipe which poked out from the back of the car, from where it trailed round the side and fed inside through the top of the rear window. He slowly edged forward, crouching down on his heels and approached the driver's door. His little heart started pounding with excitement and apprehension. As he reached the window, he rested for a couple of minutes beneath it, then, with his pulse racing, turned slowly and stretched upwards to peer in through the glass.

A man sat silently at the wheel, staring solemnly ahead of him. The boy dived flat onto the ground and swiftly slithered round to the back of the car and lay quaking, with his hands over his head. When he realised there was no movement from within, he became more courageous and stealthily returned to the window to peep again. He held fast but the man seem to be totally unaware of his presence so he continued to stare. He noticed with concern that the man seemed terribly sad, and after a few minutes a single tear rolled down the man's cheek. How could he possibly be unhappy? He had this marvellous vehicle and must therefore have lots of money. What more could he need? Nonetheless, the boy felt sorry for the melancholic figure, and wanted to do something to cheer him up. He reached up a small fist and was just preparing to knock on the window when the man suddenly leant forward and turned on the ignition causing the engine to start. The boy started and jumped back. He noticed immediately, with amazement, that small puffs of grey smoke appeared at irregular intervals in the back of the inside of the car. What a disaster he thought, the car has caught fire and the strange young man doesn't seem to have noticed. He threw caution to the wind and started banging wildly on the window, screaming,

'*Incendio! Incendio!*' (fire! fire!)

'*What on earth was going on?*' Nick wondered. Here he was, peacefully trying to commit suicide, and suddenly, he was torn from his self pity by loud screaming and wild rapping noises. He turned the engine off and simultaneously looked through the window. He was completely nonplussed when he saw a small tanned face that was wildly distorted, as a young child incoherently shrieked and banged on the window.

'*What on earth was he saying?*' He certainly looked deeply distressed. His wide open, soft brown eyes seemed to be glistening with un-spilled tears, and he jumped up and down excitedly whilst his tufted black hair flopped about on his forehead. Nick opened the door and stepped out. To his utter amazement, the small boy had completely disappeared. He looked around, and was further startled by the sight of a wizened old goat, standing in a corner of the clearing, nonchalantly chewing on a mouthful of vegetation. He stared wordlessly at the goat for several minutes, then he felt and irresistible sensation twitching at the corners of his mouth. First he started smiling, and then before he knew it he was laughing uncontrollably. He sank to the ground and pounded the earth mercilessly in an attempt to get a grip on the wave of unremitting hysteria that had swept over him. Eventually, realising that he was fighting a losing battle, he rolled over onto his back and roared at the incandescent blue sky.

Some considerable minutes after the farcical incident in the woods, Nick had finally recovered and got up to see that he had been left quite alone in the forest. He smiled, wryly, and walked to the car, then proceeded to rip off the pipe and attachments before hurling them into the surrounding trees. This wasn't the answer; there must be a way through the black cloud that had descended upon him. He had no idea if the little boy and his goat actually existed or had been a figment of his troubled mind. Real or imagined, they had brought him back to his senses.

Twenty minutes later Nick found himself back on the 125, heading for Luz in a strangely light-headed frame of mind. As he approached home, he mulled over recent events as he seemed to have decided to stay in the land of the living for a little while longer. He hoped that this meant that he was coming to terms with his situation. He wasn't stupid enough to think that all his problems were over. This was simply one battle that he had won. The rest of the war stretched out before him. But maybe, just maybe, he had turned the corner.

## Return to England

November 2004

The ticket office at Lagos train station is housed in a beautiful Portuguese Colonial listed building. It boasts a green tiled façade and intricate roof. In Portuguese the name for railway is "*Caminho de Ferro*" which translates into "Track of Iron" a title which Nick found amusing. He paid twelve Euros for a ticket to take him on the hour-long journey to Faro from where he could get a taxi for the ten minute drive to Faro international airport. His financial situation was desperate. He was down to his last few Euros and getting back to England wasn't going to be easy. Sitting on the platform waiting for the train to arrive, he had time to think about his future. The station was busy, for the most part with young back-packers who had made it this far having achieved the last stop off point for budget travel, before continuing to make the requisite pilgrimage to Sargres and Cape St. Vincent, the most south westerly point of Europe. Most based themselves in the ancient walled town of Lagos which had, over the years, developed a vigorous night life. Now they were heading homeward. They were mostly students returning to prepare for the winter term at college or university looking tanned and healthy despite their heavy partying in the Lagos bars.

The atmosphere in the station was animated which helped to lift Nick's flagging spirits as he wasn't exactly playing the role of the returning hero. He had no idea what he was going home to; it just felt good to be heading in that direction. He had finally come to terms with his inner daemons and was determined to put the past behind him and carve out a new life for himself. The time for self-pity had passed and there was a new weapon in his armoury. He could now hypnotise people and was getting better at it day by day.

Lagos is as far west as the "Track of Iron" reaches. This is the last stop. The train backed lazily into the station announcing its arrival with a deafening blast from its horn. An almost identical mix of back packers exited the carriages as those who got in to take their places.

Nick found a seat facing forward and prepared for the journey. The carriages were basic, which didn't worry him as the view from the window more than occupied his attention. The rail track ran along the southern Algarve coast passing through quaint villages, golf courses and orange groves laden with fruit, their bright orange crop contrasting with the lush green of the leaves. The warm afternoon wind blowing in through the open windows smelled of fennel and other aromatic Atlantic herbs. Nick smiled inwardly as the train clanked along never exceeding fifty kilometres an hour. With each kilometre that passed he felt as if heavy layers of negativity were being blown away into the Algarve countryside.

As the train pulled into Faro station he was brought back to reality, jostling to grab a taxi to the airport. Finally he joined forces with two young student nurses who agreed to share the fare. When they arrived, the airport was in pandemonium with package-holiday crowds milling around the concourse.

Time to come up with a plan! So far, Nick had no plan, his prime objective being to get back to England—anywhere in England—and, from wherever he landed, on to London. Given the small amount of money he had left, he needed a miracle. He was carrying just a holdall so at least he was mobile which was more than could be said for the hundreds of holiday makers who were lugging huge suitcases, surf boards and enormous sets of golf clubs.

His attention was taken by a group of around twenty golfers all dressed in the same fire engine red polo shirts and black slacks. They were congregating around a bar which was doing a brisk trade serving them local beer at an astounding rate. These middle-aged men were making the most of their final hours of freedom, using up the remains of their "foreign" money and generally acting in a more boisterous manner than normal. The use of various versions of "air clubs" was being demonstrated by members of the group, all connoisseurs of the invisible swing. The noise increased as the beer was consumed. Nick chose a seat in the bar at a convenient distance and observed them. The most noticeable member of the group was a man who Nick guessed must be the tour leader who busied himself, checking that every member had got their passport and tied on their baggage labels. He was clucking around his charges fussing like a mother hen. Check-in was going to take longer than usual given that the golfers would need to take their bags of clubs to the oversize item counter once they had booked in. Golfers are so attached to their clubs that they encase them inside several layers of protection creating something like a mummy or a large Russian doll. The organizer moved away from the group and sat alone at a table away from the noise and gyrations of his club mates. This was Nick's opportunity; a plan was beginning to develop in his mind. Casually, he wandered over to the man who was now busy tying labels onto his own luggage. This was going to be the first real opportunity to put his hypnotic ability to the test.

'Looks as if your club mates have had a great time,' he opened the conversation.

'Yes, played six of the best courses on the Algarve we 'ave,' he replied. 'Eight competitions and won 'em all.'

Nick went along with the conversation which was predominately a list of the club's achievements and specific member's merits. Once the organizer had started, it was difficult to get him to stop. They were sitting a reasonable distance from any other people, conditions were good enough Nick judged to get this man under his influence if only he could get him to stop buzzing about and stay still for just a few seconds.

'Right bunch of pros are my lads.' he boasted. Nick was in full patronizing mode, laying it on with a trowel trying to get the organiser to stay still. The organizer decided that he needed to return to the herd for round-up and check in. It looked as if the hypnosis plan wasn't going to happen but as a last minute effort Nick made his final attempt.

'Been great talking to you.' He pumped the man's hand enthusiastically.

'I wonder if there would be any chance of one of your team shirts? They look great and my friends would be greatly impressed.'

'Shouldn't really, but I suppose it wouldn't matter this once. I always carry a couple of spares just in case one of the lads has an accident.' Can't give it to you out here. One of them might see me and complain but go into the toilets and I'll be there in a couple of minutes.'

Nick thanked him once more and walked across to the nearby toilets. Sure enough after three minutes the man came in and proudly presented him with a neatly wrapped bright red polo shirt before returning hurriedly back to his flock. *My hypnotic debut is going to have to wait until another time* thought Nick. When he was alone, he tore off the wrapper and changed from his own shirt into the gaudy new. Leaving the toilets, he circled around the gesticulating golfers and found a sufficiently good observation position. The "lads" were herded to the check-in under the shepherding skills of the organiser, they booked in and then made their way to the oversize article desk where they guardedly handed over their beloved clubs to the care for the two airline employees who unceremoniously dumped them onto a conveyor belt leaving the owners bereft like mothers leaving their children on their first day at school. The organizer took charge again and corralled the group towards the departure lounge. This was to be the first real hurdle for Nick to overcome. Taking off his jacket he tacked himself onto the end of the golf group, acting as if he was one of them. The organizer waved a bundle of boarding cards at the gate official and the red shirted group was ushered through en mass and from there on to the security check. Once inside Nick distanced himself from the crowd and watched. He was now in the departure lounge. There was no way back and no actual plan for going forward; it would just have to unfold. Like a lion stalking a herd of wildebeest Nick surveyed the group for a weakling and sure enough one gradually appeared. A little pot bellied man with huge ears was beginning to show obvious signs of wear. The combined pace of the golf holiday with its continual drinking was having effect. He drifted to the edge of the group and then headed off to the toilets. Nick followed; it didn't need a Sherlock Holmes to locate the little fellow in the toilets as he was making a fine job of throwing up the contents of his pot belly. Keeping an eye on the golfer and the rest of his mates, Nick could see a plan developing. The main group moved off through passport control still playing on their air golf clubs, totally oblivious of their missing comrade. The next move was crucially all about timing. It was obvious that the man in the toilet was going nowhere. He was now clinging to the toilet like a survivor from a shipwreck hanging onto a piece of wreckage. Nick would have to wait until the last moment to make his move. '*Time to go for it.* The airport Tannoy system was calling for the last remaining passenger Mr Canton on the flight to Luton to go to the departure gates. Nick ran towards the departure desk waving his passport, the courtesy bus was about to close its doors and the desk staff waved him through, confident that the red shirted golf team were all accounted for. He scrambled onto the bus which would take them to the aircraft much to the annoyance of the other passengers who had been kept waiting in the heat. Once on board the plane, Nick settled himself into a seat at the back of the partially full plane, quickly changing back into his own shirt. He was on his way to Luton and from there, on to a new life. He relaxed, wondering if Mr. Canton had surfaced yet.

# | 5 |

December 2004.

# Methodology for Plundering the Chancery Lane Safety Deposit Vaults

∫ o here he was, back in London, broke but not broken. Within a week he had rented a pretty minimal bed-sit in somewhat less than a slick part of the capital but that didn't matter. He was back and full of motivation. There was an overall feeling inside of him that he was once again in control of his own destiny. Best of all he knew that his hypnotic ability was tantamount to a gift from the Gods. Armed with this, he would be able to discover a new purpose in life.

## Tom Holland

Sometimes tiny insignificant events which we dismiss at the time as being inconsequential can turn out to be a pivotal thread in our lives. It was just such an event that changed the direction in which Nick's life was moving. His chance meeting with Tom Holland whilst languishing in the Algarve had given him the inspiration for an idea. Armed with his newly acquired hypnosis skill, which he had now put to the test many times and thought he had pretty much perfected, he telephoned Tom and arranged for the conducted tour of the Security vaults in Chancery Lane that Tom was in charge of. This was a promise which had been agreed in the bar of the Mirage back in the summer. Tom was obviously proud of the position that he held. During their conversations, Tom had told Nick about the premises he managed and a germ of an idea had taken root in his mind.

He was anxious to see the buildings for himself and discover if there was potential to put together a plan of action.

Tom was surprised and delighted to hear from Nick and, true to his word, arranged a date to meet. Nick's financial situation was far from healthy but his hypnotic skill did allow him to negotiate his financial affairs with a definite advantage without actually stealing from anybody. Outgoings such as his rent were delayed and his tab at the local supermarket became extended well past the point that would have been the norm.

Nevertheless he needed to create the impression that he was a successful young man. He had a respectable wardrobe of civvies left over from his days as an army officer. Suits, tweeds, regimental ties etc. but to complete the illusion, he bought a good quality Cromby overcoat which sported a moleskin collar. To complement the ensemble he added a silk scarf as a finishing touch. As he left his bed-sit, he checked his appearance in the full length mirror. He liked what he saw; he would easily pass as acceptable in London. A far cry from the miserable wreck that he had descended to being, those short months before in the Algarve. Nick probably looked a little out of place as he walked out of his cheap bed-sit, which was not in exactly the best location, but which was all that he could afford. The meeting with Tom Holland went well; first he took Nick to lunch, where they reminisced about their time in southern Portugal. Tom remarked that Nick's appearance had altered radically from the laid back look that he knew from Lagos. Nick explained that he had been enjoying a well earned rest from the pressures of London life when they had first met which Tom said he completely understood. Tom then proudly gave Nick a full tour of the impressive subterranean vaults. They were astounding, buried deep under London in a never used section of London Underground. Security was paramount as Tom frequently pointed out. He took his job very seriously. He then proudly gave Nick a conducted tour of the world famous Silver Vaults introducing him to some of the dealers who traded there. Tom gave Nick a pamphlet which gave a brief history of the vaults and which he read in detail.

## The Chancery Lane Safe Deposit Vaults

The Chancery Lane Safe Deposit vaults opened in 1876 utilising London tube tunnels which were built but never used for trains. Renting security boxes at that time was mainly to London's wealthy elite in order to safeguard their household silver, jewellery and personal documents. Entrance to the building was gained by special arrangement and the strong rooms were guarded day and night, as indeed they still are today. In fact it remains the proud boast of the Safe Deposit that there has never been a robbery within its precincts. The business remained the same for several years, but with many of the original clientele being replaced by silver dealers who required secure premises for their burgeoning stocks. This need was made more pressing by the outbreak of the Second World War.

As knowledge of the vaults began to spread, the Vaults became a "must" for visitors from overseas seeking quality silver at dealers' prices. The rapid expansion of this business led to many more dealers renting a strong room within the now well renowned Silver Vaults and it has been in its present format since 1953 when it was reopened at the completion of rebuilding necessary to repair bomb damage sustained in the London blitz. Behind the huge safe doors and within its vaulted walls, it is possible to find anything from a champagne swizzle stick to a full size silver armchair! Although English silver predominates, there are specialists who deal in silver from every corner of the world. In fact, every period and every style is catered for, in this unique setting.

The dealers of "The Vaults" have supplied the trade and public alike for over fifty years, many having supplied the most famous 'retail' stores, private collections and museums. No customer is too small to be supplied and their integrity is paramount. Merchandise is always sold with a guarantee to condition and authenticity.

The London Silver Vaults is an unusual, interesting and exciting place to explore and many regular visitors make it their first stop when arriving in the city. It is the finest centre for silver in the world today and to quote a famous collector: 'If you cannot find it in the Chancery Lane Vaults, you cannot find it anywhere."

Tom Holland had made sure that Nick was given the full five star treatment. The tour was detailed and thorough; this was a man who was extremely proud of the establishment that he was in charge of.

The visit to the silver vault section was undoubtedly interesting but Nick's real curiosity lay in the second half of this unusual building, the safety deposit vault. During the tour he had noticed that there were private secure area booths where clients could spend time with the contents of their boxes in private unhindered by cameras. Each booth was furnished with a leather topped table and two chairs. These areas were completely private away from the CCTV cameras which bristled at every corner although they were still within the high security protection of the vault. Obviously security was at the highest level but the client's privacy was also vital. The contents of the safety deposit boxes were of no particular importance to the vault company whereas their overall security was paramount. Although Nick could not see the actual clients pouring over the contents of their boxes it was a calculated guess that gemstones were the main treasure secreted away down here. The majority of other clients that he glimpsed were obviously Jewish diamond merchants from their distinctive attire, Hatton Garden being their nearby place of work and trade. It might be the oldest safety repository but technology was the key word in this establishment. The application of the latest equipment had reduced the need for employees. A remark that Nick fielded to Tom.

'Just the six of us, Nick. That's all we require to keep this place safe and sound.' Tom expounded. 'Amazing isn't it?'

The Silver Vaults were open to the general public in contrast to Safety Deposit Vaults which were under strict security. This required two receptionists who were male and ex-police or military service personnel. They were situated at the entrance and never actually entered into the Safety Deposit Vaults, so they would therefore pose no threat to his operation. The only other employee that he needed to consider was the cleaner. Due to the sensitivity of the safety deposit vaults, cleaning was not something which could be undertaken by just anyone. The vaults cleaner was a retired warrant officer from the Scots Guards but again there was little chance that he could compromise Nick's plans as his working hours were outside business hours. He would need to devise an infallible strategy which was slowly taking shape in his mind as the meeting progressed. The three key players in his plan were Tom and the two inner guards. whom he was about to meet. Nick made his opening gambit.

'Tom I have been searching for a building with facilities similar to those that you have here,' he enthused.

# The set-up

'It's actually my good fortune that we met. I need just such a place as this to keep my stamp collection.' Nick explained that he had inherited an extraordinary collection of rare stamps from his late grandfather.' Tom looked suitably impressed.

'At the moment it's in my bank and getting access is a tiresome affair. There is a lot of work necessary to categorise and catalogue the collection before I can ever think of selling it—if indeed I ever do. It's going to take months. My grandfather was an avid collector from the time he was a small boy until his death at the age of eighty-two.'

'I'm delighted that we can offer you the conditions that you are looking for. And as an additional bonus we will be able to go for a pint occasionally and continue our chats from the old days in the Mirage.' Tom sounded very happy at the prospect of having Nick around.

At the end of the tour Tom took him to his office and made coffee for them both.

'Take a look at these, Nick.' offered Tom, proudly opening one of a dozen leather bound ledgers which were housed in a cast iron Victorian bookcase. Nick could see that they were all meticulously hand written.

'Of course it's all computerised now but these ledgers go back one hundred and thirty years.' The detail in the ledgers was interesting with a large percentage of the names obviously those of European Jews which meant diamond dealers. Nick's brain was working overtime.

Tom continued his explanation enthusiastically.

'When a box has not been opened for sixty five years and the key holder cannot be traced I have the authority to break into it. We call this "Drilling". Of course apart from the locksmith there is an official presence from the City of London Police and an official from the court when the box is officially opened.

'You wouldn't believe what we find in some of them.'

'What happens to the contents after that?' queried Nick.

'It all becomes property of the court.'

As the information of the previous hour trickled into his brain, the possibilities of infiltrating the security system and gradually removing items began to formulate into a more detailed plan. His methodical mind noted every detail with keen interest. Why would someone keep items locked away in a high security vault? In the case of the everyday movement of the diamond dealers it was easily explained, high security in close proximity to Hatton Garden. This only accounted for about twenty five percent of the clients as Tom explained. The majority of the boxes contained objects which were valuable but needed to be hidden for a variety of reasons. Tom admitted that there were probably all sorts of clandestine reasons for using the vaults but the client's anonymity was always protected. The conversation continued in a relaxed manner and he began to confide in Nick a little.

'For the most part this job scores high in both boredom and repetitiousness after the army but needs must and I have to earn a living. There is a more sinister side to it—a threat that my family and I are exposed to.' Tom went on to explain the threat of Tiger Kidnapping or Tiger Robbery which is a crime where abduction is part of a robbery. A person of importance to the victim is held hostage as collateral until the victim has met the criminal's demands. They call it a Tiger Kidnapping because of the predatory stalking that precedes it—the crime often requires considerable inside information about the target. Tiger kidnap poses a threat to retail banking and financial organisations.

'There are pre-arranged code words to alert police that the victim is being held within a tiger situation. My wife hates the thought of it but the safe has a time lock system and cannot be opened outside the hours of verified business and this is publicised so I doubt that it will ever happen here. He went on to explain more details of the vaults security systems.

'The most impressive visual item is the actual vault door. It's a seven and half ton circular giant made by the John Taylor & Company who built the doors for the Bank of England and many more.' The job might be boring but Tom showed an obvious pride in the building that he controlled.

Since discovering his ability to hypnotise Nick had become chillingly proficient, honing the skill by reading and researching everything on the subject that he could get his hands on. His unmatched eye colour had never been something that he had paid much attention to. It wasn't very noticeable unless someone was close and looking straight into his eyes. But he realised that it gave him the great advantage of concentrating the subject's attention directly on his eyes.

Using hypnosis had become a tool necessary for his survival over the past months and he could now put someone under quickly and with relative confidence. Sitting alone in Tom's office gave him the perfect opportunity to get to work on Tom.

In addition to reading the book on hypnosis which he had discovered at Quinta Da Felicidade some months before, Nick had refined his knowledge by practising at every suitable opportunity. A favourite book by Lisa Selvidge had a particularly good explanation of how the mind works:

"The sub conscious is by far the larger part of the mind. Our subconscious controls much more than just our organs, it controls our entire being. It is thought that our minds are 5% conscious and 95% sub-conscious. Consider what we do automatically everyday without thinking. Walking, breathing, seeing, hearing, smell, we don't have to think about these things because our sub-conscious is dealing with it all. It just happens sub-consciously. We are uncontrollably in control of our sub-conscious. Psychologists and others have performed numerous experiments on people who are in a hypnotic trance. This research shows clearly that the subconscious mind does not make the selections and comparisons that are necessary for the reasoning process. Our subconscious mind will accept any suggestion, no matter how false. Having once accepted the suggestion, it responds according to the nature of the suggestion given. The difference between our conscious, reasoning mind and our subconscious which is impersonal, non selective and accepts as true whatever our conscious mind believes is true. Our subconscious mind does not have the ability to argue or dispute what it is told. If we give it the wrong information it will accept it as true, then it will work to make the information correct. It will bring the suggestions, even those that are false, to pass, as conditions, experiences, and events. Our conscious mind has been described as the '*Guardian of the gateway.* 'One of it's most crucial functions is to protect our subconscious mind from false information. The reason that this is so important goes back to one of the basic laws of mind. Our sub conscious mind is very sensitive to suggestions; it simply reacts to the impressions given to it by our conscious minds. It cannot pick and choose between different courses of action. It merely takes what it is given. When a subject is rendered into a hypnotic state the hypnotist has by-passed the conscious mind and entered into the sub conscious where they can implant positive autosuggestions."

An interesting and useful tool which Nick had perfected was the use of a "trigger" word. This is a word that is embedded into the subconscious of the person being hypnotised. The mention of the trigger word would immediately put the subject into a trance from where auto suggestive orders could be implanted. This he used on Tom, As soon as the two of them were comfortable in his office and Nick was sure that there would be no sudden interruptions, he began to hypnotise him. The trigger word for Tom was to be "Excalibur." It might have been heard by the subject in all manner of situations but only from his mouth would the word "Excalibur" evoke the required effect. He embedded the trigger word and in addition gave the orders to which Tom was to react. Fortunately he was very receptive to hypnosis. Then Nick brought him out of the trance and continued with the normal conversation.

'OK Nick,' Tom focused on the moment as if he had just shaken himself out of a deep daydream, 'let's get on with the boring bit, filling in the application.' This went well until they got to the question of Nick's bank account. He hadn't planned for that, '*Shit*' the details of his bank account would never stand up to scrutiny given the way the past year had evolved. There was a pregnant pause and a feeling of panic began to form in his mind. Tom's pen was poised to add the banking details to the application form; Nick had to do some fast thinking. "Excalibur!" Toms head dropped onto his chest. Although Nick had become proficient in his newly acquired skill nevertheless he was still wary of using it as it was all so new to him.

'OK Tom, I'm going to give you my bank details.' Nick inserted the required fictitious details into Tom's subconscious and brought him out of the trance. There was a pause as Tom collected his thoughts.

'So, that's that, Nick. Everything appears to be in order.' He closed the completed folder. The application was accepted. The account number and contract passed to Nick. He explained to Tom that he would be bringing his treasured stamp collection for safekeeping in one week's time. Tom said that the timing was perfect and a box and key would be waiting. The first phase of Nick's plan was successfully in place.

On the way home on the Tube, he had time to contemplate what he was getting into. He thought that he had nothing to lose and also it felt as if he was getting back at the Establishment who in his mind were responsible for his being in the situation he now found himself in.

Everything in the vaults was most probably hidden from the authorities in the first place. Furthermore his plan was only to open boxes which had been unattended for sixty years, which meant that the owners were more than likely dead. He could see no reason for repercussions. He recalled a robbery some years earlier in London when thieves had broken into a security vault. They spent the weekend working their way through half of the safety deposit boxes before they ran out of time. Later when the robbery was discovered and the clients had been contacted, no complaints were made as everything in there was clandestine and there was also never an official list compiled of what had gone missing.

The only doubt which was nagging at him was about Tom. He was a decent man and a friend. How would this affect him? Nick had no intention of dragging him down or causing him any harm. Should he ever be caught he would explain how he had pulled off the robbery and Tom could not be implicated. After much soul-searching he decided that he had to go forward with his plan.

## Preparation

The next morning was Saturday. Nick rose early and went out of London until he reached Langley a few miles west of Heathrow. He remembered from his time living in Windsor that there was a car boot sale every Saturday on the outskirts of Langley village. He wandered around the boot sale looking for something specific. After an hour he found exactly what he was looking for and a delighted stallholder willingly took his tenner in exchange for six tattered leather bound photo albums. With his new acquisitions he moved on to Slough town shopping centre where he headed straight for W.H. Smith's. There he purchased twelve starter packs of stamps, a large magnifying glass with a stand, several sets of assorted tweezers and two A4 note pads. He paid in cash and drove back to his apartment. It was a simple job to remove the photos from the albums and replace them with the stamps. He inspected his handiwork and was pleased with the outcome; the albums looked like a collection that had been assembled over many decades. It would require close scrutiny by a keen collector to discover that the stamps were virtually worthless.

As arranged, precisely one week later Nick returned to Chancery Lane. He was greeted by Tom who had finalised all of the required paperwork and ceremoniously handed Nick the key to his own personal security box. Together they went through the stringent security measures and entered one of the private booths. Over his shoulder Nick carried a finely tooled leather Victorian gentleman's holdall which was about the size of a large traditional doctor's instrument bag. He had bought the holdall in a high quality leather goods shop in Windsor. It wasn't cheap and he worried about the cost but felt that it was a necessary prop to complete his portrayal of a well to do young man. The bag contained the stamp collection plus the other items that he had purchased from WH Smith's. In addition there were two pairs of white gloves bought from a store which was dedicated to Masonry.

Tom accompanied Nick to the client's quiet area assisting him to settle in. He personally fussed around ensuring that he had everything that he needed.

## Veronica

As requested by Tom, the vault's assistant, Veronica whose official title is custodian brought out his box. He made polite conversation with her since she was soon to become an integral participant in his plan. He opened the box and carefully arranged the items inside, explaining to Tom and Veronica that he would be coming in about three times a week to work on his collection. Tom appeared duly impressed and content that he had settled Nick in nicely.

On each subsequent visit Veronica brought him his box and he soon formed a friendly rapport with her. This was a slowly, slowly procedure. He had to become established and accepted. He noticed over the following week that there was quite a few of the vaults' clients who made use of the private booth facility and although each cubicle was completely independent he knew that he would have to proceed carefully. In the second week he decided that the time was right for him to try his powers of hypnosis on Veronica. He needed to put her under and embed a trigger word into her sub conscious.

Veronica was a stereotype Essex girl, late forties, bottle blonde and a little overweight. She commuted to work each day causing her favourite conversational subject to be public transport and the "Bloody weather." She had become relaxed in his company and even tried a little light flirting.

'Oh, Nicholas you do have lovely eyes, just like that David Bowline.'

She turned out to be the person most susceptible to hypnotism that Nick had dealt with so far. Her one major vice was that she was a heavy smoker. To brighten up his visits, Nick decided to attempt a standard hypnotic procedure on Veronica. He implanted the desire to give up smoking into her subconscious. This paved the way to a new dialogue between the two of them. At every meeting he would politely ask if all was well and added a remark to see if the smoking habit had disappeared. Sure enough she kicked the habit much to her own amazement. Her trigger word was installed and ready to be called upon when needed.

Veronica had a desk at the entrance to the vault. It was her duty to coordinate and log all actions within the floor of the vault. When given the client's number she could electronically open the rack in the zone where the box was located. The client could then take their box from the rack and open it in the quiet area booths. When they had finished they placed the box back in the rack and Veronica closed the zone again. If the boxes were larger, Veronica would take them to the quiet area on a trolley.

## George

Sitting above Veronica was George, the third member of the vaults inner security team. He was positioned on a raised podium which backed onto the end wall of the vault and was surrounded by glass at the front. From this vantage point he could observe everything that happened on the floor of the vault. The only area that George couldn't watch was that of the quiet booths. The job that he did must have been boring in the extreme. His brief was to watch all of the comings and goings within the vault which appeared to Nick to be a rather old fashioned security method considering the state of the art equipment that the building boasted. Thinking about it, Nick could see the logic in the method. George was the human element and not susceptible to the foibles that computers and electrical gismos are prone to. It was a clever if not antiquated additional human system but it was efficient and Nick would need to think deeply about how to get around it. The observation cubicle bristled with gadgetry enabling George to shut down the complex in a nano second if something was out of the ordinary. Adding a human to the ultra technology was a clever move. Should all of the equipment ultimately fail there was George to take over the situation manually. Anything suspicious and he could automatically set off the alarms and close down the system. Tom had said that because the vaults posed a high security risk there were pre determined procedures and codes in place with the police. George had direct lines to the City of London Police with codes that could start an automatic course of action in seconds. George was the next hurdle for Nick to deal with and this was a potential "Beechers Brook."

# Daylight Robbery

Week Three, and Nick decided that Veronica was well and truly prepared the time was right to concentrate his attention on George. He worked late on his collection until the vault was about to close and, as they were leaving the building together, he invited George to have a drink at a local pub. The closest pub to the London Silver Vaults is the 'Knights Templar' which is also in Chancery Lane. It took little time for Nick to have George under his influence and get the key word embedded although he was far more difficult than Veronica and was the type of man whose eyes were always darting about the room never settling which was probably why he was the right man for the job that he did. They were sitting in a quiet corner of the pub; nobody was paying them any attention. Their conversation covered several subjects but usually returned to football, George's favourite subject. Nick finally had George hypnotised and the key word embedded when he noticed Veronica arrive at the bar obviously looking for George. He needed to think quickly to bring George out of his trance before Veronica spotted them, came over and noticed something unusual. By the time she had arrived and sat down, Nick had completed the reverse countdown and George was back with them again.

'What's up, George? You look puzzled—has your team lost again?' asked Veronica as she joined them at their table.

'No . . . . no, just contemplating another pint,' he replied looking a little confused.

# Initiating the plan

Now, Nick had all of the pieces in place and could move on to the next phase of his plan. Tom, Veronica and George had become comfortable with his visits. His time in the private booth varied. The fact is he was actually reading a novel, Moby Dick, a classic that he had promised himself to read for some time and which was a fine way to while away the hours. Then, after two weeks he decided that the time had come for him to make his move.

It was a beautiful spring Monday morning when he arrived at the vaults. Not that it made any difference to the employees as they were locked away in their subterranean place of work which was totally bereft of any windows. He felt nervous and rightly so. This was after all very much a hair brained scheme by anyone's estimation. He had thought about filling a hip flask with Famous Grouse to help his nerves but knew that this wasn't the answer. There was still time to walk away and nobody would know what he had been planning to do. 'Keep going!' He told himself—it'll be ok. Just keep moving forward.'

Nick stopped by for his regular chat with Tom in his office. He was chipper after having a glorious weekend doing what so many British men adore, pottering around in the garden and washing the car. The coffee was brewed in what was now becoming something of a ritual. Tom was always eager to chat and reduce the boredom of his day. When Nick thought that the time was right and Tom was sufficiently relaxed, he gave him the trigger word and he was again at his command. Tom sat silently in his chair. Nick took the office phones off their cradles and picked up Tom's mobile which was on the desk. Luck was with him. It was a model that he knew, so he quickly turned the ring tone to silent. All appeared set so he took the opportunity to study the ledgers and discovered that the oldest boxes had not been opened for a long time and were approaching their overdue period. Finding his way through the ledgers for the first time took longer than expected, Next time he would be able to do it more quickly. Making a list of the numbers of the ten oldest boxes, Nick placed the paper in his pocket. A final check of the room to be sure that everything was in place and then he put the phones back as they had been. Now he could gently waken Tom from his trance. As Nick reached the end of his reversed count-down the office phone sprang into life. From the peaceful ambience that had existed in the room the phone sounded much louder than usual causing him to jump and Tom to look startled. He answered the phone falteringly, looking around the room in bewilderment. Slowly he regained his composure. He made some obscure reference to daydreaming and finished his coffee.

Tom was completely unaware of what had happened and continued to be oblivious. They talked some more and then Tom telephoned Veronica on the internal system to tell her that Nick was on his way. Nick thanked him for the coffee and went down into the vault. When Veronica brought his box to the privacy of the booth she stopped to chat as usual discussing the events that were making the news, and of course the weather. Once he felt comfortable that the time was right, Nick gave her the trigger word and was relieved when she fell directly into the pre-ordained trance. Slowly and concisely he instructed Veronica to bring the first of the boxes from the list that he had in his pocket. Without hesitation she did as requested then returned to her desk, leaving him alone. To George everything seemed to appear quite normal.

## The First Box

Box 178 was of medium range dimensions. Much of the black paint had been worn away so that where the steel was exposed there was a light coating of rust. It looked as if it had been well used at some point in its existence but now with a liberal coating of dust it had a neglected look about it.

Nick sat looking at the metal box in front of him for some time waiting for the alarms to sound and the close down procedure to be initiated, trapping him inside the vault, a culprit, caught red handed. Three minutes passed. He decided that he had to continue—there was no going back now.

One problem that he needed to overcome was the removal of the owner's padlock. They were only standard, low priced affairs and some could be picked quite easily but the locks were old and he needed a more reliable method of removing them. To this end he had purchased a small pair of bolt croppers which just fitted into his Victorian holdall. On one of his earlier visits he had taken the bolt croppers and packed them into his security box. On a following visit he took six new padlocks of the same size as those used in the vaults. His preparations were complete.

A disadvantage of encouraging Veronica to be so friendly was that she occasionally peeked in to see how he was fairing, emphasising the boredom of her job. Apart from this Nick was quite at liberty to take his time removing the padlock although the vault had a library like atmosphere and any sudden unexplained noise would be noticeable and might alert George. He placed the jaws of the bolt croppers over the padlock's steel hasp and draped his overcoat over the croppers hoping to deaden any sudden noise. Long handled croppers would have cut through the steel like butter, but in order to fit into his holdall and then the box, he had to compromise with a more compact model. It took a lot of pressure to sever the lock. His arms were shaking with the effort. The padlock finally gave way with a sharp metallic snap. The box was open! He quickly returned the bolt croppers to his box and covered them with papers and albums. The now useless padlock he threw into his holdall. The time had come to look into the box and reveal its secrets.

## Plan successful

Disappointment! The box was full of old comics. All the preparation and planning for—this! His frustration was evident. He sat back in the chair and thought hard, and then it came to him. He knew that this box had remained unopened for more than sixty years, making the comics of some value as they were all in pristine condition. He transferred the contents of the box to his holdall. Upon uncovering the bottom of the box his eye fell upon two large manila envelopes. Opening the first envelope, he scattered the contents onto the table. There was a pile of stamps which he estimated must have numbered about a hundred. The second envelope contained a complete set of Third Reich bank notes from the period spanning the Second World War. These were stuffed into the holdall with the comics while the stamps were added to the albums. Now he really did have a valuable collection. Nick tidied up the table and snapped one of his new padlocks on the plundered box. Making a final check to see that everything looked good, he called for Veronica using the call button which was located at the entrance to the booth. While she wasn't needed Veronica sat at her desk close to the vault entrance just inside the huge steel door. She arrived at his booth.

'All done for today, Nick?' she enquired.

'Yes that's enough for one day. Come and sit down for a minute.'

Never guilty of missing an opportunity to while some time away from her boring job and flirt a little, she sat down on the seat opposite. Nick let her settle down and then uttered the embedded key word. Veronica's head dropped onto her chest.

'Veronica you will take Box 178 back to its place in the racking, lock the rack and return here.' His orders were calm and precise. Veronica placed the now slightly lighter box onto her trolley and did as she was instructed. When she came back Nick told her to sit down and she obediently obeyed.

'Veronica, when I waken you, all your memory of taking box 178 will have disappeared. You will remember nothing of bringing the box to me or of returning it to its location.' Counting backwards from six, Nick returned Veronica to her normal state of consciousness.

'What was I saying, Nick?' queried Veronica with a vacant look on her face, 'I've forgotten what we were talking about.'

'You were telling me about giving up the vile weed.' He smiled.

'Ah yes, now I remember. I can't understand it, just don't fancy a fag anymore! Bit of a pity really—don't know what to do with me 'ands these days.' Nick slung the strap of his holdall over his shoulder and said his goodbyes. He waved to George in his goldfish aquarium. He had seen nothing that looked remotely suspicious and waved back.

'See you on Wednesday!' Nick called back as he left the vault.'

He walked out of the front door of the building expecting at any moment to be stopped by a security guard or policeman but nothing happened. He walked on into Chancery Lane and was swept along with the stampede of commuters returning home. It was a cool evening and he was aware that he must have been sweating due to being worried whilst inside the vaults and the contrasting chill air made him shiver. He needed a drink but was careful not to choose a pub where George or Veronica might wander in. He turned right into Rolls Passage and slipped into the Blue Anchor pub. Sitting at the busy bar he was able to reflect upon the events of the afternoon. His first reaction had been severe disappointment at discovering the comics but the real triumph was that he had successfully pulled off what was to be the first of many such sorties to the London Safety Deposit Vaults. He looked up from gazing into his pint and saw his reflection in the mirror behind the bar. He had a smug look on his face which graduated into a huge grin. '*Cheers*' he said to himself, '*Here's to the Hypnotist.*'

The beauty of his plan was that the owners of the boxes that he systematically plundered were almost certainly dead, so nobody was going to complain and even when it the time came for the boxes to be officially opened, if they were found to be empty, who cared. It was undeniably the Perfect Crime!

The next day he set to work on converting the spoils of the previous day's work into hard cash. The Internet is a perfect location to off-load recently acquired loot. There are dozens of web-sites which are dedicated to collectors of comics and plenty of dealers scouring the net for bargains.

Three hours of checking out these sites revealed that the comics had a conservative value of approximately four thousand Pounds. Not bad and there were still the bank notes and the stamps. These must be valuable.

## Explanation of Security Within The Vault

In order to access the contents of a box there are three stages to be passed. The main obstacle to any would-be intruder is the physical vault. To begin with, it is below ground, the only entrance being a huge circular door with all the latest Hi-Tec devices fitted. This represents ninety-five percent of the security protection and is virtually impregnable. The boxes themselves come in twelve sizes and are housed in aisles according to size. The most popular and more numerous are the smaller boxes. All boxes are numbered. Each box is constructed from light gauge mild steel painted black with a hasp and clasp, secured with a standard padlock which the box owner supplies. The keys to this padlock are held only by the client.

Each of the boxes slides into a wall mounted rack which is in turn locked. It was Veronica's job to unlock the particular rack section electronically and allow the clients to carry the box to a booth where they can, add, remove or work on contents as they desire. The larger boxes are placed on a trolley which Veronica steers around the vault with the dexterity of a seasoned rally driver. With prior arrangement when a client who wishes to spend time working with the contents of their box arrives at the office to sign in, the box can be taken to the preferred booth by Veronica in preparation. This was the case with Nick. As soon as he signed in, a message was sent to Veronica so that he, Veronica and his box arrived at his favourite booth simultaneously. As the days passed the employees of the security vault became used to his ritual and thought of him as a hard working, diligent young man. He slowly added to the contents of his box with the small tools and equipment that he would need. He had considered all of the problems to be surmounted individually and in depth; he would have plenty of time to study every aspect of the vault at his leisure.

His day had been successful. Nick went to the local Internet café and placed a selection of the comics on the internet after lunch. Then he visited all of the comic book dealers that he could find within a reasonable radius of his flat and managed to sell seven comics, netting £534.00 in cash. Building his personal fortune was turning out to be harder work than he had had expected.

## Life gets better

Gradually Nick began to get back on his feet financially. Firstly paying off some debts—admittedly helped by cheating a little—using his hypnotic advantage. Then as the months passed and more money came in, he was able to move back to Windsor and buy a car. After six months of visiting the vaults his fortune had grown substantially and he moved from a one bedroom flat to a two bed luxury apartment and up-graded his car to a Jaguar Sports. He was dealing a lot in cash.

Life was looking good once again. Nick began to notice that he was becoming strangely addicted to his latest activities. He knew that although nobody was actually being harmed by what he was doing, it was no way to live his life. He was accumulating all of the toys but apart from the concern that what he was doing might be discovered and the added excitement that disposing of his "loot" created, life did seem to be very shallow. There was a huge vacuum in his existence.

His parents were oblivious of what was going on. They believed the story that he had fed to them explaining his new career as a commodities consultant. I suppose, in reality they would have believed anything, so desperate were they to see him succeed after such a disastrous episode as his ejection from the army. He saw much less of them in those days; perhaps because the lie that he was living hurt him when he was in their company.

## Nick discovers the Da Vinci sketches

The 10.45 from Windsor rolled into Waterloo Station and disgorged its human cargo. Nick joined the last of the stampeding commuters heading into the underground. He squeezed into a tube train which took him the short journey to Chancery Lane, where he thankfully re-emerged into the winter sunlight and walked to the Silver Vaults. He considered himself lucky that he didn't have to make this journey on a regular basis with a time limit and the constraints of a boring job to contend with.

This morning was slightly different from his regular routine. He needed to get a new list of numbers of all the boxes which hadn't been opened for a long period. By now, he had worked his way through the original set that he had originally obtained from Tom Holland. In order to get the new numbers he would have to get Tom into his office and under his control so that he could get the information. The task should be easier this time as the trigger word had already been implanted. Putting someone under the influence is always a little daunting as there must be no interruptions such as someone walking in or a phone ringing at the wrong moment. Tom Holland was in the foyer when Nick arrived. He always enjoyed Nick's visits since they gave him a chance to break the repetitiveness and monotony of his day.

'I'll tell Veronica that you're here,' said Tom, shaking his hand in a warm welcome.

'No hurry! Still got loads to do on the stamp collection—probably a couple of months or more. It's turned out to be a much bigger project than I at first envisaged.' Nick embroidered his cover story.

'Fancy a cup of coffee?' suggested Tom, eager for the opportunity to chat.

'Just what I need.' Nick agreed. *'Thought that you would never ask.'* The two of them walked down the steps which led to the underground tunnels, then into the office where Tom switched on the electric kettle in the tiny executive kitchen.

'Problem with this job is that we have state of the art security, so sophisticated that it has practically eliminated the need for personnel. This can make life a little boring. I'm always glad of an excuse to break the monotony.' admitted Tom. Coffee made, he sat down at his desk while Nick wandered around the office pretending to admire the various framed prints. Just as well things are so efficient, he thought. Tom didn't even have a secretary such was the nature of this particular branch of the Security business.

'I can see why you need to get out of here on occasions. Having no windows does make for a claustrophobic environment.' Nick wandered over to the desk, coffee cup in hand, and sat down opposite Tom. He waited for Tom to drink his first mouthful of coffee and put his cup down.

'Tom, listen to me carefully, "Excalibur."' Nick said in a commanding voice. The embedded trigger word worked immediately and Tom was under. Nick had become adept at hypnotising people by now but was still surprised at the ease and speed with which the trigger word worked. He went over to the desk and took the telephone receiver off the hook. One wall of the office was made over completely to shelving which housed a series of impressive old leather bound ledgers. He walked across to the ledgers and took down one marked 1941. Tom made no movement; he stared unblinkingly at the coffee cup on the blotter in front of him.

Nick took a pencil and paper and worked his way through the ledger looking for likely possibilities. He had watched carefully on his first visit when Tom explained the system which had been adopted by the company. It was a mixture of the old and the new, the old ledgers were still relevant as safety deposit boxes were generally taken in perpetuity, and the cut-off age was set at one hundred and ten years to alleviate the chances of error. The period of time that a box was considered unattended was sixty five years. He made a list of twelve likely boxes and then went to the computer where he checked out the last time that they had been opened. Six boxes fitted the criteria that he had set.

This was good news! There would be plenty to be getting on with over the next week. The first number on his list was 1276 and the absent owner was a Mr Alfred Horn who hadn't bothered to pick up his booty for the past sixty four years. A far off distant bell rang in the back of Nick's mind for this was a name that he had come across before but it was insignificant enough to be pushed to the back of his mind. *'Well, Mr Horn, whoever and wherever you are, let me give you a helping hand.'* Nick thought. He tidied up everything that he had touched and reset the phones and returned to his seat. Time to bring Tom back to the land of the living.

Tom Holland blinked and picked up his coffee cup wondering how he had managed to go off into such a deep daydream while someone was with him in his office. Daydreaming and reminiscing was something that he did fairly frequently these days, but always when he was alone; and why was his coffee nearly cold—surely he'd only just made it?

'Never mind.' he heard himself say aloud.

'So, Nick, you were saying that your stamp collection will need some time yet to knock into shape.' He picked up the conversation where he thought it had left off.

'Probably at least two months at the pace that I'm going. There is so much that has to be researched.' Nick replied, allowing himself the merest hint of a smile.

'Better get on with it I suppose,' he said, 'got a lot to do.'

'I'll call Veronica and get your box taken to your usual booth.' Tom suggested picking up the phone,

Nick thanked him for the coffee and went down to the vaults where his box was waiting. There was the usual polite exchange of pleasantries with Veronica and George and then he got on with the pretence of working on his precious stamp collection. He allowed ten minutes to pass before calling Veronica into the booth. It was easy to put her under using the pre-set trigger word and then to give the instructions for the box that he wanted her to bring to him.

'I want you to bring me Box 1276.' Nick instructed and Veronica went off pushing her trolley to return five minutes later with the box. It was oblong, 20cm X 30cm with a depth of 10cm. It was always exciting when he opened a new box and today was no exception. Every box contained items that were there for some clandestine or devious reason. Opening them was like checking a winning lottery ticket.

At first glance the contents of Box 1276 were notably uninteresting, just a brown envelope which appeared to hold very little, hardly worth bothering with. Perhaps as it was still early Nick had time to return this box and try another one. The envelope was marked "War Office." It had originally been sealed but had subsequently been roughly torn open. The contents consisted of six old sheets of paper a little smaller than A4 with rudimentary diagrams and strange illegible writing. It was obvious that they were very old but he could understand nothing of their meaning. He examined the outside of the envelope again. The "War Office" mark had been made with a rubber stamp but underneath there was something written in pencil. Age had caused the writing to deteriorate making it barely legible. In his bag of stamp collectors' equipment there was a magnifying glass. Nick adjusted the focal length and the faint writing came into focus. The writing consisted of two words. He assumed that it must be a name but the lines were blurred and the rubber stamp was exactly on top, which added to the difficulty. Finally he deciphered the name and sat back in the leather chair bewildered.

"Rudolf Hess!" What the hell was all this about?

Nick had a degree in modern history and had specialised in twentieth century warfare which had been the theme of his dissertation so this was a subject that he had studied and knew quite well. Suddenly he remembered the name in the ledger. Alfred Horn. This was the name that Hess had given when he was captured by the two Home Guards who had first discovered him when he parachuted into Scotland in 1941.

There had been occasions in his new career when he had discovered items which, although valuable, could not easily be sold without arousing suspicion and had to be returned to their original boxes. The decision which now faced him was, do I keep these papers or lock them away again and move on? Finally the temptation was too great and he decided to take them with him and attempt to unravel the history at his leisure. Placing the envelope into his leather bag, he called Veronica who replaced the now empty box back in the rack where it had spent the last six decades. Nick then brought her out of trance and she returned to her desk at the entrance to the vaults. He packed up his equipment and called Veronica back again to lock away his own box.

'That's enough stamp collecting for one day. he joked. He bid her and George a cheery good afternoon and did the same to Tom Holland as he passed his office.

'See you in a couple of days, Tom.' he called as he left the building and headed back to Chancery Lane tube station.

There is plenty of reference on Rudolf Hess and many theories as to why he made that dramatic flight in 1941 but it was all conjecture. This was an historical enigma which had attracted more conspiracy theories than most. It appeared to Nick extraordinary that someone of high status in an opposing army could be offered such a degree of freedom within the country that he had so recently been playing a pivotal part to conquer. Post Nuremburg he was submitted to what must have been the most costly incarceration in the history of mankind.

It was quite obvious that the story of Rudolf Hess held far more secrets than were common knowledge. So where then did the strange papers that Nick had recently liberated from their hiding place in the centre of London fit into the equation? He focused his attention on the sketches. There was something about them which had a familiar look, but what was it? There was a distinct medieval feel to the drawings but what was the link to the Second World War? Why would Rudolf Hess hide something so old in London? The mystery deepened. If Nick had acquired the sketches in an honest manner, it would have been easy to take them to a museum or a reputable dealer in antique manuscripts for valuation but that would be too dangerous given the circumstances.

The papers stayed in his flat hidden in the bottom of a wardrobe. From time to time he would take them out and attempt to unravel their origins. But it was obvious that the mystery could not be solved by him alone. He was going to need outside help.

## The Struggling Student

Finding a lucky parking space Nick decided to drop into the nearby Starbucks for a well earned coffee. The café was busy; he queued, got a latté and looked around for a seat. He got lucky again and settled himself into one of the larger armchairs. Adjacent to his position was a group of students. They appeared reasonable but were making more noise than was comfortable. He paid the students little attention; after all they were causing him no problems. As the raucous chatter continued it was impossible for anyone it the vicinity not to hear. The butt of their joking was a pimply faced youth who was trying to verbally defend himself, but his stutter was so distinct that he stood little chance. The more agitated he became the more he stuttered and the more he stuttered the more his contemporaries piled on the pressure. Nick tried to block out the barracking that the young man was suffering but it was difficult. Eventually, bored with the sport, the group left and Nick relaxed. His latté finished, he stood up and prepared to leave. Glancing over to where the rowdy group had been sitting he was surprised to see the youth was still at the table. Nick walked over and sat down in the booth opposite the young man. It was plain to see that he had been crying and he looked uncomfortable and embarrassed to have a stranger sitting in front of him, perhaps to add insult to injury. He made a move as if to leave but Nick reached across the table putting his hand on his shoulder gently pushing him back onto the chair.

'Look at me please.' it was a request not an order. The lad looked at Nick with eyes like a startled fawn.

'What is your name?' he asked gently but firmly.

'Robert.' he mouthed not quite knowing how to deal with this tall stranger who had suddenly entered into his space. He looked confused, probably more scared to run away than to stay

'OK Robert, look into my eyes just for a second.'

Nick could see the puzzled expression on his face as he noticed his unmatched eyes. His forehead wrinkled into a frown as his focus darted from his left eye to his right. Instinctively he wanted to stand up and walk away but his flight and fight mechanism had been short circuited, the message from his brain to his legs wasn't getting through. Another altogether stronger factor was stopping him. The Guardian at the gates had been disarmed. It happened in an instant Robert was now completely at his will.

'Robert, I want you to remember a time when you felt really good about yourself. Perhaps you had accomplished something you were proud of, or maybe you were being complimented for your effort. The actual incident is not important. What is important now is the feeling that this memory generates within you. When you have that memory; focus on your feelings and your emotions. I want you to remember how it felt inside enjoying those emotions. Allow those feelings to grow stronger and more positive while you take in a long, deep breath through your nose and press the thumb and the middle finger of your left hand together. In future Robert, whenever you do this those confident feelings will be there for you. You can feel them anytime, anywhere, in any situation; these feelings are now becoming more and more a part of you. You are growing into a stronger, more confident person. Remember, any time you want to feel confident, take a deep breath through your nose and press together the thumb and the middle finger of your left hand. You will never stutter again because you are in control. Robert I am going to count back from six to one and when I have finished you will be wide awake feeling more confident than you have ever done before in your life.'

The counting over, Robert was sitting with a huge grin spread across his face. Nick eased back into the chair.

'Hey Robert you were just telling me about the course you are taking and your mind must have wandered.' Nick broke the silence.

'I'm sorry, err don't know what happened there.' Robert replied in a bewildered tone.

'I'm doing a four year media studies course. This is my second year.' There was no trace of a stutter.

'*Bloody Hell,*' Nick thought, *'I'll be walking on water next.*'

'I'm sorry to run but I have to meet some friends.' Robert apologized.

'I have enjoyed our conversation.' He lied as he really had no idea of what he must have been talking about.

'See you again some time.' Nick replied with a goodbye wave.

With that Robert rushed out through Starbucks' door and into the street looking happy but dazed. The last thing that Nick saw him do as he walked away was to press his thumb to the middle finger of his left hand. He held the hand in front of his face, looking at it as if it belonged to someone else. Nick let out a sigh of relief and sank back even deeper into the chair.

'That was the kindest thing that I have ever witnessed.'

A woman's voice spoke from the next table. Her back must have been almost against Nick's but he had been so focused on the event with Robert that he hadn't noticed.

'Would you mind if I came round and sat with you?' the woman inquired. A hundred thoughts flashed through Nick's mind. Had he compromised himself? He had decided that his ability to hypnotize would be his secret and his alone. More than that, if his plans were to work no other person must know that he had the ability to hypnotize. Now he had blown the whole deal to some nosey woman in Starbucks. At a guess she would ask him to hypnotize her and stop her from eating four pounds of chocolate a day. Nick groaned inwardly and didn't answer hoping that she would disappear. She wasn't to be so easily put off and moved around to sit in the seat so recently occupied by the youth. His eyes moved slowly up from the table and onto the face of the woman in front of him.

It would be difficult to judge which of the two was the more surprised. They had been sitting almost back to back for over fifteen minutes, neither having seen the other's face. Nick blinked, struggling to retain his composure. Sitting before him was a stunning woman of a comparable age to his own. Her long dark hair framed a strong aristocratic face which showed an obvious compassionate nature. The green eyes were perfectly complimented by the soft glow of her flawless tanned skin. Her mouth was full and sensuous, her neck elegant and long. She was tall and slim with an athletic figure. The clothes she was wearing were sophisticated, a sober suit with a crisp white blouse which I assumed must be her working attire. There was a long pause, whilst they each composed themselves. Neither had been expecting this, finally;

'Hi! I'm Tamsen Richards. I really am sorry to barge in like this but I genuinely wanted to say well done for the way that you helped that poor boy.' Tamsen, although having regained her composure was still slightly unsteady herself.

'I'm Nicholas Trevelyan and I really—.' his answer was cut short.

'Don't be modest, that was a wonderful thing to have done.' Tamsen interrupted.

'I think that I could do with another coffee.' Nick suggested. 'Would you like one?'

## Tamsen Richards

From the moment that they met, there seemed to be unmistakable, exhilarating electricity between them. Tamsen apologised for listening to his conversation with the young man but she had found it impossible not to hear. Nick sat there mesmerised listening to the sound of her voice. There was a distinctive air of confidence about her which was tinged with modesty. Unprompted, Tamsen began to tell him about herself:

As he had deduced from her accent, she had spent a lot of time in the States. Her father was from Washington which was where she had spent the first twelve years of her life. Her mother was English and after her parents became divorced she came to live in England where she continued her education, going on to university. She had studied for five years and was now a practising solicitor. Her mother had wanted her to become a doctor but as her education progressed it became apparent to all that her real love and interest lay with the law. She had found the studying and training fascinating and after successfully acquiring her degree had moved to London to share an apartment with her oldest and dearest friend Gemma who had graduated with her. Tamsen had been accepted by Digby & Short, Solicitors, in Battersea, as a junior and had recently been made a partner. She loved her work and was encouraged all the way by her employers who could see her potential.

All of the time that Tamsen was talking, Nick found it impossible to take his eyes off her. Ironically it was he who was mesmerised by her; he imagined caressing her and stroking her beautiful long shiny hair. He was abruptly bought back to reality with a jolt, when she asked him to tell her something about himself. This might be a problem as his recent history was less than applaudable.

'Perhaps we could discuss "me" over dinner tonight.' he said slightly nervously. Tamsen appeared to be faintly taken aback by the boldness of his offer but agreed. There was something about him that apparently intrigued her and she was eager to find out more.

'That would be lovely, thank you.'

'If you let me have your mobile number, I'll call you at around 7-30. Do you have a preference for food?' I was now playing the game by the prescribed rules. Tamsen laughed,

'I'll eat absolutely anything, thank you.'

After giving me the number of her mobile, her mind appeared to revert to feminine mode, as she wondered what she would wear; Nick appeared to have really fired up her interest and he wanted to tell her that she would still look great even if she was wearing a burkha but this wasn't the time. Who was to know from such a chance meeting where this would lead? Tamsen explained that she had not been very successful with the men she had met in the past, mainly because her studying had taken so much of her time and energy. Now her life had moved along. He deduced from the conversation that she was well and truly in the market for a man and Nick fully intended to make himself a prime candidate. The next weeks were exciting and soon the couple were dating on a regular basis.

## Hatton Garden, London's famous Diamond Centre and Jewellery Quarter

Nick's systematic plundering of the London Silver Vaults continued at a steady pace. The items that he liberated (this was how he preferred to view his actions) were many and varied but by far the largest percentage was made up of diamonds, due to the proximity of Hatton Garden which had been the centre of London's jewellery trade for centuries. This posed a problem that he needed to deal with quickly and efficiently. He studied the diamond trade in detail and learned all he could about the intricacies of the business. As the months progressed his haul from the vaults grew. Bizarrely the actual liberating of his loot was the easy part. Disposing of it was another matter and required a lot of thought. Again the Internet proved to be invaluable in discovering information. Nick Googled diamonds and found masses on the subject and printed off the following.

"In the past, the South African mining and marketing company DeBeers had controlled about sixty percent of the rough-diamond market; they would sell diamonds to a chosen two hundred dealers, who would in turn redistribute to cutters. The cutters sent them to wholesalers, who would then sell them to retailers. In the year 2000 the DeBeers diamond cartel ended as the group made its biggest change in focus for more than seventy years. From then on, it ceased to support world diamond prices by buying up and stockpiling diamonds and gems, concentrating instead on enhancing the demand for gems by persuading the jewellery industry to spend much more on advertising. This change was in some degree encouraged by the continuing wars raging in Africa, and in particular the twenty seven year Angolan civil war which had caused a flood of diamonds onto the market; these were called 'Blood' or 'Conflict' diamonds. A Conflict diamond is one mined in a war zone and sold, usually clandestinely, in order to finance an insurgent or invading arhis's war efforts. Contemporary examples may be found in Angola or Sierra Leone, where the sale of diamonds has funded rebel groups in both countries' brutal civil wars. This has led to the Diamond Registry's policy on 'Conflict Diamonds' in February 2003. All members of the World Federation of Diamond Bourses were required to subscribe to the 'Kimberley Process', which requires that all rough diamonds purchased comply with United Nations resolutions and come with the following statement:

"The diamonds herein invoiced have been purchased from legitimate sources not involved in the funding of conflict and in compliance with United Nations resolutions. The seller hereby guarantees that these diamonds are conflict free, based on personal knowledge and/or written guarantees provided by the supplier of these diamonds."

## American Trip Set Up

All of this added to his difficulties. His diamonds had been out of circulation for at least sixty years. Some were quite large and could be traced back to the original cutting company. On the positive side, this was a business where some dealers would ask few questions as long as the price was right. Through a careful process of elimination he had whittled his buyers down to two in London, three in New York and three in Amsterdam. If he was going to smuggle—and eventually sell—anything, then precious stones had to be the chosen items, the smallest objects with the highest value. Conversely, the hardest substance known to man showed up beautifully on x-ray machines. On his two previous visits to New York he had carried smaller amounts and taken a chance of simply concealing them in his hold luggage but now he needed to come up with a better plan. He drove over to Slough on a shopping trip to get an unusual array of items. His first stop was a toy shop where he purchased three ten inch porcelain figures: Fireman Sam, Postman Pat and Bob the Builder, all nicely packaged in sturdy display boxes with cellophane fronts. Next he visited an arts and craft shop for silicone mould-making equipment, plaster of Paris, an acrylic paint set, brushes and craft knives. In the town centre he dropped into Boots and made his most unusual purchase, a box of condoms. His next destination was the local builder's merchant where he bought a roll of roofer's lead and a soldering iron.

Once home, Nick smiled to himself as he unloaded the shopping. It was an eclectic assortment. That evening he got to work. Carefully opening the three cartoon character boxes so that they could be re-used, he set them aside. Then he then made a two-section mould from the silicone for each of the porcelain figures. As the moulds were setting he selected the diamonds to be taken to New York and divided them into three groups. He slipped each group inside one of the condoms. Using the craft knife, he fashioned the lead sheet into envelopes and placed the diamond-loaded condom inside, then sealed each package with the soldering iron. This would make them indiscernible as separate items and appear as just a blob on the scanners. The silicone moulds were now set and ready for pouring. As the plaster was setting he placed the lead envelopes into the moulds so that their flat bottoms were level with the figurines' bases. This was as much as he could do that the evening; it would take several hours for the moulds to dry completely.

Nick stretched his legs and yawned; on the desk beside him was a small black pebble about the size of a blackbird's egg. He had picked it up on the beach at Praia-da-Luz. He took the pebble and weighed it in his hand. It was a convenient reminder of the depths to which he had sunk, not so long ago. His determination to never again return to those depths was strong. He was filled with a new resolve. He checked his watch; it was 1am. Time to go to bed and allow his evening's work to dry. The next morning, he opened the moulds with some trepidation but all three figures were a good reproduction of the original. Trimming off the casting flash, he prepared them for painting. Using the original figurines for reference he painstakingly painted the copies and by 3pm his work was complete. This was the method he used to transport his diamond collection over a period of twelve months and it never let him down. He made his excuses to Tamsen saying that he needed to go to New York on business but leaving out the real reason for his visit. She accepted this and wished him a safe journey.

# | 6 |

# NEW YORK

Nick walked out of passport control and through the security check at Heathrow Airport's Terminal Four. This was always a nerve-racking time. In his baggage, already checked-in at the British Airways desk, he had carefully concealed a considerable fortune in diamonds in their toy town containers. This was the point of no return; if he were to be stopped from now on the game would be up.

"*Shit!*" The alarm sounded.

'Hands to your sides and spread your feet, please Sir!' he co-operated. The security guard ran his hands very professionally over Nick's body. 'It's the metal buckle on your belt, Sir. Best take it off next time, to save any further inconvenience.' suggested the guard.

'Thanks very much.' Nick replied, trying to sound as cool and collected as possible.

An international Trans Atlantic flight is always something of a lottery if you are travelling tourist class. However, Nick had booked himself into Club Class; the way things in his life were proceeding, he would soon be travelling first class. The flight to New York passed without too much distress and the British Airways jet touched down at Newark on time. Getting through US customs is a long, drawn out procedure post 9/11 but he passed through without difficulty. Nick pushed his loaded baggage trolley over to the bank of telephones dedicated to local hotels and located the phone for the Plaza Hotel, 1155 Broadway, situated on the corner of Broadway and West Twenty Seventh Street. After twenty minutes the courtesy bus arrived and, in the company of other travellers' he settled down for the ride across the Holland Bridge, over the Hudson River and into Manhattan.

## Plaza Hotel

The Plaza Hotel could only boast a three star rating but it gave him everything he needed. He booked in at 7.30pm and settled into his single room. After unpacking, he took a shower and, feeling a lot more refreshed, dressed and went down to the lobby where he bought a copy of the New York Times and a magazine.

'I wonder if you would mind putting that into a plastic sack for me? Newsprint is so dirty, it ruins clothing.' he politely asked the young girl who was serving.

'Why certainly, Sir.' came the equally polite reply. She had met her fair share of eccentrics and knew how to handle them. Nick wandered into the restaurant and asked for a table for one in a dimly-lit corner. The meal was good; by British standards it was enormous. He slipped a butter knife into his pocket and after dinner, satisfied and tired from the flight, took the lift to his room on the eighth floor. He spread the newspaper on the bed and placed the three plaster figurines in the centre. By knocking one against the other he broke off the legs of the plaster cartoon characters and prized out the lead envelopes with the butter knife. The whole operation took just five minutes but made a mess which he wrapped in the newspaper and placed in the plastic sack. It took another five minutes to open the envelopes and extract the condoms protecting the diamonds. He would dispose of the rubbish himself since he imagined that the chambermaid would quite rightly become suspicious if she discovered three broken figurines and three used condoms after only one night in the hotel. Before finally getting into bed he took his cell phone and sent a text message to Tamsen, telling her that he had arrived safely. Then he changed the UK SIM card to a US 'pay-as-you-go' SIM that he had purchased on a previous visit.

## Disposing of the Diamonds

Next morning, carrying the plastic sack with its unusual contents, Nick stepped out into the bright Broadway sunlight and walked two blocks down the street. Off to the right was an alleyway with several dumpsters. He threw the sack into one, then walked briskly back to the hotel for breakfast. The waiter showed him to the same table as the previous evening. While waiting for the food he made three phone calls from his mobile. The first was to Bert Bergheart, a diamond dealer whom he had done business with before and who was always willing to deal. Bert was greedy but dependable, he haggled all the way but it invariably culminated in a deal. Nick arranged a meeting for eleven o'clock that morning.

The second call was to Moses Litherman. Mosses was the kind of guy a casting director would choose to play a stereotype Broadway Jew. Nick liked Mosses. His opening line was to regularly tell Nick that he had wasted his time crossing the Atlantic to bring 'such rubbish', but after an hour of bartering Nick always walked out of Mosses' office with a smile on his face and a bulging bundle of dollar bills in his pocket. The meeting was arranged for 3.00pm that afternoon. The third call was to the Chase Manhattan Bank, where he had established an account on his two previous visits to New York and needed to talk about his investments. This appointment was scheduled for the day before he was to leave New York, three days hence. Breakfast arrived and he tucked into another enormous meal. Little wonder, he thought, that America was a nation with an obesity problem. Returning to his room, he took two of the three packets of diamonds and carefully poured each into a Plaza Hotel envelope, which he then placed inside a leather wallet he had brought with him. The third package was placed in a secret pocket sewn into the front of his trousers, only accessible from the inside. When he checked out later that morning, he asked the concierge to put the wallet in the hotel safe. He wished the desk clerk good morning and walked out onto Broadway to hail a taxi.

The United States is the world's largest consumer market for diamonds and over ninety percent go through New York City. More than two thousand six hundred independent businesses are located on this block, nearly all of them related to diamonds or jewellery. Located close to where jewellery is made and where diamonds are cut and traded, the Diamond District is centred on West 47th Street between Fifth Avenue and Avenue of the Americas (Sixth Avenue).

# Bert Bergheart

It was too far to walk to West 47<sup>th</sup> Street. But fortunately, cabs in New York are readily available and cheap. It was also safer, considering that Nick was carrying a healthy hoard of precious gemstones. The swarthy cab driver grunted and pulled out into the Broadway traffic to the usual accompaniment of disgruntled drivers' horns. Within ten minutes they had arrived at Bert Burgheart's offices. When the office suite had been last decorated in 1970 it may have looked fashionable but now it seemed decidedly jaded. If the style-police had raided they would have loved it! Nevertheless it served its purpose as every visitor was from the jewellery trade; Burt didn't deal with the general public. The receptionist was the same vintage as the décor, her hair piled high and apparently powdered. It must have taken hours to arrange initially and thereafter maintenance was minimal and infrequent. Nick mused that it would not have looked out of place in the Court of Louis XIV at Versailles.

'Is Mr. Bergheart expecting you?' He smiled inwardly again. Was that accent for real or was this lady doing an impersonation of Barbra Streisand?

'Yes he is. I'm Mr. Trevelyan. Meeting booked for eleven o'clock.' It was 10.55am.

'Could I use your toilet please?' Nick was delighting in the secretary's accent.

'The bathroom is back into the corridor, first door on your right.'

'Many thanks.' He did an about turn and headed off to the toilets.

In order to get to the hidden pocket he had to actually take off his trousers.

*"OK my beauties, nicely warmed up for Uncle Burt." He* thought to himself.

One hour later Nick was in a taxi heading back to the Plaza Hotel. The bulge in his trousers had disappeared but now he had a bulge in his inside breast pocket made up of American dollar bills. He stopped off at the reception desk to pick up his key and the leather wallet. Back in his room he took the second parcel of diamonds from the wallet and replaced them with the dollar bills from Burt Bergheart. It was time for lunch.

# Moses Litherman

That afternoon Nick set off for the second of his meetings. Mosses Litherman's office was in the same block as Burt's but one hundred meters west. The procedure was the same. Arrive five minutes early, retrieve the diamonds from where they nestled in his secret trouser pocket and enter the fray with Moses. It was like a well-rehearsed script. Moses would go to great lengths to tell Nick that he had wasted his time buying an air ticket. He would field the remark and reply with something on the lines of;

'Well, Mosses, there are plenty who will be more than eager to have them.' And so the match was played out like a game of tennis until both parties were satisfied with the eventual result. Mosses loved the sport. For his part, Nick went along with the charade. He often thought about hypnotizing Mosses but that would have felt like cheating, somehow breaking the unspoken rules of the game. He walked out of Mosses' office and onto Forty Seventh Street with another healthy bulge in his inside pocket. The time was five-thirty. The tennis match with Mosses had taken longer than anticipated, but so what, he wasn't on a tight schedule. It had been in the back of his thoughts to buy a present for Tamsen. Where better than the jewellery centre of New York? He wandered along the street looking for a likely shop. His concentration was focused on Tamsen and the gift. Everything had been going to plan so far and his guard had dropped.

# The Muggers

'Hey man, could you spare a couple of dimes for a coffee?' A huge American was blocking his way. With dreadlocks and scruffy clothes, the smell of his rancid breath and body odour was immediately sickening. Before Nick could think, another smaller man hemmed him in from the other side and pushed a gun under his chin. The big man pushed another gun into his ribs.

'Move or we'll shoot you right here!' the smaller man was doing all the talking.

They bundled him into an alley, the sort of locale he had seen hundreds of times in American movies, the kind of alleyway that you should never, never go into. He was roughly jostled along, falling over dustbins and tripping over rotting garbage until they finally stopped. How the hell could he have allowed this to happen? He just wasn't streetwise to the level necessary in New York. The street was only a hundred feet away but it might as well have been a mile. He could see at the entrance to the alley people and cars passing by in the bright winter sunlight but this dank smelling hell hole never saw the sun. This was their territory. Nick prepared to fight his way out and make a run for it but the look in his attackers' eyes was frightening. They were both obviously high on drugs and very dangerous.

'OK, give us all you've got,' the shorter man demanded in a menacing manner. Nick measured the distance to the street. He was fit and felt sure that he could outrun these two, but the guns! With two guns in a closed environment like this, he was sure to be shot in the back. What a place to die! Play for time, get them closer. Nick had never attempted to hypnotize two people at the same time but he knew that it could be done. The three of them now formed a triangle. His back was against a crumbling damp brick wall and his attackers were standing back with their arms raised, guns pointing at his head. He spoke quietly.

'What did he say?' the big guy asked. Nick whispered again.

'What are we playing about at?' said the shorter man.

'Waste him now and get it the hell over with.' They moved in closer, perhaps to hear what Nick was saying or maybe just to get a better shot. They were now about three meters away. His heart was pounding as he started to talk to the men and attempt to influence them. Any second they could have decided they had heard enough, pull the trigger then rob his dying body of more than they could ever have dreamed of. But luck was on his side. He was gaining control. Cautiously he began the procedure which would put his attackers under his influence. When certain that they were both hypnotized, he gave himself a few seconds to regain his composure. Now, how best to conclude this affair?

'Tell me your name.' He concentrated his attention on the shorter man.

'Winston.' with a feeling of relief, Nick could see the aggression had disappeared from the man's eyes. He was standing like a partially-deflated doll.

'Move over there, Winston,' he ordered.

Moving Winston further down the alley away from his partner, Nick then walked back to the bigger man.

'What's your name?' He felt confident now but anger still bubbled in his mind.

'Joshua.' said the bigger man.

'OK Joshua, I have something important to tell you, something that you have to act upon as soon as I give you the signal. Do you understand me?' Joshua nodded his large head like a naughty child.

'Joshua, Winston is going to kill you! He wants everything for himself. As soon as you hear three blasts from a car horn you must shoot him before he shoots you. Do you understand Joshua? You must shoot Winston before he shoots you. The signal is three blasts from a car horn.'

Nick walked over to Winston and repeated the message.

'Winston, Joshua is not your friend. He will shoot you as soon as he hears three blasts from a car's horn. You must shoot him first. Remember, three blasts on a car's horn. On the last blast, you must kill him.'

Then Nick led Winston over to Joshua so that they were two metres apart.

'Winston, point your gun at Joshua's head!' he ordered. The response was slow.

'Joshua, point your gun at Winston's head!' another slow but deliberate response.

The two men's wrists were almost touching, their arms rock steady but their eyes were glazed, bereft of the anger that had burned there previously. Nick surveyed the scene. For the first time since he had entered the ugly alleyway, he looked up to check if there was anyone witnessing the bizarre scene that was being played out below. The walls which flanked the alley were solid with no openings or windows. At the far end there was a chain-link fence piled high with rubbish. Nobody could pass or see through. Time to leave. He walked towards the street, stopping at the end of the alley to check out his two attackers, almost expecting them to have walked away. But no, they were still standing like two statues, guns pointing at each other's heads. Walking out onto 47th Street, there was a battered yellow cab sitting at the kerb with its window open. Nick leaned in and pumped the horn three times.

'Hey what the fuck are you doing, man?' The taxi driver was irate but his words were drowned by two simultaneous gunshots from the nearby alley. Nick walked a block then took a taxi back to the Plaza. He fell onto his bed like a sack of potatoes. It had been a busy day and he felt very tired. Perhaps he slept for half an hour; he wasn't sure. The spectre of the two men in the alley flashed through his mind and played with his conscience, although in his heart, he knew they would not have hesitated to end his life. Relieving the planet of two undesirables did not unduly worry him; nevertheless he was conscious of snuffing out two lives, no matter how objectionable they may have been. It was simply a case of kill or be killed.

## Plaza Hotel—Enter Mercedes

The lift arrived at the ground floor. Nick stepped out, walked across the foyer and into the hotel restaurant. After the events of the day he was relieved to swap the solitude of his single room for the bustle of the restaurant.

The hotel was a small to medium affair; the restaurant could only boast fifty to sixty covers and he had never seen it more than a quarter full. The serving staff had become familiar with his dining habits; as soon as he entered, the head waiter swooped and showed Nick to his favourite table. Danny had quickly acknowledged that this Englishman was a client who wasn't afraid to tip well.

'How was your day, Mr. Trevelyan?' inquired the head waiter 'Fine thanks, Danny, just a couple of annoying interruptions but nothing that couldn't be sorted out,.' Nick replied genially. He ordered a vodka and tonic and studied the menu. Having made his opening gesture, Danny allowed the other waiters to look after the "Englishman in New York" while he busied himself elsewhere.

Nick ordered a steak, explaining that I didn't want half a steer. A bottle of good red wine was added to the order before he settled back to enjoy his vodka and tonic and indulge himself in a mixture of daydreaming and people-watching. He allowed his thoughts to drift towards the following day's agenda when he would cross swords with Mario Burlace. This was a character who needed treating with caution. Nick had only dealt with Mario once before and although the meeting had gone to plan, his sixth sense told him that this was a man not to be trusted. He had paid up but he wanted to know more, too much more. Where was Nick getting these high class diamonds from? If he could find out and cut Nick out of the loop, then he could make an even bigger profit; the driving force in his life.

After about fifteen minutes the steak arrived and Nick realized that he was quite hungry. His attention was attracted by a flurry of movement at the restaurant entrance. Danny had suddenly become highly animated and was gesticulating in a plausible impression of Basil Fawlty. Nick was curious as to why this usually urbane man should have undergone such a rapid transformation. The answer was soon evident. Danny was moving in reverse, traversing the tables with a high degree of dexterity while ushering a tall, elegant woman to her table. There was obviously not a shortage of options where she could sit but eventually the decision was reached and she chose a table not too far from his.

All heads in the restaurant turned furtively to observe the arrival of this remarkably beautiful woman. Once her seating arrangements had been resolved, Danny turned his attention to making an unnecessary fuss over the table lay-out. Most of these events Nick viewed with a certain disinterest concentrating on the huge steak that would have served four people in the UK.

The woman was tall, slender and elegant. There are women, and then there are women, but the apparition not twelve feet away from him was something special. In common with most heterosexual red blooded men, he considered himself a connoisseur of the female form and the woman standing so tantalizingly close was as fine an example as he ever had the good fortune to observe. She wore an immaculately tailored charcoal grey business suit. The front was low cut allowing her lace bra to be seen. The cleavage, while not huge, was certainly adequate. The tight fitting skirt was cut slightly above the knee with a side slit which allowed alluring glimpses of shapely legs. Her body looked toned to the extent of being hard. Nick decided that she must be an athlete of some description. The skin had a Mediterranean olive tone and her long black hair was tied back in a severe classical style. Her features were elegantly sophisticated and she exuded self confidence. He guessed her age to be about twenty-eight.

Two observations puzzled him vaguely. Her eye makeup was theatrical: dark and somewhat heavy. Secondly; she wore far too much expensive jewellery, The flurry of the mystery woman's initial entrance was over and the restaurant returned to normality. Nick continued with his meal, acutely aware of the beauty sitting and facing him two tables away. Danny enquired if the lady would like a drink while she studied the menu. The reply was for a Caipirosca, which confused Danny. She politely explained that this was a Caipirinha with a shot of vodka, a new trendy drink which

Danny hadn't yet encountered. He accepted the information enjoying any opportunity of engaging her in conversation. When the drink arrived she sipped it delicately. Holding the glass in front of her, she gazed across the rim in Nick's direction. He decided not to make eye contact and continued with his meal. A mobile phone ended the stand-off, causing the woman to retrieve the telephone from her Gucci handbag. The distance between them was no more than twelve feet and she made no effort to be discreet when answering the call.

'Yes, I understand completely Mr . . . . Symonds. If your daughter is ill then of course you cannot make the meeting. Please call me tomorrow and we will arrange another date.'

Her accent was cultured Middle American. Something seriously important must have occurred to cancel an appointment with a woman like this, Nick mused. Conversation over, the mystery woman returned to her Caipirinha/vodka and continued to look in Nick's direction, obviously deep in thought. Danny hovered attentively close by.

'Is everything OK with your meal Mr. Trevelyan?' he asked, hardly taking his eyes off the woman.

'Fine thanks Danny, just fine.' Nick replied. This short exchange appeared to trigger an opportunity, for without warning she got up from her seat and walked over to his table and stood facing him. He placed his napkin on the table and stood.

'I do hope that you will excuse this impoliteness but I feel that we have met before. My name is Mercedes; I am one of the principal dancers with the New York Ballet Company. We recently visited London and when I heard your English accent I felt convinced that we had met there.' Nick was obviously delighted at the opportunity to talk to this woman, particularly as she had opened the conversation even if the reasoning was slightly contrived.

We all have little fantasies of using a particular line such as jumping into a cab and saying, 'Follow that car in front and don't lose him!' This was just such an opportunity and he wasn't going to miss it.

'Mercedes, I'm delighted to meet you.' He held out his hand and felt her strong handshake.

'My name is Nicholas Trevelyan and sad to say we have never met; I could never be so remiss as to forget meeting such a beautiful woman.' He accentuated his British accent for effect. There was a slight pause for the initial impact to settle. He left it to Mercedes to make the next move, feeling that perhaps his luck was just a little contrived.

'Nicholas you are going to think this awfully forward of me but my business dinner appointment has called off and I detest eating alone. Would you mind if I joined your table? "*What a daft question,* he thought.

'I'd be delighted and honoured! Please take a seat.'

Mercedes moved her things to his table, much to the annoyance of Danny and several other men in the restaurant. And so the evening progressed. Mercedes had a light dinner and together they worked their way through two bottles of red wine, followed by brandies. The conversation flowed easily. Mercedes' life in the New York cultural scene sounded interesting and Nick made his life as a worldwide commodities dealer as exciting as he could dream up at such short notice. Begrudgingly, Danny brought the bill and Mercedes' coat; together they walked out into the foyer.

'Do you like jazz, Nick?' Asked Mercedes,'I'm having such a great time and it's too early to go home yet. On the next block there's a great blues bar that I'd love to show you.'

'Sounds fine to me.' He was having a pretty good time himself.

And so the evening progressed. The drinks changed to Jack Daniels and the music was all that you would expect from a New York basement blues club. It was one thirty in the morning when they left the smoky atmosphere and walked out into the invigorating night air. As they walked along the sidewalk towards his hotel, Mercedes slipped her arm through his.

'Wow, you Englishmen certainly do have charm.' Mercedes whispered. There was a mixture of emotions running through his brain: flattery at such a high level was slightly intimidating although thoroughly agreeable. But the warning signs were flashing up. '*Let's take it to the next level*' he thought '*This promises to be fun!*' Standing outside the hotel it was 'make or break' time. How to suggest going up to his room for a nightcap without sounding too forward? He needn't have worried; it was Mercedes who was making the running and suggested the next move.

'Nick, I can see that you are a perfect gentleman who wouldn't dream of asking a lady up to his hotel room at this hour so I'll spare you the embarrassment and invite myself. How does that sit with you?'

'How could he resist such an offer? It could irrevocably damage Anglo/American relationships.' He agreed.

Arm in arm they walked up into the hotel, across the foyer and into the lift. They were the only passengers. Nick hit the button for the eighth floor. As soon as the lift started to move, Mercedes pushed him roughly against the back wall of the lift. Taking his face in her hands she kissed him passionately, her tongue exploring every region of his mouth. Her right leg curled around his left thigh, demonstrating her athletic prowess. She pulled him onto her, ardently. The embrace lasted until the lift bell announced their arrival on the sixth floor. Along the corridor and then, while Nick fumbled with the door lock, Mercedes continued fondling, kissing his neck and pushing her warm, moist tongue into his ear. They fell into the room.

Nick needed a little time to catch his breath, so sudden had been Mercedes' passionate advance. He flopped into the only single armchair where he felt safe for the moment. She sat opposite on the two-seater couch. For a minute or two she sat, simply looking at him and then she slowly stood up. Taking a stance with her legs slightly apart, she slowly unbuttoned the front of her immaculately tailored suit, pushed the jacket back over her shoulders and let it fall to the floor. Her hands went behind her back and undid the bra clip. She took the bra by a shoulder strap and flung it teasingly into his face. Her breasts were delightful, certainly not large but of prefect dimensions; in contrast the nipples were large, dark and extremely pert.

Mercedes hand disappeared behind her back again; there was a sound of a zip being opened. The skirt fell to the floor revealing that she was wearing nothing beneath the skirt apart from black hold-up stockings, the tops of which were made of delicate lace which gripped the well-muscled sleek thighs. Her stomach was perfectly flat; below, the pubic mound was shaved and inviting. She stepped out of the skirt and with her toes flicked it towards him, the movement causing her breasts to quiver exotically. This was a woman who knew how to tease a man. Balancing on one leg she removed one shoe and then the other. Apart from the stockings and jewellery she was completely naked.

Again her hand disappeared behind her head and her beautiful hair cascaded down onto her shoulders. She shook her head to allow the hair to fall naturally and again her breasts quivered pleasingly.

'Like what you see, Nick?' Marina had asked the same question under the same circumstances in what seemed a lifetime ago.

'I consider that to be a superfluous question.' Nick continued to play the English gentleman. What happened next, he hadn't been prepared for. Mercedes walked over to the hotel radio selector, scanned through a couple of channels and found one dedicated to classical music. The volume was turned up high. Nick was convinced that the whole eighth floor could hear but he couldn't have cared less, Mercedes began to dance.

Their conversation so far had been something of a farce as far as he was concerned. He had been lying from the start, making up his background as he went along, and he assumed that Mercedes might have equally been playing a similar game. Whatever she had told him to date, the dancing part was certainly true. She was quite obviously a trained dancer. She performed as if he wasn't in the room, her beautiful naked body conveying the beauty of ballet with the subtlety of a concert pianist playing a classical masterpiece. She had the poise of a ballerina combined with the savage grace of a lioness. Nick looked on, mesmerized. Finally the music ended. Mercedes stood in front of him, her chest heaving from the exertion, her gorgeous body glistening with a thin covering of sweat. She extended her arms in a gesture for him to stand up. He complied. Sensuously she opened the buttons of his shirt and it fell to the floor, she moved down to his trousers and they too fell to the floor. He was standing in only his boxer shorts. Her hand slid down and his penis was hers. Her neck arched backwards in sheer delight; her eyes flickered.

Standing in front of him was one of the most beautiful women that he had ever seen. She was offering herself and it was a temptation that few heterosexual men could refuse. Nick had convinced himself that he needed to discover the reason why she had so obviously come on to him so readily,

There must be more to it. Up to this point the conditions hadn't been convenient for him to attempt to hypnotise her, or perhaps that was the excuse that he was making to himself to cover his guilt at allowing this to progress the way it had. Her company was pure golden honey. Tamsen was in his mind and he was tormented by that thought which motivated him to make his next move.

*"Oh Lord, forgive me for what I am about to do! This is as close to heaven as a man can be and I'm about to jump off."*

'Mercedes, look into my eyes." Nick began the procedure for hypnosis and within ten seconds she was under. Her lovely head sank onto her chest. An amusing thought flashed through his mind. This was the first time he had hypnotized someone who was simultaneously holding his wedding tackle. Allowing himself time to adjust to the situation, he continued.

'Mercedes, who sent you here?'

'I was sent by Mario Burlace.' Not too much of a surprise there.

'What did he want you to do?'

'I am to find out where you get your diamonds.'

'And what else?'

'Nothing else. Just give you a good time and learn where your diamonds come from.' Nick needed to think about this.

'Mercedes, why are you working for Burlace?' Their time together had been brief but he had actually developed affection for this obviously talented woman. Whatever she was, she was not a hooker.

'I have two addictions which Mario knows about and uses to manipulate me.'

'What are they?' Nick expected the answer to be drug-related but was astounded by the reply.

'I have an insatiable addiction to expensive jewellery. I just have to buy the things that I see. Mario has a beautiful store and allows me to run up a heavy account there as long as I help him on occasions.' This answered a lot of questions.

'And what is the other addiction Mercedes?'

'I also have in insatiable appetite for sex.' Quite a revelation, although not completely unexpected, Nick thought. His next move was crucial in ensuring his safety while in New York and maintaining a useful business contact for the future.

'Mercedes, when you report to Mr Burlace you will tell him that we had an enjoyable evening together. We spoke of many things and I explained that I was in New York to sell diamonds. These were from my father's business in London. Occasionally there is a surplus of diamonds which the company do not want sold on the European market and so I am sent to the U.S. to dispose of them.' Nick thought that the explanation was simple and plausible and decided to leave it at that.

'Now Mercedes, I want you to think about jewellery.' It was more than probable that he would never again meet Mercedes but the memory of her dancing and their night together in New York would be burned forever on his memory. He couldn't help but like her and he wanted to help. He implanted thoughts deep into Mercedes mind which would rid her of the craving for expensive jewellery. He considered giving the same treatment for her sex problem but decided to leave well alone. It was something that she would have to deal with herself.

'I'm going to wake you up now. When you are awake you will feel content but tired. Then you will make your excuses and leave.'

He took her through the reverse countdown and Mercedes was awake, sitting naked on the couch.

'Wow Nick, did the booze catch up with me? I must have dozed off.'

Her nakedness now appeared to be a concern and she quickly gathered up her clothes, made polite goodbyes and was gone. Nick checked the time, it was 4.30 am. Time to crawl into bed. It had been a memorable night.

# Mario Burlace

The next morning Nick walked into the restaurant for breakfast as usual and went through the ritual of being shown to his favourite table. However, it was obvious from his attitude that Danny was seething with jealousy. In any hotel the gossip mechanism is super-efficient and the Plaza was no exception. The night staff would have seen Mercedes going up to his room and doubtless witnessed her coming down again an hour and a half later. While he was waiting for his breakfast to arrive, he made a phone call. This was to Mario Burlace, the third of his New York diamond dealers.

Burt and Mosses had been relatively uncomplicated to deal with, but Mario Burlace was a very different matter. Mario was of obvious Italian, possible Sicilian extraction which in this city generally heralded sinister overtones. Mario Burlace had attempted to infiltrate Nick's operation without success so far, but he would need all of his guile to keep ahead of the game and he knew it.

The Burlace offices, while in the same district as his previous appointments, were a million miles away in style. The offices were above a lavish jewellery store which wouldn't have looked out of place on Fifth Avenue. There was a separate entrance to the offices immediately to the side of the shop front.

Five minutes before his appointed time, Nick entered the building and took the lift to the fourth floor where Mario's offices were located. The reception area was modern and expensively decorated. The receptionist looked efficient. He introduced himself and asked for the gents' toilets.

Once safely inside a cubicle, he removed the diamonds from their snug hiding place, returned to the reception area and took a seat. After about ten minutes the receptionist announced.

'Mr. Burlace will see you now, Mr. Trevelyan.' The door to an office opened and Nick walked in.

'Hi, Nicholas, how are you?'

Mario's office was lavish. Hardwood panelled walls, expensive 'repro' furniture and deep pile carpet. Probably not the height of good taste but nevertheless, lavish. Mario sat behind a huge walnut desk with tooled leather facings. He was an overweight Neapolitan in a shiny designer suit and over-the-top expensive jewellery. Why not? He did own a jewellery store. His thinning hair was slicked down with gel and he sported a large black moustache. Nick estimated his age to be about ten years older than his own. On either side stood two men who did not look like diamond dealers.

'Good to see you again, Nick.' Mario stood up and offered his hand across the large expanse of desk. Nick reached across and shook hands with him. He made no effort to introduce the two men. Nick wondered how the de-brief with Mercedes had gone. There was nothing of any significance to report—he had seen to that—and he imagined that Mario would have been less than pleased. Nick sat down in the seat adjacent to Mario's.

'So—are we going to do business again? I hope so.' There was a distinct air of insincerity about everything that Mario said, making Nick feel increasingly ill at ease.

'Yes Mario, I think that we can perhaps achieve something this morning but I'd rather that we talked in private.'

'Don't you just love the way that these Limeys talk? Hey Tommy, Chuck, go take a coffee break!'

The two men did as their boss demanded. Nick felt more comfortable when they had left the room.

'Mario, you are looking a little tired,' he observed, sympathetically.

'Lot of work lately, Nick, Yeah, I suppose I am a little tired if the truth be known.'

This was easy! He had Mario just where he wanted him and within thirty seconds he was under.

'Mario, are there any CCTV cameras or microphones in this room?'

Mario's head had slumped onto his chest. It bumped up and down as he spoke.

'Yes, but they're not working—waiting to be upgraded.'

'Mario, what are your plans for me?'

'Tommy and Chuck are going to follow you to see if we can find out where you are getting the stones from. If they discover nothing then they will jump you and get back the money I pay you.' Nick gave the situation time to sink in. He needed to think fast.

'OK Mario, I'm going to tell you something that is very important. Listen to every word that I say.' Nick began his preposterous story.

'Mario how many brothers did your father have?'

'Five.'

'What was the middle brother's name?'

'Antonio.'

'Did you know that Antonio was a Second World War hero?'

'No, my uncle Antonio spent most of his life in Alcatraz. You must mean Uncle Frank. He died on the beaches in the "D Day" landings.' Mario's voice was slow and laborious.

'Yes, Uncle Frank, Mario. Well your uncle Frank was in England before the 'D Day' landings and he fell in love with an English girl. He promised to come back after the war and marry her but sadly he was killed. That girl was pregnant with his child. That child grew up and became my father. So you see Mario, we are cousins.'

Nick knew the story was ridiculous but planted deeply into Mario's subconscious it would have total credibility. Nick had passed the "Guardian at the gateway" and was now dealing directly with Mario's subconscious mind. "For as a man thinks in his subconscious mind, so he is. What has been planted into your subconscious you will make reality."

'We are cousins, Mario, that's why I came to New York to find you.' A smile spread across Mario's face.

'Cousins.' Mario whispered the word like a six year old boy.

'So Mario, you see that you have to look after me and make sure that I have everything that I want because I'm family. Give me a good deal on my diamonds and tell Tommy and Chuck to look after me while I'm in the city.'

'Yes, cousins . . . family.' Mario's head bobbed on his chest.

'All of this is our secret, Mario, only you and I know the truth. It must be our secret, Do you understand? Our secret.'

'I'm going to waken you up now and when you are awake you will remember all that I have told you but it will remain our secret. Ten . . . nine . . . eight . . . waking slowly and feeling relaxed, seven . . . six . . . five . . . more and more awake and ready to do a good deal on the diamonds, four . . . three . . . two, feeling good and contented, one . . . wide awake.'

Mario sat back in his walnut and leather armchair; a childlike grin cracked his swarthy face and a tear began to well at the corner of his eye.

'Nick, I always look forward to seeing you. Why don't you come over more often and hey, bring your Mom and Dad next time?' Nick relished the thought of his father meeting Mario.

'I might just do that, next trip. By the way they send their love,' he lied.

The tear in the corner of Mario's eye trickled down his pockmarked cheek.

'Mario, I have a lot to get done while I'm in town, so can we get on with the deal?" Nick made a mental note. "*Send Mario a Christmas card and a boxed copy of 'Saving Private Ryan'*". The dealing over, Mario called the two heavies back into the room. The third wad of US dollars was safely tucked into his inside breast pocket.

'Now, is there anything else that I can help you with?' asked Mario eagerly.

'Well there is one thing, Mario. I'd like to buy a present for my girlfriend.' Nick replied.

'Got a girl, hey Nick, bet she's a stunner. Love to meet her some time'.

'You will, you will. I'll make sure of that, I know that she would love to meet you and your family. Mario, we must keep in touch more in the future there is so much for us to catch up with.' Nick was enjoying the charade, feeling that he had done his work capably. Any pressure that had existed disappeared from the meeting, turning it into something of a family reunion. All of this was much to the confusion of Tommy and Chuck.

'Tommy, take Nicky down into the showroom and let him pick out a present for his girl. Tell Abe not to write a bill. It's on the house.'

'OK boss.' If Tommy was confused before, he was doubly confused now. Mario jumped up from his chair and walked enthusiastically around the desk. First he pumped Nick's hand and then almost uncontrollably he converted the handshake into a hug. Nick went along with the scene. Tommy and Chuck looked on in bewilderment. As he left the room, Nick saw Mario wiping away a tear with the cuff of his Armani suit. In the lift Tommy muttered that Mario was a little emotional today, as if he was hoping for an answer to the conundrum.

In the glittering showroom, Nick browsed the display cases, followed by the over-attentive manager who he assumed must be Abe. His thoughts were tinged by the vision of Mercedes, browsing these same show cases. Tommy hadn't spoken to Abe yet and the manager was anticipating a good sale and a fat commission from the well-dressed and well-spoken Englishman. Nick finally decided upon an unpretentious gold and platinum bracelet. Abe fussed about packaging the gift but was noticeably deflated when Tommy walked over and explained that Mr Burlace had sent orders not to charge this client. Abe was transformed, almost off-handed in his approach from then on, but Nick put the package into his overcoat pocket and walked out onto Forty Seventh Street. This time he was well aware of who walked near to him. He didn't want a repeat of yesterday's fiasco. The alley was across the street and crime scene tape fluttered in the afternoon breeze. He hailed a cab and drove back to the Plaza.

## Checking out of the Plaza hotel

Picking up his room key and the wallet from Reception, Nick asked for his bill to be made up and went straight up to his room. He tucked the dollar notes from Mario Burlace into the wallet which was now bulging. Then he changed his clothes to something more casual and went to lunch. This was to be the last lunch of this trip; he would be booking out the next day at noon. He paid the hotel bill in advance and in cash. In the afternoon he took a sightseeing tour of the Big Apple to justify his visit should questions ever be asked.

The morning breakfast ritual was played out as before, Danny's jealousy was uncontrollable. He would have loved to have been the one to spend time with the delectable Mercedes and he was having trouble disguising the fact. He allowed the junior staff to serve at Nick's table. Nick told the subordinate waiter that this was his final meal for this trip and tipped handsomely. Returning to his room, he completed the last of his packing and then divided the money from the wallet into two piles, leaving some dollar notes. He put on a suit, placing half of the money into his inside pocket. The rest he put back into the wallet which he returned to the reception desk for locking into the hotel safe for the final time. He reached the Chase Manhattan Bank five minutes before his appointment but this time he didn't need the excuse of finding the toilets. It was also quite refreshing to have a meeting where there was no hidden agenda, just banking and investment options. Banks are always happy to take your money. The meeting was over in forty minutes. He took a cab back to the Plaza where he changed into comfortable clothes for the flight, retrieved his wallet and checked out. The courtesy coach headed back across the Hudson River, via the Holland Bridge and on to Newark airport. Nick allowed himself to relax. He had achieved all he had come to do.

Later, when he had settled into his seat on the BA jet, he reflected on the events of the past four days. Life was certainly unpredictable. He was eternally thankful that he had picked up the book on hypnotism at Quinta Da Felicidade all those months before.

## Timothy Harcourt

Second Lieutenant Timothy Harcourt walked across the drill square at the regimental headquarters of the Shropshire Regiment with a certain amount of trepidation. This was hallowed ground and although he actually outranked the regimental sergeant major, he was well aware that he was considered nothing but a nonentity, a Rupert playing at being a soldier who was openly despised by the entire senior non-commissioned staff. The Regimental Sergeant Major had an annoying knack of belittling him when he was in his presence and the drill ground was his territory and his alone. Anyone who walked across the square did so at their peril. Should there be one small item of uniform that was incorrect or even minutely scruffy it would be seen from the regimental's office which perched like an eagle's eyrie at the head of the square next to that of the Colonel.

These offices were adorned with colourful, neat gardens edged with white painted stones, flanked by two flag poles, all of which looked strangely out of place in this testosterone rich environment. Timothy's demons tormented him; the other junior officers appeared capable of taking the situation in their stride but Timothy was always on the back foot where the 'Regimental' was concerned. And so it was with some relief that he finally reached the verge that marked the boundary of the drill square and the neatly edged pathway which led to the colonel's office.

One ordeal over, he now faced a second of the morning. Colonel Mike Evans had summoned him to his office for what he supposed was to be a statutory periodical interview for he had now completed almost three years in the army and his promotion to captain was a possibility which lurked fondly in the back of his mind.

Colonel Mike, as he was popularly and affectionately known, was a grammar school boy who had been born to be a soldier and a leader of men. From the day that Timothy had arrived at the regiment, it was patently obvious that Colonel Mike had taken an instant dislike to him. Timothy had made numerous attempts to win the Colonel's approval but whatever he did only resulted in a disaster which aggravated the situation even more. In the outer office which doubled as the regimental clerk's domain, the adjutant and the 'Regimental' stood talking in a corner.

'Good morning, Timothy,' came a polite greeting from the adjutant before he returned to his conversation with the 'Regimental' who was a bull of a man, prone to explode into seemingly uncontrollable rage at the most trivial incident. Thankfully the Regimental made no comment.

'Go straight in, Timothy.' the adjutant said in a friendly tone, 'The colonel's waiting for you'.

The Regimental and the adjutant glanced over their shoulders as Timothy made his way to the door of the colonel's office. The clerk, a certain Lance Corporal Doyle peered over his counter like an expectant Meercat waiting to see its cousins swept up in the talons of a swooping eagle. Timothy was receiving negative vibrations that he didn't much like. Colonel Mike was sitting behind his desk, legs stretched out before him and hands clasped behind his neck. He fixed Timothy with his iron gaze, got up from his chair and walked round the desk. His eyes never left Timothy's as he sat down on the corner of the desk. It had always been a mystery to Timothy why rugby players allowed themselves to be disfigured in such a gruesome way. Cauliflower ears and broken noses did not figure highly in the scheme of things in his world and Colonel Mike had both. It had to be something akin to German officers and their love of sporting duelling scars. He was brought abruptly out of his thoughts.

'Timothy. Your time with the regiment has not been a happy one, I fear.' the colonel opened. 'Neither for you, I suspect, nor for your platoon. Perhaps your choice of regiment could be at fault as I feel that you would have been better suited to a regiment that was rooted more in the past than we are. You have almost completed your first three years of service with the colours and now you must decide what you are going to do next. One option would be to sign on for a further nine years and make a career of the army. The other would be to leave when your three years are up and return to Civvie Street with a clean record from the army and take up a new career. There followed a long pause.

'I recommend that you choose the second option.'

Colonel Mike had a reputation for being forthright, but this was brutal. It was a bombshell but not an altogether unexpected one.

'I am going to give you twenty four hours to consider what I have said, after which time I expect an answer. As you know, we are training up for a second tour in Iraq and I need my platoon leaders to be working well in advance with their men.'

A stunned Lieutenant Harcourt marched out of the colonel's office. No need to think about getting that third pip sewn onto his uniforms now, he reflected.

And so it was that Lieutenant Harcourt left the Shropshire Regiment with the minimum amount of ceremony and returned to London to pursue a civilian profession. He had a clean army record even if he hadn't scaled too many dizzy heights; and there was his qualification in accountancy to fall back upon. Timothy was many things but it must be said that he was never one to let the grass grow under his feet. Within a month he was starting a new career with The National Criminal Intelligence Service as fast track officer. He had maintained his friendship with Tristram Wrath-Bingham whose own career in the army was moving at a spanking pace, helped somewhat by the patronage of his father. Wrath-Bingham tolerated him as a useful lackey but never allowed him to get too close, occasionally inviting him to parties where he was useful to make up the numbers. And so the years passed and Timothy rose through the ranks as a criminal investigator, his cunning and guile equipping him perfectly for the job.

## Britain's National Criminal Intelligence Service

"Britain's National Criminal Intelligence Service (NCIS) was launched in April 1992 to provide leadership and excellence in criminal intelligence. The organization aims to combat the top echelons of crime and seeks the ultimate arrest or disruption of major criminals in the UK. NCIS is one of the first services to be set up in Europe to deal with the development of criminal intelligence on a national scale with approximately 500 staff drawn from the Police, Customs and Excise and the Home Office and of course the armed forces. It aims to help law enforcement and other agencies, at home and abroad, by processing and disseminating information, giving guidance and direction, and analyzing major criminal activity. Apart from a resources division, NCIS comprises the Headquarters (HQ), United Kingdom (UK) and International divisions. HQ Division includes an operational support unit, an intelligence co-ordination unit, policy, research unit and a strategic and specialist intelligence branch. The latter's responsibilities vary from organised crime to football hooliganism. Five regional offices in London, Birmingham, Bristol, Manchester and Wakefield are overseen by the UK Division which also includes a Scottish/Irish Liaison Unit, currently based in London.

The International division manages a network of European Drugs Liaison officers (DLOs) and is linked up with the world-wide DLO network managed by Customs and Excise. The UK Bureau of Interpol is also based within this division enabling NCIS to have direct access to Interpol's 176 member countries. Information processed by NCIS plays a vital part in tackling serious crime in Britain, and is used to assist police forces in other countries. The service gathers intelligence on offenders ranging from drug traffickers, money launderers and organized criminal groups to paedophiles and football hooligans. 9/11 had brought about many changes. Money laundering by drug barons had become a high profile target which affected anyone with a bank account. Any money moved around the world which might be used to finance terrorist activities received high priority scrutinisation Everything which passed through banks and building societies had to be accounted for."

Timothy's job kept him on his toes and so his delight was hard to disguise when one day a file landed on his desk which was to make not only his day, but his whole year. The file was not unlike others that had ended up on his desk in recent months now that the authorities had decided to clamp down on unexplained large amounts of money finding their way into British bank accounts. This was just such a file—a man whom the banks had flagged up as amassing a fortune with no obvious source of income. Nothing outstanding in that, until Timothy read the name of the suspect—Nicholas Trevelyan!

'Oh thank you, God, thank you.' Delight surged through Timothy's body, he scrutinised the report in every detail. Apparently several banks had become suspicious and reported the matter to the authorities. There had been some investigative work carried out but the file was fresh and the suspect had no idea that he was the subject of an inquiry. Timothy wasted no time at all in contacting Wrath—Bingham. No point in explaining the details of his windfall over the phone when he could milk it to the limit.

'Hello Tristram, it's Timothy.' He made every effort to remain cool and collected although he could hardly contain himself.

'I have something that I know you will want to see! Can we meet?' the response was dismissive.

'Busy time of year, old boy, Trooping of the Colour is coming up, it's the silly season, state visits etc. Much to do, you know.'

Timothy played his ace.

'Pity really as I have recently received a file on an old friend of yours and I thought that you might just be interested.'

A slight curiosity registered in Tristram voice.

'Old friend eh? Tell me more.'

Timothy was revelling in the charade.

'Someone from your past, Tristram.'

'And who might that be, pray tell me?'

'Someone from both our pasts.'

Another pause to draw out the drama that was to follow. Timothy was well aware of Tristram's loathing of the man who had broken his jaw in Edinburgh and knew that he would go to any lengths to wreak his revenge.

'Nicholas Trevelyan!'

'Bloody hell!!'

Tristram's delight was complete as he considered the implications of a file being on Harcourt's desk knowing what he did for his living these days.

'Can you make it to the mess here in Knightsbridge this evening, Timothy?' he asked in an altogether more friendly tone.

'Yes, of course, Tristram,' a smugly confident response.

Dinner in the Household Cavalry officers mess was an opportunity not to be missed. Especially as he had never before been invited.

'Seven for seven thirty, don't forget to bring the file. Nice to hear from you.' the conversation ended.

The officer's mess of the Household Cavalry in Knightsbridge was a undeniably privileged invitation. Timothy was in his element. This is where he should have been, and not slogging it out with a line regiment like the Shropshire's where mere grammar school boys ruled the roost. He felt that fate had dealt with him cruelly. His day dreaming was brought to an end when the now Captain Tristram Wrath-Bingham took him by the elbow and led him to an ante-room. Tristram was resplendent in his immaculate mess dress. Scarlet bolero jacket bedecked with gold trimmings, right down to the gold accoutrements on his spurs. If ever Timothy had been guilty of jealousy this was the time.

'So tell me Timothy, what do you have on Trevelyan?'

The next hour was taken up with the details of the file and further enquiries that Timothy had made.

'There is no record of where the deposits have come from and it looks evident to me that our mutual friend is acquiring money from some suspect source. I have permission to carry out a full enquiry into all aspects of his life, including phone taps.'

'Excellent Timothy, excellent, I couldn't be more delighted.' encouraged Tristram. 'Let's have a brandy shall we?'

And so the events that were to lead to Nick Trevelyan's second downfall were set in motion and, by a strange twist of fate, the perpetrators were the same as on the previous occasion. The hounds were baying and they could smell blood. As they saw it, Nick was culpable, he had lain his head on the axeman's block and they could barely wait for the axe to fall on his neck.

Timothy Harcourt delighted in his visits to the Knightsbridge mess. He thrilled at experiencing the lavish, exaggerated life style that he wanted so much to be part of and if it were to be only for brief interludes then he would take whatever he was given. 'He would love to be as close to Tristram, again, as he had been at Sandhurst.

It was wholly unfair that he had been assigned to a line regiment. He knew that Tristram only tolerated him for his intermittent usefulness but this didn't matter. In fact he enjoyed being abused by him and in a perverse way; he actually wanted Tristram to mistreat him. Because Timothy was hopelessly in love with him, but only in his private thoughts. This was something that he alone knew. Timothy's homosexuality was a secret that he had kept well hidden. Very few knew of his preference for men and his obsession with domination. There were professional people with whom he used to play out his own depraved caprice. These were well paid not just for the service that they administered but for the anonymity that was a hallmark of their trade. Strange how the veiled abuse that he received whilst with the Shropshire's did nothing to excite his strange sexual eccentricity. It had to be an aristocratic male or even female to push all of his perverted buttons. There were to be many visits to the Household Cavalry Officers' Mess over the next months when Timothy reported to Tristram. They were both deriving great pleasure from the exercise.

And so the hunt progressed. Timothy focussed his attention on pursuing Nick, keeping the file away from his colleagues in the intelligence service lest they became interested and moved the case out of his control. He wanted nobody else involved. Timothy thrived on the situation and squeezed it for the last drop of blood. Although his visits to the cavalry mess had become more frequent Tristram was becoming impatient, relishing the delicious thought of Nick Trevelyan being dragged through the courts and ruined financially. Timothy sensed that this current set of circumstances was to be only a temporary pleasure. He knew that when the case reached its finale, Tristram would cast him aside with contempt like a worn shoe from one of his magnificent cavalry horses.

The phone taps had revealed nothing. As far as they could ascertain, Nick was living a reasonably normal lifestyle. His relationship with Tamsen Richardson checked out. They found that she was whiter than white. Nothing unusual there. Unbeknown to Nick, he was followed for ten days but his movements showed nothing spectacular apart from regular visits to the London safety deposit vaults which were a mystery. Timothy finally decided that some positive action was needed; he visited the vaults to interview the manager Mr. Tom Holland on the pretence of a regulation call. Timothy danced around the topic of general security, broaching the subject of money laundering but eventually he was forced to open up and asks questions about Nicholas Trevelyan. Tom Holland appeared a little surprised

'Yes I know Nicholas Trevelyan quite well as it happens, both as a client and socially. A very industrious young man, no doubt he'll go far,' enthused Tom as the interview progressed.

'As far as anybody tampering with the security,' Tom laughed aloud, 'No-no, never been the slightest hint of a problem in over one hundred and thirty years'.

Timothy ended the meeting and left the building feeling thoroughly confused. There was obviously something deeply suspicious about Nick's involvement with the vaults but with no crime having been committed, he had no case. But where was the money coming from?

There were the occasional overseas visits but Timothy's remit didn't give him the resources to follow the suspect out of the British Isles unless he up-graded the case and that would mean that it could be taken out of his hands. Timothy found himself in an impossible 'catch 22' situation. Soon he would have to make a move but his options for action were decreasing. There was one alternative, which was to arrest his suspect, search his house and take the chance that enough evidence could be discovered to make the charge stick. At a meeting in the Knightsbridge mess, Timothy explained the details of his dilemma to Tristram.

'Absolutely no argument, Old Boy, go in and bag the bastard.' Tristram advised.

'Yes, but if there is no evidence to support the case, then I'm in big trouble.' whimpered Timothy.

'Got to be done, just has to be done, old man.' Tristram sensed blood. With that, Marina joined the two men and the subject was closed. Tristram had given an order and Timothy was obliged to obey.

## The Tamsen Year

The setup was simple and worked well for both of them. Tamsen commuted into Knightsbridge from her new flat in Windsor where she had moved to be closer to Nick. Some nights she slept at his apartment and other nights she stayed at her own place. It was an arrangement which they both agreed to. Tamsen was a career lawyer and dedicated to her job; burning the candle wasn't always an option for her, so on the occasions when she had an important day ahead and a good night's sleep was required she gave Nick advance warning. For his part the agreement was perfect. He was able to continue with his scam at the vaults and still enjoy the company of the beautiful Tamsen. Perhaps it just didn't occur to Tamsen to look further into his financial affairs; a romantic would say that she was blinded by love—after all it had happened to many women before her. Nick was astounded by the contrast in the relationship with Tamsen. The only other full-on romance he had experienced had been with Marina. His time with the voluptuous Marina had been steamy in the extreme even bordering on the animalistic but shallow, without meaning or depth. This was a new experience, something completely different. That's not to say that making love was less fulfilling because it was, but in a completely different way: now, it was sensuous, loving and intense. Their social life, too, was a world away from his previous experience. Tamsen introduced him to the finer things of life. The arts had been by and large something of a vacuum, that he had missed out on during his education. Tamsen opened up a whole new world, visiting art galleries, attending the theatre and listening to classical music. Much to his surprise, he loved it all and embraced it with enthusiasm. Their social life was hectic and their love life, exquisite. They slipped deeper into the relationship, each having a strong appreciation of the others achievements. On another level the unrestrained chemical magnetism worked its magic on each of them.

However, as weeks melted into months, Nick began to develop doubts. He was becoming troubled by the lie that he was playing out. The daily pretence that he was living an ordinary lifestyle began to worry him and lying to Tamsen was becoming more and more difficult. He wanted her to know everything about who he was and how his path through life had brought him to this point. Nick wanted so much to come clean, sit Tamsen down and tell her all of his dark secrets. But it would be an enormous risk which he found impossible to take. She would then become implicated in a crime and could be considered to be an accessory after the fact. What if then she rejected him? His happiness with her was something that he had never before known; to risk losing her love was an unacceptable option. And so the charade continued. Several times his cover story wore thin and he thought that he would have to face up to admitting his deceit, but the tempest subsided and the love boat returned to an even keel.

'Nicholas Trevelyan: why a man who epitomises the macho male should have statues of Fireman Sam, Postman Pat and Bob the builder in his bedroom confuses me. I get the feeling that your army buddies would have loved to be privy to that snippet of information.' Tamsen had been tidying up his apartment and discovered the figurines.

'If I were to snoop around your bedroom I have no doubt that I'd discover the odd Barbie doll.' Nick joked, thinking quickly. Considering the circumstances that was as close as Tamsen got to discovering his hidden life.

On his next visit to the vaults he took the Hess documents with him and locked them away with his stamp collection. He didn't know what the documents meant but as Tamsen was checking out things in his bedroom in a cleaning frenzy it would be better for them to be kept elsewhere and he could spare himself the worry of having to invent some believable explanation of what the papers were and more to the point how they came to be in his possession.

Friday evening arrived and he was looking forward to a relaxing weekend. He got home first and cooked a risotto which they washed down with a good bottle of red wine. They had decided to have a lazy evening listening to a new classical CD that Tamsen had bought that day. After dinner they cleaned up the kitchen, loaded the dishwasher and flopped out on the sofa.

'You have never told me any more about your hypnotic skills. Could you hypnotise me?' That evening Tamsen was back in an inquiring mode. It was a question that Nick had been expecting for some time but he was in fact surprised that she had waited so long to ask it.

'That's simply my party trick, nothing more.' He added blandly—an answer that Tamsen seemed to accept. After a busy week they were both tired and went to bed early. They made love but somehow it was different from the previous occasions. Nick felt that there was something wrong but he was unable to decide just what it could be. He was naturally a light sleeper; the wine had put him into a troubled, restless sleep.

## Busted

As dawn broke, he was wakened by a tremendous crash followed by all hell breaking loose in his flat. More than a dozen burly armed policemen broke into the building shouting like maniacs. As he leapt out of bed the door to the bedroom burst open and the room flooded with armed police. Nick was wrestled naked to the floor, unable initially to retaliate, overwhelmed by the number of his attackers. His face was rammed into the floor, two men sat on his shoulders. He was still able to see that Tamsen had found time to cover herself with a bath robe. She was standing by the bed talking to one of the police officers in such a reserved manner that she could have been chatting to her uncle. What the hell was happening? She should have been screaming her lungs out. Then even stranger, what the fuck was Timothy Harcourt doing in his bedroom? His world slipped into slow motion. It was like a scene from a low budget badly directed "B" movie. Then the adrenaline kicked in and he erupted from the floor like a human volcano. He was a seasoned rugby player; this was just like being in the middle of a collapsed scrum. He knew the feeling well, and he was certainly the centre of attention. He regained his feet and threw off two attackers, His arms were free. As he glanced to the right, a man's face was at shoulder level and at a convenient distance so he gave the man the full ferocity of a back elbow jab which connected with his nose. He toppled backwards screaming and holding two hands over what was obviously a broken nose. Another man was conveniently standing squarely in front of Nick so he gave that one a short arm jab to the throat which put him out of the game. All of this new action brought a fresh face to the party. Standing in the doorway was a policeman in body armour, Nick noticed that he had two pips on his shoulders. He never had understood the police rank structure but this was obviously the man in charge. Heads turned towards him.

'Stand back you bunch of wankers! Taser!' He gave the order with authority and everyone obeyed, knowing what was coming. Now the craziness of the scene took a further twist. All the policemen scurried away as if Nick had suddenly contracted rabies. He was standing in the middle of his now destroyed bedroom, naked, and as if this wasn't bizarre enough, the 'two pipper' took something from his belt which resembled a child's toy gun. All eyes were on the officer holding the bright yellow toy space Taser. The eye contact between Nick and 'two pips' was intense. He could feel an uncontrollable smile breaking out in the corners of his mouth, so surreal was the situation and so ridiculous was the yellow toy gun. 'Two pips' was smiling too. When 40,000 volts hits your nervous system, all smiling stops. Nick felt as if all the Christmas lights in Oxford Street had been re-routed through his body. Every muscle went into spasm and that was before he had fallen to the floor. The fight was over and he lay on the floor, a twitching mess. The pain was excruciating, then slowly faded. He attempted to get back on his feet again and continue the fight. This was only a momentary situation as three more policemen pulled him down again. He was shouting with rage, indignation and total surprise. The thought flashed through his mind that this might actually be a terrible nightmare and he would soon wake to find Tamsen lying beside him. He heard one of his attackers shout.

'Just do it!'

Two pips was shouting orders again. Nick felt a sudden sharp pain in his right buttock and knew that I had been injected. His head began to arch backwards; there was a loud buzzing in his ears. It became louder and louder. His head continued to arch backwards making him feel as if he were falling into a chasm. Backwards, backwards, more buzzing, louder and louder. Then the muscles in his calves went into spasm; the pain was agonizing, backwards, backwards and then darkness and silence.

He finally came out of the anaesthetic to find himself in a prison cell; he was still naked, lying on a minimal bed, covered with an itchy army issue blanket. On the floor was a neat pile of prisoner style clothing. In a corner there was a stainless steel toilet and washbasin. *'Not quite' Four Star, he thought.* Nothing else for it but to get up and wash and dress. Room service would undoubtedly be along soon. His head was banging and his mouth felt like the bottom of a gerbil's cage. He decided that the only way to deal with this was, keep it light, don't let them grind you down and say as little as possible. What could they possibly have on him? Nick almost relished the thought of the inevitable interrogation. After all, there was little incriminating evidence in the apartment and nobody was going to make a case against him. But where did Tamsen fit into all of this? Oh yes, and that slimy little turd, Harcourt—what was his role in this charade? Nick's head felt like a cement mixer full if bricks. The spy hole in the cell door scraped open and he could feel himself being watched. Ten minutes later the door opened and two police officers came in.

'You bastards drugged me!' he shouted as they entered his 'hotel suite'. They read Nick his rights and officially cautioned him.

'So where am I?' he asked. The reply was something of a shock.

'Paddington Green Maximum Security Police Station. Mr. Trevelyan, you are being held under the proceeds of crime act.' This was serious stuff but Nick felt confident that this was an over-kill situation that would soon be resolved. He tried to remain up-beat.

'I'd like my one telephone call now', he demanded.

'I'm afraid that that's only in American TV shows, Mr. Trevelyan. But nevertheless we will allow you to make a call if you give us the name.'

## Steve to the Rescue

Nick gave the name of his close friend, Steve Craig. The police officers checked it out and he was allowed to make the call.

'Good morning, Nick. Good to hear from you. How are you?'

'You might well ask, Mate. I'm currently being held at Her Majesty's pleasure in a cosy little abode in the charming location of Paddington Green.'

'What! I'll be there in twenty minutes.' and he was. Because of who he was, Steve was allowed immediate access.

'Before we start, Steve, can you get me a drink and perhaps a Panadol or two?'

'Don't even think of asking for a Pimm's number 1—it's tea, coffee or nothing.'

'Any chance of a bacon sandwich? I'm starving and appear to have inadvertently missed breakfast this morning.' Steve went out of the cell and was away for thirty minutes. When he returned it was with a mug of coffee, a bacon sandwich and a load of information not all of which Nick was going to enjoy hearing.

'OK—so what's happening?'

'Well Nick it appears that the CIA have been interested in you for some months. You are an ex-British army officer, highly trained and of some considerable experience, with a serious grudge against the establishment. In recent months, after arriving back from abroad, you have amassed a substantial, undisclosed fortune. They thought that you had gone rogue. You have all the traits of a "broken arrow".'

'A broken what?'

'Broken arrow', that's the Yank's terminology for someone with clout who changes sides. A more sophisticated English description would be, "Arrows from within." Or in simple terms you are considered to have gone rogue. You have to admit, Nick, your profile does tick all of the boxes and our American cousins were bound to pick up on you. I'm afraid to have to tell you that Tamsen, if that's her real name, was sent by the CIA to check you out.' Nick's attitude was suddenly and viciously transformed. Anger stepped in.

'You mean that the whole thing between us was a lie? I can't believe it.'

'I'm sorry, buddy, but you had better get used to it because it's a fact.' Steve was brutally frank but there was no other way.

'Are you telling me that she is just going to walk away?'

'Nick, she is at this moment on a jet headed for the US. Later today she will be getting a de-brief from the CIA director of intelligence in Langley, Virginia.' Nick slumped back on the bed. Steve continued: 'If you think back you will remember that the days when you made your trips into London always coincided with Tamsen being in town for the day. The fact of the matter was that she and her colleagues were tracking your every move. Everything that you said was being listened to; everything that is, apart from the moment you entered the Chancery Lane vaults. Their surveillance equipment was certainly sophisticated but not good enough to follow you down into the vaults. Once you were inside the building they lost contact. This infuriated them and made them even more suspicious. Half of the legitimate diamond dealers in Hatton Garden have been scrutinised by the CIA over the past couple of months. In addition to all of this and in parallel, Timothy Harcourt was also leading an enquiry into your activities completely unbeknown to the CIA and vice-versa. Classic case of the right hand not knowing what the left hand is doing. The dawn raid was orchestrated by Harcourt. The CIA knew nothing of it but clearly it has blown Tamsen's cover and she has been withdrawn.'

'Withdrawn!' Nick was verging on the emotional. The feelings he had felt for Tamsen had been entirely real. His biggest problem had been guilt for keeping his true activities from her when in reality this was her only reason for being there with him.

'Steve, she was the only woman that I have come anything near to caring for' I just can't believe that it was all a charade; no woman could possibly lie to such an extent. I also sense the hand of Wrath-Bingham in this. Wherever Harcourt is, Wrath—Bingham is never far away and vice versa. I know that my instinct will prove me right.

'I know, Nick, you and Tamsen looked well together—the happiest that I have ever seen you. The few times that the three of us had dinner together you looked like a perfect couple.'

## The End, or is this the beginning

At the age of thirty Nick would be the first to admit that his life, so far, had been anything but ordinary. However, the situation in which he now found himself was bizarre in the extreme. Twenty-four hours earlier, after a long hunt, he had been caught by the Fraud Squad and charged with stealing from the London Safety Deposit Vaults, Chancery Lane. His only phone call had been to his old friend and fellow Sandhurst cadet, Steve Craig who was now in the SAS and was security adviser to the Cabinet. Steve immediately pulled the requisite strings and visited Nick in his cell.

'I don't know if I can get you out of this mess, Nick, I'll do everything that I can to help but you have to tell me everything, in detail.' Steve advised. Nick then told him the whole story from beginning to end, missing nothing out, including his ability to hypnotize.

'Are you telling me, Nick, that you can hypnotise someone to order?'

'Pretty much, as long as the conditions are all ok, yes.'

'And are you prepared to demonstrate this ability to me?'

'What, do you want me to hypnotise you?'

'No, that wouldn't work, I'll send in a guard with some more coffee and tell him that you are cleared and will be released later without charges. You can work your magic on him, if you really can that is.'

'Deal! Just put another bacon sandwich on that order. And yes—one more question: what was that daft ray-gun that they zapped me with?'

'Since you were keeping an entire section of the Met's CO19 busy, the decision was taken to hit you with a Taser gun. It's the latest hi-tec demobiliser. You should feel honoured—it appears you are the first prisoner to be captured using this weapon.'

'Yeah, thanks. I feel like a rogue rhino from Zoo Quest.'

Steve left the cell and after thirty minutes a guard came in armed with a steaming mug of coffee and a bacon sandwich. He was alone and had obviously been primed that Nick wasn't any sort of a threat. He was quite ready to enter into conversation. When Steve returned fifteen minutes later, Nick was finishing the remains of his sandwich and coffee. Sitting opposite, in his underpants was the guard having a great time singing Bohemian Rhapsody in a very bad voice.

'Wow, I knew that you were a strange bird, but this takes the biscuit.' was Steve's amazed comment as he stood surveying the scene. 'But for God's sake, sort him out. He's one of my lads and if anyone else sees this, he'll never live it down.'

Three hours later, Nick was taken from the cell by four tough looking guards in a closed van. He was driven for about twenty minutes across London. Then he was hurried through the back entrance of what looked like a government building and unexpectedly, after checking the view from a window, found himself in a musty ante-room at the War Office, surrounded by a new team of four guards who were evidently highly professional and had obviously been made aware of his hypnotic ability and refused to talk to him. After half an hour the door opened and Steve Craig walked in. He was dressed in his uniform and Nick noted with admiration that Steve was now a full Colonel.

'Come with me please, Nick.' said Steve, in a firm tone. Together they walked into the inner sanctum. The surprise on Nick's face was impossible to hide, for besides Steve and the other six high ranking army officers gathered in the room, sitting at an imposing desk, was the Home Secretary.

'Mr. Trevelyan.' began the Home Secretary, 'before we start I must warn you that we are aware of your, shall I say, 'talents'. Should you make an attempt to influence me in any way during this interview the meeting will be terminated immediately?' Nick nodded his acceptance.

'Mr. Trevelyan, I will be brief. You have been caught red handed misappropriating large amounts of what we can only assume were very valuable assets. According to your lifestyle and the bank deposits that we have so far been able to discover, this has amounted to a considerable fortune. You could be facing an extremely long jail sentence. It is true that there will be no complaints from the people that you have robbed, as they are, for the greater part, dead. And besides, for all we know, the items may have been stolen in the first place or hidden to avoid tax implications, or something similar. Additionally, the vaults from which you took these valuables have no idea that anything is missing and they are certainly none the wiser concerning what has been happening on their premises. The Home Secretary paused.

'Mr. Trevelyan, we have studied your army records and your friend Colonel Craig has filled us in with some further details. You are a lucky man to have such a loyal friend. I am a politician and it is in the nature of my job to make deals. I am prepared to offer you a deal. We realize the importance of your abilities. Together with your military training and experience, these abilities could have remarkable advantages for this country, particularly in the field of espionage. I am therefore offering you the possibility of exoneration from the serious charges that you are presently facing. In addition you will be given back your commission with the rank of full Colonel and assigned to the Army Intelligence Corp.

Mr. Trevelyan, we all know that there is no such thing as a free lunch. We will require, in return for this arrangement, your services as a special agent. We feel that this is an area to which your . . . er . . . particular skills may be well utilized.' All of this will be probationary and can be withdrawn if you fail to meet our expectations. Colonel Craig will be your probationary officer.

The Home Sectary had never overly impressed Nick as a politician, and he had considered him to be rather a weak, type. But now, the man suddenly rocketed in his estimation. He was tough, thorough and to the point. The deal that he had laid on the table looked good—reinstatement with promotion—while the alternative could be very bleak indeed. Really this offer was pretty much a no-brainer.

'If you are successful, we will expunge the misdemeanours that you have perpetrated. We ask one more thing from you today in order to seal this agreement. Since we are prepared to make you this generous offer, I want to see for myself the extent of your ability to hypnotize people. Much hinges upon this. Therefore, in order to kill two birds with one stone, we have devised a small test for you.

Mr. Timothy Harcourt has become something of a thorn in our side regarding this matter; therefore we have decided to allow you to deal with the problem in your own particular manner. At this time he believes that he has you cornered and is champing at the bit to bring charges against you. He is waiting in an interrogation room within this building as we speak. The room has a one way mirror system which will enable myself and the other gentlemen here to see and hear how you will deal with Mr. Harcourt.'

With that, the assembled group moved off to reconvene again in fifteen minutes at the interrogation room.

'Just time for a coffee and then you're on, Nick.' suggested Steve.

'Think I need more than a coffee.' Nick replied.

The two Colonels walked into the staff canteen, bought two coffees and sat down. The canteen was almost deserted and they were able to talk freely.

'There's a lot riding on this, Nick, so for God's sake get it right, I've staked my reputation on the outcome of this travesty.'

'Don't worry, Steve. I want what you have created for me and I have no intention of screwing things up either for you or for me.'

'By the way, the coffee in Paddington nick was much better than here.'

As agreed, the group re-convened in a basement area where the bare concrete walled interrogation room was housed. Its most striking feature was a window which was ten feet long but only two feet high; it looked onto a room with very little furniture. Centrally placed was a flat table about the size of a normal dining room table that was firmly bolted to the floor. There were two chairs at adjacent sides and sitting at one of the chairs was the unmistakable Timothy Harcourt. In front of him, strewn across the table, were piles of photocopied papers which he was arranging nervously. It had been some time since Nick had seen Timothy, apart from the rapid glimpse that he had caught of him when Timothy and his buddies had so annoyingly disturbed his sleep yesterday morning. He had changed little over the years. His weasel ways were just as evident now as they had been years before at Sandhurst.

'Ready for it?' Steve whispered in his ear. 'Some of the brass here think that I've lost my marbles, so for Christ's sake do a good job.'

'Let's get on with it shall we?' Nick walked to the door and entered the room.

The initial meeting was tense. Timothy apologized profusely explaining that he had made several attempts to pass this unhappy affair on to a colleague, one who didn't have such a close history with the accused but his superiors had insisted that he must see the case through. And so, unhappily, it had fallen to him to interview Nick—much against his wishes.

'*Yeah, my heart bleeds for you.*' Nick thought as he sat down in the vacant chair.

'Nick, I have no option but to get on with this sad situation, odious as it may be,' squirmed Harcourt.

Nick sat forward in his chair and focused his attention on Timothy.

'Before we start, Timothy, I was wondering if you were feeling ok, you look a little tired to me.' Nick commenced his work.

'Yes, well actually I have rather been burning the midnight oil lately.' 'Your eyes must be feeling heavy, you must be feeling sleepy, Nick continued.

Steve told Nick later that the sceptical onlookers were all amazed at the speed with which he took control of the situation and total control of Timothy who was now sitting quietly looking like a pensioner taking a nap on a park bench. Nick got up from his chair and walked out of the room leaving him to his siesta.

'Very good, Colonel Trevelyan. I am impressed.' The Home Secretary was obviously happy with what he had witnessed; it was the first time that

Nick had been addressed as 'Colonel' and he enjoyed the feeling. The brass were all chatting amongst themselves. Nick felt as if he were heading the bill at the London Palladium.

'And how long will the subject remain in that state?' the Home Secretary inquired.

'About twelve to fifteen minutes if I leave him alone. He will automatically waken as if he had just dozed off. I can now implant suggestions into his subconscious which he will act upon so long as the suggestions are acceptable.' Nick explained. The Home Sectary continued,'The gentlemen here will tell you what implanted suggestion they want you to put into agent Harcourt's mind. After all he was really only doing his job. Colonel Trevelyan, I have enjoyed this afternoon's diversion and I have no doubt that you will be an impressive addition to the SIS. Colonel Craig will keep me informed of your progress; I expect superlative results from you in the future.'

The whole meeting was over in less than an hour. The Home Secretary excused himself and left, taking with him his entourage, explaining that he had many other affairs to deal with but as a parting remark he added that he doubted that his next engagement would be as agreeable as the episode that he had just witnessed.

Timothy was given the information that had been concocted which rendered him inert as far as his case was concerned. He left feeling a little confused about the morning's business. Steve and Nick found themselves standing in the ante-room again once the guards had gone.

'Well Colonel Trevelyan, I guess we had better get to work and sort out the Harcourt aftermath.' grinned Steve.

'OK Colonel Trevelyan let's get on with the rest of your life.' mused Steve as we walked down the steps of the War Office and out into the sunlight of Whitehall.

'I think that dinner would be in order, and it's your shout'.

'You name it; I'll pay it.' Nick replied. 'I certainly owe you that, just for openers.'

# | 7 |

# NEW LIFE

Over dinner, there was much to be discussed. Steve had been given the responsibility of organizing the advanced training that Nick would require.

'To begin with, you will be spending six weeks with the regiment in Hereford. This will bring you up to a very high level of proficiency in all aspects of weaponry. You aren't going to thank me for that too much as you need to get prepared to get your knees dirty down there with the lads. And don't think that the rank of Colonel will give you any privileges; you will be wasting your time with those guys. It will also get you back into the machine; after all you have become a little soft recently. During your time there you will make six HALO (High altitude low opening) jumps just in case we need to slip you into a locale in secret. Another reason for bogeying you away in Beacon is to let the heat die down here in London. That little shit Harcourt, will have to have a keen eye kept on him but with what you have put into his mind, I'm convinced that you have sorted him out. I have no doubt that the people in GCHQ will be able to dig up some dirt on the squirming turd that can be used to have him develop amnesia where you are concerned, should the need arise. Then I have you booked on a week's advanced driving course with the Met police. That should be fun. After that, it's all brain work. Three months in Cheltenham at GCHQ learning the marvels of the technology that those fellows love so much. And finally six months in London getting to grips with the wondrous workings of MI6. They will be the people whom you will be immediately answerable to, apart from myself and my bosses. While all this is going on, the aftermath of your recent escapades needs to be tidied up.' Steve paused as he was obviously thinking on his feet, thinking out loud.

'We have people who will see to that. I have mentioned Harcourt but there are other matters that need to be addressed. We have to establish an impeccable background for you that cannot be cracked. You are to become an independent financial advisor so you will need to "mug-up" on that subject whilst all the other stuff is going on.'

Steve was deep in thought but lightened up as he came to the next subject on the agenda.

'Now we come to something that has posed a major dilemma. The proceeds from your surreptitious visits to Chancery Lane have created something of a problem'. There was evidence of a smile at the corners of Steve's mouth.

'We know that you have amassed quite a reasonable fortune over the past year or so. There is your property in Windsor, various bank accounts, works of art, diamonds and more, including a rather nice Jaguar. God only knows what you have stuck in the vaults that we haven't been able to get at—and to tell you the truth, we would rather not know. Steve stopped to reflect.

'Yes we know about most of it. The problem is that although we know that you stole these items, there is nobody to make a case against you. You have in fact committed the perfect crime. It has been decided that to attempt to return the property would open up an unnecessary can of worms. Far better to leave things as they are, which has the advantage of giving you a strong cover from which to undertake your new role.'

Steve leaned back in his chair and stretched.

'Nick, you really are a lucky fucker. For millennia, military strategists around the globe have been pumping countless millions into discovering the secrets of paranormal subjects such as remote viewing, hypnosis, ESP and parapsychology. There is little doubt that, if these subjects could be mastered, their potential in warfare would be phenomenal. The remote viewing project in the US attempted to gather information about distant or unseen targets using paranormal means or extra-sensory perception and ran for years. It was eventually abandoned never having reached a satisfactory conclusion. The military hierarchy knew that if they could crack the understanding of these extraordinary subjects creating a network of "Psychic Spies" they would have added an immensely powerful weapon to their arsenal. The CIA and the US Army thought enough of remote viewing to spend millions of taxpayers' dollars on "Stargate" The program involved using psychics for such operations as trying to locate Gaddafi of Libya and the locating of a missing airplane in Africa. And now due to a catalogue of bizarre circumstances Nick, you have perfected a technique that the CIA would pay a king's ransom for. Even more uncanny is the fact that you have landed in the lap of MI6 which explains why they were swift to recruit you into their ranks'.

In order for Nick to sustain a plausible cover story, it was decided that he ought to maintain the same level of lifestyle that he had become accustomed to from the proceeds of his exploits at the London Security Vaults. He wasn't going to argue. He

Knew that MI6 desperately needed operatives who could infiltrate society at all levels. His two bedroom flat in Windsor was paid for and he had to admit that he liked his Jaguar and designer clothes. All this would have been difficult on the salary of a British Army Colonel. MI6 had tidied up a lot of loose ends, but handing back the proceeds of his exploits was considered to be virtually impossible. And so it was concluded that he should continue to live the life of a successful investment consultant.

The year long specialist training had taken him away from his flat but he had returned whenever possible to maintain the cover story. Nick cleared the flat of anything that reminded him of Tamsen. Her treachery had cut deep. This was the first time that he had really been hurt by a woman. Steve yet again proved what a sincere friend he was; their friendship went back years. Fate had thrown them together at Sandhurst and fate in its own unfathomable way had caused them to finally work together. Steve knew Nick better than he knew himself. The training that he threw him headlong into was so intense that Nick had little time to dwell on the past. The scars were slowly healing. The vacuum which had existed in his life was now filled.

So here he was, a new agent, part of SIS working out of Thames House and yet to prove himself. He had been assigned to a team made up of boffin types who trawled cyber space looking for indications of potential terrorist activity, or "*local chatter*" and who could make a computer do just about anything. There were other agents in his team, male and female, some of who looked nothing like the stereotypes he had expected. Nick was assigned to a head of section but his overall handler was Steve. He and a very few other people knew of Nick's ability which was kept secret for there is always a possibility of internal moles whom it was thought Nick would be useful at detecting.

His training was not all action. He spent hours in the basement of Thames House where the paper archives were housed, studying old cases and documents. He had to learn the location of safe houses, how to break into cars and buildings undetected and dozens of ways of killing someone quietly and without the use of violence. There was a whole new language to be learnt i.e., the banter that these people used to communicate. Surveillance gadgetry was constantly being up-dated and all operatives were regularly brought up to speed with the latest technology.

## The New Agent

Walking along the Albert Embankment on his way to the office, Nick slowed his pace as he passed curious locals and tourists gathered along the Embankment parapet wall. His attention was drawn to an animated girl among the group, pointing excitedly towards the grey January river waters. Some people had cameras ready, others were videoing the spectacle or capturing it on their mobiles.

A TV news crew, newly arrived on the scene, were preparing themselves. The attractive presenter checked her notes, collecting herself for the live broadcast. Nick was close enough to hear her piece to camera.

" . . . Initial sightings of the Northern Bottle-nosed whale were reported several days ago, although her wayward journey up the Thames River to visit the City of London may be this whale's last port of call. Rescuers have had little success redirecting her to the open seas . . . ." Nick watched the river. Across the water on the other bank he could see the MI6 building, known to those in the business as "Legoland". That's where he worked.

He couldn't believe what he was seeing. Dozens of the building's supposedly "top secret" employees were out on its balconies, in full view of the general public, all attempting to glimpse the spectacle of the lost creature's final hours. *'Bloody idiots!'* How the hell can they be so dumb? Nick knew that if he ran, he could be there in five minutes and get them back inside. Getting a man on the spot so quickly would have been difficult but not impossible. Once the opposition had seen the error they would have seized the opportunity and taken full advantage. Nick was edgy and the repercussions that could result from such a simple lack of thought could have severe consequences particularly for the more junior staff if they were recognised by the bad guys. His attention was now focused on getting to the balcony and clearing it of its spectators.

His cell-phone signalled a call. It was Steve. He sounded troubled.

'Nick, get yourself into the office as quick as you can. I need you back on the grid.'

'I'll be there in five.' With the Thames between him and his destination he set off at a run in the direction of Vauxhall Bridge. Maybe Nick should have told Steve about the whale watchers but he felt that he could better deal with it himself and prevent what might be a prickly scene from occurring.

The River Thames was the unlikely stage for the whale drama and it played to a captivated audience. The four ton bottle-nosed whale surfaced exhausted in bewilderment. It slapped the surface of the murky Thames with its sickle shaped tail and disconsolately blew a fountain of spray into the chill morning air. It was an extraordinary sight and a heartrending one, even in a city like London, where the curious is more often the rule these days. It was obvious to all watching that these were the final hours of a remarkable creature.

On the balcony of Thames House the assembled whale watchers watched with intent, oblivious of the danger that they were exposing themselves to. As he walked out onto the balcony a nerdy cipher clerk popped up next to him like a Meercat on patrol. He shouted angrily, arguing that something should have been done sooner as if Nick had a direct line to "Whales in crisis". Nick nodded, but knew that the whale's survival was impossible; her battle was lost as soon as she had passed the Thames Barrier.

The vantage point on the embankment was the mysterious MI6 building. Nick had visited the office block many times in recent months but was amazed to see so many employees crowding the balconies; He had no idea that so many people worked here in Thames House as each section was a secretive business which tended to cause each department to keep themselves to themselves.

Nick looked back across the river to the embankment where he had been standing five minutes earlier. Crowds were gathering in the winter sunshine to watch the distressing spectacle. TV news stations were running minute-by-minute coverage, crowding out all other stories. This was cheap TV. His eyes were focused upon London's lost whale but his thoughts were temporarily elsewhere. It was sixteen months since he had been caught red-handed relieving the Chancery Lane Safety Deposit Vaults of their clandestine treasures and he had then been unceremoniously hauled before the Home Secretary. It had felt like the end of the line and most likely would have been but for the intervention of his old Sandhurst buddy, Steve Craig. Steve was serving in the Special Air Service and was now Chief Security Advisor to the Cabinet. He had risen to the rank of Lieutenant Colonel. After hours of bizarre negotiations which included some not too veiled threats and very few options on his part, Nick had been given what pretty much resembled an ultimatum and was recruited into a little known group operating out of MI6—called the SIS. It was not just a case of walking in on his first day and saying.

'Hi!—I'm the new bloke!'

Oh no. Nothing so easy. He had been thrown straight into an intensive training regime which lasted a year and involved working with several of the intelligence agencies and a lot of time spent at Hereford with the SAS. The course was rugged but he loved every minute of it. He was a soldier again, something that he felt born to be. His daydreaming was suddenly interrupted when Steve appeared from an office and strode out onto the terrace. He was a well-known and highly respected individual at Legoland.

'What the fuck are you all doing out here?' Steve Craig barked at the whale watchers.

'Don't you think half the Islamic world would love to know who works in this building? Idiots! Fucking idiots! Get inside! Your ugly mugs could be all over Al-Jazeera by tomorrow.'

Steve had positioned himself so that no happy snapper could get a mug shot of him. The whale watchers shuffled not quite knowing how to react.

'If I had wanted you to do this in slow motion I would have told you. Now move!'

They all filed sheepishly back to their various hidey holes and within fifteen seconds the balcony was cleared leaving Steve and Nick alone. Nick knew only too well that inside this man beat a heart the size of a polar bear's but when he reverted to anger mode he was a fearsome character.

'Not too sure those people are used to your way of putting over a point. They're civvies not squaddies, you know,' Nick grinned.

'And you, Nick, you should know better,' chastised Steve. There seemed little point in explaining to Steve that he had been about to get the people inside, having seen the danger himself but he didn't get a chance as the action moved swiftly forward.

'No time for this crap. We have business to attend to; get out of that suit and into a sweater, jeans and trainers! I'll get us a car and driver.' Steve's anger had suddenly abated as he switched seamlessly into a different high-efficiency mode.

'Where are we going?' Nick inquired to the back of Steve's head as he ran off along the corridor shouting over his shoulder.

'I'll brief you in the car.'

While Nick changed from his sober office suit into casual clothes, he was perceptively aware of all the pressures that would surface when the call eventually came to go into action for the first time in the new role that he had been groomed for. Military action was not new to him. He had seen combat many times as an infantry platoon leader with all of the support that goes with modern warfare, but this was different. He was a Special Operations Agent now and couldn't help but wonder if, when the time came, he would be able to repay all of the trust that Steve had shown in him and measure up to the job.

Nick met Steve again in the underground car park where a driver was waiting. The car was a two year-old BMW 7 series; the man who drove it wore scruffy civilian clothes and looked as if he had just walked off a building site. Mick was on secondment from Hereford, a complete non-conformist and exactly the guy that you would want by your side when the going got tough. Steve gave the order to move off.

## The Hostage Siege

'London Heliport, Mick, normal speed. We don't want to attract attention.' The car pulled out of the side entrance and slid into London traffic.

'OK Nick. The situation is this. A group of Islamic fundamentalists have taken over the Cheshire home of Sir Humphrey Taggart; he was the last British ambassador to Iraq and subsequently Islamic advisor to the government during the second Gulf war. Fortunately for us it's an old manor house, totally concealed within its own grounds. We have had the place completely sealed off by the local constabulary, plus five

SAS four-man teams bogeyed away at strategic positions ready to go at a second's notice. The big plus in our favour is that the media haven't received wind of this yet; they are too busy watching your bottle-nosed friend.'

'Sounds as if the pigs have taken over the farm,' observed Nick.

By the time Steve had finished the briefing, they had reached the heliport. They walked briskly through the departure lounge and out to the waiting private helicopter. The flight to Cheshire took fifty-five minutes, during which time Steve outlined his plan and the specific part Nick was to play in it. Helicopters are noisy beasts and Steve shouted the information rather than spoke it.

'What are they demanding?' Nick asked.

'Release of eight detainees from Guantanamo, ten million Pounds Sterling and an unhindered flight to Iran.'

'And what cards are they holding?'

'The hostages: Sir Humphrey and his wife, their two daughters, a cook and a manservant. There is also an unfortunate postman who just happened to be there when the attack took place,' added Steve.

'How do we categorize their intentions?' he asked

'Deadly serious. They have stated a willingness to martyr themselves for their cause. We know they have Sir Humphrey and the eldest daughter strapped into suicide bomb waistcoats. We have top level Cabinet clearance to use whatever force is deemed necessary, so if we have to waste them all, then so be it.'

'And my part in this pantomime?'

'You, my friend, are to be the negotiator. We have telephone contact. Their leader is one Abdul Kharmi, a Pakistani, born in England, educated at Sheffield University and trained in Pakistan and Iran. He's a radical zealot indoctrinated with a hatred of all Western culture.'

'Just my kind of guy.'

'They have agreed to a meeting between our negotiator and Abdul. Your brief is to go in and buy us some time. You can use the excuse that gathering ten million in Sterling and getting flight clearance takes time, not to mention the deal in Guantanamo and the need to win over our American cousins. By the way, we have no intention of meeting any of their demands. It's government policy as you know. Never give in to terrorists' demands. While you are inside, assess the situation and report back every detail. And now the biggie . . . I want you to use that special hypnotic ability of yours to control this man. What do you think—are you up to it?'

'The first part I am trained for. I know I can do what you want, and I don't expect any problems there. Now for the hypnosis part. I'm certain that if I can get Abdul alone for just one minute, no more than three metres away from me without interruptions, I can get to him. There has to be nobody else within hearing distance for just one minute. You must also understand that I can only plant suggestions which are subtle; direct orders won't work if they are against what the subject would normally believe. So I'll need time to devise a viable story and get these suggestions, which must be restrained, embedded. I can activate these implants with a trigger word, but given the conditions, we have to accept that the outcome will be very sudden. I will only be able to make Abdul carry out one task. It has to be backed up by an all-out attack from your men. We are only going to get one go at this.' Nick stared at Steve as he delivered his options. It wasn't going to be easy.

'One more thing—there are no guarantees.'

The helicopter landed in a field a mile away from the Taggart house, They were transported to the target area in an unmarked police car which was waiting for them. By the time they had reached the stable block, which acted as a forward base for Steve's men, the final details of a plan had been cobbled together.

'Something else that you need to know, Nick: you go in unarmed, un-wired and the targets are out of range of our marksmen.'

'Any other good news, Mate?'

The stable block had been hastily furnished with field equipment, radios, and even a desk. All conversation ended abruptly when the red phone on the desk sprang into life.

'That'll be him! Are you ready to go in?' asked Steve. Nick nodded acceptance.

'Hello Abdul, Colonel Craig. As you can see we have met your demands. There are no armed personnel within shooting distance,' Steve lied. The voice on the other end sounded agitated, which accentuated the Sheffield accent.

'Where's the money and the coach to take us to the airport?' Abdul was screaming his demands into the phone.

'Abdul' Steve attempted to answer but was cut short.

'Listen to me, Western Pig. These people will die if you don't do exactly what I say.'

'OK Abdul. Take it easy; we don't want any bloodshed. We can end this amicably but it will just take a little time. You know what bureaucracy is like. We have to get a lot of signatures in order to do what you are asking.' Steve sounded conspiratorial.

'Stop stalling and get on with it or you will have these people's blood on your hands. Allah is great!' Abdul ended the conversation abruptly.

'They're getting stressed in there; these are young arrogant men who are convinced they will be martyrs for the cause. Their indoctrination has been thorough; a deep, vicious hatred has been implanted in their minds.'

Steve picked up the red phone; it was answered immediately.

'Abdul, this is Colonel Craig, I have news concerning your demands. This line cannot be guaranteed secure and we need to know that all of the hostages are alive so I am sending in a mediator to clarify the details. Will that be OK with you?' Steve looked meaningfully at Nick. There was an uneasy pause.

'Send him in but if I suspect anything, he will be shot.' replied Abdul.

'You are calling the shots, Abdul. We'll do it your way.' The brief conversation ended.

'Ready to go, Nick?' asked Steve looking a little apprehensive.

'I guess I'm as ready as I will ever be.' Nick didn't want to appear nervous. He tried hard to look confident. The culmination of a lot of training and more importantly, his abilities, were about to be seriously put to the test.

Sir Humphrey Taggart's country home was an imposing Tudor manor house. On a summer's day and under happier circumstances a visit would have been a pleasurable affair; but today, in midwinter, and given the prevailing circumstances, it was anything but pleasant. Nick's trainers crunched the gravel on the path leading to the Elizabethan porch. He was six metres from the front door when a heavily accented northern voice ordered him to stop.

'Take everything off; I don't trust you, you bastard!' demanded a voice. Nick shrugged his shoulders and did as he was ordered.

January in Cheshire is not a good time to be standing in someone's front garden, naked. Nick decided that allowing them all their demands was a negative approach, so he made a demand of his own:

'OK, you can see that I'm unarmed; would you mind if I put my clothes back on? It's bloody freezing!' Having attended several lectures at GCHQ on the art of hostage negotiating, Nick knew that it was considered beneficial to keep the mood as light as was practical. He also realised that his body temperature was dropping dramatically and he would soon start to shiver—a bad position from which to negotiate. Grudgingly, the voice agreed. He dressed, immediately feeling the benefit of his clothing. The door was pushed open.

'Keep to the middle of the hall!' ordered the voice. 'Any suspicious move and I'll shoot you.' So they definitely did have a gun—or perhaps guns—in addition to explosives. Nick began to mentally compile the list that Steve had asked for.

'No need for that, Abdul. I'm just the negotiator.'

He entered the house. The porch hallway was small but opened onto a central room which echoed the exterior of the building: exposed beams and white plaster walls. It was well furnished; there was a minstrel gallery, accessed by a magnificent oak staircase, Nick took in the scene, trying to observe as much as possible. Standing in the centre, his eyes were immediately drawn to four figures above in the gallery. Two of them were quite obviously Sir Humphrey, with his distinguished silver hair, and his eldest daughter; each was strapped into a harness which held what must be explosives. Two Asian youths were pushing their captives' heads forward, forcing them against the gallery railing. Sir Humphrey, although dishevelled, looked relatively calm but his daughter was sobbing uncontrollably. Nick made eye contact with Sir Humphrey; how could he let him know that they were going to do everything possible to get him and his family out alive and that the teams surrounding his home were the best in the business? He could only allow himself a hint of a nod which he hoped Sir Humphrey interpreted as positive.

Nick was aware that two other men were behind him but continued to stand in the centre of the room, facing the way he had entered. There was no need to aggravate the situation. The two men circled and flanked him from behind, entering his peripheral vision. His first impression was they were all young and typical of the many Muslim men who can be seen in any number of British towns and cities: shaven heads, designer jeans, shirts and trainers. The leader stood out he was older, perhaps thirty-two, with a shaven head and long beard. He wore a robe that reached the ground. In his right hand was a Browning 9mm automatic.

'Abdul, my name is Nick, I'm here solely as a negotiator, I'm not from the police or military.' *Better to start with a good lie,'* he thought.

'I work for the government; I'm here to see that everyone gets what they want and we end up with a solution that all parties agree to, a happy ending.' Nick pulled back, thinking that perhaps he was being too patronizing. So far the atmosphere had remained fairly calm. From his profile Abdul appeared to be prone to sudden dramatic tantrums. This had to be avoided at all costs.

'All of your demands are being dealt with but you must understand that a great deal of negotiating has to be worked through. The main sticking point at the moment is with the American government. I'm sure you appreciate that what we are asking them for is, in their estimation, a lot. We have to convince them it's the right thing to do.' Nick could hear the sound of his own voice as if he was an outside observer looking in at the scene which was unfolding and concluded that he sounded remarkably convincing. A thought flashed through his head. *'So far so good. Keep it up, Nick.'* The fact of the matter was that neither the Americans, nor anyone else, had any idea of the drama being played out in this pleasant English backwater.

'Americans are capitalist pigs! Allah will have his revenge upon them.' Abdul shouted. Nick nodded feigned agreement. The negotiating was moving along OK so far, but where were the other five hostages and the two Asians? Abdul was obviously far from dim; he was not allowing all of his cards to be seen. Was this the time for Nick to make his move? He lowered his voice so that the two men closest could not hear.

'Abdul, I would like to talk to you in private; it would be better if the hostages didn't hear this.'

'If you think that you can overpower me, then think again! I have no reservations about using this gun. You would also do well to remember that Rashid here has the remote control which will send everyone in this house to their maker. We are all armed and it is our wish to die a warrior's death.'

Given this opportunity Nick took time to study Rashid. The youth was wearing cargo pants and around his skinny right thigh was duck-taped a large red plunger button which was pointing upwards. The youth looked twitchy and nervous. Abdul said a few words to Rashid in Urdu and with the barrel of his pistol, motioned for Nick to move towards the door. He obeyed and walked into the library. It was an imposing room lined from floor to ceiling with shelves of books. The furniture was heavy but functional. He noticed two computers and a lap-top plus a photo-copier and fax machines as well as other office equipment. Obviously Sir Humphrey, his wife and daughters, used this room on a regular basis. Nick had read all of their profiles in detail. They were all academics—the family of a senior Foreign Office official would have to be and one of the toughest postings that anyone in that business could have, experenced, to be Iraq during the reign of Saddam Hussein. Abdul would have discovered this room as soon as he had taken over the house and doubtless used the computers to maintain contact with any outside accomplices that he might have.

Nick turned to face Abdul; they were approximately three metres apart.

'So what do you want to talk to me 'in private' about, Mr Negotiator Nicholas?' sneered Abdul.

His gun was levelled at Nick's chest; it was cocked. The safety catch was in the off position. Abdul meant business and had obviously been trained to use small arms. He picked up on Nick's eye movement.

'Yes, Nicholas, the safety is off, there's a round in the chamber and the trigger is set to a hair pressure. I feel that for the sake of your health you had better keep your distance. That's if you don't want a neatly-drilled nine millimetre hole in your chest.' Abdul was in control and enjoying the power that holding a weapon gives.

'Don't worry Abdul; I'll stay where I am.' Nick remained calm. Was this the moment to make his move?

Every time that he had attempted to hypnotize someone it had been successful but there was always a nagging doubt that there could be a time when it might not work or could just go wrong. He had read that there were people not susceptible to hypnotism and Abdul might just be one of them! Or worse. Although Nick's odd coloured eye seemed to give him a great edge on getting his subjects' attention focused—what if Abdul was colour blind?

'I have noticed that you are looking tired, Abdul. This must be a stressful time for you.'

'Did you get me in here to talk about my bloody health? What is this crap?' There was a great deal of annoyance in Abdul's voice and Nick needed him to be calm.

'No nonsense Abdul, I have to look at every aspect of what is happening here and I can see that you really are looking very tired. We want this matter to be dealt with in a way that is acceptable to both sides and as you're calling the shots, it's important that you are as calm and cool-headed as possible. You are under a lot of stress. Just look at me for a second. I can imagine that your eyelids are feeling heavy?' Nick spoke slowly, taking the conversation to a calmer level.

'Can you feel yourself getting even more tired?' The stage was set for Nick to do his stuff. Just as long as Rashid didn't walk in, Abdul would go under. It just needed a few more soothing words to establish a complete state of hypnosis and then the suggestions could be implanted into his subconscious. Nick noticed the signs that he had come to know. Abdul's eyes were flicking from his left to his right eye. Although standing, his stance took on a more relaxed appearance, the muscles in his neck eased and his eyes glazed. The gun however remained steady in his hand and continued to point directly at Nicks heart. It was now or never. Suddenly, Nick could see that he was now under his influence and began to implant his suggestions.

'Abdul, I want you to keep a close watch on Rashid. He is an infiltrator and will betray you all. He is being paid by the CIA and when the time comes he will see you all die before walking away himself. You must kill him if your mission is to succeed. I will give you three words. When you hear them you must shoot him immediately. It has to be done for Allah and the cause. The words that you will hear from my lips only will be "Sword of Freedom." I repeat, when you hear me say "Sword of Freedom," you must shoot Rashid immediately. Then you will have avenged Allah and your name will be written in the Hall of the Righteous forever.' Nick allowed himself a brief micro-second, flicking his attention from Abdul to the door through which Rashid might walk into the room at any moment and ruin the whole plan.

'I am going to count slowly backwards from ten to one and when I am finished you will be wide awake and ready to send me back to talk to your superiors. Ten . . . nine . . . eight . . . you are slowly waking. Seven . . . six . . . five . . . . more awake and feeling that you are in a winning position. Four . . . three . . . two . . . almost completely awake and ready to move on: One.' Abdul blinked several times and looked down at the pistol in his hand. He looked like a child reading aloud at school and losing his place in a book. He quickly recovered and regained his confidence. Nick stroked his ego a little to make the transition as seamless as possible.

'As we were saying, Abdul, I am here to ensure that your demands are met but we need a little more time to sort out the details. In the meantime, is there anything that you need?'

'No. Nothing, I have stated my demands. Just go back to your capitalist bosses and tell them that if there is no agreement by 10 am tomorrow we start killing hostages.'

Nick walked out of the library into the main room and looked up at the despairing hostages still hunched over the balcony. He saw the haunting desperation in the eyes of Sir Humphrey's sobbing daughter and, feeling helpless to intervene at that moment, he walked on into the porch. As he left the room, he noticed Abdul looking strangely at Rashid.

*'For God's sake! Not now Abdul. Wait for the signal,'* he thought.

Walking out into the crisp winter sunshine was a welcome liberation from the desperation that hung like a fog from the walls inside the house. Nick continued up the drive and turned a corner, out of sight from the house, where Steve was waiting for him

'Well?' he inquired.

'Yes. It's done.' Nick reported despondently. 'But the next stage ain't gonna be easy'.

## The Attack

Inside the stable block there was a flurry of action as Nick began his debrief.

'You have until 10 am tomorrow before they start murdering the hostages'.

'OK, so we hit them at dawn. Did you manage to implant the trigger word?

'Yes, but it will only take out one mark—he's the one with the detonator duck-taped to his leg and he's a nervy bugger. I calculate that you will have approximately sixty seconds to hit them before they work out what's happening.'

'Not a worry. We estimate we will have the building swamped in forty seconds.'

'One problem—if I have been successful in making Abdul shoot Rashid, we have no way of knowing if he will make a clean kill. Also, when Rashid hits the deck there is a strong possibility that he could land on the detonator button. It's a big brute and could easily be activated unintentionally.'

'That's a risk we are going to have to live with.'

'By the way Steve, there's a considerable computer set-up in the library. Make sure that they can't access the outside world with it and alert the whole bloody planet to what they're doing.'

Steve called in his men for a briefing. Those who had been watching the house with sniper rifles and infrared night scopes were replaced by police marksmen, giving Steve a team of twenty men from the Regiment, all of whom had spent months training for a scenario just like this. In the aftermath of the Iranian Embassy siege this was standard procedure. In addition to the stable block forward command there was a rear command post set up in a commandeered house, far enough away and completely out of sight and sound of the Taggart house. Here the county constabulary and other units were based with direct lines to the Cabinet.

'I want a bomb disposal team ready to move in as soon as I give the signal. They will need six men: two for Sir Humphrey, two for his daughter and a final two to deal with Rashid. Once they have dealt with the walking bombs, I want them to concentrate on locating the fixed explosives and disarming them. We will need ambulances and the fire brigade at the rear command post. For God's sake, tell them to approach quietly. No sirens!'

The SAS were an undemonstrative group. Not much in the way of conversation passed between them. Each had a file which consisted of photocopied photographs of the hostages and plans of the house and gardens. These they had studied in earnest while sitting around in various corners of the stables. Dressed in black coveralls, they now busied themselves checking and re-checking their equipment. Their weapons were individual to each man, their own personal choice, not standard issue. The only time they became more animated was when food arrived. This they devoured with obvious delight. There was a scale model of the house with cutaway sections on a central makeshift desk. Occasionally one of the SAS men would go over to the model and scrutinize the layout. Nick marvelled at how this could have been built in such a short time. As dusk set in, some of the men camouflaged their faces and hands, then slid off into the darkness without saying a word. Their job was to get close to the house during the night without being detected by the hostage takers. They needed no further orders; each man knew exactly what he would be required to do.

'OK Nick. This is how it's going to work. I'll lead the frontal assault with three men.' Steve nodded at the three men who were sitting together. We'll go in through the front door to monopolize their attention. At the same time another team will go in through the back.' Another nod to a group of men who were leaning against a wall. The rest of our guys will enter from wherever they can, mostly from first floor windows.' Steve turned to Nick. 'You will be here to make the call to Abdul. As soon as we hear the shot, we let all hell lose. We'll hit the house with stun grenades and smoke. I can't tell for sure how close the men who have gone out tonight will have got to their fire locations but they are good. By dawn I expect at least three to be on the roof. As soon as you make the call, leg it up to me and follow me in. You have the best idea of the layout and know some of the faces. I want all bodies outside—hostages and terrorists alike—so that we can divide them up. You will be particularly useful in that. The three who are bombed-up will have to be taken to the area I have marked. It's a sunken terrace isolated from the rest of the gardens and the bomb squad boys can do their work without hindrance. So what weapon do you want? I know that you have a preference for a Glock 17; but there's also a Browning 9mm here if you want it.'

'I'll stick with the Glock, if you don't mind,'

And so the die was cast. Thus far, Nick had acquitted himself admirably; but would he be up to it when the brown stuff hit the fan? Steve had gone out on a limb and Nick didn't want to let him down but there was an overriding incentive which hung over him. The Home Secretary had added a clause concerning his future career which simply stated that if he didn't cut the mustard within his first six months as a special operative, his commission would be terminated. There was a lot riding on the forthcoming action.

The stable was reasonably clean and sleeping bags had been sent in at Steve's request. The SAS men appeared to be able to sleep anywhere; their needs were minimal apart from a continuous stream of pizzas, McDonalds and KFC, which were devoured with enthusiasm. They didn't so much sleep as rest; all their senses were heightened as the adrenaline flowed. It was possible that at any moment the whole thing could "kick-off" so they had to be instantly ready to go into action. The stable had no heating and the January night was cold, but the service issue sleeping bags were adequate. Nick slept fitfully, convinced that Steve's plan was sound and there were no soldiers on the planet who were as capable of carrying it out as well as these guys. Nick had no doubt on that score. His concern was that when the time came, would he be up to it? The soldiering part he was born for but, if the hypnotism let him down, his part in the op. would be compromised and he would be on his way back to Civvie Street yet again. One hour before dawn, Steve paced around his assembled team. There was no need to rouse them as all were wide awake and raring to get on with the job.

'OK, Troops, cammy up, and then one final briefing in fifteen minutes.'

There followed the usual scratching and farting that all soldiers excel at in the early morning but little was said. Nick went over his kit for the final time. He smeared his face and hands with army issue camouflage cream. Like the SAS men he wore a black jump suit and a dark blue seaman's woolly hat was pulled down over his ears. An ear defender was in his right hand, ready to be rammed into place as soon as he had made the decisive phone call; his left ear was already protected. He had chosen a reverse shoulder holster on the outside of the jumpsuit to carry the Glock 17 and a respirator was slung around his waist on an issue forty-five pattern webbing belt. If the smoke and stun grenades didn't do the trick they would resort to gas. Hanging from the left side of the belt in a webbing sheath was a twelve inch hunting knife. A spare magazine of nineteen rounds in his front pocket gave him thirty-eight shots. If he needed more ammunition that this it would be because they had botched it and been forced into a stand-off situation. That was "deep-shit" too terrible to be contemplated.

The back door team was in position and apart from the bomb squad only three SAS men remained; they would go through the front door with Steve. The first silvery-grey chinks of dawn were illuminating the chill Cheshire morning; perfect conditions for a dawn attack.

'Give me three minutes to get as close as I can, then make the call.' instructed Steve. The door of the stable opened onto the grey early morning light and Steve and his men were gone. Nick checked his watch and looked around the stable, now empty apart from the six bomb squad men sitting quietly, looking slightly dubious. Nick guessed that he looked more than a little terrifying in his latest fashion creation. The second hand of his watch swept to the three-minute mark. He lifted the red telephone receiver and the number rang immediately. There was no answer. Hopefully Abdul and his cronies were all sleeping.

'Come on Abdul, pick up!' His voice sounded irritated, then . . .

'What the fuck trick do you think you bastards are playing?' Abdul sounded angry.

'Abdul, it's Nick Trevelyan Abdul—"Sword of Freedom". Nicks voice was calm, clear and concise, speaking the words that he hoped would drop the key domino and set the rescue plan into action, triggering the commands implanted into Abdul's subconscious. Nothing happened. Nick's heart pounded. He fixed his eyes on the bomb disposal men who looked at each other, totally confused. Taking the Glock 17 from its shoulder holster he cocked it, hearing the satisfactory sound of a round slamming into the breach, then checked the safety catch and replaced it in its holster. Still nothing, then he heard the receiver at the other end hit something hard. There was another pause when in the distance Abdul's voice shouted out:

'Traitor! Bastard! Traitor! 'The next sound was three shots fired in quick succession from what sounded like a 9mm handgun. All hell broke loose.

## Release the dogs of war.

A cacophony of sound broke the tranquillity of the quiet Cheshire countryside: explosions, gunshots, breaking glass, women's screams and ferocious shouting from wild, angry, crazy men. Nick dropped the handset, kicked the door open and started to sprint the three hundred metres to the house, ramming the remaining ear defender into his right ear as he went. There were more explosions from stun grenades, more gunshots and still the screaming continued. He covered the first two hundred metres without difficulty but slowed as he hit the gravel drive; he removed the Glock from its holster and flicked off the safety catch. Bounding up the front stairs and through the porch he launched himself into the main room.

What he found was a scene from hell; within such a short time the destruction was incredible. Smoke hung everywhere, the intermittent explosions from the G60 stun grenades and the gunshots were deafening. But worse was the screaming from both men and women. Nick wondered who was doing the screaming. The tactic to create maximum was being achieved in a spectacular manner.

Nick attempted to make sense of the scene in which he was now a principal actor. At the top of the oak staircase an SAS man appeared, manhandling a young woman who Nick assumed must be Sir Humphrey's other daughter whom he hadn't seen earlier; the SAS man's left hand gripped her upper right bicep whilst his right held an Uzi machine gun. He dragged the screaming woman down the stairs, shouting at her all of the way. She was on the verge of collapse, perhaps the shouting was the only thing keeping her going. She was being rescued from a nightmare by a madman. Finesse was not the order of the day. Their regiment has a saying. "Maximum force, maximum aggression".

Where was Abdul and, more to the point, where was Rashid?

Nick had turned to make for the library when his question was answered. Rashid was lying on the floor, staring into space with three neat 9mm. holes in his forehead. A pool of deep crimson blood formed the shape of a halo reminiscent of a Russian icon on the floor around his head. The detonator button looked intact. '*Thank God for that!*' Nick thought. There was a movement to his right. It was Abdul lurching forward like a crazed maniac, his gun blazing but not aimed at any specific target; his thoughts were focused on Rashid's body and the detonator. The only redemption for him now was to reach it and send them all to Allah. Nick dropped to one knee, reducing his target size, took aim and squeezed the trigger. The Glock barked three times. Abdul spun backwards like a contorted ballerina with the impact of the bullets. Two torso shots and one throat shot had done their job; He was dead before he hit the floor.

Then silence, uncanny silence. Nick felt a hand on his shoulder. It was Steve. There was blood on his jump suit but Nick could see that it wasn't his own. Steve motioned to him to take out his ear defenders, which he did, only to notice that all was not so quiet. There were still the sounds of women screaming and crying. Even with the protection of ear defenders his hearing had been impaired from the power of the stun grenades. But thankfully it was over.

'What's the butcher's bill, Steve?' he inquired hesitantly.

'All aliens dead.'

'No operatives dead or injured?'

'One hostage fatality. A solemn list.' Steve grimaced. 'That's seven dead in all.' his voice must have betrayed his revulsion.

'Which one of the hostages bought it?'

'Poor old Postman Pat. He was cuffed to a radiator in an upstairs bedroom. When one of our men came through the window, an alien managed to get off a shot. Pat was in the way and stopped it—a classic case of being in the wrong place at the wrong time.'

A Captain from the Bomb Squad arrived and reported that all the bombs had been neutralized.

'Thank you, Captain. Tell your lads 'well done,' said Steve. The house and garden were filling with police, fire-fighters and paramedics.

'Nothing more for us here', he said. More police had arrived and were taking over the situation; Steve handed over responsibility to the senior officer. The SAS team had congregated in the main room.

'OK lads, back to the stable for a quick debrief.'

In the stable, all the documentation from the event was being bundled into black bin liners and then thrown into the back of an RAF coach, commandeered from a local air base. The SAS team had changed clothes and cleaned themselves up as much as they could. They filed onto the coach, looking more like a group of cabbage-picking agricultural workers than an elite fighting force. Steve gave instructions to the sergeant major and the bus moved off, leaving Steve and Nick in front of the stable. Nick was about to inquire how they were getting back to London when the BMW with Mick at the wheel came around the corner.

'Take us back to London, Mick.'

'OK Guv. Did everything go well?'

'Yes, good job, Mick. By the way, what happened to that whale in the Thames?'

'I'm afraid she died, Sir.'

Mick was an excellent driver; the BMW sped along the M6 keeping well within the speed limit which, Nick guessed, was not his normal method of driving. No need to draw attention to themselves considering the mini arsenal inside the car boot which would require a lot of explaining if they were stopped. The three of them settled into the journey. Getting back to London by car was going to take a lot longer than getting there by helicopter. Mick produced an I-Pod, from which occasional snatches of Santana, Guns and Roses and Meatloaf could be heard. The car was fitted with the latest high-tech communication gadgetry. Several phones which Nick knew would be scrambled rang constantly. Steve was busy de-briefing the hierarchy, which was only to be expected in the aftermath of an operation of this magnitude. For his part there was nothing more to do other than sit back and relax. Nick managed to sleep a little while Steve busied himself on the phones.

His thoughts focused on Steve. He really was on top of his job, the British Government was fortunate to have such a dedicated professional man in the team. Over the years Nick had come to know Steve perhaps better than anyone. He knew his history; as a youngster he had been a tear-away but the army had sorted him out. He had started his army career in the Junior Leaders' Regiment at sixteen and worked his way up. But for this fortunate break he would most likely have been thrown onto the scrap heap of British society and like so many others never achieving his full potential. More and more a new breed of officer was passing through Sandhurst. Men who displayed ability over nobility of which Steve was a fine example.

Finally as they cruised along the M42 through Oxfordshire the calls to Steve ended and he was able to talk.

'You did an excellent job there, Nick.'

'Happy to be of assistance.' Nick replied. Nothing more needed to be said such was their friendship.

His first assignment as an agent had been a success and the future looked bright, but it had been a long, rocky path that had brought him to this conclusion.

# Knightsbridge

Steve's car wove its way expertly through the London traffic. His personal driver and right hand man, Mick, was at the wheel mumbling a continuous stream of abuse at all of the other road users, and taxi drivers in particular.

'If you keep on like that, Mick, you will be a prime candidate for a heart attack.' Steve advised his driver.

Mick took no notice and continued to sling incoherent abuse. Steve turned to the other passenger in the back of the vehicle.

'Got a nice little task for tomorrow morning if you're interested.' Steve smiled in a wickedly childlike manner exposing another side of his character.

'Oh yeah, and what would that be?' Nick's suspicions were immediately aroused.

'Nothing heavy. In fact quite the opposite. This could prove to be a light diversion after today's action.'

Steve went on to explain that on the top floor of the twelve storey accommodation block at Knightsbridge Barracks, located on the edge of Hyde Park. there is a clandestine location which houses secret surveillance equipment. 'We need to go there and inspect the place. It's a periodical event and I have volunteered us for the job.'

Nick could see from Steve's face that this was something of a set-up but agreed to go along with the plan.

'Eight-thirty tomorrow morning at Legoland,' he added, leaning forward and pulling the ear-piece from Mick's ear.

'Eight o'clock tomorrow morning at Legoland, Mick!' he shouted into the driver's ear.

'OK Boss, where are we going?'

'To see the "Piccadilly Cowboys" at Knightsbridge Barracks,'

'Oh by the way, Nick, full number two dress for us; we will be having breakfast in the officer's mess.'

Next morning they met at Number 85, Albert Embankment. They were both dressed in their respective Khaki uniforms and looked very much the part. Mick still looked as if he had been mixing concrete.

'Bloody hell, Guv! We don't get to see you in the ginger suit too much these days—you look quite respectable.'

'Where's your khaki suit, Mick?' asked Steve.

'Sold it at a car boot sale. Some young trendy must be walking around dressed as a Grenadier Guard colour sergeant.'

'Remind me to have you locked up sometime, will you please, Mick?'

'Yes Guv.'

As they were from slightly unusual units the guard at the gates of Knightsbridge Barracks must have been puzzled but even so, he flung up a smart salute as they drove in, having seemingly worked out who they were. Nick considered the advantages that his new position was affording him. His insignia was less well known than Steve's but never the less it impressed.

'Christ, Guv, this place stinks of horse shit,' observed Mick in his own inimitable way as we parked close to the stables.

'Behave yourself Mick, go and have a walk around Harrods. There is some lovely totty in the perfume department. I'll call you on your mobile when we're ready to go, and do your best to keep out of trouble.'

The NCO guard commander had immediately recognized that they were something special. He knew that the light grey beret of an SAS officer is a rare sight as is the green beret of the Intelligence Corps. The SAS beret badge of inverted wings and dagger commands total respect in any sector of the armed forces. He flung up a smart salute, booked them in and pointed them in the direction of the Officers' Mess.

The present Knightsbridge Barracks was re-built in 1970 on the site of the original one. It is a modern building incorporating some of the features from the previous barracks. The officer's mess, as would be expected, is lavish. In the entrance foyer, Steve and Nick placed their berets on a long, highly polished antique table. The table had been with the Household Cavalry for centuries and over the years the headgear of kings, princes and generals had adorned it. Such illustrious characters as The Duke of Wellington would undoubtedly have placed their hats upon it. In more recent times, The Princess Royal would have put her hat there as the Colonel of The Blues and Royals and Princes William and Harry would have done the same as young officers in the same regiment. Steve and Nick were from units whose officers wore berets. There were already a dozen or so cavalry officers' forage caps heavily adorned with gold braid laid on the table. Next to these their berets looked like no more than two pieces of grey and green cloth, decidedly shabby in comparison emulating a poor relative syndrome. They looked at each other, a look which spoke a thousand words. The table seemed to epitomize the struggle that together they had fought against for so long. This was one of the inner sanctums of the aristocratic elite.

'The Colonel is expecting us, Nick, so we can anticipate excellent eggs and bacon.'

'Do you think that they will have 'Daddies' Sauce?' Nick enquired.

They walked into the dining room. There were about a dozen officers sitting at the long table. All looked up as they walked in, the insignia on their guests uniforms causing interest. Steve allowed Nick to walk ahead, a little in expectation of the next event. He wasn't to be disappointed. Nick's old adversary Tristram Wrath-Bingham was sitting at the far end of the table. Bloody hell. Nick should have seen this coming. Steve had set him up, good and proper. Immediately Tristram saw Nick he sprang to his feet.

'What the fuck are you doing here, Trevelyan? Nick allowed time for a pause before answering; he could feel Steve standing two paces behind. There was a total hush in the room. All eyes focused on him.

'You might like to re-think that statement CAPTAIN.

What the fuck are you doing here COLONEL TREVELYAN?' Nick answered. The moment was exquisite. Tristram threw down his napkin and stormed out of the room like a schoolboy in a fierce tantrum. Nick watched him leave, relishing the moment. Steve took a few paces forward and stood by his side, clearing his throat in a theatrical manner. Nick took a half glance sideways and could see that he was grinning like a Cheshire cat. The silence was broken by a cavalry officer who stood up and welcomed them to the table. They were soon engrossed in conversation. Nick got the feeling that anyone who put the dislikeable TR-B in his place was welcome in this mess. This was a case of revenge being best served on an empty stomach. Nick sat down at the seat, still warm, so recently vacated by RR-B and enjoyed a breakfast that he would remember for a long time. Steve and Nick carried out the inspection which was the reason for their visit and later walked out into the winter sunshine and onto the Knightsbridge Barracks parade ground. Steve turned to Nick and put out his hand for him to shake, looking him straight in the eyes.

'Well my old friend, today we have finally laid the ghost that has been your worst demon ever since I have known you. More good news is that after I reported your part in yesterday's little Cheshire drama to my superiors, I am delighted to be able to tell you that your commission is confirmed and irrevocable, unless that is you decide to chin the wrong person again.'

There didn't seem much that Nick could say apart from 'thanks' but such was the deep bond of friendship between them that nothing else was necessary.

While Steve busied himself booking them out of the guardroom and trying to locate Mike, Nick strolled out through the ornate front gates of the barracks, across the road and into Hyde Park. He walked across Rotten Row and stood looking out across the park towards central London. Alone, he had time to consider the events of the past. His future was set, he was doing what he was born to do and it felt good. "Raison d'être". Looking back even further to the crazy series of events that had brought him to where he was now, it was impossible to stop himself from laughing out loud. The past years had certainly been one hell of a roller coaster. As we tread the bumpy path of life we encounter many individuals. They all leave an impression upon us, good or bad, some more than others. Nick had just won a small battle over his nemesis Tristram Wrath—Bingham but he wondered if this was the end of their war or just a temporary ceasefire. His mind wandered back to that day at Sandhurst and the first time that he had the misfortune to encounter TR-B. In contemplating our personal history it's easy to look back and wonder, what if? But life isn't like that. It is lived forward.

## The new agent

Nick's success at the hostage siege had set him off at a cracking pace in his new role as a special operative. His superiors were delighted that their gamble had paid off so handsomely. They were convinced that they had a special ace up their sleeves with Colonel Nicholas Trevelyan but it was imperative that his skill as a hypnotist should remain a close guarded secret in order for it to be used to its full potential.

MI6 had tidied up all of the loose ends but handing back the proceeds of his exploits was considered to be virtually impossible. And so it was decided that he should continue to live the life of a successful financial consultant which was to be his new cover story. Nick cracked open a bottle of champagne soon after hearing this and shared it with Steve. He was financially off the hook, life looked rosy and he had been saved from who knows what. Most likely jail.

'Make no mistakes, Nick; there will be times when to do so might make you regret taking the Queen's Shilling again. This isn't the Boy Scouts.'

'Yes, I know that, but I'm more than happy to take my chances.' He didn't need to think too long about his answer as he loved his new career.

The year-long specialist training had taken him away from his flat but he had returned whenever possible to maintain the cover story.

As the dust of the proceeding years and the stress of the intensive training settled, Nick found himself fitting comfortably into his new way of life. As for Tamsen, well it was as if his memory possessed an internal protection system which had automatically kicked in; he actually found it difficult to conjure up and sustain pictures of her in his mind. They were there and then they were gone, like bubbles. No matter how hard he tried to evoke a vision of her, it was there only for a second and then it drifted away.

Everything from his adventures in the vaults had been cleared up; his bank accounts were left as they had been without noticeable intervention. All of his assets remained in his ownership. In fact he was now whiter than white. The team from MI6 had been thorough but the only place that they hadn't managed to penetrate was his own deposit box at the vaults. Opening up the "can of worms" which was his financial life had caused them untold problems which made them arrive at the decision that the safety deposit cache was far better left alone.

Living in Windsor gave Nick a great base; he was able to get into the West End of London where all of the best exclusive clubs and restaurants were located. He had been given a list by his section leader of several people who were of interest to MI6. He was to attempt to befriend them and the easiest way to do this was to be seen at these exclusive locations as a frequent punter and cultivate a circle of friends who would in turn move him onto the targets that he was aiming for. There were many mornings when he found himself driving back to Windsor, along the M4, as the dawn was breaking.

## A little self examination

The enigma of the strange papers that he had discovered—and liberated—from the vaults over a year previously was eating away at him; he could see that the sketches were old and therefore most probably valuable. They could also have historical significance but how could he establish their authenticity? Furthermore, what were they describing? From what he could see, they appeared to be depicting the Earth. There were parallels of latitude and meridians of longitude.

From schoolboy science, Nick recognised the representation of the poles and the earth's magnetic fields. But it was all slightly naively drawn. The text, on the other hand, looked complex but in what language? Although the spacing between the words was uniform, the actual letters were strange, appearing to be almost inside out. Perhaps they were from a time when little was known about the solar system. Galileo came to mind. Nick looked him up and found that he lived from 1564-1642.

The sketches certainly looked as if they could be from that era. This was a riddle wrapped within a mystery.

The spy game turned out to be less intensive than Nick had expected. His training alongside the other operatives was vigorously kept up; they were updated regularly on any new surveillance equipment and weaponry that became available. He was shown the location of all safe houses and other places that might be needed in an emergency. All of this was interesting and allowed him to get out and about but there were also plenty of tedious hours spent in 'The Paper Archives' which were housed in the basement of Thames House. This was where the pre computer files were kept and Nick was expected to spend any free working hour mugging up on old cases and contacts. His predecessors had signed hundreds of contracts and set up dozens of spy networks recruiting sleeper agents as far back as WW2. Any of these agents—who were still alive of course might be of potential use and he was expected to acquaint himself with all of this information.

This for Nick was purgatory. He hated sitting at any desk let alone one in a basement. Weekly, he could book himself an hour on the ranges where he honed his shooting ability. There was one advantage to spending time in the paper archives which was that he was mostly alone and contrary to the title, there were computers. This gave him the opportunity to access files that would not have been available to the general public. He looked into everything that he could find on Rudolf Hess and indeed Alfred Horne but his frustration was only compounded by the endless dead ends that he was encountering. He even looked into Leonardo Da Vinci and Galileo but he discovered nothing new.

If nothing was happening then his weekends were clear. It was on just such a weekend, a bright sunny day that Nick took his Jag for a spin with the top down. There was something that was bothering him and driving allowed him to focus and concentrate on this quandary with more clarity.

As he headed back towards home, things were beginning to resolve themselves in his mind. His route had taken him out of Windsor to the west and as he returned, his course brought him through The Great Park along the road which passes directly through the centre of the park. He pulled the car over, turned off the engine and allowed the silence to envelope him. In the distance was the castle where he could see the royal standard fluttering on the Round Tower in the light breeze. HM the Queen was at home. His mind wandered as he gazed at the gnarled oak trees that lined the main road through the park. These were trees that he had never seen in any location other than in the park. Any one of them would not have looked out of place in a Tolkien story. Their planting must have been deliberate but for what purpose? No sawmill in the world could have cut a straight plank out of them. He mentally made a note to check out the reason for their existence. Meanwhile his mind returned to more relevant matters. The dilemma which was bugging him was three fold. Should he go back to the vaults? Could this somehow implicate Tom Holland if he were to be discovered? He had confided all of his misdemeanours to Steve—all except one—the mysterious papers in the vaults. Was withholding this fact a betrayal of their friendship?

Inwardly he knew what his final decision would be but he needed to put himself through the mental process of questioning his actions. Tom Holland was an honourable man who had shown Nick total trust and his loyalty to his employer was without question. Nick knew that he had taken advantage of their friendship, something of which he wasn't proud. He could reason with himself that it had been to manipulate Tom in order to get to the contents of the vaults; but the final vindication for Nick was that Tom's integrity had never in any way been compromised because of what he had done. Not telling Steve about the papers in the vaults was, he decided, immaterial; after all they could turn out to be nothing, little more than worthless. He was beating himself up on this account for nothing! The sun was now setting behind Ascot to the west and the evening was beginning to get chilly. Nick hit the automatic hood button; the convertible did what it said on the label; folding itself up like something from a Transformers movie. He was cosy inside his sleek roadster. His mind was made up. He would go back to the vaults.

## Return to the Vaults

Tom Holland was elated when Nick called him.

'Hi, Nick! Where the hell have you been?' he asked excitedly. Nick wondered if there would be any animosity which might have been caused by the visit he had received from Timothy Harcourt, but Tom sounded genuinely delighted to hear from him.

'It's a long story Tom, which I'd be delighted to tell you all about over lunch if you can find the time to be my guest.' A convenient time was arranged later in the week. 'I look forward to seeing you, Nick, and hearing all about your adventures.'

And so Thursday morning found Nick joining the ranks of the commuters taking the train from Windsor to Slough, and on to Paddington where he took the underground to Chancery Lane. Parking in London was something of a nightmare. When he was officially in London, he could use the underground parking in Thames House but today was different. This venture was a private affair and if anyone did feel like following him, they would need to be good to keep up with him on the underground.

Tom was waiting on the steps in front of the vaults. His delight at seeing Nick was obvious and dispelled any worries that he had about his being suspicious of Nick's long disappearance. They walked out along Chancery Lane heading south towards Fleet Street and on to Tom's favourite restaurant.

Once they were settled, Nick began to tell his story. He would have had to admit that he felt a little guilty that what he was about to relate was a pack of lies but as far as he could see, no harm could come from it.

'So you see, Tom, the call came from out of the blue. An uncle who was a plantation owner in Malaya died suddenly and as I was the only relative whose life style was flexible enough to allow me to go and administer his estate, I was volunteered by the family.' Rather a good story, Nick thought.

'Actually my first reaction was that this was going to be something of a nuisance but in reality it turned out to be a super little adventure.' Since Tom seemed to be buying the story, Nick added a few embellishments.

'The estate was just outside Mersing on the east cost of Malaysia, just north of Kuala Lumpur—a really beautiful place.' He had done his homework but was getting just a little too clever.

'Yes, I know it.' Tom interrupted; 'I was there in the late sixties attached to the Ghurkhas'

Oh-no, how unlucky can you get? This was going to need some quick thinking.

'Late sixties eh? You wouldn't know the place now, Tom, and K.L. has been transformed into a modern city in the past decades.'

'Yes I know, I've seen documentaries and the Sean Connery film which featured the twin towers. It was little more than a tatty village when I was there.'

The panic was over, Tom had accepted his story. Nick could feel that Tom was happy to see him again and remarked that he looked forward to their little chats when he told him that he would be starting work again on his long abandoned stamp collection.

Lunch over, they walked back to the vaults and Tom took him down to see Veronica and George who seemed equally pleased to see him again.

'Thought that you had left and forgotten all about us!' Veronica feigned grief.

'How could you think that?' Nick replied, mimicking her grief.

'Know what, Nick? I'm still not smoking. Been over eighteen months now,' she proudly announced.

'I'm delighted to hear it.' was his honest reply because she did look better for having kicked the habit. A sudden realisation hit him; he actually did miss them all.

'Well, while I'm here, I suppose I'd better get on with some work. My stamp collection isn't going to sort itself out. With this, their little reunion broke up and Veronica went off to fetch his security box.

Opening the box after a year was exciting. Nick knew exactly what was inside but the brown envelope with the mysterious papers had been gnawing away at him for months and was a mystery that he was determined to solve.

Saying his goodbyes and promising not to stay away so long in future, he left the vaults with the brown envelope tucked inside his overcoat. Once again he joined the early commuter rush returning to the suburbs and, in his case, his bachelor flat.

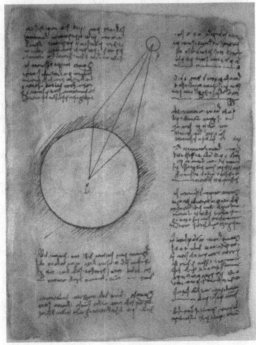

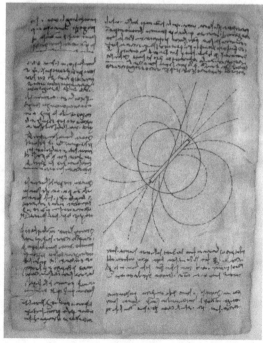

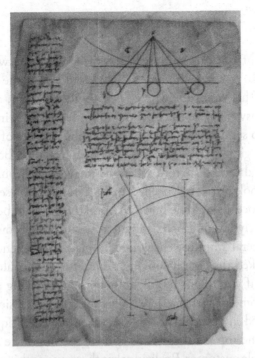

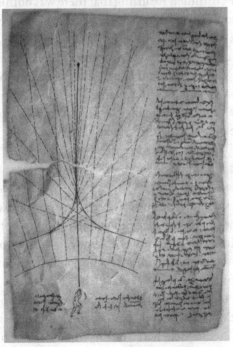

# The Oxford Bookshop

Weeks went by and the puzzle prevailed. When he was alone in his apartment with a spare moment, Nick would take the sketches from the bottom of his wardrobe where he had hidden them, and attempt to discover the answer to the riddle, but with little success. Finally, he gave in and decided to seek outside help. He made photocopies of all six sketches and put the originals back in his Chancery Lane security box. Armed with the copies, he drove to Oxford where he knew there would be plenty of antiquarian bookshops. He needed to be careful. If these artefacts were perhaps the proceeds of some previous burglary, he could be in deep water. He chose a likely looking book shop and went in; he browsed the musty shelves for several minutes checking the place out; then, when he was satisfied, he asked the elderly looking proprietor if he could help.

'I wonder if you might be able to help me, I'm trying to authenticate the origin of some papers that have come into my possession.' Nick asked the man dressed in tweeds who looked rather like an antique himself. He glanced over the top of his bifocals and then around the store in which Nick was the sole customer. Realizing that there was nothing of significance happening, he somewhat begrudgingly agreed to oblige. Nick produced the photocopies, and images of the Antiques Road Show flashed through his mind. The next six minutes were excruciating. 'Tweedy' said nothing; he grunted many times leafing through the pages until Nick thought that he would crack and shout at the man. '*Well what do you think?*' but he managed to stay calm until finally the expert looked up from the pages, his piercing blue eyes staring directly at him.

'Mr. er . . . .' 'Tweedy' was searching for a name.

'My name is Thomas Holland,' Nick said, using the first name that came into his head.

'Well, Mr. Holland, you have chosen wisely this morning, I assume that you took pot luck when deciding which shop to come into?' He was getting to be a little too inquisitive. If the worst came to the worst, Nick might be forced to do nothing more than snatch the photocopies and run off into the Oxford traffic.

'My name is Dr. Marcus Oatley. I am, as you have correctly surmised, an expert on antique books and manuscripts, my specialist subject being Leonardo Da Vinci.' Nick had another memory flash which featured 'Mastermind'.

'I have to tell you, young man, that in my, may I say learned opinion, these photocopies could be of sketches drawn by none other than Leonardo himself.' Nick tried hard not to gulp visibly. This was obviously a man not given to joking. He continued, 'I pride myself on knowing all of the da Vinci notebooks and sketches, of which there are many. These sketches, if they are indeed genuine, and I would need to examine the originals myself to confirm their authenticity, would have never been seen before.' The full magnitude of what Dr Oatley had just said was beginning to sink in.

'Do you have any idea, Mr. Holland, of the potential value of these articles?' The Antique Road Show flashed through his mind again.

'Well I was rather wondering.' he said, feeling decidedly greedy.

'The fact of the matter is that, if they are genuine, then the value is whatever you would care to ask for them. They are practically priceless.' The statement hit Nick straight between the eyes like a cricket bat.

'The existing known da Vinci sketches are owned by such distinguished places as Musee du Louvre, Paris; The Royal Library-Windsor Castle, Budapest-Szepmmuveszeti Museum, Biblioteca Nacional, Madrid which might give you some idea of the level of esteem at which this work is held. You might also be interested in the subject matter Mr Holland.' Dr. Oatley continued. He was in his element now and getting quite excitedly fired up.

'Da Vinci was interested in the solar system and these diagrams depict the rotation of the earth on its axis, the gravitational pull and magnetic poles. He was way ahead of his time as I'm sure you know from your school days.' explained the connoisseur. This was astounding news indeed and might shed some light upon the Hess connection but that information was not for the ears of the learned doctor at this point.

'Da Vinci was convinced of the negative gravity theory at the poles and these are the diagrams which he used to demonstrate his supposition.' enthused the expert.

'Wow, Dr. Oatley, that certainly is a revelation. I'm slightly shocked.' Nick could bring himself to utter nothing but his truthful feelings. He was actually warming to the wily old antiquarian and he guessed from the way he was smiling now that the feeling was mutual.

'Mr. Holland, if that is in fact your name, I'm going to be totally frank with you.' Nick saw a twinkle in the old man's eyes that he hadn't noticed before.

'I would hazard a guess that you have come by these extraordinary artefacts by surreptitious means. That is of no consequence to me. I am now an old man. I have very little by the way of family, and my only true love is Renaissance books and manuscripts. In all of my years exploring historical literature I have never encountered anything as astonishing as what you have shown me today. I have no interest in how you came by these treasures but I would beg you to treat them with the utmost care because they could be of immense historical value to the entire world. You must understand that at a very conservative estimate each of the sketches would be worth a minimum of a million pounds and combined, ten million would be considered an extremely low figure.'

Any fear that Dr. Oatley would blow the whistle on Nick disappeared with the last statement. He considered himself a good judge of character and his gut reaction was that this man was being totally honest.

'Dr. Oatley, it is obvious that you are an astute man and I would guess that you are also a good judge of character.' Nick said. 'Your idea that my getting hold of the drawings less than honestly is correct but then I would like to think that it was also not entirely shameful because, if it hadn't been for me they would still be hidden.' I continued. 'You can rest assured that I will take good care of them and do the right thing whatever that might be' his voice was calm and sincere because he meant what he was saying.

'However they came into your possession is of no interest to me.' continued the expert. My only wish is that you find a way of bringing them into public view so that they can be analysed and enjoyed by all. Here is my card. I would ask you to please keep me informed regarding the progress you make. Please do not hesitate to call me should you need help on the matter. I will be more than happy to assist.' They shook hands and Nick walked out of the quiet mustiness of the shop and into the bustling Oxford street.

During the drive home the real significance of what he had just heard began to impact. He had managed to solve half of the puzzle but there still remained the Hess connection and he now carried the burden of disposing of something that was worth several millions of Pounds. He felt some comfort in the knowledge that the originals were locked away safely in his safety deposit box under the watchful eyes of Tom, Veronica and George.

As the days passed, he pieced together the facts that he had collected. They were purely a list of information and known events. The story of

Hess's involvement could only be speculation. He listed the facts that he knew.

- Hess flew to Scotland in 1941.
- His treatment by the British authorities could only be considered bizarre.
- Somehow Hess managed to put the documents in the Chancery Lane Safety Deposit.
- The Da Vinci sketches depicted;
1. Angle of earth's tilt on axis.
2. Earth's magnetic field. Object entering orbit, due to earth's gravitational pull.
3. Object leaving earth, not affected by earth's gravitational pull.
4. Orbital satellites. E.g. Moon.
5. Parallels of latitude; effects of gravitational pull lessening towards poles.
6. Diagram of the vortex effect present at the North and south poles.

Somehow these facts were the ingredients that caused Hess to make a life altering decision, but Nick could only guess at the missing pieces of the jigsaw. Germany at that time was making tremendous advances in rocket science. They were also close to perfecting an atomic bomb.

If da Vinci's assumption was correct and the negative gravity theory of the poles actually existed then if the German V rockets could somehow be launched from the poles there would be significantly less fuel required to send them into space and from there to orbit the planet. They would be able to carry a heavier pay-load which could be the almost completed atom bomb. All of this added up but why then did Hess take the papers out of Germany?

Nick felt as if he had solved part of the puzzle but there were still plenty of pieces missing. He had made some progress in the paper archives on his Hess riddle but the answers still continued to elude him. He knew that if he was to enlist the services of Orville, the section computer genius, he would come up with the answer but at this moment this was his problem and his alone.

# Juliet Section

As a new operative in SIS, Nick had been assigned to Juliet Section which consisted of himself and five other agents. His first impressions were that his new colleagues were less than obvious 'spooks'. There were three operatives who more or less fitted the bill, i.e., two women and one man, fit, active and more than capable of looking after themselves in a tight spot. The fifth member of the team was a million miles away from the James Bond image that Nick had in his mind at that time. Orville Skippings was downright scruffy, which was actually a conservative description. Orville was bordering on rancid which was particularly evident towards the end of the week—leading Nick to the conclusion that Saturday or Sunday must have been his bath night. None of this mattered to the Section, for Orville was a genius. He epitomised the absent minded professor in every detail but none of this mattered once he got behind a computer. It was a joy to watch him practically make the computer sing and dance. Orville could hack into a cuckoo clock and make it bark. This man was a rare asset in the world of espionage. He could break codes and hack into anything and everything in seconds.

Juliet Section was led by Edward Fitzpatrick. Edward was a quietly spoken Irishman, a scholar and very much a gentleman. His role involved liaising with the Home Office and heads of security organisations on a global level. Nick estimated that he was in his early sixties which meant that his service had spanned decades of world conflict, in particular, the Cold War period. All of this made his knowledge base remarkable.

This, then, was his new group of workmates. Steve was based in the same building but his remit was more at Cabinet level attending all Cobra meetings. When the nasty stuff happened it was Steve who was called for; he dealt with the heavy details and his SAS teams were regularly in action. Nick was a sort of floater between Juliet Section and Steve's unit.

# Tamsen Returns

Six weeks passed. Nick was involved in several minor operations but his specialist ability hadn't been called upon. He was getting used to his new role and enjoying life again. It was important that he became established as a part of the West London scene. Terrorism operated at all levels and it was imperative to have operatives implanted into every plane of the social scale.

Starbucks was one of his favourite local coffee venues. He enjoyed walking through Windsor, buying the everyday things that he needed and stopping for a coffee before returning to the flat. His training had covered all aspects of intelligence work including surveillance. That day, there was something different, Being a Tuesday, he had made his customary visit to his bank and as it was raining he lingered a little longer in WH Smith looking for something to read. Something that he couldn't quite get a handle on was worrying him. Within the depths of his sixth sense, a distant warning bell was beginning to ring. The coffee house felt warm and cosy after the miserable rainy day outside, he ordered a latte and sat down at a window seat. From here he could observe people coming in and out of the coffee house.

'Hello, Nick.' Tamsen appeared next to the table; she must have been in the building when he arrived.

'Tamsen!' His surprise was impossible to hide. It took a while to regain his composure; 'Or is it really 'Tamsen'? Everything else about you was a lie so I imagine your name was, too'

'Yes—you're right, Nick, my real name is Sian. Nick, I am so sorry for what I did to you. I know that you will never forgive me—but I just had to see you again and tell you that my feelings for you were real.'

His emotions were confused. Seeing Tamsen again was a shock; she was just as beautiful as ever. During the months that had passed since she so callously walked out, he had had plenty of time to think about the cruelty of her actions and yet so much had changed in his life over the last twelve months. He recalled one of the lecturers at GCHQ telling them:

*"Once someone is recruited into an intelligence agency albeit the KGB or CIA or whatever, they will never be allowed to leave."*

And now, Tamsen/Sian was playing him. He could feel it. But what did she want? Did she know what his role in the cloak and dagger world of espionage was now? He needed to find out more. He went along with the game; this had to be checked out, it was all too pat.

'I want you to know that I was being controlled by the CIA, and you were my first assignment. If it's any consolation to you, after that mission I was taken off field duties as it was thought that I had allowed myself to become too deeply involved with my 'mark'. They put me behind a desk.

I stuck it for almost a year, then resigned.' Acting as casually as he could, Nick drank the remains of his coffee.

'Sian, saying the name made him feel uncomfortable I'm afraid that I have to go now. I'm late for an appointment, but I'd love to talk to you more. How about dinner tonight? Are you in town for long?'

'That would be lovely! Can we meet here at seven thirty?'

The date was fixed and they each walked out into the street and went their separate ways while the pipes and drums of the Grenadier Guards marched up the hill from Victoria Barracks to change the guard at the castle. Nick needed to call Steve urgently but couldn't take the risk of calling from his flat which he now suspected could have been bugged. The sudden appearance of someone with Sian's background was far too suspicious. His cell phone was secure; he sat on a bench in front of the castle and made the call to Steve. Nick explained what had happened.

'Were you at the de-briefing when I was raided last year?' he asked

'Yes of course I was. After you called me from Paddington Green, I demanded to be there.'

'Did Tamsen ever know the full extent of what I was up to?'

'No, we kept them in the dark as much as we could. Once it was established that you were simply a serial criminal and not a terrorist risk, the CIA immediately lost interest in you and pulled out.'

'So she doesn't know the full extent of your hypnotic ability and what went on in the vaults?'

'No they were severely frustrated when their highly sophisticated listening devices didn't work underground. They went dead as soon as you entered the vaults.'

'What do you think she's after, Steve?'

'No idea, mate. Could be that suave charm of yours—but I would guess that there is a deeper motive. You will have to play along but, this time, don't get burned.'

'Don't worry, my memory is good. I can still see her face when we got hit; her only reaction was annoyance at having her cover blown.'

He returned to the flat. Steve had sent over a two-man team and the building was swept for bugs. None were found. At the same time, they installed minute surveillance cameras which covered the living room. Any intruder would have to pass through there.

'All done, Guv—, no bugs here,' said the operative in charge who looked rather like the senior of two regular GPO engineers. His admiration for the organization that Nick had become part of, was increasing by the day. Steve's ability to call up operatives and have them on his doorstep within the hour was impressive. In the comfort of knowing that the flat was not bugged, Nick relaxed, wondering how best to deal with the situation. He put on some classical music and immersed himself in thought. Ironically he realized that he was listening to Nigel Kennedy playing Vivaldi's '*Four Seasons*' music that Tamsen had introduced him to, in what now seemed like a lifetime ago.

That evening he picked her up in his Jag and drove to a trendy restaurant in Ascot. They decided on a secluded table and took their time eating, enjoying the meal. The wine was excellent, the atmosphere was relaxed and Nick chose his time to make the next move. There was nobody within earshot and the waiters had completed the greater part of their work. It was now time to attempt to hypnotize Sian. He had to be very subtle and, as always, the feeling that this might be the time when it didn't work, was gnawing at his insides.

'Sian, look at me, look into my eyes.' slowly and gently he soothed her into a feeling of calm comfort.

'You know, Nick, I can't tell you how many times I have thought about you over the last year, but the most memorable and lasting image has to be your eyes. I have never seen anyone with eyes like yours. Two separate colours is weird but with you it has a wonderfully haunting effect.' Flattery is usually acceptable but this wasn't the time or place. He got her full concentration and continued with his work.

'Your eyes look quite tired, Sian, your legs and arms are feeling heavy too. Allow them to relax. Just let your eyes close.' Twenty seconds and she was under. Her head slumped slightly forward but to any of the other diners in the restaurant they appeared to be a couple deep in conversation. Nick waited for another two minutes to be sure that she was in deep hypnosis.

'Sian, I am going to ask you some questions which you will answer completely honestly.'

'Yes.' mumbled Sian.

'What do you think happened to me when you went back to the States?'

'You were caught stealing from the Chancery Lane vaults. You were not a terrorist and so the CIA had no further interest in you. I made enquires and no charges were ever made against you as the whole affair

211

was too embarrassing for the authorities and was dropped.' Nick now knew that his cover was intact.

'Sian, why have you come back?'

'I have come for the da Vinci Papers.' Now this was a bombshell. He had to think fast for this was something that he hadn't anticipated.

'How do you know about the da Vinci Papers, Sian?'

'I went through your apartment, cleaning, when you were in London. Don't you remember, I found your funny little painted toy figures and gave you a hard time over them. Then I discovered the papers. I made photocopies and at first thought nothing of them. Later I researched them and discovered that they are worth millions.' This all fitted, but how did she expect to get the papers from him?

'Sian, what is your next move?'

'Mr Palestroni wants me to gain your confidence and get more information about the papers.'

'Mr Who?'

'Caesar Palestroni. He is paying me to do this. He is very powerful. His men are watching everything that I do.'

Nick looked around the restaurant worried that he had been negligent. There was no one who looked suspicious but he decided that for now, he had enough information. His sixth sense had been right after all.

'Sian, I am going to waken you up, but before I do, I want you to remember these two words, *"Four Seasons"* and in the future whenever you hear me say them, you will immediately return to the state of trance that you are in now.'

He implanted the trigger words into Sian's subconscious which at any time in the future would render her instantly hypnotized. Before he was able to start the count down to bring Sian out of her trance a waiter suddenly arrived at the table.

'Would you like coffee, sir?' Nick glanced nervously at Sian but he had no need to worry. The waiter noticed nothing; he was busy concentrating on the forthcoming tip.

'No thank you, just the bill please.'

When he had gone, Nick bought Sian out of the trance. She blinked nervously several times and looked slightly embarrassed as if she had started a sentence and forgotten what she was talking about. Nick smiled inwardly as it appeared that whenever people were brought out of a trance they felt as if they were guilty of a temporary memory lapse. The evening ended on an affable note.

In the pub car park it didn't take a genius to spot a black Audi pulling out onto the Winkfield Row road at a discrete distance behind them as they left. It maintained that distance and stayed with them all the way back to Windsor. Nick wasn't unduly worried as Sian had told him that she was being followed and at this point there was no significant threat. Sian gave him her mobile number and they agreed to meet again soon. Nick dropped her off where he had picked her up in front of the castle.

Early next morning he met Steve at Thames House and told him what had happened the previous night. 'Steve, I have something to tell you that I think you ought to know.' It was time to tell Steve the whole story concerning the now authenticated da Vinci Papers. 'When I first discovered them I had no idea of exactly what they were.' Nick explained.

'They certainly looked authentic and were most undoubtedly old but it has only been recently that I have verified their origins.' Nick went on to recount his visit to Oxford and his meeting with Dr Marcus Oatley.

'Bloody hell, Nick, you certainly do have a knack for falling into shit and coming up smelling like a Chelsea Flower Show garden.'

'Yes I know all about that but what about this Italian connection?'

'Caesar Palestroni. Yes, we have masses on him.' Steve's secretary was sent to get the file on Signor Palestroni.

'I get the feeling that Sian is acting on her own in this matter. Seems as if she has her own agenda and may well have moved on from the CIA. I can have that checked out.' Steve surmised.

When the file arrived, it was huge. Palestroni was wanted by Interpol for a multitude of reasons: fraud, money laundering, political corruption, illegal arms dealing and, drugs. He was certainly not above resorting to homicide in order to achieve his ends. In his native Italy he was extremely high profile, half the country loved him and the other half hated him. He was undoubtedly corrupt but extradition laws protected him. France, Germany, Britain and the U.S.A. would all love to get their hands on him but he stayed within the protection of Italian law. He was immensely wealthy, his acquisitions stretching across all spheres of business from mining to technology. His principal residence was a villa in Sabina on the outskirts of Rome which was said to be extraordinary, housing what must be one of the world's greatest private art collections.

'He's a wily old bird by all accounts.' Steve mused. 'There have been plenty of attempts to entrap him and get him out of Italy but he is always one step ahead.'

In his mind a plan was beginning to emerge.

'We know that he wants the da Vinci Papers.' Nick concluded. 'Sian knows that they exist and that I have them. Remember, she took photo-copies. She is working independently for her own gain, which has to be why she is here. Palestroni is bank—rolling the operation. Steve, we are going to need copies. Can the boffins at GCHQ come up with something?'

'I'll get onto it right away.' Steve went off to make the calls. Nick poured himself a coffee from the peculator in Steve's office. It tasted awful. He read more of the Palestroni files; this was certainly a dangerous man if only half of the contents of the files were true. Dealing with him was going to be high risk. Steve returned after half an hour.

'This coffee is bloody awful.' Nick chided.

'Home Office issue—what do you expect?'

While you were away Steve, I contacted Orville and brought him up to speed on the Hess/Horne puzzle. He is looking into it and will have a report ready by eight this evening.

The da Vinci papers were playing a leading role in the Sian case and Nick had briefed Steve on all that he had managed to discover. It was now time to release the indomitable Orville onto the subject. If the mystery could be solved then the best brain in the world was now on the case.

'Good call, Nick. If that egghead can't sort it out, then it can't be sorted.'

'OK, the news from GCHQ is this. They have no problem with reproducing believable forgeries from the originals which will stand up to high levels of scrutiny. You will need to make photo-copies for the boffins to work from. The bad news is that they will have to be made on paper which is contemporary to the Da Vinci period, late 15th century. As you can imagine this is going to be difficult to source but not impossible. The first test Palestroni's experts will run will be on the paper. There is no way that this can be faked, so it has to be genuine.' Steve relayed the details of his enquiries.

'So tell me, Nick, what are you intending to do?'

'I want good copies of the da Vinci Papers that will keep Palestroni's academic specialists occupied long enough for me to get close to him. I

will use Sian to get me into his villa and I will have to play it by ear from that point. My intention is to get him out of the country to England or, better still, the States where he can stand trial. From what I have read in your files, he has supplied arms to most of the terrorist organizations in the world. He has to be stopped.'

'Just run that by me again. You intend getting yourself invited into the lion's den where you will serve him a set of counterfeit papers and then get him to give himself up?'

'That's more or less the idea.'

'Nick, you have had some pretty half-arsed plans in your time but this one wins the lottery. Once you go inside his villa we will have no way if getting you out. You will be completely alone. No wires, no weapons and no back-up.' Steve looked dismayed.

'Do you have any good news?' Nick asked.

'Yeah! Italian food is great and they do a mean line in wine,' he joked 'I can do it Steve, trust me, and just supply me with what I need.'

'I would give you more chance of success if you were to get yourself an invite to his next birthday party and arrive with a suicide bomber's waistcoat strapped around your middle. Anyway I have rather enjoyed working with you over the past twelve months. I might actually miss you.'

'Yeah, miss me buying your beers most weekends! But I will leave the keys of my car with you. I've noticed you drooling over it. I can cure you of that if you let me hypnotize you.' There was a pause while Steve was immersed in thought.

'Hang on, hang on; I've just had a notion. If you hypnotized me, I wouldn't know would I?'

'Nope!'

'So have you ever . . . .?'

'Have I ever what?'

'Hypnotized me, you dickhead.'

'Well, my old friend, that's for me to know and for you to worry about.'

Nick walked over to the window and looked out onto the drizzly London day and across the waters of the river Thames. What was he letting himself in for? If he were to be brutally honest with himself, well he didn't really know but the plan such as it was had been given the green light and was being put into action. Against all of his training Nick had no plan "B" to fall back on.

True to his word and on the dot, Orville walked into Steve's office. He plonked two folders onto the desk. Niceties were something that Orville didn't spend much time worrying about. He was a man of few words.

'It's all there. I've hacked into German archives and British WW2 intelligence files and I think that you are going to enjoy reading about Herr Hess and his adventures.' With that he was gone.

Steve sprayed the room with an air spray that he kept for just such visits. They looked at each other and laughed. Nick picked up the files and shook off a dusting of biscuit crumbs, then tossed one of the files over to Steve. They settled down to read. Within four days, the da Vinci Papers were copied and placed in the vaults with the originals. Nick called Sian and arranged to meet her for dinner the following Saturday.

She agreed and Nick used his time reading everything that he could on Palestroni plus familiarizing himself with the part of Italy where the villa was located.

## Germany, 1941

Rudolf Hess. Third in line as leader of the Glorious Reich (eyes only.)

Gravel crunched under the tyres of the sleek Mercedes Benz staff car as it pulled in a long curve and drove up to the heavily guarded crash barrier. An immaculate young SS officer snapped to attention opposite the driver and delivered an impressive salute to the high-ranking occupants in the rear of the vehicle.

The officer meticulously checked the identification of each of the car's occupants, even though all of the participants in the two-minute drama knew full well that the senior of the vehicles passengers was, after the Fuhrer, one of the best-known men in Germany and in fact the western world.

Rudolf Hess was impatient to leave the confines of Berchasgarden, the Fuhrer's Bavarian mountain retreat. The weekends when he was expected to attend the Fuhrer's social gatherings always left him feeling oddly frustrated, confused and disgusted. The frustration that had been steadily growing over the past months had become far stronger in recent weeks, as he realised that his role in the Fuhrer's plan was nothing more than that of a puppet. Hess was of use to Hitler simply as a figurehead. A hero of the First World War when he had served the Fatherland with gallantry and distinction, he epitomized all that was expected of a soldier of the Third Reich.

He felt like and indeed was, little more than a tailor's dummy, parading in the magnificent uniforms that his rank demanded; making stirring but empty speeches that were written for him by the Fuhrer's advisors, to the Fuhrer's requirements. Meeting only the people that the Fuhrer allowed him to meet, knowing that his every move would be reported back within hours or even minutes.

The disgust that he felt was disgust for himself. He knew full well that his military role was an empty one. As empty as the countless millions of spent shell cases which littered the landscape in the war-torn countries into which Germany had carried the Swastika. Disgust in himself as he displayed mock admiration for the man who, day by day, displayed the advancing ravings of a maniac, and was leading his beloved Germany to certain defeat, humiliation and perhaps even annihilation. And yet he, like so many others, did nothing to make a stand against this tyrant.

The adulation of the masses was hypnotic and the total admiration of his fellow officers massaged Hitler's ego and inflated his pride, beyond reason. For Hess, the weekends spent at Berchasgarden had become increasingly intolerable. Hitler surrounded himself with an inner circle of generals and government ministers, all of whom were forced to agree with, and act upon, his every whim. Otherwise strong men were silent in his presence and acted out the charade that their unhappy fate had made them part of.

The un-balancing of Adolf Hitler's mind was becoming more and more obvious during these nightmare weekends. He would change his uniform up to six times a day; he involved everyone present in the making of his home movies, much to their embarrassment' except for Eva Braun, who loved being photographed whenever the opportunity arose and the ever present children of Himmler, the Chancellor.

The retreat was a fortress, sixty miles southwest of Munich, garrisoned by Hitler's elite guard who were in evidence practically every six feet. Hitler was becoming increasingly paranoid about being assassinated. In this, there were many who agreed that there was indeed a threat to the life of the Fuhrer and many, many more who would have loved to see him dead.

The staff car wound its way down from the magnificent Bavarian mountains to the foothills, where the scenery changed from the ruggedness of the German Alps to the spectacular countryside known as the "Golden Land."

Rudolf Hess gazed through the window of the limousine, barely blinking as the beautiful countryside glided past. Here the trappings of the Third Reich and the evidence of war were less in evidence causing the motorcade of the vice Fuhrer's car and its escorts to bring a dramatic contrast to the otherwise idyllic rural scene.

The only other passenger in the car was Colonel Hann who was Hess's aide-de-camp. He was only too aware of the mood of his immediate superior, and knew from experience that the best policy was to keep as quiet as possible hoping that Hess would forget that he was even present. He knew from previous visits to Berchasgartten that, on the return journey as the kilometers slid past and Hess distanced himself from Hitler, he would slowly return to his former self.

Eventually Hess broke the uncomfortable silence. He enquired about the coming week's appointments and listened disinterestedly as his aide read out his coming engagements. As he had expected there was nothing of substance. Nothing in which he might be able to contribute to his nation's war strategy. Hitler as ever had made sure of that.

The only glimmer of interest was aroused by Tuesday's engagement. Hess had been given the task of supervising the unloading and cataloguing of several road and train convoys which were laden with art treasures that had been brought back to the Fatherland in an attempt to keep them safe from Allied bombs. This lame excuse appeased any sceptics who were offended by the operation which amounted to little more than looting in the name of The Third Reich. It was common knowledge that many of the treasures would never reach Berlin but would instead find their way into the numerous private hiding places known only to senior rich SS officers.

On Tuesday Hess the cavernous warehouse was already stacked high with every form of art treasure imaginable. And still the lorries rolled in, to disgorge their loot. Many of the artifacts had been professionally crated whilst others were simply wrapped in blankets. A team of historians and art experts would start pouring over the treasures as soon as they arrived. Occasionally something of particular importance would be un-crated or un-wrapped, creating a murmur of excitement causing everyone to congregate around the latest discovery.

The civilians present were highly educated academics and for the most part had little interest in the war. They were forced to be party to this twentieth century Aladdin's cave which was totally alien to their fundamental beliefs. Hess wandered from one group to another. The atmosphere in the warehouse was not difficult for him to detect. The art experts who found themselves part of the peculiar scenario all absolutely disagreed with the spectacle that was unfolding before them.

The magnificent collection of stolen art treasures, plundered from the greater part of Europe, represented centuries of culture and were now being greedily hoarded and stacked like so many sacks of corn. Hess himself greatly appreciated the beauty of art and was appalled by what he was witnessing. It would have been so easy for him to voice his agreement with those present and to decry the cultural rape that was being carried out in the name of *The Fatherland*. But to do so would be tantamount to suicide. Instead he had to maintain a strong facade of superiority which was to be expected of him, and refrained from being drawn into a discussion which might move towards disagreement of the matter in hand.

The morning passed while everyone got on with their work. Before too long the novelty of being under the same roof as the Deputy Fuhrer wore off and the art aficionados continued to fuss over the ever mounting treasure trove.

Lunch was a decidedly morbid affair; with art experts who were lucky or unlucky enough to find themselves seated at the top table with Hess remaining very guarded for fear of incriminating themselves. Hess himself was decidedly uneasy and guided the conversation towards obscure niceties of polite rhetoric. For his part he would have liked nothing more than to make full use of this unusual opportunity and immerse himself in a free flowing discussion with such a gathering of distinguished academics. But he needed to be guarded. All at the table were profoundly grateful when the meal had ended and each could return to their allotted tasks.

Rudolf Hess felt that he was an outcast amongst these people and he knew precisely why. He was a soldier, he dealt in death, whilst the academics were interested predominately in art, history and beauty. The strange thing was that he was in agreement with their sentiments. He wandered to a quiet corner of the warehouse and lit a cigarette. Whilst enjoying the seclusion that this particular calm corner afforded, Hess casually rummaged through one of the crates. It had already been opened but seemingly abandoned by the academics before its contents had been checked—perhaps for a more interesting find.

Inside the crate an old leather portfolio caught his eye. Hess noted with some surprise that some sketches within bore an uncanny resemblance to similar work that he had seen once before by Leonardo Da Vinci. The portfolio fitted easily into his briefcase and Hess slipped the package inside. He took the documents with him and later enlisted the services of Prof. Von Rorritz, an eminent historian with whose help the documents were authenticated. What he found caused him to abandon his family and country. and, on the 10th of May 1941, he flew to Britain, creating one of the most intriguing unsolved enigmas of modern history.

## THE DA VINCI PAPERS

In a series of sketches, diagrams and articles, Leonardo da Vinci described his discoveries which, if published, would without any doubt have a devastatingly apocalyptic effect on mankind, at that point in the evolution of human history and for the following fifty years.

Man has long known that the earth is spinning on its axis. If we spin any ball or globe we create a centrifugal force which is much stronger at the outer peripheral or equator than at its point of axis. At the axis or polar points it is a logical conclusion to assume that the centrifugal and therefore gravitational pull will be far less or even eliminated completely. Da Vinci discovered and analyzed this phenomena proving beyond doubt that his discoveries were factual.

The twin invisible vortexes which exist at the north and south poles magnetic and gravitational create an area of zero gravity. As da Vinci explained; if a rock were to be catapulted up into the vortex it would simply continue to go up and up as it would not be returned to earth by the gravitational pull. Another example given by da Vinci is the eye of a tornado or cyclone, where whatever is in the path is sucked up due to the temporary removal of gravity through natural forces. In Hess's hands, The da Vinci Papers were explosive.

Germany at that time, with the fanatical support of Hitler, was developing its lethal V1 and V2 rockets. Hitler was well aware of their importance to Germany. If they could be made operational in time, they would give him the power to bring the world to its knees. Hess had been privy to several meetings when the rocket scientists had been subjected to all manner of threats to hasten the preparation of the rockets. But regardless of the threats, the scientists had argued that breaking free of the earth's gravitational pull was a major obstacle and the enormous quantity of fuel required in order to achieve this appeared at that point a seemingly unsolvable problem. This problem had been anticipated much earlier and a research facility had been set up by the Nazis in Poland to examine the theory of negative gravity. Once free of the gravitational pull and in orbit the power required to manoeuvre the rockets or direct them back to earth was minimal. They could be used to bomb any point on the planet that Hitler desired.

Imagine if the da Vinci Papers information were to be delivered into the hands of Hitler's scientists. Launch platforms could be positioned at the poles and a minute fraction of the fuel to power ratio would be required to launch the deadly V2's which would send them out through the earth's gravitational pull to orbit the planet. From there they could be directed back to deliver destruction on any give point on the planet as decided by the Fuhrer with little effort and deadly accuracy.

The initial response of Vice Chancellor Rudolf Hess was elation, for he alone held in his hands the one piece of the jigsaw that would undoubtedly give Germany the means with which to beat the Allies. And more. Once the Fatherland had perfected the Atomic bomb. Which according to Hitler, was just a matter of years even months away the whole world would be paralyzed by the grip of the Third Reich and all this could be achieved, with no massive troop deployment necessary, other than defending and holding the vortex sites. The implications and potential of the documents was inconceivable and yet there was huge doubt in his mind. The doubt posed by Adolph Hitler himself. There was no question that he was entirely mad but his grip on the country and the military was total. What would he do if he were allowed to achieve his goal of world domination? Hess deliberated over the papers for some days, during which time he was constantly harassed by Von Rorritz who could not understand the reason for the delay in showing the crucial documents to the Fuhrer.

Von Rorritz knew that Hitler's obvious delight in the discovery would undoubtedly mean huge recognition for him personally, assuredly securing him a place in history as the genius academic who first uncovered the secrets of Leonardo da Vinci's work.

A meeting between Hess and Von Rorritz deteriorated into an argument and from there finally to a fight. Hess attempted to make clear his fears explaining what might be outcome should the papers reach the hands of Hitler. But Von Rorritz could see his opportunity for recognition slipping away and refused to listen. Hess, the soldier and far the stronger of the two killed the professor and later disposed of his body. This was not achieved without arousing some suspicion and after much deliberation, feeling that his time in Germany was running out, Hess made the momentous and epic decision to fly to Scotland on the now historic date.

At 5.45 pm on Saturday 10 May 1941, Hess, a pilot with more than twenty years experience, took off from the Messerschmitt works airfield at Augsburg, Bavaria, in a twin-engined Bf 110 fighter-bomber. After a journey of almost a thousand miles lasting four hours, he crossed the British coast over Ainwick in Northumberland, then flew on towards his objective, Dungavel House, eventually baling out at 11 pm to land near the village of Eaglesham. Detained by the local Home Guard, Hess gave his name as 'Alfred Horn' and demanded to see the Duke of Hamilton, then a serving RAF officer.

A deal was struck with Winston Churchill who withheld the full extent of the matter from both his American and Russian counterparts, Roosevelt and Stalin. The only three people who knew the deadly secret were Hess, Churchill and Von Rorritz.

Von Rorritz was dead, killed by Hess who was by this time himself showing significant signs of madness, and besides, who would believe such an incredible story? Churchill decided that the only solution to the dilemma was to bury the story as deeply as possibly. By the time of the Nuremburg trials Hess demonstrated just how unsound his mind had become. Finally the verdict of the trials was reached which resulted in committing Hess to solitary confinement in the Spandau Prison on a life sentence. Churchill himself carried the burden of the knowledge to his grave, convinced that he had tidied up all of the loose ends to the best of his ability.

For the duration of the initial negotiations with Winston Churchill in London, Hess was given certain freedoms and liberties. Later during the period pre to the Nuremburg trials he was held under light guard at Maindiff Court near Abergavenny, initially two Welsh Guard sergeants' were always in attendance and latterly two male nurses from the hospital were charged with the responsibility of his security. A strange and unexplainably lenient treatment for such a high ranking officer from an opposing army that was determined to crush Great Britain. Particularly as he was, post Nuremburg, incarcerated for what must have been the most costly imprisonment of one person in the history of mankind. During the period he spent in Abergavenny, it was relatively simple for him to arrange for the de Vinci Papers to be taken to a safety deposit box in the London Safety Deposit Centre underground in Chancery Lane, and there the secret lay undisturbed until discovered by Nicholas Trevelyan almost sixty years later."

By the time Nick and Steve had finished reading, they looked at each other in amazement. Orville had done a superb job. The extracts came from multiple sources. Some sections read like a novel which must have been written by someone with inside knowledge whilst other details were compiled almost as a list of facts. Perhaps a novel had been written but withheld from publication as the material was too politically explosive. Orville's research was expansive and detailed he had done a magnificent job as usual.

'I think I need a drink after that,' said Steve and Nick was in complete agreement. They took his car and drove to a pub a little way from Thames House. It was Saturday evening and London was quiet. With two pints set on a corner table. they began to discuss the information that we had just read. Steve opened the conversation.

'That really is one hell of a story and I can see why Rudolf would not have wanted Adolf to get his hands on it.'

'The irony of it is that it's pretty much irrelevant today since the Berlin Wall came down and with all of the space junk that's floating about in orbit.' he mused. Orville had done a sterling job but we now needed to digest the material and decide what should be done. Steve considered the options,

'I guess that enough time has now passed for the implications to be of far less relevance that they were sixty odd years ago. But if the da Vinci negative gravity theory holds up then I had better pass this info onto my superiors.'

They called in another two pints and the debate continued. Much of this was now of little interest to Nick. His sights were set on the infamous Signor Palestroni; He wanted him so badly he could taste it.

# ITALY

Saturday evening arrived; Nick picked Sian up from the taxi rank outside Windsor Castle. He had purposely not enquired about where she was staying, not wishing to add more confusion to the issues. They drove to Ascot where Nick had made reservations at the same restaurant as before. The evening went well, the conversation was kept general and it soon became obvious to Nick that Sian was playing the romantic card. He allowed it to happen and simply ordered more wine, enjoying being seduced by a beautiful woman in the line of duty. What more could a man ask for?

They both danced around some issues, avoiding too many references to their past. After the meal they went back to Nick's flat and drank some more. Then the inevitable happened. The love making started in the living room but, aware of the surveillance cameras, Nick moved into the bedroom where there were none. He knew that he was playing out a role and it was more than likely that she did too. Previously, their sex had been good but quite conservative, particularly when Nick made the inevitable comparison with Marina who had no inhibitions at all. Tamsen had been a completely different deal and, as at the time he had believed her to be somewhat of a newcomer to sex, he was content to experience the difference. Now he decided to push things. How far could he get her to go? She was setting the pace and Nick fell into the game enthusiastically. He wasn't disappointed. Sian was prepared to do whatever he wanted; she must have considered the da Vinci papers worth it. The sex, because it really couldn't be considered love making, continued until four in the morning, when, exhausted, they both fell into a deep sleep.

Nick woke to find that Sian had been up for some time; she had showered and made tea. She brought the tea to bed, they talked, and Nick decided that he wanted some more sex. It was obvious that Sian wasn't as keen as he was, but he insisted and she wasn't about to disagree, Nick guessed that she considered she had invested too much by this time to turn back. Later they went into town and had lunch at the converted Victorian railway station commercial complex. They ate at a French restaurant which Nick thought was a bit of a contradiction in terms considering the locale. Sian made her excuses and left. Then he returned home to watch the rugby on TV feeling rather relaxed and pleased with himself.

Next morning he was at Legoland discussing details of his plan with Steve when a call came in from the surveillance team watching his flat.

'They are just going to patch through some interesting images from your pad,' said Steve. They settled in front of a monitor.

'This was taken half an hour ago.' Steve explained

The surveillance camera had captured two men entering his flat via the patio door.

'That's always locked,' Nick complained.

'Hang on, Nick—there's more.' said Steve.

The two men went on to search the rooms very professionally without disturbing anything. It took them ten minutes and they were gone. The monitor flickered and flashed and then new images settled. The lovely naked body of Sian appeared from the bedroom and walked over to the patio doors. She slipped open the catch which locked the fixed side of the doors so that, although it looked more or less the same, it was locking nothing. The time counter flashed 09-30 Sunday morning.

'You certainly do have to suffer for your country my friend,' laughed Steve, the images of the delicious Sian still in his head.

'So now that she knows the da Vinci Papers aren't at my home—where it would have been a simple operation to have stolen them—she will have to make a fresh move to get me to bring them out of hiding. She would have expected the deal to be closed after the break-in. If the papers were still hidden in my flat, they would have been stolen and that would have been the end of the matter'

'Do you think that you will have to suffer more sex with this Mata Hari in order to bring this to a conclusion? You really are a fine example to us all.'

'Bollocks.'

Nick left Legoland early in order to miss the commuter traffic. He arrived home feeling dirty and grumpy from the commuting. He took a shower, dressed in a bath robe and crashed out on the sofa. He dozed a little until the ring tone of his mobile brought him back to the present.

'Hi Nick, it's Sian, I was wondering if we could meet for a drink tonight?' She was about to play her next and crucial card.

'Yes, of course. Tell me a time and a place.'

'Eight at the castle taxi rank would be fine.'

After hanging up, Nick called Steve to tell him that things were on the move.

'Keep it in your trousers for as long as you can manage.' was his only remark.

'Bollocks.' was Nicks

Eight o'clock on the dot, Nick pulled up at the castle taxi rank and Sian jumped into the car. She looked more beautiful than ever. Her jet black hair, which was usually tied back, was loose and flowing. She wore casual clothes which were obviously designer and the aroma of her perfume which he remembered was Opium caused his passions to be aroused.

'Anywhere in particular?' Nick asked.

'Just a quiet pub where we can be alone and talk.'

They drove along the Thames to Runnymede where he knew a secluded pub. It was quite early and the place was only about a quarter full. He went to the bar and ordered drinks while Sian settled at a quiet table in the garden. How was she going to make the next move, he wondered? When they had settled, she made her opening gambit.

'Nick I have to admit I have been less than honest with you,' Sian opened.

'*Now there's a surprise . . .*' Nick could have made a dozen sarcastic replies but decided to keep quiet and give her a chance.

'And?'

'Nick I know that you have some very important papers which are by Leonardo Da Vinci.' He feigned surprise.

'I discovered them by mistake in your apartment when I was tidying up. I never thought much about them but I have since discovered their true value.' '*Just conveniently leaving out the fact that you had them photo-*copied,' Nick thought.

'I have a client who is prepared to pay you a large sum of money for them.'

'Suppose I don't want to sell them?' He played her at her own game.

'Nick, I know that what I did to you was unforgivable but I've got myself into a dangerous hole and I don't know how to get out. I have promised my client something which he has now become obsessed by and he won't take no for an answer. I'm really scared, Nick. All that you have to do is sell them to him! He's filthy rich and you will be rich yourself.'

'And how do we pull off this deal?'

'We don't need to worry about anything. My client will arrange everything. The money will be deposited in an account of your choice or my client will open an account for you in Switzerland or wherever you wish.'

'And what do you get out of this, Sian?'

'I get a percentage of the agreed sale price. Surely that's fair?'

'And your client, who is he?' Nick knew the answer but reckoned that Sian would be suspicious if he didn't ask.

'I'm afraid I can't tell you that at this point. I can only tell you that he's Italian.'

'Give me time to think about it.'

'Sure, Nick, but please don't take too long. My client is a very impatient man.' Nick allowed two days to pass before contacting Sian again.

'OK, tell your client that I want one million Pounds Sterling for each of the six sketches, money to be deposited in a numbered Swiss bank account.'

'Nick, thanks so much. You won't regret this. Where are the da Vinci Papers now?'

'In the London Safety Deposit vaults. I thought you might have guessed that.'

Next day the plans were laid out. Sian and Nick would be picked up and driven to Chancery Lane where he would pick up the papers from his security box. They would then be driven to Heathrow; from there they would be flown first class to Rome. For the final stage of the journey, the client's private helicopter would take them to his estate. Naturally the documents would have to be authenticated which was not a problem as there were apparently substantial laboratories at the client's villa. Nick could see plenty of problems but he needed to act naively to keep the action flowing.

'Perhaps you had better stay at my place the night before we go. It will make things less complicated,' he suggested. *And it will give me another night of super sex with Sian,* he thought—given that she will surely disappear again once the deal is completed. At this point she could hardly disagree. It felt rather mercenary but then again it was she who had written the original script.

Sian arrived that evening with a large suitcase. They went out to a Thai restaurant, followed by a play at the Theatre Royal. Nick loved the theatre which Sian, then Tamsen, had introduced him to. It was a superb evening. The production was Agatha Christie's "Murder on Air", a play set in the 1930's which perfectly complemented the musty old theatre.

Back at his flat Sian proved once again what an excellent lover she could be, attentive, willing and accommodating. They slept soundly and awoke refreshed and ready for the adventure ahead.

At 10 am, a black Mercedes with smoked glass windows arrived and they were whisked off along the motorway and into the London traffic. The Mercedes double parked in Chancery Lane while Nick went inside to retrieve the documents. Parking tickets appeared not to be an issue for these people; it took no more than ten minutes. He had purchased a good quality briefcase for the occasion which now held the precious papers.

They left the city centre via the Hammersmith flyover, back onto the M4 and on to Heathrow. At the airport they were greeted by what Nick assumed were employees of the mystery client and their cases were checked into first class. Nick kept a secure grip on the briefcase. Ten minutes into the flight and it was obvious that Sian was nervous. She found it hard to stop talking and constantly repeated herself, asking numerous questions about the da Vinci Papers. Nick was becoming irritated; he needed quiet in order to think. A solution came to mind which might kill the two proverbial birds with one stone.

'Sian.'

'Yes Nick.'

'*Four Seasons.*' Immediately Sian's head slumped forward. 'Sian, you are going to enjoy a deep sleep until I waken you.' And she did.

How many men would love to be able to silence their partners so easily, he wondered. The flight gave him the space that he needed plus the affirmation that the trigger word was firmly implanted for immediate activation, when needed.

## Alexis

The flight to Rome took about two hours. Once again, at the airport, they were fast tracked through customs and another black Mercedes—an exact replica of the last which took them the short journey to the section of the tarmac reserved for private aircraft and helicopters.

A new character had entered the arena. Waiting for them at the airport, an immaculately dressed man introduced himself as Signor Palestroni's personal assistant. He politely gave his name as Alexis. So Nick was now being allowed to know the name of his mystery buyer. He acted as if the name had no significance to him. He made a swift assumption from his accent that Alexis must be of German descent; He also made another immediate assessment. This was an extremely calculating and dangerous individual. Although he was outwardly polite, this was clearly just a thin veneer. Alexis was a man in his estimation who had the capability of horrendous violence. A man not to turn your back on. His arrogant attitude to everybody he came into contact with was evident. He got exactly what he wanted in an efficient manner. Alexis nodded to two guards who were standing close by and Nick and Sian were given a highly professional body search. A smaller Mercedes drove over from the official arrivals building and their luggage was transferred to the helicopter undoubtedly having been scanned for anything suspicious.

The helicopter flight took about fifteen minutes flying over exquisite country roads lined with poplar trees which were flanked by the rolling green terraces of the region's famous vineyards. Finally they touched down on the villa's private helipad. Nick noted two other helicopters, each sporting the Palestroni crest. He was impressed. Time to meet the family, he thought, as they stepped down from the helicopter and walked across the sweeping lawns towards a magnificent villa.

## The Villa

"Magnificent villa" was something of an understatement, for in reality, there were three superlative buildings encompassing three sides of a square. The central, lower and for the most part single storey building must have been Roman. From the exterior it was evident that it had been painstakingly, sympathetically and lovingly restored to its former glory. Nick guessed that this must have been the country estate of a very high ranking Roman official, at the very least a senator. To the South there was another magnificent building but from a different period in Italian architecture. This was a Renaissance mansion rather than a villa. It towered over the Roman structure rising in the central section to five stories. The third building was again from a completely different period. This was a modern design with minimal architectural embellishments. It was clearly not built as living accommodation, having a far more functional appearance.

In the centre of the three buildings was an immaculately manicured Italian Renaissance garden, which looked as if it would have been laid out at the time the south building was constructed. Probably at that point in the history of the site the Roman building would have been just a ruin. Nick could not help but be impressed. He brought himself back to reality by reminding himself that all of this was most likely to have been financed by corrupt means.

Alexis led them towards the central Renaissance mansion. Nick made a mental note of everything that might be useful should he need to make a hasty retreat. One thing was very noticeable: there were a lot of guards patrolling, they were all armed and most had dogs. he also noted that his exit routes were beginning to close. The central doorway was magnificent. Enormous wooden doors opened onto a huge entrance hall. The décor was as fresh as the day the building was first opened. There was far too much to take in during the short time it took to pass through the hallway. Alexis led them to a side chamber where Nick was surprised to see a lift. This modern piece of equipment was so well designed that it fitted in completely unobtrusively with the rest of the architecture. Sian, Nick and Alexis got into the lift and Alexis pushed the button for the fifth floor.

## Caesar Palestroni

The silent elevator came to an almost imperceptible halt and the doors slid open with a sound like silk curtains over a Persian carpet. The three of them walked out into a magnificent room. Once again Nick was stunned by the splendour and opulence of the room which was oval with a vaulted ceiling. To the front there was a semi circle of windows which overlooked the formal gardens and beyond, far beyond. Nick made a mental calculation that he might have to run at a fast pace for the best part of an hour just to get off of the property! Standing in the centre of the semi circle of windows looking out over his domain stood Caesar Palestroni. Nick had done his homework well and knew a great deal about the man who stood there. His hands were clasped behind his back, seemingly oblivious that anyone had entered his inner sanctum.

'Signor Palestroni?' Alexis spoke quietly as if afraid to disturb his master. 'Signor Palestroni, I have Mr. Trevelyan here.' Alexis, demonstrating the true arrogance that he transmitted, did not bother to announce Sian.

'Ah, yes. Alexis, Mr Nicholas Trevelyan and the beautiful Sian.' Caesar was an Italian and Sian was beautiful, he would not be so negligent as his employee; it quite simply wasn't in his genes. He turned around to face his newly arrived guests.

The dossier on him back at Legoland had been spot on. Caesar Palestroni was not a tall man. His file said that he was about 5'6" but his overall appearance was so well presented that he gave the impression of being taller. The dossier suggested that it was likely Palestroni had been under the surgeon's knife on several occasions for cosmetic reasons, the last operation being a full face lift. He was slim and well proportioned which might have been accredited to a tummy tuck.

His one failing feature was his hair which was thinning. In an attempt to hide this, it had been dyed black, combed backwards and slicked down. He had a stereotypical macho Italian appearance. His immaculate dark blue suit was worn with the jacket draped over his shoulders.

Nick knew that this man was sixty-five but he could have fooled most people and easily dropped ten years from his age. There was another feature that epitomized this man's strength which was his overall demeanour. He spoke with total confidence assuming that whatever passed his lips was an unarguable fact. Totally confident that nobody would interrupt. His accent was delightful and his command of English immaculate.

The semi circle of windows where Caesar was standing was a raised area, five steps higher than the main part of the room. In order to get to where Caesar was and to shake his hand, Nick needed to climb these steps but made a point of staying two steps lower than Palestroni so not to antagonise this extremely vain man with his superior height. He had noted that Alexis never went up the steps as if this was hallowed ground and not for employees.

'So, Mr. Trevelyan, you have brought me the elusive da Vinci Papers?'

'Yes, Mr. Palestroni. I have.'

'That is, of course, if they are indeed original.' Nick knew that he would have seen Sian's photo-copies but decided he would not allow himself to be drawn into any argument at this point.

'Mr Trevelyan, it might interest you to know that I have a superb collection of Italian masters from all periods of my country's illustrious history. Later, perhaps tomorrow, when you are settled I will personally take you on a tour of my gallery. But alas there is something which is missing from this magnificent collection. Something which grieves me deeply. With all of the beauty that I have collected under my roof, I do not have one work by the most famous of all Italian and arguable world painters, Leonardo da Vinci. One of Italy's most famous sons and where

is the bulk of da Vinci's work to be found, do you know Mr. Trevelyan?'
Nick did, in fact, know much about da Vinci. He had made a strong point
of learning all that he could over the past days but this was neither the
time nor place to demonstrate his newly acquired knowledge.

'I'm afraid I can't give you an answer to that.' he admitted.

'Let me enlighten you, Mr. Trevelyan.' Palestroni was getting noticeably
agitated by his own rhetoric. 'Madrid, Paris, London and other locations
far from these shores.' he allowed himself a little pause.

'And now finally, thanks to you and the beautiful Sian, I shall soon
own my own da Vinci.'

Nick handed the briefcase to Palestroni who placed it upon a huge
Napoleonic style desk. Gently he opened it. He then opened a drawer in
the desk and took out a pair of white cotton gloves. Lovingly, one by one
he removed the tissue wrapped documents and placed them on the desk.
His joy in what lay before him was palpable.

'The man who drew these was a painter, inventor, visionary,
mathematician, philosopher and engineer—but above all he was born
in Tuscany.' Tears were visible in Palestroni's eyes before he recovered
his composure. Placing his hand under the edge of the desk he pushed
what Nick assumed must be a hidden call button. Within fifteen seconds
two guards entered the room. Nick made a mental note of this action.
Palestroni reverently returned the sketches to the briefcase and snapped
the lock closed.

'Take these to the laboratory and make sure that you give them only
to Professor Marietto.' he said to a guard.

'Now, my friends, you must forgive me for my lack of hospitality.
Alexis, will you please take our guests to their rooms. You must be tired
and will need to refresh yourselves before dinner.' Palestroni turned his
back and returned to his gazing at the tranquil view. It was evident that
the meeting was over. Nick considered asking for a receipt but decided
that, given the circumstances, it might be considered slightly trivial. He
had been granted an audience with Palestroni and that was the best that
he could expect for the time being.

Alexis took Sian and Nick to the west wing of the mansion. This was
again a contradiction in architectural styles. Externally the building had
the appearance of a Renaissance mansion but internally the west wing
was much more like an ultra modern hotel. Palestroni was obviously

accustomed to receiving large parties of guests and he dealt with them in an efficient manner.

Sian and Nick were each given separate suites. He showered, wondering how much of his activities were being monitored. He had never suffered from bashfulness; if he had been, army life would have cured him. He wandered around naked for most of the time before dressing as the time for dining approached. The internal phone rang. It was Alexis.

'Mr. Palestroni requests your company for dinner: eight pm sharp in the east wing dining room.' adding 'Signor Palestroni doesn't accept lateness.'

'I'll be there, thank you Alexis.' Nick replied curtly. 'That's if I can find it in time in this huge building,' he added, thinking this would give him an opportunity to wander around with a perfectly plausible excuse.

At 7.45 he was dressed and feeling hungry. He set off and purposely took what he knew was the wrong direction. Nick played the bumbling guest and by the time he had finally found the east wing dining room, he had explored much of the building. Remarkably there was nothing 'out of the ordinary' if that could be said in such an extraordinary house.

The dinner guests were mingling, drinks were being offered by uniformed staff and the whole affair had the appearance of a small gathering in a smart hotel. His attention was attracted by the entrance of Sian who had obviously made a special effort and looked stunning. What a pity she was such a femme fatale and that, sadly there could be no romantic future with her.

Palestroni called Nick over and introduced him to Professor Marietto. He explained that the professor was leading the team authenticating the da Vinci Papers. Nick shook his hand, inwardly wishing him the very best of bad luck. What would happen if the documents were proven to be forgeries? He would be compromised but could do nothing more than hope the eggheads at GCHQ had done a good job. If only Nick could have manoeuvred the learned Prof to a location where he could manipulate him to give the thumbs up on the papers his worries would have been greatly reduced but he knew that this wasn't going to happen.

'I will have reached my decision by mid-afternoon tomorrow but I have to say that from the data which I have analyzed so far, things are looking most promising.' said the professor.

Everything at the villa was first class and the dinner was no exception. The conversation was principally concerned with art which precluded

Sian and Nick somewhat. When he was brought into the conversation he felt as if he were being patronized by Palestroni to the extent of being talked down to, simply tolerated. After all, in his eyes, Nick was nothing more than a common thief.

When finally the dinner party ended, Nick felt relieved. Pleasant good nights were exchanged and when Palestroni had left the dining room, the other guests gradually drifted away. Nick walked Sian back to her room; he suggested a nightcap and whatever else might transpire. Sian feigned exhaustion after the events of the day. Nick decided that this wasn't the time and certainly not the place, tempting as it was. He needed to be one hundred percent alert as Steve had warned he was now in the lion's den. He said good night to Sian and went to his suite.

Punctually at 8.00 the next morning there was a knock on his door and a maid pushed a trolley into the room with a mixture of breakfasts that would have delighted the most finicky tastes. He ate heartily, showered and dressed. At 8.30 his internal phone rang. It was Alexis.

'Mr Palestroni would like you to join him on a tour of his art gallery. Be in the entrance hall at ten.' An invitation from Alexis had the annoying ring of a command. On the dot of ten Nick walked into the entrance hall as requested. Sian was already there. They were immediately joined by Palestroni. Walking six paces behind him, as ever, was Alexis. The four walked out and down through the formal garden. The exotic scents of the flowers wafted through the air causing an aromatic invasion of their senses. They walked across the grounds and into the gallery, the interior of which was as high-tec as any building that Nick had ever encountered. It was also as large as any public art gallery he had ever seen. All of this for one man and his occasional guests. There were even guards walking unobtrusively around in a livery which wouldn't have looked out of place in The National Gallery in London or the Louvre in Paris. Proudly, Palestroni strutted around like a peacock in his own Taj-Mahal showing off his treasures. Nick felt almost guilty for taking little notice of the truly magnificent collection that he was privileged to see, so self indulgent was this egotistical maniac that his monumental arrogance was becoming more and more evident with each minute that passed. Once the tour was over, Sian and Nick made all of the polite noises expected and headed back to the tranquillity of their suites. At two thirty, the internal telephone rang again. It was Alexis.

'Mr Palestroni would like you to join him in the turret room at 3pm. Be in the entrance hall at 2.55.pm sharp.'

Again on the dot, the three of them met in the entrance hall. Alexis did not speak but nervously checked his watch, waiting until thirty seconds before the hour when he abruptly herded Sian and Nick into the lift. It arrived at the fifth floor precisely at 3pm Palestroni was standing as before, gazing out of the windows. Again he ignored their presence until Alexis gingerly announced their arrival. Caesar Palestroni turned to survey his visitors. Alexis positioned himself by the elevator whilst Sian and Nick walked forward.

Finally when he decided that the theatrical interlude had produced sufficient dramatic tension Palestroni spoke.

'Mr. Trevelyan, I have some good news for you. Professor Marietto has carried out extensive tests and assures me that the da Vinci Papers are indeed genuine.' Nick looked across at Sian who was smiling. He felt massively relieved that one of the highest hurdles had been cleared. But there was something not quite right. In his peripheral vision, he noticed that Alexis had quietly taken the pistol from his shoulder holster and was holding it down to his side. Palestroni continued.

'Unfortunately in the difficult and troubled world that we live in; good news is quite often followed by bad. Today is one such day for you Mr Trevelyan. You have brought to me the finest treasure in the world of art to be discovered this century for which you are to be commended. But in reality your part in the overall affair is as nothing. You are simply the messenger. Even less! You are no more than a common thief. And so, regrettably you are to be eliminated.' Palestroni's statement was icy cold and to the point. He was judge, jury but not the executioner. He was now in possession of the da Vinci Papers and hadn't paid out a penny. Nick also realised that the drama which Palestroni was about to instigate satisfied both his dual twisted sense of the theatrical and total greed.

'Come here, my dear.' His attention was now focussed on Sian. She cautiously walked towards him. He opened a drawer of the huge desk and took out a hand gun.

'Are you familiar with this weapon?' He enquired, 'You should be. As a CIA agent you will have spent many hours practicing with one just like it.' Sian took the weapon and expertly checked it. Nick immediately recognized the gun as a Glock 17, ironically his favourite hand-gun.

'And now I want you to kill Mr. Trevelyan. He has become surplus to requirements and is rather a nuisance.' The order was delivered without emotion. Nick saw the blood drain from Sian's face. She looked at Palestroni and then at him.

'I must also mention that, should you not carry out this request, Alexis will kill Mr Trevelyan and then regrettably he will kill you, too. That would be such a pity for you are a beautiful creature. Sadly Alexis does not share my love of beautiful things.' There was silence.

Nick watched as Sian released the magazine clip, checked to see that there were actually rounds in the magazine, and replaced it, snapping the clip shut by hitting the butt of the weapon onto the palm of her left hand. She then cocked the pistol, loading a round into the chamber and thumbed the safety catch forward. The weapon was now ready to kill.

Watching the expert way that Sian handled the gun, Nick was suddenly aware of a facet in her character that he had never seen. This was a woman whom he thought he knew but obviously he didn't know her at all. There was a cold realization that the woman whom he had so recently had sex with, was now cast in the role of his executioner.

Her eyes glanced around the room; to Nick, it looked as if she was thinking of shooting her way out of what was an impossible situation. Alexis sensed the advanced tension, his gun hand moved from his side to his chest and Nick heard the unmistakable sound of the weapon being cocked. To Palestroni and Alexis it looked as if she was preparing to kill Nick. But what was actually running through Sian's mind is something that Nick would never know.

He needed to think fast. Slowly, trying not to arouse suspicion, he moved to position himself between Sian and Alexis. It appeared as if he was about to plead with Sian. Palestroni was expecting to see a spectacular drama played out in his exquisite private turret room theatre. He surmised that Nick was weak and would break down, pleading for his life. Actually he wasn't too far from the truth and Nick needed to dig deeply into his reserves to continue. He moved closer to Sian. The gun was held in her right hand which now hung at her side. When he thought that the distance between the four people playing out this drama was right, he whispered to Sian words that only she could hear.

'*Four Seasons!*' Sian's head sank slowly onto her chest. Nick was nervous that it might have appeared suspicious but he needn't have worried. It simply looked as if she were saddened by what she was about to do which added to the keen sense of theatre which flooded the room. Palestroni looked on, perversely enjoying each second of the drama that he had created. The gun was still in her hand and Alexis was in a position to finish him in an instant if Nick made any sudden moves. He whispered.

'Sian, when Palestroni tells you to kill me you will disobey him, raise your gun and shoot over my shoulder at Alexis. You must kill him or he will kill you. You must be quick and accurate. One shot to the head, three shots to the body.'

'Enough!' Palestroni was getting impatient, like a Roman emperor. He had ordered Nick's death and was ready for the action.

'Sian! Kill Trevelyan.' Sian's beautiful head straightened slowly, her arm came up, the gun hand was rock steady. The point of aim moved from his crotch to his stomach and up to his heart. This was when Nick closed his eyes. Had he actually done a good enough job in planting the new instruction? Perhaps under stress, hypnotism loses its potency. He had no way of knowing. The gun came level with his eyes, which remained semi-closed. Could this be how it was to end for him? Had Steve been right? Going into the lion's den was a stupid idea, tantamount to suicide.

Bang!

The first shot rang out, closely followed by three more. Nick spun around to see Alexis on the floor in a heap. He ran over and picked up his gun. Another Glock 17.

Sian was standing motionless, still hypnotized. She had been given no other instructions and her head was slumped forward. Palestroni made a sudden move and hit the emergency button on the corner of his desk. Nick had just enough time to re-position himself. A door at the western corner of the room burst open and two guards rushed in. There had been four shots fired. Alexis was in a heap on the floor, Sian was standing with a gun in her hand. The guards made an instant assumption and fired. Eight shots thumped into Sian's torso. She was dead before she hit the floor. The guards' attention was concentrated on the scene before them. In a split second they noticed Nick but it was too late. He pumped two shots into each of them before they could get off one themselves. Palestroni's Praetorian Guard had been eliminated. There was no time for sympathetic feelings. Nick knew that he had only seconds before the second group of guards would arrive. He ran towards Palestroni. It was evident that he was not a fighter. Why should he be when he could employ someone else to do his dirty work for him? Nick wanted to tear him limb from limb but needed him unharmed in order to carry out the rest of his plan. Nick charged up the steps like a raging bull, lowered his shoulders and surged forward with his head, delivering a ferocious head butt to Palestroni's sternum. He went down like a sack of potatoes. Nick stood over him and dragged him to his feet. Nick was far taller. He cupped Caesar's chin in his right hand and stared into his eyes. He needed to control his rage and above all he needed to be quick.

'Caesar, look deeply into my eyes.'

'*Oh God!*' This part always sounded so corny whenever Nick said it, but right now and under these conditions it was bordering upon insanity. He started the procedure to hypnotise Caesar Palestroni who was groaning and whimpering in an uncontrollable manner. He had totally lost his confident aura of power and arrogance. He sobbed like a child and suddenly he looked every year of his usually well disguised age. The groaning continued but he wasn't responding to Nick's well tried formula. '*Shit!*'

What the hell was going on? This had never happened before. Time was running out. Sirens were wailing all over the building, the turret room was bound to be one of the first locations that the guards would check. His only hope was that the secondary guards would expect their boss to be safe in the knowledge that his hand picked Praetorian Guard were there to protect him plus Alexis, the head of security. They had no way of knowing that all three were lying dead on the floor of the turret room. '*Think Nick think!*' He was too pumped up with anger that could be it. '*Calm down, calm down!*' Palestroni was also so scared that he wasn't receptive to anything. '*Slow the action down, breath deeply, take it easy.*' Slowly the situation calmed. Caesar was still sobbing like a baby but he was calmer. Nick started again.

'Caesar, look into my eyes.' Caesar did what he was told for the first time possibly in his entire life. Now the technique began to take hold and his head slid down onto his chest. The sobbing stopped and he relaxed. Nick sighed a huge sigh of relief. Palestroni was under but this was only the beginning and Nick still had much to do.

The door at the western end of the turret room burst open and four guards rushed in. Nick turned towards them, presenting Caesar's back to them. He was his human shield; they could not take a shot without risking hitting their boss. They advanced slowly, maximizing their target and fanning out to improve the angle. The laser beams from their sights flashed across Nick's face searching out any exposed area at which to shoot as soon as the order was given, but Caesar Palestroni remained silent. Nick's forearms were burning with the pain of supporting the weight of his body; Palestroni was all that was shielding him from a hail of bullets. He knew that he couldn't hold on for much longer and as soon as he released his grip and Palestroni slid to the ground, Nick would be dead. The time left was measured in seconds not minutes. The hyenas were closing in for the kill.

'Caesar! All that has just happened will be wiped out of your memory. When you regain consciousness you will remember that I saved your life when Alexis and Sian attempted to kill you. They shot your two guards and I shot them. It was me that saved you from being murdered by Alexis and Sian. They have been plotting to do this for months. You know that Sian was a CIA agent. She told you that she had resigned but that was a lie, she was still very active and was in collusion with Alexis. I killed them! I saved your life!' The story was preposterous enough to be believable. Palestroni's confidence was returning and growing in strength.

'Caesar you owe me a tremendous favour. I will now be your head of security; you will rely on me for everything, as you did with Alexis. From now on you will not make a move without me.' Palestroni mumbled.

'This man saved my life.' he whimpered.

The guards were moving in and were close enough to hear his voice. Nick prayed that they couldn't speak English.

'One more thing Caesar, whenever you hear me say the words, "*Caligula*" you will return to this deep state of hypnosis. Remember, Caesar, "Caligula" only from my lips, my voice. Now I am going to bring you back to consciousness.'

The guards surveyed the scene of carnage before them. Their leader was in the arms of a tall man who was whispering to him. Four weapons ware trained on his head. Soon they were going to have to make their move and blowing Nick away was the only option open to them.

'Six-five-four you are feeling relaxed and waking to remember all that I have just told you. Three-two—one. Wide awake and ready to clear up the aftermath of the unsuccessful assassination attempt on your life which I foiled.' The guards were confused. Was the tall man attacking or helping their boss? It would be too dangerous to shoot him. He was far too close to the stranger. The guard leader called to Palestroni in Italian. Nick couldn't understand what he said but his best guess was 'Do you want us to shoot this man? Palestroni groaned. Nick helped him to stand up.

'Put down your weapons,' he ordered. He walked over unsteadily to survey the scene. Slowly his composure returned.

'Nicholas, how can I ever thank you enough?'

'Caesar, I'm delighted that I was here when the attempt on your life was made.' Nick said, feeling better now that he knew that the suggestions that he had implanted into Caesar's mind were working to full effect.

'I knew from your file that you were a superb soldier but this is phenomenal. Alexis was the best. I never suspected him for a moment. A traitor in my team, right by my side. Nicholas, I want you to take over Alexis's job! Name your price.' *First name terms so soon;* Nick was delighted at the way his plan was working out although there were elements that he had never expected.

'We can talk about that later, Caesar. For now we have to clear up this mess.'

Palestroni ordered his doctor to be called immediately and slouched down into a huge armchair. Nick could see him rubbing his chest with a confused look on his face. He went over to the body of Alexis and checked for a pulse. There was none. He removed Alexis's shoulder holster and put it on. Then he made the Glock safe and checked the magazine: four rounds expended from a magazine of ten. Then he slid the gun into the holster. It gave Nick a feeling of security that had been missing since his arrival at the Villa.

Ordering the guards to check on the bodies of the two guards who had died, he went over to Sian. Even in death she was beautiful. Perhaps if she had not been hypnotized she could have fought on and perhaps she might still be alive. Nick felt a massive pang of guilt because it was him who had rendered her motionless after she had killed Alexis. From the way that he had seen her handle the gun, he knew that she would have been more than capable of putting up a hell of a fight. He took the magazine from her gun; four rounds expended and put it in his jacket pocket. He now had a dozen rounds with which to defend himself if things turned nasty.

The doctor came, fussed around Palestroni and declared him stressed but in good health. He recommended rest. The doctor wanted Palestroni to go to his bed where he would administer a sedative. Before they left, Nick enquired:

'How do you want me to dispose of the bodies, Caesar?'

'We usually just bury them in the grounds in deep lime filled pits. The guards know what to do. Please take care of it, Nicholas. I am feeling very tired.'

How many bodies had been disposed of in this manner? Who would ever know the full extent of this tyrant's previous exploits? Nick called the guards over;. One looked as if he was superior to his colleagues. Nick ordered him to fetch all CCTV tapes of the last day. Caesar watched his efficient manner and Nick could see that he was pleased that he had made such a fine choice of a substitute for Alexis.

With Caesar in bed and out of the way for a while, Nick could move more freely. Word had passed amongst the employees that he was now head of security which gave him free range of the buildings but he dared not allow Caesar Palestroni out of his sight for long. The senior guard returned with the video tapes. Nick explained that the tapes would stay with him and busied them with the disposal of the bodies. For the first time since entering the estate, he was able to use his mobile. He called Steve.

'Hi Nick, thank God. Are you OK?'

'Roger to that Steve. All is well but I have a list of requests before I can deliver the turkey in time for Christmas.'

'Fire away.'

'I want clearance for Mr P's private jet to land at Northolt airport in six days time. He is then to be given a tour of the best national fine art galleries at the highest level including the Windsor Castle collection. We will need the leading fine art experts in the country to stroke and pamper our guest and massage his over inflated ego. You must send the invitation in three days time via diplomatic courier with as many official looking bells and whistles as you can think of. This invitation is to be over a two day period. We have just six days to prepare our mark. Arrange all accommodation and transportation at a minimum five star level. In addition please inform our colleagues in the CIA that their operative's body will be found tomorrow on the outskirts of Rome. Tell them to pick her up and take her home with minimum fuss. I'll call again in three hours.'

Nick had no intention of allowing Sian's body to be planted in Italy no matter how beautiful the location, where her relatives would never know what had become of her. The body must go home to her family for the grieving process to take its natural course. He owed her that at the very least. The orders were given and that night the body of Sian was dumped on parkland on the outskirts of Rome. Not the highest level of respect but the best that he could manage considering the circumstances.

When Palestroni emerged from sedation he busied himself preparing his gallery for the installation of the da Vinci sketches in a place of honour within his remarkable collection. He wasted no time, personally making sure that the art world knew of the spectacular coup that he had achieved in securing the most momentous discovery in decades.

Nick stuck to Caesar like a shadow. He couldn't take the chance that his hypnotic implantation might deteriorate or even disappear allowing Palestroni to remember what had really happened. A couple of times he talked to Nick about the shooting.

'It's all very cloudy, Nick. I can't remember clearly exactly what happened. Why did my chest hurt so much?'

'Ah, that would have been when I knocked you to the floor when they tried to shoot you; it was a very close thing'. Nick was enjoying himself, playing out the charade, embellishing his fabric of lies, deceiving the man who had himself used lies and deceit to his advantage for so long.

On the afternoon of the day after the shooting, a special diplomatic delivery arrived for Palestroni. Nick watched as he read the official looking document. He looked unhappy but said nothing. Later when they were sitting quietly alone, Nick activated the trigger word.

'Caesar—*Caligula.*' The man's head sunk to his chest.

'What was in the documents that arrived this afternoon?'

'I have been invited to London to be the honoured guest of the highest society of art aficionados in the world.'

'So why were you so unhappy about being invited?'

'I can't go and take the risk of being arrested.' Nick looked around. The cameras were off and there was little chance that they would be disturbed. Caesar Palestroni was probably one of the richest and most powerful men in Western Europe but at that moment he was totally at Nick's mercy.

'Caesar, you are considered a supreme authority in the art world, your collection and knowledge of Italian art is well respected. If you go to England you will be completely safe. In addition, you will be accorded all of the honours associated with a man of your eminence. Caesar, go to

England and enjoy the glory which is rightly yours.' Nick then turned to some other more rather personal business.

'Caesar, with all that has happened you appear to have overlooked the little matter of transferring the six million Pounds into my Swiss bank account.'

This was a debt that Palestroni had never anticipated paying so Nick needed to be subtle. As far as Palestroni was concerned, the da Vinci Papers were in his possession and no payment needed to be made.

'You will give instructions for this to be done today.' Nick thought that he had done enough for this session to alter the man's mind so he slowly brought him out of his trance. Caesar sat gazing out of the window for several minutes and then he suddenly slapped the arm of his chair.

'I will go to England. This is a rare opportunity and too good to be missed. Make all of the preparations, Nicholas. We fly tomorrow.' Nick went off to inform the pilots who would need to file a flight plan for Northolt which was a specialist airport. Then he called Steve.

'Hi, mate; all systems go for tomorrow! I'll see you at Northolt at midday. Has the circus been organised?'

'Everything's in place. It should be a splendid show.'

Being an integral part of the Palestroni entourage, Nick was privy to view the day to day workings of the slick business machine which was Caesar's empire. There was a constant stream of secretaries and accountants continually bringing documents/faxes and e-mails that were ceremoniously laid before their master, which he then read with all the pomp of a Roman senator. Nick noted that Caesar never made notes; everything was stored in the remarkable, if not devious, mind. Before any document was shown to Palestroni it had first to be scrutinized by Gregory who was the chief accountant. During all hours of business Gregory was sewn to his master like a shadow. Everything had to receive his seal of approval before it could be submitted to the master. The whole scenario had a medieval feel which was accentuated by Gregory who was reminiscent of the character created by Bella Lugosi in the earliest black and white horror movies. When he moved he gave the impression that he was hovering rather than walking. His elongated pale face was bordering upon frightening. A long hooked nose pinched at the tip dominated his features with a pair of deep set hooded eyes which darted from person to person creating an impression of mistrust in whoever they fell upon. It was evident to Nick that Gregory did not like or trust him. This was about to be compounded when Caesar gave Gregory the order for a Swiss bank account to be created and six million pounds to be deposited therein. The steam was practically visible emitting from the chief accountants pointed pixie-like ears and Nick reveled it.

# | 8 |

# THE VISIT TO ENGLAND

Caesar Palestroni's private Lear jet touched down at Northolt airport on the western outskirts of London. A gaggle of eminent art historians who genuinely thought that this was an auspicious occasion were in attendance. Several were considering cornering Palestroni who had triumphantly heralded the news that he was now the proud owner of hither—to unknown works by Leonardo da Vinci—news that had set the art world alight. If they were lucky, he might make a generous loan of the sketches to their respective galleries thereby gaining notoriety for them. Among the crowd, Steve mingled with the art fraternity. Caesar was in his glory. Steve came over and quietly shook Nick's hand.

'Bloody hell, Mate! This is a real achievement. You really are the man, I have to admit.'

'I appreciate that, Steve.'

'You wouldn't believe the hassle I have had getting the Home Secretary to approve this pantomime, so seeing you touch down with your new buddy has meant that I can keep my job. I was thinking that I could have ended up counting gas masks and pick axe handles in some MOD warehouse miles away from civilization if you hadn't come up with the goods.'

'Thanks for having faith in me, Steve.'

'Oh by the way, does this mean that I will have to give you your car keys back?'

'Bloody right it does. I'm all done here, off back to my flat for a well earned rest.'

'Ah, well I wanted to talk to you about that.'

'Oh no! What the hell now do you have planned now?'

'Well it's not exactly me, Nick, it's our American cousins. They want you to stick with Palestroni while he is in London and then get him to go to New York. It's all a matter of extradition laws. They can do a far better job on him over there than we can here. You just have to get him to fly on across the Atlantic of his own accord.'

'Bloody hell, I detest the man and now you want me to stick around with him for another week. I thought my part in this was over.'

'Sorry Nick but we need you. This is a very special case and we can't allow him to slip through the net again.'

'OK, so what's the plan?'

'Stay with Palestroni while he does his tour of the galleries and then hypnotize him so that the CIA can dig out all of the information to put together a watertight case. None of the information extracted under hypnosis would be admissible in a court of law either here or in the States but if we can poke about in Caesar's brain and get as many leads as possible, we will have him banged to rights and nobody will know how the information was gathered.'

'Ok Steve. I'll do it. But only two operatives plus you and I'll tell you when and where.'

'Whatever you say, Nick. You're holding all the cards. By the way, Sian's body was picked up in Rome and taken back to her home town. The director of the CIA has sent his personal thanks.' Nick had no time to answer. The convoy of limousines was preparing to move off and he needed to be next to his mark.

Caesar Palestroni was a happy man. Wherever he went, he was the centre of attention. The art world appeared to adore him. Steve, as always, had done a remarkable job at very short notice. The grand tour of all the capital's major art galleries was spectacular and the accommodation first rate. Nick busied himself for Palestroni's approval as an efficient head of security. In reality he had nothing to do as Steve had security as tight as a drum. Steve was always close by. Nick grabbed an opportunity to talk with him.

'It has to be tonight. Be ready for my call in the hotel after 10 pm.'

'Leave it with me; I'll be in the next suite with the two CIA operatives revved up and ready to go.'

The agenda for the day was hectic. The motorcade swept from one gallery to the next. Palestroni's feet hardly touched the ground. In the evening there was a dinner in his honour given at the hotel and attended by even more arty folk. Nick was amazed that Steve had found so many suitable people. Caesar was not a late night man. Probably the fear of wrinkles spoiling his latest facelift was too great for him. At 9.45 pm he bade his guests good night and retired to his suite. Naturally, Nick accompanied him. His personal maid and manservant had prepared everything the way he liked it. Nick told them that they could leave. Caesar sat in an armchair where Nick brought him a Brandy which was his nightly ritual.

'Nicholas, I am so happy that I decided to come here. The threat of arrest was probably all paranoia on my part. I wouldn't have missed this for the world.' Nick sat down in a chair adjacent to Caesar.

'Caesar, I want you to listen carefully *'Caligula.'* His head slumped forward onto his chest. Nick took out his cell phone and called Steve. Before he had replaced the phone in his pocket there was a soft knock at the door. He walked over and opened it. With Steve there were two other people, a man and a woman. Neither looked anything like agents. They were more like lawyers, which was more than likely exactly what they were. No introductions were made for none were expected. Nick checked them for the conditions that he had agreed with Steve earlier: no cell phones, no excessive smells like perfume, no after-shave and definitely no smoking. There could be no mistakes.

'Ask him whatever you want but do it through me. Keep your voices low.'

The woman asked if the conversation could be taped and she produced a small recorder from her bag. Steve positioned himself at the door and the bizarre interview began. Two hours later, Nick decided to call the meeting to a halt. He had never held anyone in a hypnotic trance for anything like this period of time before. Silently, the trio left the room. Nick waited for a while and then brought Caesar out of his trance.

'What time is it, Nicholas?' enquired Caesar sleepily.

'Midnight. I'm afraid you fell asleep which is not surprising after the day that you have had.' Caesar made no comment and wandered off to his bedroom. Downstairs in the empty hotel bar, Steve and I talked.

'Our American friends are delighted. They have enough to send Palestroni away for the rest of his days.'

'So all that we have to do now is get him through tomorrow and you convince him to continue the grand tour in New York.'

'That will be tomorrow's agenda.'

'You need to find a convincing American art aficionado who will make the offer of a continuation of the wonderfully successful tour. Someone from the Smithsonian or the Paul Getty Museum. And all of that by tomorrow afternoon. A bloody good actor might be the answer. I will add his weight to the story to make it believable.'

The next day was, if anything, more intensive than the first. Caesar and his entourage were whisked around gallery after gallery. By lunchtime even Nick's head was spinning and he was relieved to go back to the relative calm of the hotel where they had lunch.

'Nicholas, our hosts appear to have saved the best until last. This afternoon we will be taken to Windsor Castle where a unique collection of da Vinci's work is housed. Can you imagine a more fabulous location for an art gallery.' Nick smiled inwardly. Palestroni had achieved most things in his life but royalty had so far eluded him. Before they set off they were presented to the President of the *American Fine Art Foundation*. Walter Skorjefski was a stereotypical art critic from his goatee beard to the leather patches on his tweed jacket.

'Mr. Palestroni I am here on behalf of the Fine Art Foundation of America.

We have been following with great interest your truly amazing UK tour and in the wake of the phenomenal success we would like to invite you to continue the tour in the Unites States as a guest of the American Fine Art Foundation. Naturally all expenses will be met by ourselves and we are considering a two day visit along the lines of what you have graciously agreed to, here in London.' Initially, Caesar looked delighted but as the full repercussions settled in his mind he backed off a little.

'Mr. Skorjefski I am deeply honoured by your generous offer which I have to say is somewhat sudden.' Skorjefski interjected.

'Please don't make any immediate decisions Mr. Palestroni. I realize that this is an offer made at very short notice and that you are of course an extremely busy man but our thinking is that as the success of your British tour has been so well received by the art world an immediate continuation would be advantageous.'

'You are most kind; please give me time to consider the offer. I will call later with a decision.'

With that Skorjefski left and the motorcade set off for Windsor. So believable was Skorjefski that Nick was left wondering if he was in fact the real thing or just someone that Steve had set up for the occasion.

Windsor Castle's art treasures were astounding but the da Vinci section focused Caesar's attention. He appeared to be close to tears such was his admiration of Leonardo. Nick walked towards the Rolls Royce that was to take them back to their hotel, Caesar was some distance behind basking in the waves of adoration which were being lavished on him by who knows who and did a double take.

'Mick, what the hell are you doing here'? Sitting in the driving seat was Steve's wing man looking uncharacteristically neat and tidy.

'Bloody hell Mick I hardly recognised you someone's done a good job on you, you're almost human.

'The boss said that I had to look the part. Any special requests?'

'Yes I need time to work on our Italian friend so keep an eye on me as I might want some extra time'.

In the back of the car, driving back to the hotel, Caesar was deep in thought. Eventually he confided:

'Nicholas these past days have been supreme. The invitation to America would give me double the pleasure but I cannot take the chance of going to the United States. It would be far too dangerous.'

It seemed to Nick that every time he used his hypnotic influence on someone the circumstances were always different and slightly unusual. Here he was sitting in the back of a Rolls Royce. He was not facing the subject; both of them were looking ahead. The limousine had been supplied by Steve and, at Nick's request; the glass partition between the driver and passengers was soundproof.

'Caesar, *Caligula*.' The much cosmetically enhanced Italian head slumped onto his chest.

'Caesar, you must go to America tomorrow. You were worried about coming to England and nothing awful has happened. You will tell Skorjefski that you will accept his generous offer and you will fly to New York tomorrow.

Nick could see that they were almost at the hotel. Mick's eyes flashed from the rear view mirror to the road ahead. Nick held up five fingers and the limousine glided past the hotel on a five minute trip around the block.

Nick rounded up the hypnotic session and gave the thumbs up to Mick. I will now waken you from this trance and when you are fully awake you will start making plans for the flight. You will tell me to give orders to all of your staff to prepare for the US.' Nick commenced the countdown sequence and slowly Caesar came out of the hypnotic trance.

'Nicholas please get me a drink. I must have fallen asleep. The last days have been exciting but tiring in the extreme.' Nick poured a tonic water from the drinks cabinet and Palestroni returned to his daydreaming. As the journey to the hotel was coming to an end, he began to give Nick orders, saying that he had decided to take up the offer of going to America.

'Nick, please tell my pilot to file a flight plan for New York, leaving midday tomorrow.'

'Yes, of course Caesar. Leave it with me.'

That evening there was a final dinner at the hotel. Steve bobbed about among the guests and when the opportunity arose, they talked.

'All set. He will be leaving for New York sometime tomorrow afternoon.' Nick reported.

'Well done, Nick.'

'So when do I get to go home?'

'Not until Palestroni's jet has touched down in the Big Apple and you have handed him over to the CIA, I'm afraid.'

'I'm beginning to think that this could all be a ploy on your part. I'll be getting deep vein thrombosis from all of the flying around or is this how you intend getting your hands on my car?'

'We'll fly you back first class, airline of your choice. Stop bellyaching.' Later when dinner was over, Caesar retired to his suite.

'This has been a wonderful experience for me, Nicholas, one I shall never forget.'

'Mr. Palestroni, I have a feeling that you may be right.'

As planned, the next day at noon, the Lear jet took off for the east coast of America. The flight across the Atlantic was uneventful. Caesar busied himself with the computers and fax machine in the on-board office which spat out a continuous stream of documentation. He was happy in the knowledge that the capable Gregory was holding the fort back in Italy. He had become so calm over the preceding few days that his bodyguards had been reduced to just four, who were relaxing at the back of the aircraft. Nick sat in a deeply cushioned leather chair and considered the situation. When he reckoned that they were closing in on the final approach to New

York, he made his way to the flight cockpit and started a conversation with the pilot and co-pilot. It appeared that the jet had sufficient fuel to reach its destination but not much more in reserve. Refuelling would be necessary as soon as it landed.

The time was right for Nick to have a little chat with his boss. Something that he had been waiting for since the first moment that he had the dubious pleasure of meeting Caesar Palestroni.

Caesar was sitting in the main cabin sipping a Martini. Nick sat down in the adjacent seat. He had noticed that the stewards had remained remarkably inconspicuous throughout the flight. Almost magically, one appeared and advised Palestroni that the captain was about to make his final decent into JFK airport.

'Well Caesar, I guess that this is the end of the line.' Nick relished this moment.

'What do you mean by that remark, Nicholas?' quizzed Caesar.

'I thought that this would be a good time to tell you of a few truths which I feel you aren't going to like.' Nobody had ever spoken to him like this before and it took a little while for the reality to sink in.

'Am I missing something here, Nicholas? What are you saying?'

'Shall we start with the da Vinci Papers?' Nick allowed a pause for effect.

'They are all forgeries. I have to admit that they are dammed good but nevertheless, forgeries.' The full extent of his words wasn't hitting home as what Nick was saying was, to Palestroni, too preposterous. Nick continued.

'I am sincerely grateful for the six million Pounds that you have so kindly deposited in Switzerland for me.' He allowed himself a hint of a smile. The truth was beginning to hit home and Caesar's mind went into overdrive.

'My scientific team authenticated the papers.' Caesar delivered this as a statement of fact.

'Ah, but your boffins were fooled, Caesar. Believe me, your da Vinci Papers are nothing but elaborate forgeries. The real ones are safely locked away in my safety deposit box in London waiting for me to return.' This was turning out to be more fun than Nick could have imagined. And as a special bonus to me they will be worth at least four times as much as soon as this little pantomime hits the presses'.

'I can call Gregory and have the Swiss bank account terminated.' Caesar was still supremely confident.

'I have to admit that could be a distinct possibility apart for one thing.'

'Ah! And what could that possibly be?'

'Well, Mr Palestroni—that would be me!' Caesar laughed out loud.

'You—what can you do to stop me?'

'I control you, Caesar! Difficult as it might be for you to believe, it's a fact.'

This was all too much for Caesar to comprehend. How could a mere employee dare to talk to him in this way? Nick twisted the knife a little more.

'We are on the approach to JFK airport. There isn't sufficient fuel left in the aircraft to take you out of United States airspace. When the plane lands you will be arrested for a range of crimes that would have made Al Capone's head spin.' The veins in Palestroni's neck were clearly visible; blood was pumping at high pressure into the brain of the man who was probably the most wanted on the planet.

'No need for a coronary at this point, Caesar. I want to be able to deliver you in good condition. '*Caligula*.' The Lear jet touched down at New York's Kennedy airport. A cavalcade of limousines was waiting to escort Caesar Palestroni—but not to visit art galleries.

## The End
### Step aside Commander James Bond R.N. Colonel Nick Trevelyan Intelligence Corp has arrived.

# About the Author

Dave Jones was born in London during the 'Blitz'. Upon leaving school at fifteen he tried various jobs, at eighteen he joined the Middlesex Fire Brigade serving three years until eventually leaving for Australia on the ten pound assisted passage scheme. Returning some years later he joined the Household Cavalry and served in Malaya with the armored reconnaissance squadron. Back home to the UK after his tour of duty overseas he became part of the mounted ceremonial squadron, based in Knightsbridge serving on several prestigious events, including the investiture of Prince Charles at Caernarvon Castle. Upon leaving the army he worked at various jobs mostly as a carpenter but also driving trucks. Eventually he found unlikely employment as a personal bodyguard to an American millionaire, entrepreneur travelling throughout Europe. Upon reaching Portugal he left this employment met and married his Portuguese wife. David has four children from that marriage, three living in Portugal and one in the UK. He later returned to London and re-joined the fire service. Serving for a further eleven years. It was during this time that he had the idea to develop a children's character Fireman Sam, now an international success as a children's TV series. Upon his departure from the fire service he returned to his beloved Portugal, eventually building and running a bar/restaurant complex on the Algarve. It was at this point that he became divorced. After bringing up his children using part of the proceeds from the sale of the rights to Fireman Sam he bought an ocean going sailing boat and sailed from the U.K to Portugal/Africa. He has continued to develop as a writer over the past years, and several of his ideas have been considered for TV and film both in the UK and America. His latest venture 'The Hypnotist' is the result of a chance re-union with an old guards colleague who visited him at his Algarve home. His style of writing and ability to develop a good story line makes his work hard to put down. 'The Hypnotist' is a story which is a compelling read with many twists and turns that keep the reader guessing until the last chapter. As a sailor myself I met Dave Jones some years back in Lagos marina. The chance meeting has developed into long term friendship often sailing together we have spent many hours discussing possible ideas for story lines. I wish David success with this his latest venture and look forward to more stories from him in the future.

Clive Pearson Evans.
Welshman & poet.

# DAVID S JONES & FIREMAN SAM.

David S Jones is the originator of the popular children's animated television character Fireman Sam.

Some of the many successes up to the point when he sold his shares in the company 2002 are;

- Three series, twenty-eight episodes, one hour long Christmas special, several public safety episodes. Further series proposed.

- Live stage show, which has played at most of the principal British theatres over the past years.

- BAFTA nominated.

- Over six million books <u>sold</u>.

- One point four million videos <u>sold</u>.

- Transmitted in over forty countries.

- Twenty five years of BBC TV broadcasting.

- Merchandising in all fields.

- Co originator producer of 'Joshua Jones' animated children's series broadcast by BBC.

Fireman Sam is a much loved evergreen children's TV favorite, which has endured for more than twenty five years and will be around to entertain many generations of children to come. The new owners have taken the character from stop frame animation to CGI and the new series has made the concept more popular than ever.